Critical Acclaim for Laura Pedersen

Buffalo Gal

"This book is compulsively readable, and owes its deadpan delivery to the fact that she has performed standup comedy on national television (*The Oprah Winfrey Show, Late Night with David Letterman, Today, Primetime,* etc.)."

—*ForeWord Magazine*

The Big Shuffle

"Although it's a laugh-out-loud read, it's an appealing, sensitive, superbly written book. One you won't want to put down. I loved it."

—*The Lakeland Times*

"This is an excellent portrait of one family's journey through a time of crisis; and of coming out on the other side."

—*CA Reviews*

"Be prepared to fall in love with a story as wise as it is witty."

—*The Compulsive Reader*

The Sweetest Hours

"To call *The Sweetest Hours* a book of short stories would be like calling the *Mona Lisa* a painting."

—*Front Street Reviews*

"Pedersen weaves tales that blend humor, sorrow, and sometimes surprise endings in the games of life and love."

—*Book Loons*

Heart's Desire

"Funny, tender, and poignant, *Heart's Desire* should appeal to a wide range of readers."

—*Booklist*

"Prepare to fall in love again because Laura Pedersen is giving you your 'Heart's Desire' by bringing back Hallie Palmer and her entire endearing crew. In a story as wise as it is witty, Pedersen captures the joy of love found, the ache of love lost, and how friends can get you through it all—win or lose."

—*Sarah Bird, author of The Yokata Officer's Club*

"This book will make you laugh and cry and like a good friend, you'll be happy to have made its acquaintance."

—*Lorna Landvik, author of Angry Housewives Eating Bon Bons*

Last Call

"Pedersen writes vividly of characters so interesting, so funny and warm that they defy staying on the page."

—*The Hartford Courant*

"This book is a rare, humorous exploration of death that affirms life is a gift and tomorrow is never guaranteed. Pedersen writes an exquisitely emotional story. A must-have book to start the new year."

—*Romantic Times*

Beginner's Luck

"Laura Pedersen delivers...If this book hasn't been made into a screenplay already, it should be soon. Throughout, you can't help but think how hilarious some of the scenes would play on the big screen."

—*The Hartford Courant*

"Funny, sweet-natured, and well-crafted…Pedersen has created a wonderful assemblage of…whimsical characters and charm."

—*Kirkus Reviews*

"A fresh and funny look at not fitting in."

—*Seventeen*

"This novel is funny and just quirky enough to become a word-of-mouth favorite….Pedersen has a knack for capturing tart teenage observations in witty asides, and Hallie's naiveté, combined with her gambling and numbers savvy, make her a winning protagonist."

—*Publishers Weekly*

"A breezy coming-of-age novel with an appealing cast of characters."

—*Booklist*

Going Away Party

"Pedersen shows off her verbal buoyancy. Their quips are witty and so are Pedersen's amusing characterizations of the eccentric MacGuires. Sentence by sentence, Pedersen's debut can certainly entertain."

—*Publishers Weekly*

Play Money

"A savvy insider's vastly entertaining line on aspects of the money game."

—*Kirkus Reviews (starred review)*

Also by Laura Pedersen

Nonfiction
Play Money
Buffalo Gal

Fiction
Going Away Party
Beginner's Luck
Last Call
Heart's Desire
The Sweetest Hours
The Big Shuffle

www.laurapedersenbooks.com

Best Bet

a novel by

LAURA PEDERSEN

The fourth and final book in the Hallie Palmer series after

Beginner's Luck, Heart's Desire, and *The Big Shuffle.*

iUniverse, Inc.
New York   Bloomington

iUniverse books may be ordered through booksellers or by contacting:

iUniverse
1663 Liberty Drive
Bloomington, IN 47403
www.iuniverse.com
1-800-Authors (1-800-288-4677)

Because of the dynamic nature of the Internet, any Web addresses or links
contained in this book may have changed since publication and may no longer be
valid. The views expressed in this work are solely those of the author and do not
necessarily reflect the views of the publisher, and the publisher hereby disclaims
any responsibility for them.

ISBN: 978-1-4401-7017-1 (sc)
ISBN: 978-1-4401-7018-8 (ebook)
ISBN: 978-1-4401-6962-5 (dj)

Printed in the United States of America

iUniverse rev. date: 10/20/2009

For another daughter and son of life,

Maya Elizabeth and Lucas Robert,

and

Rev. Leroy Ricksy (1936–2006)

Founder of the Booker T. Washington Learning Center

in East Harlem, NY,

who carried Christ in his heart and a plunger in his hand.

Life is worthwhile, for it is full of dreams and peace,

gentleness and ecstasy,

and faith that burns like a clear white flame

on a grim dark altar.

—*Nathaniel West*

Chapter 1

The good news is that I've had only one roommate this past semester. The bad news is that she plays Enya night and day. At this point, it's questionable what's going to happen first—graduation from college or drowning myself in the Orinoco Flow.

Everyone else is either studying for final exams or preparing to go home for the holidays. I, on the other hand, am packing up for good. By attending summer school the past two years, it was possible to make up the semesters I missed after Dad died.

I check my e-mails one last time before unplugging the computer. Craig Larkin has sent one simply saying: Lark N. Larkin. As a goof, we sometimes toss each other ridiculous names that we could use for our children, though we're not even engaged. It's just for fun. Craig has been my on and off boyfriend since high school, but for the past two years we've been seeing each other exclusively. He was a straight-A student and star athlete, while I won the award for most days missed to go and bet on the horses at the racetrack. But my older and wiser friend Olivia Stockton insists that Craig is a closet Bohemian because he talks to trees when he thinks no one is around. I respect him most for following his heart, like when he dropped out of college to start a pond-building business and everyone was against the idea at the time. (Including me, big idiot that I am.)

There's a message saying that my cap and gown will be shipped to my home address, and also one asking me to stop by the Dean's Office. It must be about unpaid library fines. Last year my roommate owed almost two hundred dollars, so we had to buy a couple of kegs and hold a Fine Party.

In the lobby of my dorm, I use the pay phone to call Craig since I'm the only person on the planet without a cell phone.

"Where are you?" he asks. "For lunch I'm making chocolate chip pancakes with hot fudge and whipped cream!"

"Filling all the holes in the walls with toothpaste took longer than I thought," I explain. "And now I have to go and deal with an unpaid fine, which I really don't understand, since I wasn't anywhere near the library this past semester."

"Should I reschedule my appointment for this afternoon, so I can be there to help you unpack?" asks Craig.

"Gosh, no," I say. "From now on we're going to be together for...well, a lot of the time." Craig and I have rented an apartment in Cincinnati, where I landed an entry-level job with an Internet marketing firm, and he'll continue to run his pond-building business, which has really taken off over the past year.

"All right," says Craig. "I'll take you out to dinner tonight to celebrate, and we'll have chocolate chip pancakes tomorrow and every day after that."

"Absolutely," I say. "Save that recipe!"

Walking across the Quad and over to the administrative building does not present the usual *study in campus life*, where students mill around laughing and chatting, sip coffee on a bench, or play hacky-sack near the fountain. Instead, young men and women stumble along with books clutched to their chests and baseball caps pushed low on their foreheads, glancing neither left nor right. The freshmen are the worst looking of the lot, absolute zombies. After three months of hard partying, muddled minds now have to cash all those blank checks written by their bodies back in the fall.

While waiting my turn in the Dean's Office, I actually get

excited about the future. Finally, a place of my own where I can put any darn thing I want on the wall and leave it up until I get tired of it or it falls down. And no more having to pack a bag on weekends to see Craig, forgetting to include the books I need, or the right clothes for whatever we end up doing.

Finally, the secretary's voice calls out, "Hallie Palmer," and I'm ushered into Mr. Muller's office. Mr. Dakin, my regular advisor, retired this past fall, and Mr. Muller has replaced him.

"Good afternoon, Ms. Palmer. I'm glad you could make it on such short notice." A second chin takes up a third of his face and almost a quarter of his entire body.

"Hey." I sit down in the chair opposite his desk.

"Please make yourself comfortable. We have an interesting situation." Mr. Muller's eyebrows rise as he finishes each sentence.

Uh-oh. I immediately assume that I've failed one of my final exams. But even if that's the case, my grades were good going into them.

He glances down at a file on his desk. "You took psychology as a science in the second semester of your freshman year."

I recall wanting to get the required courses out of the way as soon as possible and memorizing a bunch of stuff about trained rats and Pavlov's dogs. "The professor gave me a B," I say. You only need to earn Cs in the basic requirements.

"Yes, but by taking psychology as a *science*, you fulfilled the natural science requirement but not the social science requirement," says Mr. Muller. "It can't be used for both."

I'm confused. "Before planning the last two semesters, Mr. Dakin went over my transcript and said I'd completed all the required classes and only needed to worry about finishing up my major."

"Yes, well, that seems to have been an oversight." Mr. Muller offers me a weak "smile," only it's more like what you get from squinting into harsh sunlight. "Mr. Dakin, was…well…he probably should have retired a little earlier."

I'd thought there was something a little odd about Mr. Dakin during that last meeting. A sixty-foot paperclip chain took up a good portion of his office and he kept turning the conversation to the weaponization of space.

"The bottom line is that you need one more four-credit class to graduate," says Mr. Muller.

"What?!"

"Yes, I'm very sorry to be the bearer of bad news." The eyebrows go up, and the squint is more pained, less smiley.

"But I have a *job* in Cincinnati! They hired someone with a *college degree.*"

In a calming voice Mr. Muller says, "Don't worry. I'll explain what happened to your new employer. Take the class at a college in Cincinnati and simply transfer the credits back here. You can still walk the stage at graduation this January if you like."

I breathe a sigh of relief. It's bad, but not *that* bad.

"The only thing is that if you complete the course here, we won't charge you, because of the *misunderstanding*," says Mr. Muller. "But if you decide to take it elsewhere, the school can't reimburse you."

"Huh?"

"You need a social science worth four credits—something like economics, anthropology, or political science. Or…if you want to use the psych class you already took to fulfill your social sciences requirement, then you can take another science course. He picks up a catalogue and begins reading, "Biology, chemistry, physics…"

No way! I haven't been in a real science class since tenth grade, and that was something horrible about rocks. "Don't get me wrong, Mr. Muller, I've really enjoyed college. But I turned twenty-one in September and am ready to move on with my life. I'm tired of classes, homework, and commuting every other weekend."

"I'm so sorry," he says. "I realize we have some responsibility here, and we're trying to do what we can to help. But unfortunately, I can't just give you credits that you didn't earn."

"Would it be okay if I take some time to think about this?"

Mr. Muller squints—this time as if he smells something

unpleasant. "Registration for the spring semester was a month ago and our offices close on Friday for the holidays. You'll need to let me know by tomorrow. If you want to stay here, I can extend your dorm for a semester at no charge. I've already checked and no one is scheduled to move in."

"Yeah, it's safe to say that everyone on campus has heard Enya blasting from our room at two o'clock in the morning."

Mr. Muller walks me to the door. Based on the stack of folders on his desk, Mr. Dakin apparently made a few other *oversights*. Like about two hundred.

It feels as if I'm walking out of a doctor's office after receiving some horrible diagnosis. I can't even remember which way to turn in order to leave the building. Guys are up on ladders fixing panels in the ceiling. Suddenly my feet fly out from under me and the next thing I know, I'm sliding through a puddle on my butt.

Chapter 2

"Whoops-a-daisy!" a janitor shouts as he drops his mop and comes running over.

While helping me to my feet he asks, "Didn't you see the signs?"

I glance around. "You mean the half-dozen three-foot-high bright yellow ones that say WET FLOOR?"

"The roof is leaking," he explains.

"I wasn't paying attention."

"You'll have to use the doors on the other side of the building."

I must look confused because he points me in the right direction and then continues shouting encouragement as I stumble off.

The outside air is crisp but not really all that cold for the middle of December. It's the longest fall I can remember. Some of the trees still have a few leaves bravely hanging in there and the wind whips around scattered bits of paper.

Approaching the Quad, I run into Josh, who is now attending classes here for what must be his *sixth* year. He's changed his major about once a month, and so now we're both seniors—only he has *a lot* of minors. Despite my big crush on Josh two years ago, we'd ended up just being friends. By the time I arrived back at school after Dad died, I was going steady with Craig, and Josh had a girlfriend.

"Hey, Hallie—you look terrible!" says Josh, who has somehow completely dodged acne and remains boy-band cute. "Everything okay?"

"About five minutes ago I was told that I'm not graduating."

"What?" From the look on his face, I can tell he thinks that I've been expelled. This is not surprising, since there was a run of pranks this fall, including dismantling the president's Mercedes and reassembling it on top of the field house.

"No, I mean I'm four credits short, a social science—a stupid mix-up because Mr. Dakin had Alzheimer's during his final year as my advisor. I should have known something was up when he kept showing me photos of the Soap Box Derby cars he was building."

"I heard about that!" says Josh. "He wrote a fellowship recommendation for my friend Isabel and said she was 'in possession of a pulchritudinous posterior.'"

My eyes widen. "The administration has obviously known about this for a while! It doesn't seem fair. I feel like I should be able to sue them...or something."

"Just stay for one more semester." Josh, who seems intent upon becoming a permanent student, sounds enthusiastic about the prospect.

"I have a job lined up in Cincinnati. I mean, it isn't first prize—an assistant in the marketing department at this speakers' bureau, laying out brochures and stuff, but it would give me some experience." I don't tell Josh the worst thing about the job, which is that the women are required to wear pantsuits and even skirts sometimes!

"I thought you wanted to work on product design."

"I *do*," I reply. "But I don't have so much as an internship on my résumé. I've worked as a gardener every summer since I was sixteen."

"Take the class in Cincinnati and transfer it back here," says Josh.

"I guess that's the solution," I say. "Craig is planning to move there with me. We've already found an apartment."

"That's the guy I see you with sometimes, from back home?"

I know he doesn't mean *back home* to sound negative, but it does, as if I never really grew up at college. I rub my fingers on my temples. "It's just that in my head I was finished with school, you know?"

"Hey, I've got an idea!" Josh says with the same thrill that probably overcomes him every time he switches majors. "Next semester I'm going around the world with a team from the sociology department. A professor has grant money to do a study."

"Around the world?"

"To a dozen different countries," says Josh. "We leave wallets on the ground containing money and I.D. to see if people return them, and if so, whether the money is still there."

It sounds ridiculous, but I'm so confused at this moment that I doubt anything would make much sense.

Taking my arm, Josh leads me toward the humanities building. "Oh, my gosh, Hallie, this is perfect! One of the girls on the team broke her leg playing Frisbee yesterday, and we didn't think we could replace her on such short notice. It totally messes up the hotel arrangements, because she was supposed to room with Amanda, and I'm in with this guy who's a grad student at Ohio State."

"How do you break a leg playing Frisbee?" I ask.

"Maybe it was dark," says Josh.

There were crazier stories, like the freshman who went hang gliding from the bell tower in order to ask some girl to homecoming. To make a long story short, he got a "yes" and also a concussion.

Josh leads me to a group of offices I've never before been inside. We go right past the secretary and to a room in the back with a green nameplate that says Ms. PRITCHETT on it in white letters. Inside, a woman who can't be older than twenty-eight sits at a desk heaped with paperwork.

Josh knocks on the door but then walks right in, pushing me ahead of him as if delivering a virgin for the altar sacrifice. "Ms.

Pritchett, you'll never believe this! Hallie needs four credits in social sciences to graduate—she could take Lenore's place."

Ms. Pritchett doesn't look nearly as thrilled as Josh. In fact, for a woman who is naturally attractive, her pinched expression and furrowed brow make her appear anything but.

"Are you a student here?" Ms. Pritchett peers at me over the top of her wire-rimmed glasses like a librarian on the prowl for sticky fingers and overdue books.

Even though my excitable apricot-colored curls are secured by a maximum-strength ponytail, I smooth the sides of my head just in case. Then I begin to explain the crazy mix-up. Only when Ms. Pritchett hears the words "Mr. Dakin," she stops me as if that explains *everything.*

"Bummer," throws in Josh.

"Please have a seat," says Ms. Pritchett.

Clearing some file folders off a chair, I sit down.

Ms. Pritchett repeats what Josh told me, only in slightly greater detail. For her PhD, she's studying the honesty of ordinary people in different countries and how their social structures, mores, and religion can impact integrity. Josh wasn't kidding—this small group is traveling to a dozen different countries, all expenses paid.

It sounds totally crazy. I don't know what to say and just sit there as if I've been abducted by aliens and am waiting for the mind melds or the body probes to begin.

"Would it fill Hallie's requirement?" asks Josh.

Ms. Pritchett phones the department. She places her hand over the receiver for a second. "Who's your new advisor?"

"Mr. Muller," I reply.

After a short conversation, Ms. Pritchett establishes that the project would be considered a pass/fail independent study in sociology and make me eligible for graduation in the spring. Only she still doesn't appear all that eager to have me on board. When Ms. Pritchett presents her formal offer, it sounds more like she merely *needs* me so there will be enough worker bees to complete her all-important research.

"You'll need a doctor's certificate," she states, as if it's a done deal. "Can you be ready to leave on January fifth?" She hands me a folder with the name "Lenore Gomez" typed at the top.

"Uh, can I think about it?"

"You're not afraid to fly, are you?"

"No, of course not." The truth is that I've never been on a plane before, and so how would I even know. But I'd applied for a passport junior year while having hallucinations about spending spring break in Cancún. "I…uh…made some other plans that I'd have to change. Mr. Muller just told me about this mess a half an hour ago."

Ms. Pritchett keeps checking her watch like the officious rabbit in *Alice in Wonderland*. You'd think the plane was departing in fifteen minutes. "I have to switch the flight reservations to your name, get an insurance card, and submit my final list to the administration. You have exactly one week to decide." She jots something on the back of a business card and hands it to me. "Here's my home number."

Josh and I walk out together. "Hallie, you just have to come! It's going to be awesome—we're traveling to Australia and Morocco and Hawaii. Three weeks from now you could be lying on the beach in the sun." He waves his arms in the direction of the naked branches that will soon be frosted with snow. "Look at the list: Egypt is on there—you can see the pyramids! And India—the Taj Mahal!"

"Yeah, but aren't we supposed to be dropping wallets all over town?"

"I talked to one of the guys who went on the last trip and they had plenty of time for sightseeing." He smiles and laughs. "And partying!"

"Ms. Pritchett seems rather young, mean, and ambitious."

"Oh, she's not so bad once you get to know her," says Josh. "She had a fight with her department head at Ohio State before coming here and this project is really important for her career. There's only one more group after us and then she can write her paper, earn her PhD, publish, apply for tenure somewhere—all that academic crap."

The tower clock bongs out the noon hour and Josh flashes panic. "I've got an exam!" He races off in the direction of the math building.

Other students scramble past me. I glance down at the folder in my hand and read the words "WINTER EXPERIMENT" written on the outside in black magic marker. *Wow, a trip around the world.* Only what about the job in Cincinnati and the start of my career? And what about Craig? Sure, we've had our problems in the past, but everything is going great now, and we've finally decided to start a real life together. Okay, so maybe my budgeting and bill-paying skills aren't all that wonderful, and Craig, the beloved only child of well-to-do parents, has never made a bed or vacuumed in his life, but surely these things can be worked out. I could get one of those computer programs to help with the finances. If it's really good, there might even be money left over for a housekeeper!

I can't help but wonder if all this would've happened if the door I'd originally tried when leaving the administrative offices hadn't been cordoned off. It's doubtful I'd have run into Josh. And so I wouldn't have found out about the trip. Or what if Lenore hadn't been playing Frisbee in the dark? Or if Mr. Dakin hadn't mucked up my schedule in the first place?

Pastor Costello is always saying, "Coincidence is God's way of being anonymous." At moments like this, I wonder if maybe there really is such a thing as fate.

Chapter 3

My first thought is that I need to talk to Craig. Until we discuss vital matters, there's always this odd sense that they haven't really happened. Before climbing into the car, I stop at the student union. The one good thing about everyone else in the world but me having a cell phone is that the pay phones are now all mine. Craig's voicemail picks up, and I remember he has a meeting about building a waterfall for some big Hong Kong bank that's opening a branch in Northfield. It's always funny when Craig recounts these talks with the manager in charge. Craig says the guy begins almost every sentence by saying, "It's not about the money but the principle of the thing," and yet it's always about the money.

Maybe it's just as well that I take the drive home to think over whether or not to go on this trip. Something tells me that Craig isn't going to be very happy about my opportunity to see the world without having to become a flight attendant or infantrywoman, and postponing our plans to live together. Once Craig makes a life decision, he really gets behind it so things work, whereas I seem to doubt myself right up until the moment I change my mind. For instance, every time I had a chance to do an internship in graphic design, I found a way to sabotage it at the last minute. The comfort and familiarity of working in the yard at the Stocktons', a job I've had since I was sixteen, always won out over opportunities that would've helped my career.

Driving the hour it takes to get home, my mind is awash with *Should I or Shouldn't I?* A chance to travel to a dozen different countries is pretty exciting. On the other hand, Craig and I are supposed to sign the lease next week. He's already packed up most of his pond-building stuff and printed change of address cards. Plus, we're both looking forward to knowing his parents aren't just down the hall when we make love and not having to listen to the best and worst of Enya when Craig sleeps over in my dorm room.

But it isn't *my* fault the school made a mistake and I need one more class!

On the outskirts of town, a tow truck hooks up a car with a dented front end, and I see my friend Officer Rich's squad car pulled onto the shoulder of the road. He's collecting some orange cones that must have been used to divert traffic. There's shattered glass in the road, but I don't see any blood or guts, so hopefully nobody was injured.

I pull up behind the tan and white squad car and walk over to where he's loading his trunk. Officer Rich, who is now in his early fifties, was my favorite adult when I was growing up here because (1) he never judges a person without hard evidence; (2) he treats everyone the same—rich or poor, young or old; and most important (3) I can usually beat him at poker.

"Hey there, Hallie, welcome to the next place we need a Deer Crossing sign."

"I didn't know that deer could read."

"They can in Cosgrove County. It's part of the 'No Deer Left Behind' program," jokes Officer Rich. But then he turns serious. "Honestly, with all the construction since the commuter train started running, there's no place for the poor creatures to go. They're in everyone's backyard, tearing up the golf course, and grazing on the high school playing fields like it's a buffet."

"What can you do about them?" I ask.

"Make hunting season longer," replies Officer Rich.

"Ohhh," I say. "Don't let Olivia Stockton hear about that."

Officer Rich smiles upon hearing the name of the woman he likes to describe as being "to the left of the salad fork." Surely, he's imagining the blazing editorials and protests our local social and political firebrand would organize in front of Town Hall. "You're right. Maybe I can interest the deer in a one-way all-expenses-paid trip to Pennsylvania."

"Bernard will bake some corn and carrot muffins for the trip," I say. "That's his latest." Olivia's adult son is not only my longtime mentor and employer, but an excellent cook.

"The good news is that property taxes from the new developments are bringing in extra revenue. I've hired two new police officers to start in January, and our friend Al got his job back at the Water Authority. Actually, it's a better one—his boss retired and they offered him the position."

"Terrific!"

"There's even talk of building another elementary school across from the park."

"Wow," I say. "If the town keeps growing, maybe you'll actually get some murderers and serial killers."

"One can only hope," he says, kidding. "So I hear you're moving to Cincinnati next week. No more living like a boxcar hobo."

"Yeah, well, there's been a mistake with my transcript, and it turns out that I need one more class." I look down at the gravel. "Hey, Officer Rich, what do you think about this? A professor is doing a sociology experiment and taking some students on a trip around the world to help her with it. They just invited me to go along. And it would give me the credits I need to graduate."

Being that Officer Rich is in law enforcement, I assume he's going to lecture me on the countless dangers of such a crazy undertaking.

He glances over at the row of houses that just went up along the main road into town. "Do it while you can—before you have kids and a mortgage. They sneak up on you real fast."

"Really?" I ask.

"Only you can't keep 'em down on the farm after they've seen the bright lights of the big city," says Officer Rich. "You were always too adventurous for this place anyway. You'll probably end up living in Tokyo or somewhere exciting like that."

"I can't imagine living that far away from home, but it *would* be cool to see some other places. I've never even been on a plane."

Officer Rich slowly lowers his bulky frame into the squad car. "I have to go check the holiday decorations on Main Street. We had some heavy winds this morning. All I need is another giant plastic angel bonking some old woman on the noggin while she's out buying her Bailey's Irish Cream."

I head toward my house in order to store some stuff in the garage. My sister, Louise, who is three years younger, wants my refrigerator for when she starts Yale in January. Louise took classes at the local community college while performing in some plays and has been accepted in the drama program there. I wish there was a way to tell Dad that his demise has led to better financial aid packages for all his offspring, and that a Palmer child is actually going to an Ivy League school! Although if he knew that one of us was going to college to study acting, he'd most likely have that fatal heart attack all over again.

On the street where my family lives the houses are close together, almost all two-story and painted white with a tarnished brass American eagle pounded in above the garage. When spring arrives, the flags will come out—usually the same weekend that the storm windows are put away and the screens installed.

While walking through the garage, I hear the unmistakable grind and chug of the school bus turning up our street. A few moments later my eighteen-year-old brother Teddy and the thirteen-year-old twins, Davy and Darlene, barge into the house, drop their book bags and coats in a heap by the back door, and head for the freshly baked brownies on the counter.

"Hey, Hallie," says Teddy. "Congratulations! Looks like the Palmers are two for two." Our older brother, Eric, graduated from

Indiana University and was now finishing an MBA at Vanderbilt University in Nashville, Tennessee.

"What's going on with your applications?" I ask Teddy, who is a senior at the local high school. Teddy has been *very* mysterious about where he wants to attend college.

"They're all in," he replies.

"In *where?*"

"Here and there," he says while taking an entire stack of brownies. Teddy is now officially the tallest member of the Palmer family, at six foot five and, though he's not nearly as skinny as he was during the string bean years, I wouldn't quite say he's filled out yet.

"Mom is going to have a fit if you applied to some military academy," I say. Mom isn't exactly a pacifist, but unless the draft is reinstated, I don't think we'll see her standing quietly by while her offspring sign up to become soldiers. It's bad enough she holds her breath through entire football and basketball games, certain that one of her kids is going to break a back or neck. Mom places war right up there with dodgeball, which has been the cause of substantial injuries in this family and is now strictly off-limits for her children, along with biking while listening to music and paint-splatter art.

Teddy removes a gallon of milk from the refrigerator. My energetic younger sister, Francie, who possesses such a stunning record of accidents that we're not entirely convinced she'll live to see her tenth birthday, comes barreling into the kitchen wearing only a T-shirt and sweatpants, no socks or shoes.

"Didn't you go to school today?" I ask. "Are you sick?"

"Franthie is thuthpended," announces Darlene, a slight note of triumph in her voice.

"Oh *no*. Not *again*," I say. "Who did you beat up this time?"

"Thexual harathment!" Darlene gleefully informs me. At age twelve, her lisp is considerably better, but still noticeable when she becomes excited, especially where the *s*'s are concerned.

"She kissed a boy," Davy clarifies.

"I think Mom is actually relieved," teases Teddy.

Being that Francie refuses to wear what she disparagingly refers to as "girl clothes" and constantly has *Xena: Warrior Princess* reruns playing on the TV, Mom has no doubt been thinking "possible lesbian."

Our mother enters the kitchen through the garage door. "Welcome home, Hallie!" She looks cheerful and remarkably fit for having had ten children and then losing her husband and the father to us all, after he had a heart attack only two years ago. Mom still doesn't wear makeup on her eyes or face, but I've noticed that ever since Pastor Costello declared himself as a suitor, she finds time to put on lipstick and earrings.

After giving her a kiss on the cheek, I say, "I thought you were downstairs doing laundry."

"I was over helping Mrs. Muldoon clean out her fridge," says Mom. "The poor dear, she's been having such flare-ups with her arthritis, but she won't hear of asking someone to stop by and help. It was all her daughter could do to get a housekeeper in once a week to clean and do the wash."

"Does Barbara still want her to move out to Arizona?"

"Yes, but she doesn't want to go," says Mom. "Your twin baby brothers are like sons to her now. I'm looking forward to when Roddy and Reggie start kindergarten, but I'm afraid she's going to be devastated."

"What's all this stuff?" I ask. The counter is loaded with party decorations, cake pans, the mixer is in the ready position, and two chickens are thawing out.

"Oh dear, you weren't supposed to see any of this," frets Mom. "I thought you'd go directly to the Stocktons', and then Craig was going to bring you here tonight instead of the restaurant. It's a graduation party!"

"It's still a nice surprise." In a family with many children and few bedrooms, we're all used to the fact that surprises, secrets, and sweets all have a very short shelf-life.

"There's some other news," says Mom.

Darlene, Davy, Teddy, and even Francie all stop shoving brownies into their mouths and look over at us. I can tell that it's something serious.

"You're pregnant!" I try not to sound horrified.

A round of giggles comes from the table.

"Goodness no!" Mom says this as if she hadn't managed to already give birth to ten children.

My siblings are now staring at us as if glued to the final episode of a reality TV show. Mom suddenly looks all embarrassed. "Arthur has asked me to marry him," she exclaims.

"Oh!" I'm aware that the other kids are watching my reaction. Forcing a huge smile onto my face, I give Mom a big hug and say, "That's fantastic! Congratulations!" And the truth is, I am happy for her. I knew this day was coming. A few weeks ago, Pastor Costello had more or less told me he wanted to propose—that he'd never try and take my dad's place and all that stuff. It's just a little weird, that's all. Especially on top of everything else. And marriage…it's so *permanent*.

We end our hug and Mom brushes away a tear.

"So when is the big day?" I ask.

"Well…actually…Christmas," says Mom.

"My gosh, that's in less than a week! Are you sure you're not pregnant?"

"Of course not!" insists Mom.

I sigh with relief. Not that I don't love kids, but ten seems like enough.

"If anything, I imagine we'd adopt some, knowing Arthur's commitment to orphans." Okay, two words here that catch my imagination, "adopt" of course being the first, and "some" being the other, which, last time I checked, the dictionary defined as more than one—an unspecified number or quantity.

"Having the wedding on Christmas Day is the only way that Eric can attend," continues Mom. "He has a project due, and his girlfriend has to work."

"Okay," I say. "Count me in."

Mom looks incredibly happy.

I feel incredibly faint. "I'm just going to run over to the Stocktons' to uh...you know..."

"Hallie, would you be my maid of honor?"

"Me?" The word "honor" is not often used in conjunction with my name. At least not in this town. There've been a few misunderstandings in the past.

"Of course, *you*," says Mom. "Eric is going to be the best man, Louise and Teddy are witnesses, and the little ones are flower girls and ring boys."

"Isn't Aunt Lala coming?" I inquire about my mother's well-meaning, but *extremely* absentminded, younger sister.

"It's too short notice. And your cousin Marci is...going through another phase."

"I guess it's no problem to book the church on such short notice," I joke.

"The reception will be downstairs in Fellowship Hall. Don't tell anyone, but we're going to use the flowers leftover from the Christmas Eve services." Mom giggles like a schoolgirl.

"Do I have to wear a dress?" I ask.

Mom gives me a look.

"I just meant—I only meant that I don't really have anything." I attempt to cover my error. "And there's not much time to shop." The only nice outfit I own is the black pantsuit I wore to Dad's funeral and for some reason, I don't think it will strike quite the right chord.

"We could go shopping tomorrow," suggests mom.

"That'll be great." I'm now desperate for air. "See you tomorrow then." With bedrooms being so oversubscribed in my place, I still sleep in the Stocktons' summerhouse when home from school.

"Hallie!" Mom laughs. "Aren't you coming back this evening for your graduation party?"

"Oh right. I forgot in all the excitement." Dashing out the back door, I stumble over the beanbag snake that's supposed to keep the heat from escaping and deeply inhale the fresh winter air.

Chapter 4

$\mathcal{D}$riving down the same old streets, it seems that not much has changed, including the names on the mailboxes, the cars in the driveways, and even the plastic porch furniture. No wonder all those new houses are going up. The people in the old ones don't seem to want to leave—though I notice that RVs have appeared in some driveways and so I assume that a number of retirees are becoming snowbirds. It's hard to blame them, since we get pretty much the same weather as Cleveland, which means a harsh winter. At school, my friends and I used to joke that February and March were so cold that flashers would just describe themselves.

According to the town historian (whom I had to interview for a social studies paper in ninth grade), Cosgrove County is an old farming community. Back in the 1800s, families lived on wide expanses of mineral-rich soil in this triangle between Cleveland, Youngstown, and Buffalo, New York, and rode into town once a month to buy supplies, attend political meetings at the Grange Hall, and have their teeth yanked out by the local barber. Most of the action took place on Main Street, with its bank, sheriff, property office, and one-judge courthouse, while a few adjacent streets sprang up to accommodate churches, an auction block, and yes, even a real, old-fashioned saloon (which during Prohibition became a restaurant/hotel—though the way my friend Cappy, the local bookmaker, tells it, women were the main item on the menu and came with the cost of a room). During the 1920s and '30s, factories went up in the nearby cities, while family farms started to disappear. The town remained fairly self-sufficient, yet stagnant, until the 1960s. After rioting in Cleveland and Buffalo (related to civil rights unrest and the Vietnam War), people suddenly decided this was a safer place to raise a family if you didn't mind driving an hour to work in the morning. There wasn't much diversity when I was growing up—aside from Officer Rich and his family, who are African American—but increasingly, people of different ethnicities arrived, and restaurants serving Indian, Thai, and Mexican food popped up around town. Nowadays, families with super secret meatloaf or apple-pie recipes, passed down through generations, actually go out on Friday nights for dim sum and to see movies with subtitles. And last summer, a few local Hmong women sold gorgeous handmade needlework crafts and silver jewelry at the Firemen's Picnic right next to a guy peddling Folk Art. Talk about the old and the new side by side.

In the Stocktons' neighborhood, the houses are set far apart and most have circular driveways, so there's a wide expanse of smooth rolling lawn out front. Bernard is playing catch with Rose in the last swath of daylight on grass that's stiff and silvery, the color of ice on a frozen lake . This past summer, Rose had rejected dance class in favor of softball and she plans to join a little league team of five-year-olds in the spring.

Walking over to where they're playing, I call out, "I thought that Gil was in charge of sports." Bernard and his boyfriend, Gil, live in the Stocktons' old but well-maintained Victorian house with Bernard's mother, the sixty-something Olivia, and her Italian boyfriend, Ottavio. I lived with them during my final year of high school, or The Year I Went Through My Phase, as Mom refers to it.

"He's over at the theater, and so I'm using this opportunity to get in touch with my masculine side." Bernard tosses the softball high into the air and it plops down about six feet in front of Rose. "Behind every great woman is a fabulous man!"

"Guess what?" I say. "Mom and Pastor Costello are getting married."

"Oh really!" Bernard the natural-born scene-stealer crows with exaggerated surprise.

"You already knew," I say with no surprise whatsoever.

"Evelyn was in yesterday looking for a tea caddy."

Evelyn Shapiro works at the stationery store and it's impossible to have a party that involves printed invitations without her knowing about it, along with everyone else in town.

"You're such a gossip!" I shake my head, not at Bernard so much as my own cluelessness—to have actually thought I'd find out about my own mother's wedding before he did.

"*Au contraire.* It's not gossip when you're sure that it's true." Bernard defends himself. "Then it's officially classified as *news.* Ask any editor!"

"Yeah, right."

"Besides, now that I'm approaching middle age, and possess the vast experience that comes with a life fully lived, people increasingly turn to me as their *confidante.*"

If you consider middle age to start at thirty, then Bernard approached it about eight years ago.

"Christmas Day," I add, as if Bernard wouldn't already know the date as well, and have selected an outfit.

"I *adore* a winter wedding!" A ball flies directly at Bernard's chest and he leaps out of the way. "White and white and more white!"

"With ten kids on hand, I don't think my mom will be wearing white for some reason."

The shrill cry of a peacock erupts from the backyard. A total of three are drifting and scratching about—the result of one of Bernard's many schemes to keep his two daughters, adopted from China, in touch with their culture.

"Don't the peacocks bother the new neighbors?" I ask.

"It's more like the new neighbors bother the peacocks—a phalanx of youth have turned it into the home of the all-night *soirée*. One is an entrepreneur trying to convert the old mill on Main Street into an arts center, which is fine by me, but I don't know what the rest do, aside from play loud noise and sit on the porch appearing vague or chemically dependent. There's a heap of scrap metal out back that's supposedly a sculpture. It looks more like someone dissected a jalopy."

"Where's Olivia?" I ask. There aren't any other cars in the driveway.

"If Mother didn't sneak off to wave a cell phone above her head at a Cat Power concert, then she's inside the house." He nods toward the front door and gets hit in the shoulder with the ball. "Ottavio took the *QE2*." Queen Elizabeth 2 is our codename for Olivia's cherry red Buick Park Avenue, because it's not unlike driving a medium-sized living room down the middle of the road.

Rose giggles. "Throw a pop-fly!"

"Okay, but then we're going inside," says Bernard. "It's too dark to see and we have to set the table."

I hurry up the path so that I can talk to Olivia alone for a few minutes. She's busy in her den off the back of the living room but doesn't hear me since she's plugged into her brand new pale pink iPod. This was a Christmas present from Bernard, in the hope that he'd stop waking up to Neil Diamond's soundtrack for "Jonathon Livingston Seagull" gusting through the downstairs like a seventy-mile an hour wind.

"Hello, Hallie!" Olivia removes the earbuds. "Isn't that funny, I was just sending photos of Craig's pond to a friend of mine who moved to West Virginia. They bought a big house with an enormous yard." Olivia holds up the letter. "I told her that koi are very relaxing—it's like having a Joan Miró painting in your backyard."

Olivia had actually drummed up a lot of business for Craig by talking up his ponds to her friends and also the members of her church.

The house is unusually quiet. "Where is everybody?" I ask.

"Gil is at rehearsal, and Rocky and Gigi are addicted to Baby Einstein videos, so Bernard installed a DVD player in the summerhouse." Gigi is Bernard and Gil's three-year-old adopted Chinese daughter, and Rocky is a chimpanzee that Olivia took in after he was thrown out of a program where chimps help human paraplegics with things like insulin shots. Only it wasn't really Rocky's fault, since the woman he worked for was an alcoholic and didn't like to drink alone.

"And Ottavio?"

Olivia glances out the window at the encroaching dusk as a way of determining the hour. She isn't much for clocks. "Traffic school. He should be home at any moment."

"I thought Ottavio finished traffic school in November." Ottavio, who is also sixty-something, firmly believes that experience should count when driving, and so one's age should be the speed limit.

"Those were the speeding tickets," says Olivia. "This time it's for lane changes."

"It's perfectly legal to change lanes," I say. "So long as you signal."

"Not *that* many times." Olivia releases her musical laugh. "There are only two kinds of tickets for Ottavio—moving violations and moving-even-faster violations."

Rose and Bernard can be heard entering the front hall and so I quickly lay out my dilemma to Olivia—the final class that's needed, my chance meeting with Josh, and the possibility of this trip, which would mean giving up the job and apartment in Cincinnati.

Olivia appears intrigued. "You didn't seem very enthusiastic about this position at the speakers' bureau."

"No—but everyone says it's much easier to get a job once you already have one," I reply. "My résumé looks terrible because I don't have any experience."

"The writer Katherine Mansfield once said, 'Why be given a body if you have to keep it shut up in a case like a rare, rare fiddle?'"

24

Olivia can always be counted on to come down firmly on the side of experience, of almost any kind. And although she'll never tell anyone what to do with his or her life, she usually has a few good quotes on the subject. As I like to tell my friends at school, Olivia doesn't so much change your mind as enter it.

Based on the sounds coming from the kitchen, I assume that Bernard is checking on dinner. Within a matter of minutes, he's standing in the doorway to Olivia's den holding a bunch of parsley and saying, "What's this about taking a trip around the world?"

Olivia and I look at each other as if it's no use trying to have a private conversation around here.

"Bertie, don't you have a pot to stir, or *something?*" Olivia turns back to me. "Travel is a wonderful way to broaden the mind."

Framed by the doorway, Bernard informs us, "Travel derives from *travail*, French for 'arduous toil.' Cast your gaze back farther and you'll discover the Latin word for *torture!*"

"Don't be ridiculous!" crows Olivia. "St. Augustine said that the world is a book, and those who do not travel read only a page. I quite agree."

Bernard ignores her. "Why do you need another class? I thought everything was set for you to graduate in January."

I go through the entire story about the dotty advisor who turned his attention to exploring space, both outer and inner, apparently, and then describe the sociology professor's experiment.

Bernard frowns. "Don't be ridiculous! You can't go to the Far East and South America! For one thing, what would you eat?"

"I'm pretty sure they have food in other parts of the world," I reply.

"The sort that leaves you dancing the crab apple two-step," exclaims Bernard. "No, it's out of the question. You can live here and work in the garden while you complete the missing class."

"It's the middle of winter," I say.

"We'll expand the greenhouse," says Bernard. "And that acre of forest I bought in the back—we should clear some of it and plant a proper apple orchard. That way, we can press our own cider in the fall. Wouldn't that be fun?"

"If I don't go on the trip, then Craig and I are going to take the apartment in Cincinnati and I'll start my job there," I say.

Forget going around the world; Bernard has been carping about the Cincinnati move since Thanksgiving, as if we're going to get run over by a city bus or permanently stuck in the elevator of a high-rise building.

I raise my hands as if they're scales. "I don't know…the more I think about the project, it sounds kind of interesting. I may never again have a chance to see so many places."

"If you're so desperate to take a trip, we can drive to Rush Creek Village next weekend and look at homes based on the designs of Frank Lloyd Wright," says Bernard.

"Bertie," Olivia chimes in, "will you please let Hallie decide what's best. She's not sixteen anymore. Remember the twenty-first birthday party we had here in September? I'd think it would be hard to forget seeing as the kitchen had to be repainted after your Fry Daddy burst into flames." Her voice is full of little trills and crescendos, punctuated with tremolos that serve as a wink and a nod to the audience.

Bernard scowls at his mother. "How many times need I remind everyone that the lentil patty recipe from your *Food for All Sorts* church cookbook didn't specify what kind of oil to use!"

"All *Souls*," Olivia corrects him.

"No matter. Any more of your Unitarian *recipes for disaster*, and we'll need to take out homemakers' insurance!"

"Bernard, we cannot in good conscience advise Hallie to turn down an opportunity like this when so many of our *she*roes were great travelers."

"No such word, mother."

"There needs to be," says Olivia. "Because the dictionary describes a *hero* as a man. Look at Gertrude Bell, the English writer who helped establish the Hashemite dynasty in Baghdad and create what is modern-day Iraq. Or Rebecca West traveling in

Yugoslavia, bringing to light the many underlying tensions within the Balkans?"

"And look what's happened to those countries!" counters Bernard.

"Bernard!" Olivia rarely finds humor in attacking the competence of women, unless it's televangelists, whom she claims take advantage of people's worst fears.

"But what do we know about this *professor*?" insists Bernard. "It sounds like a very peculiar project—going around dropping wallets. What about accommodations? You'll probably be crammed into some horrible *auberge* with rusty pipes and an escaped lunatic living across the hall."

"In some places we have an apartment, and in others, hotel rooms."

Bernard replies, "Only two men should ever enter a woman's bedchamber—her husband and her doctor."

Olivia and I look at each other and groan the way we always do when Bernard goes all Victorian on us.

"Yes, Bernard," says Olivia. And a lady's name should only appear in the newspaper three times—her birth, marriage, and death."

"If only we could say the same for you, Mother!"

I'm not sure if Bernard is referring to Olivia's scathing editorials or the number of times her name has been listed in the police blotter for various arrests and protests.

Olivia turns to me. "Once I arranged for Bernard to attend summer camp abroad when he was a teenager, but he wouldn't hear of it!"

"*Summer camp?*" Bernard stands up perfectly straight and his blue eyes widen. "You signed me up for a work expedition in poverty-stricken Guatemala!"

"Campfires or *campesinos*—what's the difference, so long as you're out of doors?" replies Olivia.

Bernard ignores her and begins singing from Gilbert and

Sullivan's *H.M.S. Pinafore*, "*Stick close to your desks and never go to sea, and you all may be rulers of the Queen's Navee!*"

Olivia interrupts her son's concert. "What does Craig think about all this?"

"Actually, I haven't spoken to him yet. He's sort of counting on me to help revamp the website for his business—we're going to make it interactive, so people can design their own ponds by choosing options from different categories to get an idea of how it will look—kind of like a Chinese menu."

"Oh, that's a wonderful idea," says Olivia and clasps her hands together.

"Mother, why don't you go and read your tea leaves, while I talk to Hallie sensibly about this matter?"

"Because you intend to talk her out of it, since you're afraid to travel," says Olivia. "You won't even take the girls to Disneyland."

As usual, Bernard seems unconcerned about feedback and turns his attention toward me. "I've made a delicious standing rib roast for dinner with thrice-baked potatoes and candied yams, none of which is for the faint of artery. Why don't we discuss it over the evening repast?"

"My mom is having a graduation dinner for me," I say. "I haven't told her that it's slightly premature."

"Well then, be sure to join us for lunch tomorrow, because I'm having a dry-run for Christmas," says Bernard.

"Bernard is cooking a *goose* for Christmas!" Olivia, the staunch vegetarian, looks none too happy.

"It's Peking snow goose, with rice pilaf, and a medley of winter vegetables," states Bernard. "Mother, why don't you go to the Cleveland Zoo for Christmas where you can watch all the animals and birds you want roaming around uncooked?"

"Geese mate for life, Bernard," complains Olivia.

"That's why I'm making two!" Bernard gives his mother a mock smile and then looks at me. "Mother is thinking about becoming a fallen-fruit vegetarian. She worries that cherries feel the pain of being yanked off the tree when sacrificed to become turnovers."

"I gave you perfectly good recipes for beetloaf and tofutti Alfredo!" says Olivia.

"Excuse me for being sane, but I am not having *beetloaf* and *tofutti* for Christmas dinner!" counters Bernard. "If they're anything like your recipe for last Thanksgiving's Tofurkey stuffed with soysage, the guests *might* be up for some tea and toast by New Year's Day."

"That's only because the orange juice was spoiled!" declares Olivia. "Furthermore, I have every reason to believe that you intentionally sabotaged the Tofurkey."

While the carnivore and the vegetarian continue to go at it, I slip into the kitchen and phone Craig. He may as well just meet me at my mom's, since I know about the party. On the way home, I stop at the theater where my stunning sister Louise is starring in Gil's production of *Romeo and Juliet*. Big posters out front have practically life-sized, color photographs of Louise and José, the bank teller who is playing her star-crossed lover, alongside a sign containing information about the drama workshop that Gil has started.

The theater is doing well, and it's been a boost for local business, which was declining as more people went shopping at malls, outlet centers, and superstores. Now there's a coffeehouse that sells stuff like Himalayan goji juice and specialty teas, a place where kids can make pottery, and a pet shop, all thriving. In fact, last spring Cosgrove County was written up in the *Cleveland Plain Dealer* as a great weekend getaway, so now tourists can be found strolling up and down Main Street, sometimes even taking photographs. It seems like only a year ago it was just the opposite, and locals felt they had to drive to *Cleveland* for a good time.

Gil is locking the doors as I pull up next to the curb. He's carrying a box of programs and appears to be in a hurry. I roll down the window, lean my head out, and wave.

"Hey, Hallie!" He walks toward the car and gives me the big smile and warm welcome that come from a kind heart.

Everyone loves Gil. His Southern charm and generous nature are irresistible.

"How's show business?" I ask.

"Don't forget that tomorrow is closing night!" Then he begins quoting from the prologue of *Romeo and Juliet*. "*The two hours' traffic of our stage; The which if you with patient ears attend, What here shall miss, our toil shall strive to mend.*"

Gil has been quoting The Bard for about two months straight now, and it's starting to get annoying. Especially in conjunction with the Shakespeare holiday cards featuring Willy in a Santa hat spouting something from *Henry IV, Part 1*.

"Wouldn't miss it for the world," I assure him. In truth, I'd completely forgotten about having promised to attend the final performance. "Is Louise still inside?"

"She left about twenty minutes ago," he tells me. "Did you hear that Bernard wants a panic room for Christmas? Either that or a robot butler—some choice!" Gil laughs good-naturedly, the way he usually does when discussing Bernard's latest antics. It's clear to anyone that the two of them are very happy together.

"Hey, Gil, what would you do if someone offered you a trip around the world?"

"Ha!" says Gil. "If I didn't have a husband, a job, and two kids, I'd jump at it. A great sage once wrote: *All you touch and all you see is all your life will ever be.*"

"Shakespeare?" I ask.

"Pink Floyd."

"Right," I say. Thank goodness Gil hasn't completely abandoned his rock-and-roll roots for the classics.

"See you tomorrow night!" he says.

Gil removes one hand from the box of programs to wave and then heads across the street toward his car. I guess I should be relieved that he didn't throw in the bit about parting being such sweet sorrow.

Chapter 5

$\mathcal{B}$ y the time I arrive home, a cold winter rain has begun to fall. Inside the house it's warm and cheerful. Craig is sitting on the couch helping Darlene string colored popcorn for the tree. Though honestly, with all the homemade ornaments from over the years, I don't think there's room for another thing. However, I can't help but notice how handsome Craig looks with his butterscotch hair appearing windswept even indoors and flashing green eyes that are a heavenly mixture of emeralds and seawater. Best of all, when Craig sees me, he smiles in a way that causes his whole face to ripple, like a still pond into which a pebble has been thrown.

The only person missing is the oldest Palmer child, my brother Eric, and he's arriving the day after tomorrow with his girlfriend Elizabeth. Mom pretends the two aren't living together in Nashville the same way she's been pretending that Craig and I won't be sharing an apartment in Cincinnati. Meantime, since telling her about moving in with Craig, I don't miss an opportunity to refer to Cincinnati as Sin Sin City, and then pretend it was an accident. It doesn't bother me that Mom is old-fashioned so much as that she's a lot *more* old-fashioned with her daughters than with her sons. It was the same with Dad. All of Eric's various scrapes were wink, wink, nudge, nudge, Dad smiling and saying, "Boys will be boys." But there was no "girls will be girls." No sir, not in this house, anyway.

"Surprise!" Craig says as he hurries over to greet me.

I give him a big kiss while thinking, "Oh, there's going to be a surprise all right."

Craig pulls a dozen daisies out from behind his back. Each one is a different color, ranging from the standard white and yellow to electric green, shocking red, and bright purple. "It's a psychedelic daisy bouquet. I dyed them myself."

"Wow!" I say. "These are really...hallucinatory."

Craig leans over and whispers, "I figured since we couldn't drink tonight to celebrate your finishing school, these might help create a reasonable facsimile, especially if we stand on our heads for a while."

"Amen to that!" I quote Pastor Costello's favorite refrain, which has by now become part of the household vernacular. (Unlike his oft-uttered, "Oh, fiddlesticks!")

The hypnotic aroma of home cooking automatically gathers us to the table the way harbor lights beckon small craft to safety at nightfall.

Pastor Costello sits at the head of the table and Mom takes her place at the opposite end, with one highchair on either side for the twins, Roddy and Reggie, who just turned three. They're big enough not to need the highchairs, but I think Mom is still using them for security purposes. The little kids pick up all the tricks from the older ones—kicking each other under the table during grace, adding food they don't like to one another's plates, and of course, trying to make people laugh while drinking milk so that it spurts out of their noses.

In some ways it's as if Dad never existed—only you look around the table and he's everywhere—in Louise's rich brown eyes, Francie's high cheekbones, Teddy's square jaw, and even the slightly crooked smiles of the twins.

Lillian, who is now five, does a fast but slightly garbled job of saying grace. This is a child whose bedtime prayer goes something like, "Lead us not into temptation but deliver us some e-mail." Tonight, Lillian's special intention is that there be snow for Christmas so Santa can land his sleigh on the roof.

Normally, Pastor Costello would ask if there was a special intention more "outwardly directed" (translation: less selfish), but he appears eager to add a few words himself.

Raising his milk glass, Pastor Costello says, "A hearty congratulations to Hallie who finished college today!"

Louise and Teddy begin chanting, "Go Hallie! Go Hallie!"

I interrupt them by saying, "Yeah, about that—I'm not actually graduating in January."

Mom looks stunned. Craig appears confused. Pastor Costello manages to hold his cheerful expression, suggesting that he's accustomed to hearing sudden pronouncements *much* worse.

"The school made a mistake and I'm four credits short," I explain.

Mom seems doubtful. In her book, institutions are rarely wrong. The fault more often lies in her offspring.

"It's nothing I did, honestly! You can call my new advisor." Great. I sound like an eight-year-old being accused of taking another kid's cookie when, in fact, it was given to me. Though I can't blame her. Because I played hooky so much back in high school and constantly lied about it, Mom still doesn't trust me entirely when it comes to attendance.

"So why can't you graduate if it's *the school's mistake?*" asks the more fair-minded Craig.

"Even though they totally admit it was an error on their part, the administration can't just hand me the credits because then my degree isn't 'real,' see? So they're offering to let me take the class for free. And keep my dorm room if I want to."

Mom finally appears convinced, though disappointed. "We can celebrate anyway. You'll just take the class and get your diploma in the spring, right?"

"Right," I say. "And if not, with Eric getting his master's—it still averages out to one degree per child."

Mom frowns. So much for trying to lighten the mood.

"But what about Cincinnati?" chimes in Craig.

"I could take the class there too—it's just a social science—but then I'd have to pay."

Craig furrows his wide brow underneath hair that falls across his forehead in loose strands and bayonets his chicken.

"Though at a community college it wouldn't cost that much," I add.

Craig suddenly appears HUGELY relieved. "Good. Because I've already built bookcases for the apartment."

"Only there's something else," I say. "This professor doing a sociology experiment has asked some students to help her. And I could also get the credits by participating in that."

There's silence, but for the twins slurping milk and Lillian chasing carrots around her plate with a spoon.

"It involves traveling around the world for sixteen weeks—going to different countries and dropping wallets to see how many people return them…determining how honest people are."

This time, I don't know who looks more gobsmacked—Mom or Craig.

"I don't know—I was just thinking about it," I start to backpedal. "Nothing is definite."

Pastor Costello shows his inexperience as a parent by saying, "I think it's good for a young person to see how privileged we are. I'll never forget my trip to Cambodia."

Mom is obviously thinking: Rape, Murder, Terror Attack. She stares daggers at Pastor Costello. I question whether the wedding is still on.

Apparently, he does too. "I just meant that at *some point* in one's life it's good to take a trip," Pastor Costello quickly amends his previous statement. "Though it's probably best done when you're older—in your thirties, maybe…"

He looks to Mom for a sign that he's working his way out of this hole. At the end of the day, Pastor Costello is not so much spiritual advisor as salesman, in that he's selling peace of mind. It goes without saying that his favorite Irish proverb is "a good retreat is better than a poor defense," at least where Mom is concerned.

Sure enough, Mom doesn't appear quite as stony. Only Craig continues to stare down at his plate. In five minutes, I've gone from being everyone's favorite graduate to feeling like a defendant in a lawsuit.

"So, tell me more about the wedding," I say with forced cheer. "How many people are coming?"

Mom doesn't answer, and so Teddy jumps in. "Basically everybody."

"You mean the whole family?" I ask.

"I placed a note in the bulletin that all members of the congregation are welcome to attend," Pastor Costello clarifies. "We'll have a buffet downstairs afterward."

"That reminds me, Hallie, we're going to Niagara Falls for two days on our honeymoon." Mom has returned to Earth. "Do you think that between you and Teddy and Louise you can watch the children?"

"Of course," I say.

Teddy and Louise and I all shoot one another looks that say, "Mom on a *honeymoon*?" It's a very fourth-dimension concept.

"Arthur and I thought that once school lets out we'd take a trip with the whole family—maybe to the ocean. Would you kids like to swim in the ocean?"

The little ones cheer, causing Mom and Pastor Costello to beam.

After dinner, Craig and I do the dishes. "Would you be mad if I went on this trip?" I ask.

"Just really disappointed, I guess," he replies glumly.

Leave it to Craig not to start a fight that would let me storm off feeling completely justified in my selfishness. "It wouldn't mean changing any of our plans, only postponing them by a few weeks."

"You just said four months," replies Craig. "And how do you know that the speakers' bureau would still give you a job?"

"I'll find a job somewhere else—someplace better. Like Buffalo!" This is supposed to be a joke since they just had a winter storm so bad that we weren't even certain if the city was still there.

Craig stops doing the dishes, rests his hands on the sink, and takes a deep breath before speaking. "It's just that my business is finally making money, and I've been counting on not celebrating my twenty-fourth birthday at home. But…it sounds like a good opportunity and…you know…you should do it if you want to."

"Thanks." I lean over and kiss him on the cheek. "You're the best boyfriend in the world. Let me sleep on it tonight."

I decide to stay home and crash on the couch since Mom might have to dig out my immunization record in the morning. Before he leaves, Craig reminds me that tomorrow we have lunch with his parents and then front row tickets to see Louise in *Romeo and Juliet*.

"Oh goody, men in tights," I joke.

After everyone has gone to bed, I sit in the living room making a list of pros and cons for going on the trip. The list gets longer and longer, but every time I come up with a pro, I can easily match it with a con, and vice-versa. Basically, these spreadsheets depend on (*a*) what you really want to do and (*b*) whether you're an optimist or a pessimist. By page five, the catalogue of plusses and minuses shows no sign of ending. Finally, I decide the pro/con list is a pile of crap—you can make it come out any way you want.

The cat has been scratching and meowing to go outside since the top of page two, and so I finally get up and open the front door for him. "Only you're not going to like it," I say. And sure enough, as the wet sleet hits the threshold he backs up into the comparatively warm and cozy living room.

"Told you," I say. But now, the cat runs to the back door and begins scratching at that one, as if he might have better luck using a different exit. Talk about an optimist.

Chapter 6

The next morning, I wake up to more than the usual amount of commotion in our house. Two deliverymen are walking past me with a twin bed, then another twin bed, followed by two wooden dressers and then two desks. Mom is calling out directions in a flurry of excitement. It's rare that we get anything new in this house, at least aside from children. Most of our bedroom furniture came from when Mom's parents' house was sold, and the rest we inherited when Aunt Lala moved to England.

Mom decided it would be too expensive to move to a larger house, and so she had an addition put on this past fall. I think she also had in mind that a bigger house would be farther from town and the church. I'm pretty sure that Pastor Costello guaranteed the home improvement loan with his own house and, once he sells it, they'll use that money to pay back the loan. Though he basically lives here, Pastor Costello still goes home to sleep every night, for the sake of propriety.

The deliverymen head toward Mom and Dad's old room, which is now going to be used for the youngest set of twins, Reginald and Rodney. I walk in the direction of the addition, which up until now has been taped off while they finished sanding the floors and painting. At the end of the hallway, where the linen closet was, there's now a door and then a step down that leads to a new master bedroom with a little sitting area at one end. This way, if Mom and Pastor Costello want to watch something on TV without making five or six children miserable, they can.

At first Mom bemoaned the loss of her vegetable garden, but the truth is that the backyard never really got enough sunlight for it to thrive. Besides, Pastor Costello says Mom can have any kind of garden she wants up at the church.

The extra space is terrific, but I feel bad for the little kids, because they're going to have a heck of a time sneaking in and out late at night. The window nearest Mom's new bed is right next to the rain pipe that you have to climb to get onto the roof. And if you try sneaking in through the garage, they'll either hear you coming in the back door or tiptoeing up the creaky stairs. No indeed, I wouldn't want to be young again in this house.

I follow the excited voices of Roddy and Reggie shouting about "big-boy beds." My parents' old room is unrecognizable—the double bed replaced by two twin beds, white walls painted light blue, the old beige carpeting taken up, an area rug in its place. The two wooden dressers are set up with the two desks between them, and a bookcase stands in the middle. Mom's apparently getting a head start on kindergarten.

"Good morning, Hallie," says Mom. "Isn't this a wonderful boys' room?"

I knock on the top of one desk. "All ready for homework."

"It was a good value to buy the entire set all at once," says Mom. "They were having a clearance sale."

The boys begin jumping on one bed while Francie does flips on the other. Mom quickly puts a stop to that. "Hallie, would you help me get these sheets on? I can't wait to move those cribs down to the basement."

"Why don't we just get rid of them?" I ask. The basement is already a jumble of old toys, playpens, potty seats, and highchairs.

"For *grandchildren*, of course." She looks at me and smiles.

"Hey, don't look at me!" I've never exactly seen myself having breakfast in bed and opening presents on the second Sunday in May.

Mom appears truly upset. "Why Hallie, don't you want children?"

I honestly have to stop and think for a second. My life has never lacked for "opportunities" to change diapers and feed strained peas to babies. Which is how I happen to know that babies can and will bite, without the slightest provocation from their handlers. And children are on the selfish side, if you ask me. I mean, when was the last time a five-year-old asked you how your day was?

Mom reads my mind. "I mean children of your *own*."

"Well…I guess *someday*, but not right now!"

"No, of course not!" Mom wholeheartedly agrees. "Not until you're married."

"Let's do one wedding at a time, okay?"

But Mom is still preoccupied with planning my family. "You know, with Mrs. Muldoon's daughter trying to talk her into moving to Arizona, I can't help but think how wonderful it would be if you and Craig married and moved in next door."

A comment along the lines of, *Are you currently battling an addiction to prescription drugs?* almost escapes from my lips. Which is just behind, *Not in a million years.* But I catch myself on both. The filter is working. "Wouldn't *that* be funny!" Fake laugh.

"How about we go shopping for your bridesmaid dress before lunch?" asks Mom. "Arthur is going to move some of his things over this afternoon, and I'd like to be on hand to help arrange them." (Translation: Put them where she wants.) "We can sign Francie up for karate classes on the way to the mall."

"Karate?" Then I remember Louise told me that Francie was recently thrown out of her after-school program at the local YMCA for roughhousing. I'm still a bit confused, since it was my understanding that the program was designed for overly rambunctious kids to begin with.

"Francie's energy level was too high for the Y," Mom

diplomatically explains. "But it's only because she eats right and gets plenty of sleep. All children should be so healthy."

Shopping is my worst nightmare. And looking for a dress borders on Judgment Day. "You know, I've been thinking…why don't I just borrow something from Louise? Buying a new dress is really a waste of money since I doubt it will be something I can use again." The words "waste of money" are always a surefire way to change Mom's mind.

Mom looks around the new bedroom, and I can see that she's anxious to put the boys' clothes in the dressers and move their books and toys (which are scattered all over the house) into the bookcase and toy box.

"And we have Louise's play tonight," I remind her.

"I did promise Arthur that I'd make a gingerbread Jesus for the Sunday school party," says Mom. "And the Christmas presents still need to be wrapped."

"Just let me do a few things and I'll come back and help you," I say.

Mom gives me a big hug and a kiss. "Thank you, Hallie. And thank you for being so accepting of Arthur."

I hug Mom back but don't know what to say. I'm happy that they're getting married. And it's true that at this point I can't imagine the household without "Arthur." But the fact of the matter is I don't even know what to call Pastor Costello. Roddy and Reggie automatically call him Daddy, and no one tells them otherwise. The rest of the little kids refer to him as Uncle Arthur, except for Lillian, who calls him "Uncle Otter." And Louise heard Davy tell a friend that his real dad is a mountain man in the Yukon. But I imagine they'll all switch to "Dad" soon enough too. Eric, Louise, Teddy, and I carefully avoid using any titles or proper names, sticking to the pronoun "he." And when "he" isn't around, we still refer to him as Pastor Costello. "Arthur" is just too weird. As for "Dad"—no matter how much I love Pastor Costello, there will only ever be one Dad. At least for me.

Chapter 7

"Hallie, Craig is on the phone for you!" My younger brother Davy hollers at me from the kitchen, even though he can plainly see that I'm only four feet away, standing in front of the coat closet. "And he sounds real mad."

Oh no! I was supposed to be at Craig's house at noon so we could have lunch with his parents.

Grabbing the phone from Davy, I breathlessly say, "I'm so sorry!"

"I'm not *mad*." Craig obviously heard Davy's commentary. "I was just worried that something happened. The roads can get slippery this time of year."

"I'm fine. I was just helping Mom move the new furniture into the boys' room and lost track of time." A small lie, but it'd be a lot worse to admit that I completely forgot. His mother only sent me a *save-the-date* postcard about this holiday luncheon two months ago. In fact, that's the problem—Craig's parents plan everything so far in advance that by the time the event finally rolls around a person is onto another lifetime.

"Not a crisis," says my forgiving boyfriend. "Mom is keeping everything warm. Just hurry over."

"On my way!" The receiver hits the cradle and I'm facing a Fashion Crisis of FEMA proportions. My one nice sweater and pair of slacks is at the Stocktons'. Every time Craig's parents see me I'm in the worst possible T-shirt, carpenter jeans, and high-top sneakers or boots. Basically, my wardrobe. But Craig had nicely and diplomatically asked me to dress up for the occasion. His father works as an attorney with a big Cleveland law firm, and if the man isn't wearing a suit, then it's golf clothes or khakis and an expensive sweater that appears to be straight out of the box. Craig's mother is always doing charity work or attending gardening club meetings, and so I've never seen her in anything but a skirt and at least one strand of pearls.

Meantime, this has to be the day I'm wearing a long-sleeve T-shirt from a pesticide company with the words BUG OFF printed in blood red letters above a gruesome man-eating aphid lying dead on its back, spindly legs pointing skyward. Damn. I race downstairs to see what Louise has stowed in the basement. A coral cardigan sweater is lying on top of one of the milk crates she uses as dresser drawers. It's not exactly a brilliant match with apricot colored hair, but then honestly, what is? Buttoning the sweater all the way up manages to hide everything but the gray neckline of my T-shirt, which I'd remove entirely if I didn't think the heavy wool would scratch me to death. The jeans will have to do—at least this particular pair doesn't have any actual holes, just a few bleach marks, and a small tear in the back pocket.

The Larkin house is big for three people, but both of Craig's parents use one of the extra rooms as an office. The most noticeable thing to me is not the spaciousness so much as the way that everything there actually *works*—you don't have to push the oven door just right to make it close, the windows don't leak so you wake up with a little snowdrift on the windowsill, and you don't get scalded in the shower whenever someone flushes a toilet.

Craig's parents are waiting for me in the front hall. "We were worried you'd been in an accident," says his mother.

"If I had a nickel for every drunk driver out there around the holidays," confirms his father.

"I really apologize. With my mom getting remarried, we put

an addition on the house, and the twins' new furniture arrived this morning." I attempt to make it sound as if I did the construction all by myself. Craig is an only child, even though his mom loves kids; and it seemed like the year I had to take care of my little brothers and sisters, I scored a lot of points with her, being that it was a time in my life when no sane human being going on vacation for a week would have entrusted me with a hamster. However, while visiting her son on weekends (oftentimes in his bedroom with the door closed) over the past two years, the luster appears to have worn off.

"Family comes first," says Craig's dad, as if my excuse has also flown well with him. "Why don't you let me take that sweater? With all the cooking Mary has been doing, it's awfully warm inside the house."

Oh no, not my sweater! "Hot? Really?" I try to look surprised. "The heat feels nice, I think. Very cozy."

Craig comes up from the basement, which is where he raises Japanese koi for his pond business. Glancing down at my jeans, he looks as if this wasn't exactly what he had in mind, but gives me a smile and a kiss on the lips. Craig, of course, looks perfect in gray flannel slacks and a light blue button-down shirt.

"Why don't we have a drink in the living room?" suggests Mr. Larkin. "Hallie, what would you like to wet your whistle?"

Craig and I shoot each other a quick glance to acknowledge that his father has just used another one of his country-club sayings. Sometimes we run a contest, each guessing the number of sayings he'll drop ahead of time, and then seeing who comes closest. If one of us can get Mr. Larkin to say "minding your Ps and Qs," that always counts for a double score.

"We have Merlot, Pinot Noir, Chardonnay, and the new Beaujolais, or I can make you a screwdriver."

It's just a fact that there's no chocolate Yoo-Hoo in this house. Or strawberry Nesquik for that matter. No, I've entered the gin and tonic zone. "Just some ginger ale is fine, thanks."

"Come on—you're twenty-one now, how about a glass of champagne? 'Tis the season!"

I'm never sure when Craig's parents might be pulling some sort of morals quiz on me, as in, *But is she good enough for our only begotten son?* If I say yes to the champagne does that mean they'll think I pour crème de cacao over my cereal in the morning? Ever since I (unknowingly!) dated the son of that mafia guy, the idea never appears to be far from their minds that I could just as easily have ended up a gangster's moll.

"Half a glass," I say cautiously, "if everyone else is having some."

Craig's mother brings out a big crystal bowl of shrimp cocktail, a platter of stuffed mushrooms, and some macadamia nuts. Mr. and Mrs. Larkin are in their late forties, almost ten years older than my mom, and yet they appear much less harried, as if they haven't spent large amounts of time shouting, "Take your sister's head out of the toilet this instant!" and "Stop petting the fish!" or sitting in the emergency room at nine o'clock at night with a screaming child who has managed to push a Lego all the way up his nose.

After we clink glasses and fill small china plates with hors d'oeuvres, the small talk begins. *How nice about my mom's wedding! Isn't it wonderful that Craig's business is going so well? Aren't we excited about moving to Cincinnati next week?*

What? I look over at Craig, but he is suddenly very involved with a stuffed mushroom and won't meet my gaze. So, he apparently hasn't told them that if I go on this trip our plans to live together will have to be delayed by several months.

Craig's father places his hand on top of his thighs. "Mary and I have been talking, and it seems foolish to throw money away on paying rent. All you end up with is a drawer full of rent receipts, right?" He chuckles as if this is a great joke.

We all nod in the affirmative. People tend to agree with whatever Mr. Larkin says when it comes to business matters.

"So, Craig's mother and I thought we'd buy you kids a little starter place in Cincinnati, maybe a two-bedroom condo, you'll pay the monthly maintenance, same as you would've written a rent check, and we'll make the down payment and pay the mortgage. This way, you're building equity right from the get-go!" It's easy to tell that Mr. Larkin likes the sound of the words *build equity* the same way my Dad loved to hear *buy-one-get-one-free.*

"Wow!" I must look stunned. Though not for the reasons Mr. and Mrs. Larkin think. Did Craig know about this? He must have! So why hadn't he told them there might be a slight change in plan? Or at least WARN ME that our lunch today had an agenda. On the other hand, this could be one of Craig's famous practical jokes, the way he likes to pretend the fish bite off his fingers, or call my dorm and leave a message with my roommate saying that my mother is on her way, so that I spend the next hour cleaning like a mad person, when actually it's Craig who is coming for a surprise visit and doesn't want to deal with the catastrophe that's my half of the room.

I'm desperately trying to catch Craig's eye, but he's decided it's the perfect moment to refill our glasses. Too much time elapses and the Parental Units are looking at me for a more definitive response.

"That's incredibly generous!" I finally say. "I'm not one hundred percent sure that this job is right for me, and so why don't Craig and I talk more about it and let you know." This is the moment I should tell them all about the trip, but instead I raise my champagne flute, in effect proposing a toast to the condo idea, and we all clink glasses.

Mrs. Larkin rises and clasps her hands together. "We'd better go into the dining room and start lunch or the lamb will dry out."

"Everything smells de-licious!" Mr. Larkin follows his wife out of the living room.

And that's when I pounce on Craig. "*What's* going on here? Is this some kind of setup? Why wouldn't you *look* at me?"

Craig takes my hand in his. I pull it away.

"Just listen…I knew you'd be mad, but my Dad only sprung this on me an hour ago. I hadn't mentioned the possibility of your trip to them because it's still up in the air, and quite frankly, I'm hoping you won't go. But there wasn't any way to warn you about the condo. Maybe *now* you'll finally get a cell phone—ever hear of texting!"

Craig appears so dementedly helpless that I start to laugh. Seriously, worse things can happen than your boyfriend's parents offering to buy you a starter condo. And we regularly joke about how Craig's folks are so involved in every aspect his life, right down to what type of dental floss he should use, while at my house there's a sign-out sheet posted by the backdoor in case any neighborhood lawn ornaments go missing and alibis become necessary.

"So," I whisper, "This *two-bedroom* condo—is that one room for us and one for them?"

"Craig darling, we're ready to eat," Mrs. Larkin trills from the dining room. "I've made all of your favorite vegetables and those buttermilk biscuits you love so much!"

We look at each other and cover our mouths so the giggles don't escape. I guess that answers my question.

Chapter 8

A few low white clouds linger above the trees, but nothing to suggest that we'll have snow for Christmas. There was a storm in the middle of November that left about four inches on the ground; however, it quickly melted. Since then it's been cold and clear or else gray and rainy.

It's imperative to reach Bernard's antiques shop at the corner of Main and Swan streets and catch Bernard's shop assistant June alone before he arrives. Bernard no longer works full time at the store, but I know that two days before Christmas he'll be there in the late afternoon to assist all the last minute shoppers (translation: desperate husbands ready to spend). They almost always tend to be men who don't know the price of anything and are too embarrassed to haggle in an antiques store. Plus, they're usually so grateful for Bernard's talent in suggesting items their wives always love (and usually mentioned to him beforehand), that the men are happy to pay a premium for the personalized service. Women, on the other hand, like to believe they possess better taste than Bernard, though this is largely because he continuously tells them they do. He's a practiced liar when it comes to the art of complimenting women on their choice of style and decor.

Across the street, in the empty building where the old hardware store used to be, a hand-painted sign announces that one of those places that sell bath and body products will be opening next month. A chain store in Cosgrove County! It's hard to believe. I'd left a small town and arrived home to a full-blown suburb.

Fortunately, Bernard's car is nowhere to be seen out front. Inside, a teenage girl is trying to decide between two of June's handcrafted necklaces. I see that she's greatly expanded her inventory since the last time I stopped by. She's also greatly expanded her waistline and her wardrobe. June looks like a gypsy fortuneteller in a pair of shoulder-sweeping earrings encrusted with turquoise, rainbows of frosted eye-shadow, and there's actually a fault line where heavily mascaraed lashes curl up to meet the swirls of hair gone prematurely maroon that cascade over her brow. She wears a gold lamé vest over a jade green silk blouse with a long flowing skirt that gives the appearance of being a dozen brightly-colored scarves all sewn together. Her wrists are where charm bracelets meet to form federations.

The girl is deep in conversation with June about Pisces and Taurus, and I eventually gather that she is one sign and her boyfriend the other. I busy myself looking around the shop until the girl makes a selection and starts for the door. She looks very happy on the way out.

"Another satisfied customer!" I say to June.

Only June appears doubtful. "Pisces and Taurus rarely make a good match."

"Really?" I'm still skeptical about all this astrology stuff, but whenever I'm really in a jam, I figure that it can't hurt.

June shakes her head from side to side. "Pisces is deep and mysterious, but Taurus is an open book, easily read and manipulated. These things can be overcome, but taken as a whole, it's not a good idea for the long term."

"Taurus is the end of April, beginning of May, right?" I'm asking because Craig's birthday is April thirtieth.

"Yes, the ruling planet is Venus," says June. "Taureans are typically faithful, strong-willed, and generous."

"So…uh…what do you think about a match between *Virgo* and Taurus?"

"That can succeed—both earth signs—practical and hardworking." June finishes placing the jewelry trays back inside the glass case. "If you're looking for Bernard, he just called to say that he'll be here in ten minutes—something about his pomegranate pecan muffins not rising."

"He's been really into muffins this fall," I explain. "You'd think that spiced nectarine muffins were on Maslow's Hierarchy of Needs right up there between breathing and regulating body temperature."

"Good for aromatherapy." June nods her approval.

It's necessary to hurry up if I want to escape Bernard's ridicule. "Here's the thing—I have a chance to take a really big trip… basically around the world…and I'm not sure if I should go."

"Is that so?" June turns very serious.

"And I was just wondering…" Only I'm not sure what I was wondering—if there's an astrological coin one can flip to make such decisions?

"If it's a good time for you to travel," June finishes the sentence for me.

"Yeah, exactly," I say. "Is that something…you know…that…"

"Of course!" says June. "People should never go *anywhere* without consulting their chart! How do you think most car wrecks happen?"

"Bad driving?" I guess.

"Yes, but because the motorists are distracted. And they would have known about these distractions had they consulted their horoscope before getting behind the wheel." June is already pulling down one of her enormous tomes that looks like a combination of an astronomy text and a book of spells.

"Virgo, Virgo," June flips through the large, thick pages. "They're the biggest worriers before a trip—the ones packing extra toothbrushes and a parachute."

"I sort of have to let them know really soon." I try to hurry her along, afraid that Bernard is going to pull up at any moment.

She finds a page and starts running her finger over lots of complicated circles. "Virgo is in the third house, which is commonly referred to as the House of Communication."

June begins to look doubtful. "How long is this journey?"

"Four months." I glance out the window for signs of Bernard. June shakes her head from side to side. "Maybe a weekend would be okay. Has anyone else in your family taken a trip lately?"

"Eric goes back and forth to Nashville for school," I say. "And Dad died two years ago, but I don't know if that counts as a trip." If so, it was certainly one-way.

June looks up from her charts. "When did you say your father crossed over?" She emphasizes "crossed over" as if Dad took a voyage in a time machine instead of having a fatal heart attack.

"Well...uh...two years ago on January fifth." And that's when I realize it. "The day I'm supposed to leave..."

June looks back down at her book, but by now, she's shaking her head vigorously. "No, this doesn't seem to be the right time for travel, unless it's just a few days for work or to see a sick friend or relative." She points at a part of the solar system. "Because Jupiter is—"

"How's my favorite sorceress?" calls out Bernard.

Whoa! He must have parked down the street. I quickly slam June's book closed and try to make it look like I wasn't having a consultation. "We were just discussing the weather—if there would be snow tomorrow."

"Whipping up a little incantation for a white Christmas?" jokes Bernard. "I must agree that a blanket of new-fallen snow makes the town so much more aesthetically pleasing."

"We're seeing if it's a good time for Hallie to travel." June spills the beans. And based on the sincerity of her tone, if she has any idea that others don't believe in astrology or secretly make fun of her, you'd never know it.

"Hallie, may I speak to you for a moment?"

Here we go. I follow Bernard outside into the cold.

"How many times do I have to tell you that this is all a shell game so the Crystal Queen can sell five cents worth of rocks, beads, and leather for twenty-five dollars?" Bernard talks as if trying to explain that Santa is not real to a fifteen-year-old. "She reads the obituaries and thinks there's some cosmic relevance in the fact that the people appear to have died in alphabetical order. You insisted on wearing those baubles after your father died, and I didn't say anything because it made you feel better. But I'm afraid you're tragically misguided to be hurling yourself at Morgan le Fay every time a difficult decision arises. This business of incense and charms is a crutch—just like drugs or alcohol. You'll become dependent and the next thing you know—"

"June doesn't think it's a good time for me to travel," I interrupt him.

"*Really?*" Bernard suddenly becomes quite interested in June's forecast.

"I'd be leaving on the same day that my dad died."

"Well, I guess she may have a point there." Bernard suddenly starts acting as if there's something to June's aforementioned "hocus pocus" after all.

"Yeah, but you just said—"

"I believe in listening to everyone," says Bernard. "There are, of course, signs in the universe, and June telling you not to go must be one of them."

It would appear that Bernard has the capacity to become a mystic seer himself when it complements his own agenda.

Chapter 9

That night when Craig picks me up for the final performance of *Romeo & Juliet*, he doesn't ask about the status of my travel plans, though I assume he really needs to know what to do about the apartment.

The streets are gritty with salt that was dumped in anticipation of a snowfall that never came. As we turn a particularly crunchy corner, the brakes squeal.

"Your truck needs new brake pads," I say.

Craig scowls at me. Auto maintenance is a touchy subject for us. I know a lot about cars from having worked a summer at the gas station. Meantime, Craig's family has always had brand new cars with extended warranties, and as talented as he is with building ponds, he can never figure out what's wrong with an engine, not even one in a lawnmower. Bernard says that I should pretend not to know anything about mechanics when straight men are around. But that's pretty stupid, since I can save us a lot of money by changing the oil and doing simple repairs.

Another squeal.

"It's not warmed up yet," says Craig.

I decide to leave this one alone, or we might end up having a huge fight that's purportedly about brake pads but really about something else. Why don't I tell him that despite June's dire warnings, I've made up my mind to go, and just get it over with? My whole family attends the play, except for Roddy and Reggie, who stay with Mrs. Muldoon. Eric and Elizabeth arrive from Nashville just in time and go directly to the theater, where my family takes up almost the entire front row. Looking over at Pastor Costello, I have to wonder if he's intrigued by how the theater fills up front first, as opposed to church, where the best seats seem to be in the back.

Louise is really terrific as Juliet, especially when defying her parents. And she's stunning onstage, with a magnificent aura about her, the same as in daily life. There can be no doubt in anyone's mind that Louise Palmer is a name destined to be up on a marquee in lights. Otherwise, the sword fights are entertaining and very realistic. The girls' gym teacher at the high school was a national fencing champion, and she coached the actors slated for duels.

By the look on my mom's face upon hearing the line, "Younger than she are happy mothers made," it's safe to say she firmly disagrees with the concept of thirteen-year-olds as mothers.

Louise does an amazing job of dying, probably from all that practice of hurling herself on the floor and refusing to move when she was young and didn't get her way. I can't even see Louise breathing, whereas Romeo's left foot keeps twitching.

At the conclusion of the play, everyone jumps up to give the performers a standing ovation. The town isn't so big that you can't not know at least a few people onstage, even if it's just from seeing them at the Star-Mart. During the final bows, bouquets of red roses fly at Louise from everywhere—the orchestra pit, audience members carrying them to the edge of the stage, and stagehands delivering them from the wings. There are so many flowers that Romeo has to help Juliet carry them all.

When we arrive backstage, Louise is still in her costume and makeup, accepting kudos and acknowledging admirers like Miss America. I overhear the lighting and sound guys talk about a play that Louise has been offered in New York and how maybe she can get everyone else jobs.

As the family starts listening to what's being said, Planet Louise acknowledges that we're in her orbit by announcing, "I was going to tell you at dinner last night, but..." She looks over at me as if to say, *But Hallie ruined the moment with her drama about not graduating!*

Please. Louise must have been overjoyed to find an excuse to postpone dropping this bomb for another day, especially while I was the one absorbing all the negative PR, basically a human shield for her, as usual.

"Tell us *what?*" asks Mom. Fortunately she's already sitting down, a result of Lillian falling asleep in her arms.

"I've been offered a part in an Off-Broadway play in New York." Louise flashes us her movie star smile and most everyone looks excited for a moment. But those of us over eighteen are of course thinking, *What about Yale?*

"What about Yale?" Mom asks as nicely as possible, giving Louise the benefit of the doubt—maybe she simply forgot that she's supposed to be in New Haven next week.

"Well..." begins Louise, "since I was planning to study drama... this is even better. Lots of casting agents come to Off-Broadway shows, and so it will lead to more parts."

"But how will you *live?*" asks Mom.

"By doing modeling and commercials," Louise says confidently.

People are coming by to say that the cast party is beginning. Apparently, it's being held at the old feed store, which has recently been turned into a dance club.

Mom looks confused and disoriented.

Unfortunately, I remember this look all too well from when Mom was in the mental hospital with depression for a few months after Dad died. So I jump in, "She can defer her admission for a semester."

Pastor Costello follows my lead and with an enormous smile

says, "Louise really is a terrific actress. I'm sure it will be fine." His particular brand of ministry embraces the idea that even though we can't always be happy, we can always be cheerful.

Mom looks at Eric. And why not? He's the only one around here who seems able to graduate from college. "Will you talk to her?"

Eric places his arm around Mom's shoulders. "Sure Mom, first thing in the morning."

Talk to her? Since when has anyone ever talked sense into Louise? But at least it relieves the tension for the moment. And with the wedding only two days away, Mom has plenty of other things to worry about.

Chapter 10

Christmas morning is the usual frantic shredding of paper and shrieks of delight. Only this year, we have to be at the church by noon for the wedding ceremony. As soon as the gifts are opened and the hacking, runny-nosed youngest twins have distributed two-dozen "hug coupons," everyone rushes to shower. Meantime, Darlene runs around with her new digital camera snapping photos like a crime reporter. With Eric, Louise, and me all driving our own cars, it's not a problem to transport the entire family at once. Otherwise, we'd have to use the church van.

Craig is getting out of his car in the parking lot, and I decide that I have to tell him *now*. I dash over holding my dress up so it doesn't get caught in the tops of my hiking boots. "I'm sorry Craig…but I've decided to go on the trip."

Craig smiles as if that's just fine and dandy with him—not so much as a frown or a "please, think it over" from my perfect boyfriend.

In fact, it's almost strange how easily he accepts the news. For a second, I feel bad that I'm not going to be missed nearly as much as I thought I'd be.

Craig merely looks down at my feet and asks, "Is that what you're wearing?"

"Very funny." I hurry off to the alcove to switch my shit-kickers for shiny black pumps. Mom also thought it was ridiculous that I couldn't drive the mile from home to church in the shoes that match the dress, especially since there isn't any snow on the ground, but I honestly believe my body is allergic to high heels.

Bernard pokes his head around the corner and dramatically states, "From this moment, happiness is not the question; all that concerns us is to save the remains, the fragments, the appearance—"

"What on *Earth* are you talking about?" I interrupt him.

He points at the royal blue sateen dress I've borrowed from my sister. "Louise wore that dress in Act III of *A Doll's House*."

"But of course. Sorry, I'm a little slow on the uptake today." After digging through my bag, I find a small package and hand it to Bernard. "Merry Christmas."

He rips open the DVD like a little kid. "*The Queen of England's Golden Jubilee Gala, Live from Buckingham Palace!* I had no idea it was available for purchase by commoners!"

"Sorry it doesn't come with a recipe book," I say. "But the announcer says 'an' before some of the 'h' words, like 'an historic occasion.'"

"That's how it *should* be said." Bernard is now speaking with a slight British accent. "We don't go around saying *a herb garden*, now do we?"

From out of his shopping bag he removes a small package wrapped in gold foil and hands it to me. Then he whips out his cell phone. "Excuse me for being so rude, but I have to make a quick call."

Suddenly the box in my hand starts ringing.

"A phone!" I shout. "Oh, my gosh, look out twenty-first century, here I come!"

"Complete with one year of free calls to anywhere within the contiguous United States," adds Bernard.

Wait a second. I'm just about to leave on an international trip for four months. "You just don't want me to escape your gravitational pull!"

Bernard's hand flies to his chest. "Hallie, how could you ever suggest such a thing—that I would attempt to interfere in your life with such a devious and underhanded maneuver?"

Before I can answer, Bernard has rushed out the door. I hear the "Wedding March" begin and Mom appears in the entranceway. Her cheeks are flushed and she looks stunning in an off-white tea-length gown. "Ready?"

Fortunately, there isn't time to think about how strange all this seems. I may as well be wearing a dress from an amateur theatrical, since that's what this day feels like.

I walk down the aisle toward Pastor Costello, who's waiting in front of the altar, wearing a dark gray suit and an enormous smile. In the place where he usually stands is a minister who looks to be in his late hundreds. Pastor Costello has invited the man who ordained him twenty years ago to marry them. When Pastor Anderson takes his shaky old hands off the podium and stands up straight, he appears almost lifelike.

Mom reaches the front of the church, and standing there next to Pastor Costello—they both look so *sure* of everything.

Pastor Anderson says, *Love joineth us unto God. Love covereth a multitude of sins. Love hath no division. Love doeth all things in concord. Without love, we are as empty vessels, sounding but without issue.*

He's a large man with a deep monotonous rumble, which has, at times, a soporific effect, like the distant sound of the ocean. When Pastor Anderson finally gets to the part about "Do you take this woman to be your lawful wedded wife," I'm wishing that I'd thrown back a couple of chocolate Yoo-Hoos in the alcove for staying power. This dress is feeling tighter and warmer by the minute, and my feet are dead asleep inside these horrible shoes.

At last they kiss, the organist begins pumping out "O Praise Ye the Lord," and it's off to the basement for photographs and chicken-on-sticks. I made it through the ceremony without fainting or throwing up, and that's all I was really hoping for.

Chapter 11

I've agreed to stay at the house and be primary caretaker for the paste-eaters while Mom and Pastor Costello honeymoon in Niagara Falls for two days. We all know how Louise feels about childcare, Teddy is making the most of his final year of high school, and Eric has to leave in the morning.

The holiday and wedding excitement is over, the kids are in bed, and yet I still can't sleep. Am I having second thoughts about deciding to go on the trip? If so, it's only because of Craig, since I won't regret ditching that job for a minute. However, Craig seemed fine at the reception. That's probably what I love best about him—Craig is the most understanding person in the world, always saying that you have to put yourself in the other person's shoes and not be judgmental. I should have one-tenth of his patience and compassion. He even came back to the house afterward and helped Davy set up the handheld global positioning device he received for Christmas. One thing is sure, with all the outdoor gear Davy has amassed, if he ever decides to run away from home, there's not a chance in a million that we'd find him.

It's almost one o'clock in the morning when I finally decide to give up on sleep. I wander into the kitchen, and Eric is sitting at the table drinking a beer in the dark. Since he turned twenty-one last year, Mom lets my brother keep a six-pack in the fridge when he's home visiting. She just won't buy it for him.

Outside the window tiny white flakes swirl in the darkness like dust particles. Finally, it's snowing!

I make hot chocolate in the microwave. Eric and I have always been able to read each other's minds, and this morning is no different. It's as if we're twins, even though we're a year apart. The two of us sit there silently in the dark, and for some reason, I'm reminded of the family meeting we held in the dining room after Dad died two years ago.

There's some noise on the stairs, shuffling across the carpet, and Louise appears. Her hair and face look perfect, as if she hasn't even bothered trying to sleep.

"The shower is available!" she announces, making a joking reference to the hour-long line outside the bathroom this morning, when all ten kids were scrambling to get ready for the wedding at once.

"Hot chocolate is on the counter," I offer.

"Thanks, but I'd rather have a beer," says Louise.

Eric nods toward the fridge.

Louise removes a can, sits down, looks at me, and then at Eric. "Do you think they're…you know, actually doing it?" She makes a face to suggest that answering in the affirmative might cause her to become violently ill.

Eric and I both begin to laugh. Though we may not have put it exactly in those words, it's more or less what we've both been thinking.

"If so, I'm sure it's only the missionary position," replies Eric.

This causes Louise to snort, which is possibly the only unattractive thing about her.

"Right now, maybe he's telling Mom that God is in the small things," I say.

We giggle some more.

Teddy appears, wearing torn sweatpants and a T-shirt that has a wild-haired Einstein silk-screened on the front. "What's going on? What's so funny?"

"We're picturing Mom and Pastor Costello having sex!" says Louise. She begins banging on the table. "Oh God! Oh God! Oh God!"

Teddy turns bright red. He was Mom's closest companion after Dad died, and so perhaps this whole wedding-honeymoon thing is more difficult for him. Teddy is not exactly forthcoming with regard to his thoughts and emotions. After winning a championship cross-country race, he didn't bother to tell anyone. Mom found out because Mrs. Muldoon read about it in the local newspaper and came over with a batch of cookies to congratulate him.

"All right," I say. "That's enough."

"What if Pastor Costello has committed a sin of emission?" asks Eric.

I shoot Eric a look. "So Teddy, do you have a girlfriend?" Though Teddy is a senior in high school, his awkward stage came late and despite being cute, he's still skinny and has a few pimples. The fate of the Palmer teenager is to never have completely clear skin, but not to have too many pimples all at once. It's as if they're statistically spread out to produce five a week all throughout adolescence, one for every school day.

"Cassandra!" guesses Eric.

Teddy shakes his head from side to side to indicate that this is most definitely NOT the case.

"He likes Cassandra," corrects Louise, "but he's too chicken to ask her out."

"With both Mom and Pastor Costello away, you could ask her out on a date and take the car," I offer. "They'd never know."

"Or ask her to the Morrison's New Year's Eve party, and you can kiss her," chimes in Louise.

Teddy flushes with embarrassment.

"She's right," I say. "At midnight everyone on a date has to kiss."

"By the time school starts, you're officially going out, and by prom time, you're renting a motel room!" says a gleeful Louise.

"Louise!" I say.

"What? Would you rather he go down to Nolan's where those skanky women in their twenties pick up teenage boys, to deflower them at the No-tell Motel out on Millersport Highway?"

I look to Eric for help—only at the mention of Nolan's floozies, it's his turn to become bright red and stare down at the floor.

As a result of having worked for the local bookmaker in the pool hall across the street, I happen to know that Louise is right about Nolan's.

"And I'm sure your first time was at the Ritz in Paris," Eric says to Louise.

Louise and I steal glances at each other because we both know that Louise was drunk, and her first time will always be up for debate—and possibly even a matter of public record, *somewhere.*

"Listen," I say to Teddy. "Just call Cassandra tomorrow and ask her to go bowling or to see a movie."

"I asked her to the wedding, but she says she can't go out with me because Denise Porter likes me."

"Oh," I say. "Do you like Denise Porter?"

"I never really thought about it," says Teddy. "I mean, she's nice. And sort of pretty, I guess."

"Then you have to call and ask Denise out first." Louise says this as if ordering troops into battle. "If you hit it off with her, terrific. If not, *then* you're free to call Cassandra. Or go out with Denise for a few weeks, break up, and then ask Cassandra out. Either way you'll still have a date for the prom."

Teddy shakes his head as if he needs some aspirin. "Why does it have to be so complicated?"

"For the same reason a woman isn't president," says Eric. "So that people won't find out that they're secretly running everything."

"I have a chance to go around the world for free," I blurt out. What do you think?"

"I thought you were moving in with Craig," replies Eric.

I grimace. "I was, I mean, I am, eventually. It just feels like everything is happening so fast and we're sort of young to be practically engaged and have a mortgage."

"Sounds like it could be dangerous," says Eric. "You might get kidnapped or contract some horrible disease."

"Of course you're going to go," Louise states matter-of-factly. "Who would turn down a trip around the world?"

"Mom is going to have a heart attack," says Teddy.

Louise frowns. "Not if it's for school. She's thrilled when anything has to do with school."

Chapter 12

hen Mom and Pastor Costello arrive back on Wednesday afternoon, Mom heads directly over to Mrs. Muldoon's house to pick up Roddy and Reggie. I said it would be no problem to watch them, but everyone knows that Mrs. Muldoon is always looking for any excuse to have the boys stay at her place. She's basically turned her downstairs into a giant playroom, and lets the twins sleep overnight in the bedroom her daughter occupied many years ago.

Pastor Costello is unloading the minivan while singing, "Brighten the Corner Where You Are."

"So how was the uh…trip?" I ask. *Honeymoon* sounds too much like it involves sex, and I don't think either of us wants to go there.

"I just love the Falls in winter," says Pastor Costello. "And the air was very bracing."

That's a good sign, I think. At least they went outside. Pastor Costello grabs a suitcase, and I take the stack of books next to it. The Bible is on top, but I can definitely make out at least three hardcover mysteries underneath. "Catching up on your reading?" I tease him.

"Never trust a man who studies only one book!" Pastor Costello jokes back.

Mom enters the house with the twin boys in tow.

"Everything is fine," I say. "Except Francie took her own stitches out. I called the pediatrician and he said it's okay so long as the cut doesn't open up." Last week Francie was playing "chicken" on ice skates and managed to get her hand run over.

Mom looks relieved. Mostly because any sentence beginning with "Francie" does *not* usually end with "it's okay."

"I decided to go on that trip," I say. "You know—the one I told you about—with my *school*. Where we help the *professor* with a *school project*."

"That sounds like a good opportunity," says Mom.

I can't believe it. No questions about who else is going or what professor is taking us. Even for a slumber party mom likes a deep background check.

"Okay, then. I'm heading over to the Stocktons'," I say, still fully expecting to hear, "when are we going to meet everyone you'll be traveling with?"

Nothing. Apparently, Louise was right. If it's for school, then it's cool.

"So this means you and Craig won't be taking that apartment in Cincinnati?" Mom asks with forced nonchalance.

Aha! Mom doesn't want me "living in sin" with Craig. She knows full well that Elizabeth and Eric are cohabitating in Nashville and yet she simply looks the other way. Once again, it's the old double standard around the Palmer house, as if the neighbors will think less of Mom as a parent when they find out that one of her *daughters* is shacking up.

"You just don't want me living with Craig," I say.

"If people like each other enough to set up house together, then I can't understand why they don't just get married is all," argues Mom.

Pastor Costello comes in from the garage carrying a cooler. "Who's getting married?"

"No one," says Mom. "I was only telling Hallie that I fail to see why young people are so intent on *living together* these days."

"In seminary, we were instructed to tell them that there was no reason to eat supper before saying grace," says Pastor Costello. "But nowadays, the thinking seems to be that a little getting-to-know-each-other period doesn't hurt. It may even help to build a stronger marriage."

I stare at Pastor Costello with surprise. I was certain that he was going to offer me one of his famous youth group lectures. People still quote from his abstinence talk entitled, "Mind over Mattress," though only in jest.

Pastor Costello sees Mom's unhappy expression and quickly realizes that living together is the *wrong* answer. "On the other hand, my mother, who was very wise in such matters, always said, 'Why buy the cow if you can get the milk for free?'"

Mom appears satisfied. Pastor Costello kisses her on the cheek.

The phone rings and I pick up the receiver. A guy who says he's a lawyer wants to talk to Mom.

After listening for a moment, a look of horror crosses Mom's face and she exclaims, "Lost at sea!"

Uh-oh. I hope it's not Uncle Lenny.

Another round of listening and she says, "But I don't understand."

A few minutes later, Mom is sitting at the kitchen table with tears in her eyes. "Your father's uncle was on a fishing charter in the Caribbean when a storm came up."

I become tearful as well. Uncle Lenny was the best, and he practically saved our lives when Dad died and Mom was in the hospital. Despite being a dead ringer for the Ancient Mariner, when I did the math, he only came out to be about sixty-five.

Pastor Costello sits down at the table looking despondent. He'd heard plenty about Uncle Lenny and his famous bedtime stories told in that hair-raising child-scaring Voice-of-God basso profundo. And less happily, the complete catalogue of our roguish relative's many, varied, and characteristically polysyllabic curses, the most oft repeated being "Blistering Blue Barnacles" and "Ossified Oozlebart."

"He left an education trust for the children," says Mom. "Apparently, some radar detection device he invented has just come on the market and is selling very well."

"Oh, my gosh!" I say. "That must be the crazy balloon thing that he and Teddy were working on out front."

"There's not much money in the trust right now, but the lawyer thinks it could grow considerably over the next few years," says Mom. "It was very kind of him to think of us."

But I'm remembering Uncle Lenny in his gray sweatshirt, grungy white pants and coast guard cap, leaning over this very same kitchen table to plot a course to the mall so the kids could have breakfast at the food court. He was the kind of guy who seemed to be indestructible and impervious to the elements, the ancestral version of Francie.

Chapter 13

*O*livia's cherry red Buick Park Avenue is moored in the driveway with ice-crusted windows and a Keep Your Laws Off My Body bumper sticker barely visible beneath the winter road grime. It's no secret that when the Supreme Court tilted to the right, Olivia took it personally. Filling the cavernous backseat are stacks of protest signs and sandwich boards, the topmost one hand painted to read: THE PILGRIMS WERE THE FIRST ILLEGAL ALIENS.

Bernard's latest adventure in theme parties is to have a big open house on New Year's Day. Last summer, a NEIGHBORHOOD WATCH sign went up at the end of the street, and I'm pretty sure it means that everyone is watching Bernard. So many people who don't even live on the street drive or walk past at a snail's pace, trying to get a glimpse of the gardens, peacocks wandering around screeching, and the merry-go-round on the front lawn, that they may as well just stop and gawk.

Bernard finally decided to save everyone the trouble of spying by inviting them all over. And boy do they come. The house always looks fabulous, but still, Bernard loads the place up with antiques and serving dishes so that the following week half the town is down at his shop thinking that if they buy that sort of stuff, their own homes will look just as spectacular. Since his first open house last year, Bernard has had so many requests to decorate people's homes that he's actually thinking of doing interior design as a sideline to his antiques business.

Bernard is a gambler, in the sense that he gambles on his own good taste. If there's a theme for this particular party, it's definitely Capitalism. In the middle of the buffet table, he's placed a large stack of the latest edition of his newsletter, *Decorators Without Borders*, next to embossed business cards propped up in a sterling silver holder. Gil says that Bernard could star in a docudrama called *Guess Who's Coming to Decorate?*

The living room speakers blare Jacques Brel singing in French. It may not be on my top-ten list, but I'm relieved it's not the *Rent* CD. Because if "Seasons of Love" plays one more time, Bernard is going to get 528,600 blows to the head. He's already on his second copy. Honestly, who ever heard of wearing out a CD?

When I enter the kitchen, Bernard is anxiously peering into the oven. "Sometimes I feel that if the soufflé doesn't rise, then the terrorists have won."

"The party isn't for two more days," I say. "A soufflé isn't going to last until then."

"This is a new dish for me, so I'm doing a trial run. It's called Bernard's Honey-Basted Twice-Baked Soufflé, from a recipe at Dodie's B&B. I ran across it on the Internet while researching soft-paste porcelain."

"If it's Dodie's recipe then how come it now has *your* name on it?"

"I've improved upon it by adding an extra egg, of course."

Olivia enters the kitchen and pours another cup of tea. This seems as good a time as any to tell them.

"I called the professor to say that I'm definitely going on the trip."

"*Afoot and lighthearted, I take to the open road,*" Olivia begins reciting the words of her beloved Walt Whitman.

However, Bernard doesn't look at all happy. Unlike his freethinking mother, Bernard firmly believes there's a limit to personal growth, especially when it involves crossing international borders. "Then at least have the courtesy to bring me back some raw cow's-milk Camembert made by monks at a monastery in the Aquitaine region of France. And a container of Bizac duck foie gras with truffles."

Olivia looks horrified. "Haven't you heard about the inhumane way the ducks are treated—their livers grotesquely enlarged by force-feeding them with an air pump? Some die when their stomachs burst!"

"We're not going to France," I say. "I think the only countries in Europe are Holland and Ireland. It's more like Australia, Asia, and South America."

"Then be sure to wear a hat, so you don't ruin your complexion," warns Bernard.

"It's not enough for women to escape the tyranny of the foundation garment and foot binding, but we still have to worry about having a pale complexion to be considered attractive?" complains Olivia.

"I was talking about skin cancer!" snaps Bernard.

Sitting down at the kitchen table, I open my notebook, listing the countries we're visiting and the approximate climate in each at this time of year. "Packing is almost impossible. I need something for almost every kind of weather—from boots to bathing suits."

Olivia glances down at the list. "When Peter the Great went to explore the west in 1697, he brought along twenty Russian noblemen, a host of priests, secretaries, musicians, interpreters, soldiers, cooks, pages, a troupe of dwarves, and one monkey."

On second thought, I don't think Olivia and Bernard are going to be much help with deciding what to pack. I close my notebook. "I'll check out the new sporting goods store that opened up next to Herb's pharmacy. A sign in the window says they're having a big sale."

Chapter 14

*O*n the morning of New Year's Eve, Bernard is going full
tilt preparing for his open house the next day. He'd been
possessed when it came to decking the halls for Christmas this
year, including the installation of an enormous Douglas fir tree
decorated in the Victorian style with wax ornaments shaped like
angels and children, and real candles nestled among the branches.
The tiny children are dressed in heavy layers of period clothing,
and Bernard says this helps us not only appreciate the spirit of
Christmas, but also to be thankful for the advent of Velcro, Fleece,
and Nylon.

"Why don't you have breakfast in the living room?" suggests
Bernard. "The tree is so cozy, and the girls are still asleep."

This is a nice way of saying that the kitchen and the dining
room are only missing big Red Cross signs designating them as
official disaster zones. Bernard hands me a glass of freshly squeezed
orange juice along with a big cherry scone and steers me toward a
chair next to the fireplace. He bends down and sweeps a few fallen
needles into his hand.

Olivia enters from the living room carrying her teacup. "It's
a ridiculous waste of a tree that took thirty years to grow. Not to
mention a fire hazard."

"Look who's here—it's the Anti-Christmas!" Bernard turns to

me, and as if Olivia isn't even there says (switching, as usual, to a French accent for dramatic effect), "Ever seence ze Religious Right— *la Droite religieux*—took over ze town council and attempted to make all ze shopkeepers put up les décorations de Noël and say ze Merry Christmas, ze woman has been *impossible!*"

"Don't be ridiculous," says Olivia. "The Unitarians invented Christmas to get families inside their homes during what was considered to be a very dangerous day on the streets...what with all the wassailers. It was the Universalists who went in for all the trimmings."

"Who are they?" I ask.

"The Unitarians and the Universalists merged in 1961," explains Olivia.

Bernard is placing candles among the pinecones and fir boughs along the mantelpiece and starts singing "There's Safety in Numbers" from the musical *The Boyfriend*.

"Do Unitarian-Universalists take communion?" I ask.

"Mother can't take communion," says Bernard. "The blood and body of Christ isn't vegetarian."

"No, we don't have a communion ceremony," says Olivia. "Which is probably a good thing, when you consider all the time taken up by announcements."

"How about I create a recipe for a macrobiotic gluten-free Unitarian communion wafer?" offers Bernard. "We'll call them 'I Can't Believe It's Not Jesus!'"

Ottavio walks into the living room and crosses himself upon hearing the word "Jesus." Bernard likes to say that it's probably a good thing Ottavio isn't entirely fluent in English or else he'd have run out of Olivia's church as if on fire and caught the first flight back to Italy. And that Ottavio probably thinks some of the committee meetings are to plan feasts for the saints, rather than eliminate stockpiles of nuclear weapons and have free elections around the world.

"Don't make fun of my faith." Olivia waves a warning finger.

But Bernard snorts at the word *faith*. "In God's refrigerator, there's a milk carton with your picture on it."

"If only Marx had been right and religion *was* the opiate of the masses, rather than an incendiary," says Olivia.

"I'm a Groucho Marxist myself," offers Bernard.

Finally, I manage to get a few words in. "I had the *strangest* dream last night—I was naked and had to go outside, maybe to close the shed door or something. I can't remember the exact reason. But I couldn't find any clothes to put on. Do you think it means anything?"

Bernard is now collecting the toys that the girls have left underneath the piano. "I think it means that you should go shopping for a fabulous fur coat. Possibly an ermine with a swoop cape collar, wide cuffed sleeves and stole-like crisscross styling in the front."

Olivia shoots Bernard a look at the mention of fur, but knows he's just trying to provoke her and so leaves the subject alone. "I highly doubt that Hallie's dream was meant as a call to consumerism."

"It *can* be a vocation," argues Bernard. "After Greta Garbo retired at age thirty-five, she went shopping for the next fifty years."

"Do you think dreams really mean anything?" I ask.

"Oh yes!" says Bernard. "All my best interior designs first appear while I'm asleep—sometimes even furniture that I haven't yet encountered. And then three months later, there it is at an auction—just as it was in my dream!"

"I don't think that dreams foretell the future," says Olivia. "But they can often speak about our inner selves in symbols, and so we should try and decipher them to have a better understanding of our own nature—our fears and desires. For instance, if you're naked in a dream and no one else seems to notice, this might mean you're worrying about things that no one else sees except for you. Or it might suggest that you've failed to get enough attention, and that's troubling you."

Bernard runs over and gives me a theatrical hug. "Oh Hallie, have I been ignoring you while preparing for the open house?"

I playfully push him away. "Wait a second—you both believe in dream analysis—because you never agree on anything."

"I wouldn't say we agree, exactly," counters Olivia. "Whereas Bernard dreams of Biedermeier display cabinets and roast duck l'orange, I often get ideas for poems and editorials."

I begin to laugh. It's not at Olivia's comment but something Cappy, my bookie friend, once said. He has this one client who is always making bets on these incredible long shots. The guy *never* wins. Whenever he calls, it just means more money in Cappy's pocket, and so every time Cappy hangs up the phone with the guy he says, "Put your dreams in one hand and your spit in the other and see which fills up first."

I can hear Gil and the girls getting ready upstairs. Bernard gathers up our empty plates and cups.

"You and Craig *are* coming for dinner tonight?" asks Bernard. "I've created a vegetable napoleon that's *to die for.*"

"He made it for the open house tomorrow but doesn't like the way it looks, and so he's fobbing it off on us tonight," Olivia informs me.

"Where else would we go on New Year's Eve?" I ask. Spending the holiday at the Stocktons' had become something of a tradition since the night Craig and I ended up there on our first real date five years ago. I'll always remember it as the night we had our first kiss.

"You never know," says Bernard. "Maybe you lovebirds want one of those fancy nights out with tacky cardboard hats and kazoos."

"Craig will be here about six," I say. "He's working on some huge project at a private estate outside of Akron. They're redoing the place from top to bottom."

"I'll have to see if they need any antiques or portraits of their ancestors," says Bernard, his eyes widening at the prospect of a big sale.

"And what are the chances that you'd have a portrait of one of *their* ancestors?"

"Americans are generous people." Bernard places his hand across his heart. "Those with plenty of financing, starter mansions, and no ancestors to speak of are almost always willing to adopt."

Chapter 15

*C*raig arrives at the Stocktons' and rounds off the party by passing out cardboard hats and kazoos, much to the girls' delight and Bernard's horror. My boyfriend looks amazingly handsome, wearing a navy sports jacket over a light blue sweater, with black wool pants; his butterscotch hair neatly combed back.

"You didn't have to dress up," I say.

Craig glances at my school sweatshirt and jeans. "Apparently not."

"I mean, it's just us," I say. Though as I glance around the room, Bernard, Gil, Olivia, and Ottavio *do* look rather nice. Even Gigi and Rose are cute in the matching Hello Kitty pajamas they received for Christmas.

In addition to the vegetable napoleon, Bernard is serving pork tenderloin and what he calls a "pastiche of hors d'oeuvres"— basically the rest of the food that he doesn't think looks or tastes good enough to serve at tomorrow's open house.

After dinner, Gil builds a fire and sits down at the piano to play "Old MacDonald Had a Farm," "Pop Goes the Weasel," and all the girls' favorites. Once they go to bed, he entertains us just as well by making up blues songs with all our names in them. For instance, as Hallie I can usually count on something happening to me in a dark alley, getting lost in Death Valley, or disrupting a

76

pep rally. At half past eleven, Bernard passes out "Bernardaritas," which, best I can tell, are margaritas with banana liquor.

When everyone has their glass in hand, Craig suddenly bends down on one knee, produces a ring from his pocket, and says with a slightly hoarse but passionate timbre, "Hallie, will you marry me?"

My heart skips a beat and my brain skips about three wavelengths, or whatever brains skip. The mouth opens and then it closes, but no sound escapes. The word "yes" isn't naturally bubbling to the surface, and yet "no" doesn't seem to be the right answer either.

Olivia, Gil, and even Bernard look nothing short of shocked. I think they probably expected this at a certain point, but not at least for another year. Although they are all big believers in love with a capital "L," Bernard and Gil have always made it quite clear that you need to sort out your education and career first. Even follow-your-heart Olivia likes to remind me that there's plenty of time for marriage and children, and one is likely to make a mistake by settling down for good with your first real boyfriend.

Meantime, Ottavio, the hopeless romantic, clutches his chest with both hands and shouts "Bravo! Brava!" as if Craig and I are starring in an opera.

Without even looking at the ring, I make a beeline for the door and stand on the front lawn gasping for breath while the wind whips at the branches of the oaks and maples.

Craig runs after me. "I shouldn't have done it in front of everyone, right?"

I don't know what to say. I'm spinning from the suddenness of it all and determine what might be a new law of physics—a spiral can go up or down.

"I just thought it would be romantic since we had our first kiss at midnight on New Year's Eve," says Craig. "Remember?"

My brain finally starts working again. Honestly, this is the *last* thing I expected to happen. I was under the impression that women have an idea about when a guy is going to propose so they can get their nails done and stuff like that. "You just decided—I mean, aren't we a little young?"

"I'm almost twenty-four and you'll to be twenty-two in September." Craig does the math for me. "Romeo and Juliet were only thirteen and fourteen!"

For someone who says he doesn't like Shakespeare, apparently the play made a *big* impression.

When I don't respond, Craig seems deflated. "Don't you love me?"

"Of course I do!" I say. "I—I just want to graduate and find a good job first. Craig, I'm flat broke right now—there's exactly $86.22 in my bank account."

"I'll pay for your class in Cincinnati." Craig takes my hand in his.

"There is no Cincinnati," I say. "I *told* you two days ago that I decided to earn the credits by going on the trip. And then I'll have to look for another job when I get back. Besides, I can't take your money."

"I thought since we decided to live together that it would be *our* money," argues Craig.

"Everything is too up in the air right now," I argue back.

"Things in our lives will oftentimes be uncertain—jobs, money, housing—it's the same for everyone," reasons Craig. "The idea is that we love each other and deal with it together."

"But the idea of living together was to make *sure*," I say. "To make sure we don't have annoying habits like squeezing the toothpaste tube in completely different ways."

"Hallie, we've been together for almost six years," says Craig. "We know *everything* about each other."

Craig is right about that. We'd been through a lot together—my dropping out of high school, Dad's death, Craig's quitting college to start his business. We'd broken up a few times, but in retrospect, it was probably good to date some other people. Craig is right in saying that he knows more about me than anyone, even Bernard. Likewise, he tells me all his crazy plans and ideas even when he knows I'll laugh or scoff. Maybe that's the problem—we already know everything about each other. There's nothing left to discover, and we're only in our early twenties.

"Craig, I'm sorry, but I'm just not ready to get married yet." I guess I'm thinking we can carry on as we were and then revisit the subject in six months or so.

However, Craig drops my hand and exhales deeply. "Then I think we should see other people."

There they were, the eight most dreadful words in the English language, at least when you're hearing them and not saying them.

A peacock's tail shimmers through the nearby trees, while up above, the stars glisten like crystal globes and tremble as if they're shining through a deep clear pool.

There's a tightness in my chest as if my lungs are filling with dust, and I finally manage to say, "Are you kidding me?"

"If you don't know whether or not you want to spend your life with me now, then what's going to change that?" Anger creeps into his voice.

Everything is happening so fast that I don't know how to respond. I'm not sure I even understand what's going on. "You mean you want to break up?"

"You can't seem to commit; so I don't know how I feel about spending four months alone waiting for someone who may or may not come back to me."

"Don't be ridiculous," I say. "Of course I'm coming back!"

"If you don't think you want to be with me now, then what's going to change your mind four months from now?"

"That's not what I meant," I say. "It's just that…I don't know."

Craig walks toward his car. If he just sits in it, I decide that I'll go over and we can figure this out. But he quickly switches the ignition and roars off down the street.

I turn and slowly make my way toward to the summerhouse. As I cross the backyard, the neighborhood erupts in happy shouts and buzzing kazoos, and then I hear Gil playing "Auld Lang Syne" on the piano.

Chapter 16

$\mathcal{W}$ hen I drag myself into the kitchen the following morning, after one very restless night, food is everywhere, and the smell of silver polish permeates the air. Bernard stands in the center of it all with a stack of doilies in each hand. "*Good morning, Starshine, the Earth says hello!*" I'm treated to his favorite song from the musical *Hair*.

In fact, Bernard does such an amazing job at pretending nothing has happened that I actually begin to wonder if it wasn't all just a bad dream, or more specifically, a nightmare.

"How about a Stockton Swizzle—my own fabulous combination of cran-strawberry juice, champagne, and a twist of lime." He puts down the doilies and reaches for an enormous bottle of Dom Perignon.

I continue staring at the pots and pans rack.

"*Un ange passé.*" Bernard claims that when there is a lull in the conversation, French people say, "An angel passes by in silence."

"*Bonjour, comment allez-vous?*" Olivia is carrying trays out to the dining room as Bernard finishes arranging them. Apparently, she's presumed that we're all speaking French this morning.

"Craig wants to see other people," I announce.

"I'm so sorry." Bernard quickly sets down the glass and gives me a full body bereavement hug. "I'll be the face of love for you."

He's now channeling Susan Sarandon channeling Sister Helen Prejean in the movie *Dead Man Walking*.

Olivia sighs. "Relationships are so much like the United States—they only really thrive when faced with an external threat."

I'm not exactly sure what this means, but Olivia makes it a point not to get involved in other people's affairs, and so she leaves it at that.

"The more I thought about it after Craig left last night, the more I decided he proposed because he doesn't want me to go on this trip." There's irritation in my voice because it seems more like a trick than any declaration of love. I mean, maybe there's a reason that *engagement* has the word "gag" in it.

"Did you ever think that maybe he doesn't want you to go on this 'trip,' because he loves you and wants to be with you and doesn't want you blown up by suicide bombers, stricken with disease, and consorting with retirees in sequined velour track suits?" Bernard is now using air quotes every time he says the word "trip."

Gil enters the kitchen with his coat on. "All done salting the driveway and front walk. A handful of people are already lined up waiting for the clock to strike eleven!" Gil issues a warning since, last year, a few of the early birds apparently heard Bernard referring to them as *the great unwashed*.

"Whatever happened to being fashionably late?" Bernard quickens the pace. "Hallie, go and put on the Vivaldi! Gil, bring the girls downstairs, but make sure Gigi hasn't taken off her shoes again. If they're missing in action then check the clothes dryer!"

Gil glances around at all the delicious appetizers and inhales deeply. "Everything smells delicious!"

"Everything *is* delicious!" retorts Bernard.

"Humility has never been an arrow in your quiver," remarks Olivia.

"Speaking of, did you remember to invite Estelle Johnson?" Bernard asks his mother.

"I certainly did not!" replies Olivia. "To quote Samuel Johnson, 'She's not only dull herself, but the cause of dullness in others.'"

"You just don't like Estelle because you have reason to believe she always votes against increasing the local school budget," accuses Bernard.

"And you only want to swindle Estelle's mother out of that Louis XV Revival style dining room set!" Olivia fires back.

"If they were interested in scaling back, I'd of course be obliged to present my credentials and offer my services." Bernard's newfound air of self-sacrifice makes it sound more like he's just offered to donate one of his lungs. "Dorothea cannot live in that big old house on her own for much longer. And I'd hate to see the family fleeced by some unscrupulous estate agent."

Olivia gives her son a sideways glance as if to say, *That's what I'm worried about!* She's only told Bernard a hundred times that she'll not be used as bait to bring in trade for him, the way poet and socialite Sebastian Venable employed his mother and then his cousin in Tennessee Williams' play *Suddenly Last Summer.*

"Cerberus," mutters Bernard.

"Charybdis," Olivia shoots back. She plucks a raspberry tart off an enormous silver tray and exits the room shaking her head from side to side.

While garnishing the last few serving dishes with carrot flowers and fanning the neatly pressed and folded linen napkins, Bernard begins to sing the Noel Coward song "A Marvelous Party."

Only I don't think I'm in the mood for a party, marvelous or otherwise. I need to decide fast whether this trip is a huge mistake and if I should try and get out of it. Ms. Pritchett will probably kill me because she's already rebooked the flights in my name, and I'd also turned down the job in Cincinnati. What a mess. Or *quelle horreur*, as Bernard likes to say. I head for the back door.

"Hallie, aren't you going to stay and greet everyone?" asks Bernard.

"Thanks, but I have some things to do."

As I leave, Bernard begins trilling his other favorite Noel

Coward song at my back, "Why Do All the Wrong People Travel
When the Right People Stay Back Home?"

Chapter 17

The next morning, in the half world of sleep, where dreams and consciousness collide, I hear the sound of children shrieking outside my window. For a moment, I experience a flashback to when Dad died, Mom was in the mental hospital, and I was in charge of my younger siblings. I quickly pull back the curtains to make sure no one is perishing in the backyard.

Quite the opposite. Gigi, Rose, Bernard, and Gil are all playing in the snow. A foot must have fallen overnight! And tiny star-shaped flakes continue drifting downward from low, white fluffy clouds. Ottavio drags the old wooden sled from out of the garage and starts pulling little Gigi toward the gazebo while Bernard, Rose, and Gil roll enormous balls for what must be the largest snowman in history.

"Come outside, Hallie!" calls Olivia. "We're building a snowperson!"

Pulling the covers over my head, I pretend to be asleep. Somehow, in just two days, I've gone from being totally excited about what's next in my life to positively dreading each new day. And canceling the trip now would only make things worse—it's not like I'd want to get back together with Craig under these circumstances. Let him go find some other girl! And when their car dies in a snowstorm, they can stare together at the engine for a few hours and eventually freeze to death. Happy New Year! I'll have that drink now.

The rest of the week drags along as I check things like bug spray and calamine lotion off my trip list. School starts and the buses move along slush-coated streets.

On Thursday, I have an appointment at my school clinic to get vaccinated for typhoid, hepatitis A, tetanus, and yellow fever. The place is a madhouse, so I have to sit and wait for almost an hour. Though I have a sneaking suspicion they overbook on purpose to force us to read all the scary pamphlets about sexually-transmitted diseases that are piled high on every available surface, and not a magazine in sight. If you had to wait more than an hour, it's doubtful you'd ever make love again.

The remaining décor consists of two hanging plants that are wilted and brown. Not a good sign, if you ask me.

A middle-aged doctor with prematurely gray hair and a permanent frown tends to me in one of the cubicles. He nods toward a tray covered with injections and explains that they're mostly for Malaysia. "I'd give you malaria pills for Southeast Asia, India, and Peru, but there are so many different strains nowadays, it'd be a shot in the dark. Just avoid marshy areas, use bug spray, and always wear long pants with socks. No skirts or sandals."

"You don't have to worry about me and skirts," I assure him.

"No shorts and open shoes in the Far East or the subcontinent, according to the Center for Disease Control and Prevention," he says. "Obviously, you shouldn't drink the water or eat salads anywhere outside of Europe, Canada, and the U.S., which also means washing fruit with purified water prior to ingesting it, even the kind you peel, like bananas and oranges. Avoid jellyfish in Hawaii. One of our students was there over winter break and almost died after being stung at Waikiki Beach in Honolulu. He was allergic. Bad way to find out."

Boy, listening to Dr. Doom, it's starting to sound as if Bernard was right and I *will* be lucky to return home alive. He glances at the list of countries we're visiting one more time. "I see that you'll be in Australia. You probably shouldn't even go near the ocean there. They've had a record number of shark attacks this year. That said, with the number of poisonous snakes, dry land isn't safe either."

Okay, and thanks for the nightmares. I escape with three small Band-Aids on my left arm and visions of deadly tropical diseases, stingrays, killer bees, and saber-toothed sparrows dancing in my head. I stop in the dorms to visit some friends and, by the time I arrive back at the Stocktons', the familiar line of cars out front indicates that Bernard's weekly Girl Scout meeting is in session. It crosses my mind to try to sneak around the back, but Bernard is greeting a latecomer at the door, just as I pull into the driveway.

"Oh, Hallie, can you lend a hand for a little while?" he calls out. "Gil took the girls to make pottery at that new place across from the theater. I do wish they'd learn how to craft some Imari plates and cloisonné vases rather than frogs and pencil holders." Bernard hasn't entirely given up on his program for the girls to stay in touch with their Chinese heritage, though lately it's been reduced to ordering takeout food from the Grand Wok once a week.

It would seem that my overall lack of a job, classes, and now, a boyfriend, does rather leave me without excuses. Maybe I can start telling people I have to work on my "gratitude journal." Pastor Costello says that everybody should keep one, so whenever they feel down, it's easy to remember how much they have to be thankful for.

"I suppose so," I finally say.

"Wonderful," says Bernard. "We're learning about the art of the cocktail party and so I really do need an adult at every project station."

The Bernard–Girl Scout story basically begins with, "You're never going to believe this, but…" the but being that several years ago, when a troop leader was felled in action, I believe by a mossy slope while hiking, Bernard filled in and eventually adopted the girls when the woman didn't return to her unit. Bernard is convinced that these young women (plus Andrew) are latchkey children whose working mothers do not enlighten them with regard to the finer points of etiquette and entertaining, or any points for that matter, and were living like rats in bowling alleys until he mercifully came to their rescue. The troop has experienced a seismic shift from its focus on outdoor survival skills to indoor lighting effects. (In Bernard's defense, how many high school graduates do know on which side of a place-setting the water glass belongs, or where to put your napkin when you get up to go to the lav?)

The dining room table is loaded with different styles of glasses, about fifty bottles of liquor and mixers, a martini shaker, olives, maraschino cherries, fruit slices, swizzle sticks, a variety of cocktail napkins, and a bartender's guide. I can't help but wonder if the fact that Bernard's Girl Scout troop is the only one in the area with an actual waiting list has finally gone to his head. The girls are now thirteen and fourteen, except for Andrew, the younger brother of one of the girls, who is eleven.

"Can't we get in trouble for serving them alcohol?" I ask Olivia.

"The adults are acting as tasters and Rocky the chimpanzee is demonstrating the blender drinks."

Despite his well-known drinking problem, by adopting the "moderation program," Rocky has been completely sober for a number of years, at least for the most part.

Bernard claps everyone to attention. "It makes me shudder to think how some people go their entire lives not knowing the difference between a sidecar and a gimlet. We'll have no philistines in Troop Bernard! Even if you're a teetotaler, or as an adult your tastes run to wine or beer, Aunt Mildred could rock up at any moment demanding her Harvey Wallbanger, or Uncle Oswald wanting his five o'clock highball."

A few of the girls snicker at the word "highball." Bernard shoots them a look, as if he's teaching brain surgery and there's nothing funny about the nomenclature.

"Let's first discuss the setup of the bar," says Bernard. "Can anyone tell me why that's so important when one is entertaining? Ruth Ann?"

"We're helping to make a memory," she repeats an oft-heard Bernardism.

He nods as if this isn't necessarily a *wrong* answer, but there's a *righter* one.

A girl with green glitter sprayed onto pale blond hair launches her hand into the air. "You never get a second chance to make a first impression and last impressions *last.*" Another line regularly uttered by Bernard.

"Yes, Amy," says Bernard. "But the bar also says what kind of person you are and what type of *impression* you wish to make." One by one, Bernard points to the bottles he thinks should be stocked in the abode of any young professional person, and the girls dutifully write these in their notebooks. His air of certainty suggests a past overflowing with royal regattas and family retainers.

"Of course, if you're on a budget, there are a few tricks one can employ," says Bernard. "We briefly touched on this while working on our dinner-party badge—does anyone remember?"

"Water down the booze?" suggests one girl.

"No, that's what your older brother does when he's been sneaking into the liquor cabinet with his friends."

Andrew raises his hand. "Put the good wine out first and the cheap wine later, when they're getting sloshed. By the third or fourth glass, they won't notice the difference."

"Very good, Andrew."

It's no secret that Andrew is Bernard's star pupil and protégé. In fact, I think he's even starting to dress like Bernard. Or else the vest with the silk threads is because he just came from a barbershop quartet practice.

"And when entertaining English majors, be sure to offer a Dickens martini—no olive or twist!" Bernard's splash of Charles Dickens humor is lost on everyone not old enough to vote and so he laughs at his own joke.

"Moving right along, Bernard," interjects Olivia. The meetings regularly run late, so parents wait out front in their cars either talking on cell phones or reading. But Olivia hates it that they almost always leave their engines idling.

"Yes, of course. We'll break into groups of three to mix an actual cocktail, and then each team will present their process to the rest of us and exhibit the result." Bernard has created stations for making a martini, manhattan, bloody mary, and gin and tonic. The margarita crew is sent to Rocky. At every station is the step-by-step recipe, ingredients, and, if called for, garnish and swizzle stick. Only the absence of plastic goggles differentiates the scene from a chemistry lab experiment. Andrew waits patiently by Bernard's side until all of the instructions have been issued. "Oh yes, Andrew, I almost forgot, I promised we'd work on that cosmopolitan featured in the Sex and the City boxed DVD set you purchased with your Christmas money. Go and get a chilled glass out of the refrigerator."

When my group is finished, I tell Bernard, "I really have to finish packing if we're going to poker tonight."

"That reminds me, girls. And boy." Bernard claps his hands to get everyone's attention as a few of them are pretending to be drunk. "Is anyone allergic to nuts?"

One girl says, "Bee stings."

"Good. I made out a list of nuts with everyone's name next to a particular variety and put it on the front door. Next week, we're going to talk about how to throw a card party."

"You mean like strip poker?" asks one rather well-developed girl.

"Don't be juvenile, Dana," scolds Bernard. "We're going to discuss playing cards as a social occasion, like you might organize a tennis party or a game of croquet. And Dana, my dear girl, you should make a special point of being here, since you don't know the first thing about nuts. While preparing for the holiday party, you mistook a macadamia for a Spanish peanut!"

I can't tell if Bernard means this as a double-entendre, but then he shoots Dana a look and she giggles.

Bernard turns to me. "I don't know what they're teaching

children in school these days. It's certainly nothing they can use in the real world."

That's what I love most about Bernard—I honestly don't think he's aware of the mighty chasm between his world and the "real" one.

Chapter 18

"You snooze, you lose!" barks Al Santora, who's preparing to deal the first hand as Bernard and I arrive at the church poker game. "Read 'em and weep." He refers to the blue, diamond-backed playing cards now hitting the table.

"Will you quit with the patter already!" threatens Herb Rowland.

"It's not even seven o'clock yet," I remind Al of the official start time.

The basement hasn't changed, with its rickety wooden steps and three naked yellow bulbs hanging down between the aluminum-covered pipes in the ceiling. A freshly dismantled manger sits in the corner, waiting to be boxed up, next to the washer and dryer for tablecloths and choir robes. The place smells a bit mustier, if that's possible.

It would appear that Pastor Costello notices us sniffing the air to see if some moldy undergarments are piled up nearby.

"I know, I know," says Pastor Costello. "I brought some candles to cover the smell."

Bernard glances at the two tiny white votives and then inhales deeply. "It would take at least a dozen pillar-sized Nate Berkus water-lily candles to help with *that*."

"I thought you finally got the roof fixed," I say.

"The foundation is cracked," says Herb, a local main street merchant and pharmacist who thrives on delivering bad news. "If we don't raise ten thousand dollars, the church is going to have the first ecclesiastical aquarium."

"Charge admission," I suggest.

"This is actually good material," Al says, as if taking mental notes. "Keep talking. My wife is always grilling me on these meetings, and I'm such a bad liar."

By "meetings," Al means that the wives (and this now includes my mother), think that their husbands are at a meeting of the church Buildings and Grounds Committee. Whereas there really isn't any such group, and the men just gather to play poker and gripe about their jobs, the high cost of college, how teenage daughters wear too much makeup, and there isn't a darn thing they can do about any of it. When I was fourteen, I managed to finagle my way in by threatening to blow their cover, and then later started bringing Bernard.

While Officer Rich and Pastor Costello are stacking their chips, Al lights up a cigarette. It's hard to believe that I actually welcome the smell of his Marlboro over the mildew. Pastor Costello then thanks God for the beer, oil-and-vinegar potato chips, and good fellowship, saying that everyone should be a winner tonight, which is really just wishful praying in his case since he almost always breaks even.

Bernard has brought an enormous muffin basket wrapped in orange cellophane and tied off with a big bronze ribbon. One could well ask, "Where does he find the time?" However, when he sets it on the clothes dryer, the guys just stare as if he's dropped off an infant with a dirty diaper.

Bernard removes the bow, peels back layers of cellophane, and the smell of fresh baked-goods wafts through the damp basement, whereupon the men abandon the card table and move in for the kill. No big surprise. The guys have previously been won over by Bernard's sandwich platters, artichoke fava bean dip, and other poker night delights.

"Herb, you must try this pecan brickle." Bernard begins assigning muffins. "Carrot ginger for Al and Pastor Costello, chocolate chocolate chip for Herb and Hallie, and a sugar-free blueberry for Officer Rich!"

Officer Rich's doctor warned him to cut out sugar because he's diabetic. And his wife actually searches his truck and squad cars for crumbs. Officer Rich has to dust-bust regularly and, as a result, his vehicles are much cleaner these days.

Pastor Costello and I look across the poker table at each other as stepfather and stepdaughter for the first time. It's certainly not going to change the play, but I can't help wondering if what we say here might find its way back to my mom.

Pastor Costello deftly moves me off to the side, the way he cuts a parishioner from the flock after church to discuss something private. "I was thinking of a new guideline for the games," he says quietly.

"Huh?" I'm not sure if he's wanting to change the rules or impose a curfew on me.

Pastor Costello looks to make sure that no one is close enough to hear and says, "What happens at poker stays at poker."

"Oh, like Vegas." I eagerly nod my head in agreement.

"I was thinking more along the lines of minister-parishioner confidentiality, but I suppose that's fine."

"How am I going to take all your money if we don't play cards?" the ever-anxious Al calls over to us. Pastor Costello and I are the only ones not seated at the table.

"Are you two working out some kind of father-daughter scam over there?" jokes Herb.

"Just like in that movie *Paper Moon*," says Bernard. "Doesn't Hallie remind you of Tatum O'Neal? I just loved her in that part."

Of course, none of the guys know what he's talking about, but they've grown accustomed to Bernard's movie references.

"Speaking of young people," says Officer Rich, "the mayor is worried that if we don't upgrade our Technical Institute the biggest export after cherries is going to be our youth."

"If you add on to the Institute, we'll need that new highway," says Al. "The roads are at capacity."

"We need a highway like a submarine needs screen doors," states Herb, whose family has lived in this town since it was founded way back in the 1800s.

"The population was going down, down, down for the past fifty years," says Al, who works for the town. "Then suddenly, for two years it didn't change."

"That's because every time a woman got pregnant a man had to leave town," cracks Herb.

"Anyway, it looks like when the numbers come in for last year, we'll see the first increase since 1946." Al concludes his census report.

"I don't care how many people want to move here just so long as they're responsible law abiding citizens and pay their taxes," says Officer Rich.

"Speaking of responsible citizens," says Bernard, "my neighbors rented their house to a bunch of hooligans who have parties every night and leave piles of trash all over the lawn. Is there any way I can have them evicted?"

Al laughs out loud. He knows all the town codes for zoning, building, and eviction.

Officer Rich looks dubious. "It's hard. You can only report them for disturbing the peace after 11:00 PM, and then it's just a warning. If garbage is piled up for more than a week, I could possibly issue a citation, but nothing that will persuade a judge to evict."

"Speaking of trash," says Al, "a guy who drives one of the garbage trucks backed into his own car yesterday and now he's suing himself."

"That's a new one!" says Officer Rich, letting out a rumbling guffaw. He thought he had heard just about every bizarre story that has to do with the law.

We all lay down our cards. "Nothing but some very young clubs," says Al, who was apparently hanging on in the hopes of producing a flush.

"Porn star!" announces Bernard as he spreads out sixes and nines.

"You've been dying to say that, haven't you?" I ask him.

"I couldn't decide between that and *playboy*," he readily admits. Bernard likes using the Internet to build up his poker lingo.

"Three wise men." I lay down a trio of kings.

"Ouch!" Officer Rich throws down his pair of aces as if it hurts. Likewise, Herb tosses down three sevens.

As I rake in a pot of about twenty dollars, Herb declares, "I think I liked it better when all the young people moved away."

Normally I laugh at his jokes, but tonight I feel as if I'm marking time. Or else time is marking me.

"Actually, I am going away," I announce, though Bernard and Pastor Costello already know about the trip. "For sixteen weeks, around the world to work on a school project."

Officer Rich looks up at me and says, "The number one lesson in all my safety talks is that out of the thirty-six ways to avoid disaster, running away is always the best option."

"I'm not running away from anything!" Even to me this sounds like a bad bluff.

"It's a mess out there, so be careful," says Al, who has four kids of his own scattered around the country.

"Has someone shot out your porch light?" asks Herb. "I wouldn't get on a plane these days for all the codeine Tylenol in Canada."

"I couldn't agree with you more," says Bernard, who used to be Herb's enemy until *I* got them to be friends. And now they're both ganging up on me. I swear, between the fear-of-flying lectures, a crazy old advisor ruining my life, and Craig's sudden proposal, I might decide to attend grad school for a master's degree in conspiracy theories.

Chapter 19

*A*fter giving Teddy the keys to my car and saying goodbye to everyone, I wait in the garage at my old house for Bernard to pick me up. Even with the door raised, it smells like motor oil and old tires.

Staring down at my new cell phone, I decide to call Craig and say goodbye. He doesn't answer. I'm not really surprised. What's done is done. Perhaps we're star-crossed lovers and fated not to be together. Or else love just packed up its bags and slipped away in the middle of the night like a thief. Either way, it figures that once I finally get a cell phone, I don't have anyone to talk to.

Pastor Costello opens the back door that leads from the kitchen out to the garage. Aside from the smile lines and corona of gray hair, I can tell it's him because of the sweatshirt that says, LIFE IS FRAGILE, HANDLE WITH PRAYER.

"Oh Hallie, you're still here! Have you seen Davy?"

"Negative. Did you try Jared's house?" Jared's only sibling is a baby sister and so Davy is his video game soul mate.

"He's grounded for being out in the woods after dark and supposed to be in his room," says Pastor Costello.

"Grounding doesn't work all that well around here due to the heavy traffic," I explain from experience. "Plus, you've got roof-to-ground access using the window in the older boys' room, and the small window in the basement acts as an escape hatch by climbing onto the dryer."

"Oh sweet peaches!" Pastor Costello looks exasperated after only his first week of living in the house full time. Though I must admit, with Reggie and Roddy the twin terrors having just turned three, it's hard to concentrate on anything else.

"You have to let them keep some secrets and tell a few lies," I say absentmindedly. My thoughts are more caught up in what lies ahead, and what, or rather who, I'm leaving behind.

"One falsehood leads to another, more often than not an even bigger one," states Pastor Costello in a melodic cadence that suggests he's uttered these words before. All that's missing is the cross in his left hand and the Bible in his right hand.

"Davy has always played in the woods. There's only an acre of trees before the next development starts. He knows how to use a compass and can probably even navigate by the stars."

"If we start giving on the little things, then the larger issues will soon be up for negotiation," insists Pastor Costello. "There have to be ground rules."

Oh boy, does he have a lot to learn about living in a houseful of eight kids.

"You and mom and his teachers have all the power, ordering him around every day, telling him what to do, when to eat and sleep. Grownups are like magicians, making things happen, appear, and disappear. Kids need a little power for themselves."

"I didn't read that in any of the childrearing books I've been studying," Pastor Costello says with skepticism.

"Some things you can only pick up in the trenches," I say. I'm beginning to think that love may be a bit like that too.

Pastor Costello appears to mull this. After all, I do have some solid credentials as the family runaway.

"But how can you be sure that they're on the right path if you knowingly let them get away with things?"

"Check for needle marks every once in a while."

Davy appears in the driveway carrying a large magnifying glass. He looks terrified at seeing Pastor Costello.

"I was just out in the yard showing Lillian snowflakes," stammers Davy.

Pastor Costello smiles. "You know, Davy, I've been thinking that perhaps you and I should go camping when the weather gets a little warmer."

Davy's face lights up. "Really?" he asks as if this might be some sort of a trick.

"God writes the Gospel not only in the Bible but on the trees, flowers, clouds, and stars," says Pastor Costello.

The two of them go inside the house.

Lillian comes toddling around the corner all bundled up in her snowsuit, looking not unlike the Michelin Man, if he were a midget. Though once her hood is pulled back and the scarf is down, she's a dead ringer for me at that age, with her pink complexion, long, strawberry blond curls, and light dusting of freckles. But that's as far as the similarities go. While I was always a child of action, Lillian is turning out to be our calm and pensive Zen tyke. At Dad's funeral she asked, "If they bury the body, then what do they do with the head?"

"Hey Lillian, do you think I should marry Craig?" I ask.

"I'd marry Craig. He's nice!" she says sweetly. "But I don't know if you should."

"Why not?" I ask.

"Because Hallie, people are like snowflakes, and so we're all different," she informs me, as if I'm a complete moron.

Chapter 20

ernard honks the horn of his Volvo even though he can see me sitting right there in the garage.

"You! Me! Us! Go! Let's!"

He's pretending to be English aristocracy.

After loading my stuff into the trunk, I climb in the passenger seat and Bernard hands me a book called *Journey to the East* by Hermann Hesse. "It's from Mother—some wishy-washy pre-hippie mysticism nonsense," he warns me in his fake British accent, stopping just short of singing a rousing round of "I'm Henerey the Eighth, I Am."

"Thanks." I check inside to see if Bernard has hidden a copy of *Prevention* magazine and find an inscription from Olivia. "Ships weren't built to stay in the harbor." I put it inside my carry-on knapsack.

"The car smells delicious," I say.

"Artisanal muffin basket for the intrepid travelers." Bernard nods toward the backseat. "Artisanal" is his latest for anything homemade—artisanal omelets, artisanal croutons, artisanal peanut butter and jelly sandwiches! I'm tempted to suggest that *artisanal* antipsychotic medication is next on the list.

I've never met any of the people I'm going with, aside from Josh, and so I suddenly feel embarrassed, like when Mom used to run to the bus stop with my lunch, wearing her robe and slippers and a head full of sponge rollers. But I don't say anything. It was kind of Bernard to offer to drive me to Cleveland during the workweek. Not to mention the middle of winter, when the roads can be icy.

Lost in my own thoughts, I gaze out the window while we pass my old school, the small shops on Main Street, and finally the hospital where Dad died two years ago today. Now he's in the cemetery at the other end of town. People like to joke that you can be born in the hospital at one end of Main Street, go to school and work in the middle, and then be buried at the other end, without ever leaving town. Only it's true.

As we cross the bridge into the next county, the sun slips out from behind a cloud, making the snow-covered fields sparkle like so many acres of diamonds. The majestic elm trees lining the side of the county road are now completely bare and no longer rustle with the slightest wind. Instead, they seem to be resting, as if gathering strength for what lies ahead.

Bernard leans forward and gazes heavenward. "The sky is Maxfield Parrish blue."

I laugh because something can never just be a plain old ordinary color with Bernard. There always has to be a painter or place attached, like Monet green or Pompeii red.

"And the sun is school-bus yellow, and your eyes are Windex blue," I add. Next, he's probably going to warn me that the color of the sky is a bad omen, like cows lying down in the grass before a thunderstorm.

Bernard sighs as if he's the only one who can truly appreciate the natural world, even though he won't let his Girl Scout troop go hiking anywhere except the mall.

"Did you get the catalogue of wooden swing sets I asked the company to send you?" I ask. "They're supposed to be very safe."

"Ginger Rogers that." (A Bernardism derived from the aviation phrase "Roger that.") "However, I've been thinking that the girls might benefit more from an oriental sculpture garden..."

The song, "This Nearly Was Mine," from the musical *South*

Pacific begins playing and Bernard quickly switches off the car stereo, as if this might bring up unpleasant associations for me with regard to the Craig catastrophe.

"It's okay," I say. I've never been inclined to mix real life with musical numbers the way that Bernard does. When hard times hit, a showstopper never fails to turn his frown upside-down.

"Far be it from me to meddle in anyone else's life," says Bernard, "especially when it comes to love."

Now this is hilarious. The East German Secret Police would have had nothing on Bernard when it came to getting into other people's business, *particularly* their love lives.

"Do you have a piece of tape so I can keep my right eyebrow from flying to the top of my forehead?" I ask.

Bernard scoffs as if I'm overreacting. "However, *if asked*, I would simply suggest that we put everything right before you leave—call Craig and accept his proposal and agree to sort the details out upon your return."

"And what could possibly make you think that is a good idea?"

"Matchmaking is instinctive, like knowing the difference between a full boil and a rolling boil."

"But he gave me an ultimatum!" I say. Now, I'm not sure exactly why this is such a terrible thing, other than I always hear guys like my older brother Eric complaining how they don't like it when, after a certain amount of dating, women tell them to either sit on Bachelor Beach or swim toward exclusivity.

"Hallie, did it ever occur to you that maybe he just loves you and therefore doesn't care for the idea of you trotting around the globe and being hit on by Carlos the Jackal's grandson!"

"Whose side are you on, anyway?" I ask.

"Cupid's," says Bernard. "And safety."

I turn toward the passenger window to indicate that this conversation is officially over. Similarly, Bernard stares straight ahead with his hands firmly on the steering wheel at ten and two, cloaking himself in situational martyrdom.

As instructed, we enter parking lot C at my school, and Bernard pulls behind what must be the shuttle bus that's taking us to the airport. In the lobby of the administration building, it's possible to see about a dozen people surrounded by a lot of big knapsacks and duffle bags.

"It's not too late to change your mind," says Bernard. "Alexander I of Greece contracted blood poisoning and died after being bitten by a monkey. And Sherwood Anderson died of peritonitis on an ocean liner heading for Brazil after swallowing a toothpick during a cocktail party."

Now, these stories are probably true for the most part, despite Bernard's great talent for mixing fact and fiction, a penchant he claims to share with the famous former *Vogue* fashion editor, Diana Vreeland, who labeled this particular style of information as "faction."

"I'll avoid monkeys and toothpicks," I promise.

"I'm just saying that traveling is *tres perilous*," insists Bernard. "Let's not even discuss Amelia Earhart! And what if some horrible cook doesn't clean his rusty colander and you develop lockjaw? Did you ever consider *that*?"

"Why don't you just drop me here?" I suggest this despite being certain that Bernard will want to get a good hard look at the professor and everyone else going on the trip.

Surprisingly, he hugs me goodbye at the curb, and I head toward the double glass doors and the group milling about inside.

"Don't eat seafood in months that have an "R" in their name!" Bernard calls after me. "At least in the Northern Hemisphere. And don't order the Catch-of-the-Day unless you can actually *see* the water from where you're sitting!"

I nod to indicate these will go right up there on my list with not drinking directly from the Ganges River.

Ms. Pritchett, with her tight lips and tight perm, glances at her watch. "You were almost late."

What is "almost late," I want to ask her. There's "late" and "on time," and I fall squarely into the latter category.

Ms. Pritchett raises what appears to be a bulletproof clipboard, makes a check mark, and then introduces me to a tall, slope-shouldered guy who looks to be in his late twenties. "This is my graduate assistant, Marcus Banjo Harriman."

He extends his hand and I think we're going to shake, but end up receiving a fist bump instead. "The 'Marcus' is actually silent and everyone calls me 'Banjo.'"

With his chin-length hair tucked behind his ears, scraggly moonshiner's beard, and worn cargo pants, Banjo looks like someone who just arrived back from a four-month trip.

Ms. Pritchett steers me over to a pale blond, young woman about my age wearing a plain gray dress, white tights, and black lace-up shoes. "You and Amanda will be roommates." Alongside Miss Little House on the Prairie stand two stern-looking parents and an older brother who all stare as if I'm carrying the plague.

Josh rounds the corner and offers a warm welcome. He's had his hair cut short and looks handsome in a brown leather bomber jacket over a Toledo Rockets T-shirt with acid-washed jeans.

"Oh, Hallie!" comes Bernard's singsong voice from the doorway. "You almost forgot your artisanal muffin basket."

Why me? Just when I'm meeting all these new people and seeing Josh for the first time as an unattached woman?

I dash over to Bernard and grab the basket. But rather than leave, he pulls back the gingham cloth cover to show me where the butter and jam packets are tucked in along the side and starts listing the varieties of muffins contained within. "Is anyone lactose intolerant?" he canvasses the crowd in a loud voice.

After looking momentarily perplexed, everyone is hit with the amazing scent of "perky peach" and "lusty lemon," and they start edging closer. A moment later, people are enthusing about how delicious the muffins are, even the parents right out of the *American Gothic* painting. All of a sudden, I'm very popular.

Chapter 21

Ms. Pritchett collects the medical certificates and insurance forms and carefully examines our passports. She confirms that we're all at least twenty-one and therefore no one needs a permission slip. As we load our gear onto the shuttle bus, Amanda's parents look as if they're going to change their minds, so she keeps assuring them that everything will be fine. If it weren't for the equally pale blond brother standing there, I'd think she was an only child like Craig, because they seem so worried about her.

We wait at the airport for over two hours before finally boarding the flight to Toronto. My first plane ride ever! I'm not afraid, because I really do believe that when it's your time to go, it's your time to go. On the other hand, I hope it's not the pilot's time to go while we just happen to be lounging in the back.

I was planning to sit with Josh, but end up next to Amanda. Since she and I will be roommates throughout, Ms. Pritchett has organized our plane seats together. Josh and Banjo are across the aisle, buried under a pile of Japanese-style comic books.

After a bit of general conversation, it transpires that Amanda has almost finished a degree in painting.

"I really like your necklace," says Amanda, who isn't wearing any jewelry and doesn't even have pierced ears.

"Thanks." I put my hand up to the crystals. "A woman back

home gave it to me to help me feel better after my dad died." I hold up the pearly pink stone. "And this one is supposed to help me find true love. But I'm not so sure that it works."

"Are you in a sorority?" asks Amanda.

"If you count having nine brothers and sisters a sorority, then yes," I joke.

However, she looks disappointed. "I've never been allowed to live on campus or go to any parties and so I was hoping to...you know...have some fun on this trip."

If "fun" saw this pale skinny girl, I'm quite certain he would run in the opposite direction.

"I'm sure that we'll have tons of fun." But the words echo with false hope, the way you tell people in the hospital that they're looking really good. I have a vision of my apron-clad mother asking, "Do you mean the kind of *fun* that ends in tears?"

Amanda pulls her knees up underneath the skirt of her long gray dress. "My family is Mennonite, and I hardly ever get to do anything fun."

"Do you really have barn-raisings?" I ask. "Like in that movie *Witness*?"

"They were Amish," says Amanda. "But yes, we do."

"That looks like fun," I say.

Amanda gives a halfhearted smile that suggests if you've been to one barn-raising, then you've been to them all.

"What's the difference between Amish and Mennonite?" I ask.

"It's complicated," says Amanda. "They were originally one movement, and then the Amish broke off. The doctrine is pretty much the same, but we practice differently."

"Is it true the dolls aren't allowed to have faces?" I ask. The homemade rag dolls that the women wearing old-fashioned clothes and bonnets sold at the fair never even had eyes on them.

"That's just the Amish," says Amanda. "They consider the reproduction of graven images to be unholy." Now she looks not only disappointed with me, but incredibly bored. And I realize that everyone she meets must ask her the same questions, the way people always ask me what it's like to have so many siblings, as if we're freaks.

While waiting outside the Toronto airport for transportation to our hotel, lanky Banjo gazes skyward with the air of a brooding crane. "Look! You can see the Pleiades."

Glancing up to where he's pointing, all I can make out is a jumble of stars against a black winter sky, heaven's screensaver, if you will. However, had I taken astronomy, not only would I know what he was talking about, but I'd be in Cincinnati right now with Craig. Suddenly this whole trip feels like a horrible mistake.

Mismatched laminate motel furniture, carelessly arranged atop worn beige linoleum, gives our room all the ambience of a minimum-security-prison. I don't bother to unpack, since we'll only be here for two nights. Amanda spends almost an hour in the bathroom. It's hard to imagine what's going on in there, since she wasn't wearing any makeup and her hair hangs down poker-straight to her shoulders. She eventually comes out wearing a plain muslin nightgown that looks like a longer version of her dress.

It takes me five minutes to brush my teeth, wash my face, and change into my Len's Tractor Parts T-shirt. Amanda studies me and looks intrigued. "Is that what you sleep in?"

"Yes," I say. "Well, I have different ones."

Amanda takes out the paperback with the steamy romance cover she bought at the airport. I'm relieved, because I was afraid she might want to read scripture aloud or have us work a prayer chain together. And quite frankly, as much as I love Pastor Costello, there's enough of that at home.

Settling into bed, I open the book from Olivia, Hermann Hesse's *Journey to the East*. The first line says, *It was my destiny to join in a great experience.*

So far, so bad.

Chapter 22

*I*t's hard to tell that morning has arrived in the heart of Toronto. Even when I pull back the curtains, the room doesn't get any lighter, despite the bedside clock insisting that it's almost 7:00 AM. Ms. Pritchett has instructed us to assemble (her word) in the breakfast room. She made it quite clear that 7:30 AM was more than a suggestion by saying that our return tickets could be used at *any* time—all she needs to do is call the airlines.

I look around the room and Amanda is gone. Her bed is made perfectly, as if no one even slept there, and her things are all neat and tidy. Maybe she's accustomed to rising early to milk the cows or churn butter.

There's a crowd at the front of the restaurant where the buffet is and, in the back, I can see my group gathered at two tables pushed together. Ms. Pritchett has a pile of thick manila envelopes in front of her. And there's something different about Amanda. As I get closer, it becomes clear that she's wearing makeup. Lots of it! She's still in the plain gray cotton dress, though I can't tell if it's the same one as yesterday or a different one, but from the neck up, she may as well be off to a modeling job. The rest of us are wearing jeans and sweaters, except for Ms. Pritchett, who has on dark slacks with a no-nonsense high-neck white blouse and cranberry blazer that looks like it was acquired at the bankruptcy auction of a down-market car rental agency. She'd told us not to bother with nice clothes—that we'd be working outdoors most of the time, and it was fine to look like students.

As soon as we finish eating, Ms. Pritchett passes around the envelopes and explains exactly how the project, which she's using for her doctoral thesis, will work. On the first morning in every city, we'll go out and "accidentally" drop a dozen wallets apiece, all containing twenty dollars in local currency and a slip of paper with a name, toll-free number (Ms. Pritchett has a global phone), and e-mail address. Ms. Pritchett issues us maps of Toronto with our drop locations marked by bright red *X*s. Most of our destinations require taking subways and buses, so she hands us money for that and also for two more meals.

Ms. Pritchett explains that on the second morning she'll give a sociology lecture that relates to our project. Sounds easy enough to me.

Finally, she gets to the part we've all been waiting for—rules and curfews. "Since you're all of legal age, I ask only that you behave responsibly and observe the customs and mores of whatever country we're in," she says. "When we head to the Far East, I'll review those more specifically."

Cool. We're free! This could turn out to be fun after all.

"That said, I expect everyone to be on time when we leave to drop the wallets on the first day in every city," adds Ms. Pritchett. "Same with the lectures. Not showing up will mean receiving an F and no credits."

Okay, so as long as we set an alarm clock, we can do whatever we want.

Josh and I study our maps in the lobby and determine that we're starting at the same subway stop, so we walk there together. The morning is gray and misty, as if a cloud sits on the ground, and you don't see the tall buildings until you're practically right in front of them. What I do see easily enough is a Tim Hortons donut shop on every corner. This guy Tim must be a billionaire.

"I told you this would be fun," says Josh.

"Yeah, I guess so," I say.

"Want to go out tonight?" he asks. "I found some great nightclubs on the Internet. We have forty dollars for lunch and dinner, so if we eat cheap, that leaves enough for cover charges and a couple drinks."

"Okay," I agree. This might be just what I need to feel better—a night out at a real club in a big city with a cute guy.

We split up and agree to meet back at the hotel when we're done. "Watch out for grizzly bears," jokes Josh as he disappears into the crowded subway station.

The thing about dropping a wallet is that you can't let anyone see you do it, because he might chase you down, and the whole idea is that the finder has time to check for money and decide whether or not to give it back. My first stop is the University of Toronto. I suppose the idea is that starving students may have more of an incentive to keep the money than wage earners.

Young people walk leisurely across campus with backpacks slung over their shoulders much the same as they do at my school. A guy holding a bullhorn stands alongside a card table with pamphlets and a petition while shouting about how neglected, aboriginal communities need more government help. An older Asian woman wrapped up in a parka hands me a free copy of *The Toronto Star*. In the distance, between a large gray stone rotunda and a brick building that's probably a dorm, a guy whizzes past on cross-country skis. Okay, that's something I've never seen at my college back home.

Next, I take the bus to a neighborhood called Swansea, which is several miles away from the center of downtown. I get lost a couple times, but whenever I ask someone for directions, they stop and study my map and help me. One woman actually walks me to the intersection I'm trying to find, and another guy uses his cell phone to call his wife because she grew up near the block I'm searching for. Then an entire road crew gathers around my map for about ten minutes to debate the best way to get to the zoo.

Honestly, you'd think they were all working on commission. Or else for the Chamber of Commerce.

Once back in the city proper, I have two more stops—both public parks—but they're miles apart. Based on my map, Toronto has a lot of parks. And now that the cloud of fog is lifting, I can see that there aren't many homeless people or disaffected youth hanging around on street corners, just groups of huddled office workers breathing cigarette smoke like dragons—but the air is so frigid I'm not sure how they can tell when they're finished exhaling and don't pass out.

Toronto is very clean compared to how I imagined a big city would be. The only real question I have so far is why the Queen of England is still on their money. My Canadian history isn't all that strong, but I was under the impression it's an independent country. On the other hand, there is a weird-looking bird on the one-dollar coins, so maybe they just didn't have a lot to choose from.

Chapter 23

*D*istributing all twelve wallets takes me only three hours. This project is going to be a cinch, I decide, with plenty of time to explore new places and have a good time. Back in the room, I excitedly prepare for my date with Josh. If Craig wants to see other people then fine, that's exactly what I'll do too!

When I arrive in the lobby, Josh is standing there with a young woman I don't recognize. She has jet black hair and sports one of those outfits people put together from thrift shops—a designer boob top mixed with black leather pants, an army surplus jacket, and shoes that your grandpa threw away. Oh, my gosh, it's Amanda! Not only that, but underneath all the sensible gray muslin, it was impossible to see that she's built like an hourglass!

"Hey," says Josh. "Banjo is staying to help Ms. Pritchett set up a computer tracking program for our dearly departed wallets. So it's just you, me, and Amanda."

"Call me Mandy," says the former Sarah Plain and Tall.

Okay, so I was wrong about the date. Josh invited everybody to go out. I guess that was nice. Since we'll be working together for the next sixteen weeks, it's probably a good idea to make friends. As for "Mandy," this is the moment my mother would ask, "Is *that* what you're wearing?" It's not so much that Mom is afraid her daughters won't meet men who are appropriate husband material when dressed slutty, but rather she has this strange notion that whatever outfit you die in is how you'll look while wandering around heaven for all of eternity.

We take the subway and then walk a few blocks to Richmond Street, where there's supposed to be a hot new nightspot called Moon Rocks. Outside, the doorman or bouncer or whatever he is doesn't act like those gorillas in Cleveland who resemble guys on MOST WANTED posters and get their kicks from grunting unintelligibly and turning away undesirables. The man who ushers us inside is wearing a sheepskin coat along with one of those big fur hats with earflaps, and he tells us to enjoy ourselves and "Watch out for black holes." Ha ha. A little space humor.

Inside are floor-to-ceiling lava lamps bubbling with lemon goo, dry ice underneath the dance floor, and revolving computer projections of the galaxy flashing on the walls. Blue-tinted mineshaft lights give the effect of moonbeams piercing the misty atmosphere. This is so much better than anyplace I've ever been! In Cleveland, the dance clubs don't last long, and so they're pretty basic—mirrored ceilings, strobe lights, and a drunk doing the Robot out in the middle of the floor who may or may not have a full set of chromosomes, and who may or may not be related to you.

The bartender is a friendly guy with greenish blond hair, dressed in a formfitting silver Spandex "spacesuit." He says that if we're tourists, we should try "Martians" because they're made with VO rye whisky and it's a famous Canadian drink.

A woman wearing a brown suede mini-dress overhears the conversation and asks where we're from. I tell her Ohio.

"Americans know more about England and France than they do about Canada." Her tone is more accusatory than conversational.

"That's not true," says Amanda, now Mandy. "In 2003, Canada agreed to stop exporting subsidized dairy products to the United States."

I almost shout, "Go farm girl!"

The woman looks as if she has a bone to pick with the U.S. in general, but apparently, we're the only Americans on hand. "Who's the Canadian prime minister?"

Darn. I should know this one. "Paul...maybe...or John..." I stumble.

"Or Ringo," says Josh and then giggles.

"Name ten famous Canadians!" demands Angry Young Woman.

"That's easy," says Josh. "Wayne Gretzky and that singer..."

"Celine Dion," Mandy fills the gap.

"Right," says Josh. "And Al Franken."

"I think he's from Minnesota," I say.

"Okay," continues Josh. "Then there's that group...the Ranch Addicts..."

"Cowboy Junkies," I correct him.

"Right—that's four more right there!" says Josh.

Angry Young Woman looks disgusted and walks away. We all laugh as if she's a big idiot. However, I make a mental note to brush up not just on Canadian history, but also the Canadian present. That was sort of embarrassing. I mean, the Canadians I spoke with today knew all kinds of things about the Unites States.

"Hey," says Josh. "How do you get ten Canadians out of the pool on the hottest day of the year?"

Mandy and I shake our heads.

"You say, 'Okay, everyone, get out of the pool.'"

Now we really laugh hard because the one thing we know about Canadians is that they have a reputation for behaving a lot better than Americans. Olivia is constantly saying how we can't blame the lack of gun control for all the homicides in our country because Canadians manage to have tons more firearms and yet they don't going around wasting people every five minutes.

A guy dressed like a rodeo rider comes over and offers to buy me a drink. I've never had a complete stranger offer to buy me a drink before, and I say okay without thinking how this now obligates me to talk with him while I drink it. But he does and we do. By the time the drink is finished, Josh and Mandy are out on the dance floor, gyrating together under trembling violet lights, among a tight crowd exuding pickup hormones, and looking as if they're having a really good time.

Fortunately, Urban Cowboy doesn't give me a quiz on Canadian culture or Frostback politics. He asks me to dance, but suddenly I'm not feeling all that well—perhaps I've been struck by a piece of space junk. I beg off, telling Josh and Mandy that I have jetlag. I've never had jetlag and am pretty sure you can't get it from a forty-five-minute flight, but they're having fun and don't pay much attention to my lame excuse. The place is by now jam-packed, and it takes me a full ten minutes to make my way to the door.

The city is very pretty late at night—lights twinkling, snow-covered pine boughs adorning the public square, people wandering around in big fluffy coats, laughing and saying hello to me as they pass. If things don't work out back home, maybe I'll move to Canada and feel really popular just roaming the streets by myself.

Chapter 24

"Heavens to Mergatroid!" exclaims the up-until-now unflappable Banjo, channeling cartoon cat Snagglepuss when we all meet in the hotel restaurant the following morning and he gets a shot of Made Over Mandy in tight jeans and clingy sweater.

He and Ms. Pritchett must look twice at Mandy to establish that she is indeed the same Mennonite girl they met at school just thirty-six short hours ago.

"Well, Amanda, you've certainly adapted to metropolitan culture quickly." Ms. Pritchett puts the transformation into sociological perspective for us. "Entire studies have been done on success in conjunction with rate-of-adjustment and also on early-adopters. Perhaps if we have time, I'll go through them."

"Good news!" Banjo waves a computer printout across the breakfast table. "Out of forty-eight wallets, thirty-seven have already been accounted for! This is a record. And only one was missing the money."

"What happens if we don't hear about the rest and have to leave?" asks Josh.

"People can contact us by phone or e-mail, and we'll just ask where they found it and tell them to donate the money to a good cause," says Ms. Pritchett. "Today is a free day, but I suggest that everyone stop in at some of Toronto's wonderful museums. Remember that we leave early tomorrow morning for Seattle and catch a connecting flight to the Hawaiian island of Maui."

Josh and Mandy look pretty hung over from last night, and their eyes droop as Ms. Pritchett begins her lecture on our ethics project and how exactly it relates to sociology. "Based on your encounters moving about the city yesterday, does anyone have an observation that may relate to the wallet-return rate?"

"People are really nice and helpful," I say.

"Good," says Ms. Pritchett. "But what factors drive this? What is the cultural attitude toward lost objects in Canada? Is there a dominant religion that would suggest it's bad luck to keep things you've found?"

We all look clueless. Ms. Pritchett registers annoyance. "Didn't you people read *the handout?*" The Handout is two hundred single-spaced, double-sided pages of cultural mumbo jumbo in an eight-point font that I'd planned to look at on the long flight to Hawaii. Apparently, Josh and Mandy are operating from the same playbook.

Banjo comes to our rescue. "I think it's safe to say that because Canada is a relatively new country and was built largely around the agrarian community, combined with a challenging climate, people know they have to work together in order to survive. Or at least it's a residual practice."

"Thank you, Marcus," says Ms. Pritchett. "Now Amanda, explain to us the Four Worlds model to describe the development of countries. It was on page six of your handout."

Party Girl opens her bloodshot eyes. "It's Mandy. People in the First World have computers and stuff and people in Third World countries are really poor."

Ms. Pritchett lets her off the hook, but doesn't appear satisfied. "Hallie?"

I didn't even know there were more than two worlds—first and third. Based on my blank stare, Ms. Pritchett must decide I'm living in one of those other worlds.

Fortunately, she assigns the rest of the narrative to Banjo, though Ms. Pritchett insists on calling him Marcus.

"The so-called First World refers to developed capitalist countries, the Second World is used to describe former communist and socialist states, the Third World is currently developing countries, and the Fourth World refers to ethnic groups living within or across state boundaries, such as Native Americans."

"Thank you." Ms. Pritchett furrows her brow at the rest of us. "Let me remind you that this class is pass/fail. That will be all for today, but at our next session, I expect everyone to be prepared to discuss *game theory* as applied to the social sciences and how it changed the way conflicts, such as trade wars and the arms race, are analyzed."

Ms. Pritchett slams her folder shut and storms off like a furious orchestra conductor. Banjo gathers up his spreadsheets, laughs as if the whole thing is a joke, and then casually adds, "By the way, she's not kidding about failing everyone."

Chapter 25

"The Rockies are off to your left," announces our captain as the plane heads toward Seattle.

Only I'm on the right. But if I stand up and lean over, I can see snow-capped mountains above Mandy's purple-streaked head. She certainly hadn't let yesterday afternoon go to waste. No, siree. In addition to purple highlights, with eyeliner to match, silver hoops dangle from her freshly pierced ears. I assume there wasn't enough time for tattoos.

On the flight from Seattle to Hawaii, I begin studying the dreaded handout. So much for this being an easy four science credits. A double major in particle physics and plane geometry is starting to look good.

The captain tells us to fasten our seatbelts because we're "approaching some weather." Mandy begins to ferociously crack a wad of bubblegum while reading her latest bodice ripper. I put down the handout and look out the window where Hollywood-style bolts of electricity are cracking open a darkening sky.

"Some weather" turns out to be an Armageddon-like storm. The plane hurtles from side to side while people fill airsickness bags, and a few hardy souls scribble wills and farewell letters to loved ones. The food and beverage service is cancelled, not that we could keep a mini-pretzel down anyway, and the next four hours are spent gripping the armrests and praying. If there are no atheists in foxholes, there aren't any agnostics in a tempest over the Pacific. Mandy turns out to be a marathon prayer—racing through entire pages of the Bible, pausing only long enough to inform me that, "God will protect us."

"Who do you think sent the storm?" I ask.

She looks down at her violet nail polish and has to wonder about that for a moment. From two rows behind, I can hear Banjo telling Josh how the demigod, Maui, supposedly created the Hawaiian Islands by pulling them up from the sea with a giant fishhook. If sociology doesn't work out, he can always become a tour guide.

The plane lurches, and it feels as if we plummet a hundred feet before leveling off again. I suppose this is the moment I should be making one of those promises, such as *if I live through this storm I'll devote my life to crocheting afghans for political prisoners*. Only I just don't care that much about anything right now, and if we end up as shark food, then so be it: Craig and I really will be broken up for good. I briefly imagine the funeral. Will he be sorry about dumping me? No, he'll be saying, "I told her not to go on that trip." And Bernard will be right behind him.

There's a big round of applause when we finally land. A few people throw up one last time for good measure. I'm impressed that they have anything left to puke. While collecting the airsickness bags, the flight attendants hand us different-colored plastic leis to put around our necks. A favorable exchange.

As the bus transports us to the hotel, no one says a word; and Ms. Pritchett looks the color of pond algae. Banjo pats her hand. "I'll make sure that everyone checks in—you just go to your room."

Normally I'd be excited about staying at a place right on the beach. However, after the amusement park ride to get here, the sound of waves crashing directly outside a thatched hut isn't exactly soothing. It's only eight o'clock in the evening, but Mandy and I both fall on top of our beds and pass out. I dream about being buried alive in our laundry room back home. But instead of one washing machine, there are ten. And the dryer pounds as if all of Teddy's size-fourteen sneakers are in there.

When I wake up it takes a moment to determine where I am. A bright shaft of light hits me directly in the face, and I wonder if Jesus got me for that sunbeam after all. Cracking open the door, I have to cover my eyes with my hands and peer between my fingers. The sky is fairytale blue while an endless green ocean is filled with surfers. Kids dart around the white sand beach flying kites. It's like waking up in paradise. Or at the very least, a shampoo commercial.

Josh is a few feet away, with bright tangerine trunks filling the space between a pale, but sculpted, chest and well-defined calf muscles. I'd almost forgotten that he was on the diving team. "C'mon Hallie, put your suit on. There's no lecture this morning and we don't start dropping wallets until tomorrow!"

"I'm starving," I say.

Josh points to an open-air bamboo shelter a hundred yards down the beach. "They have breakfast over there. The fruit is amazing! And they'll make any kind of omelet you want."

Eventually Banjo joins us, and a few hours later, so does Mandy—after shopping for a sexy, pink-and-white polka-dot bikini. I suddenly feel like a gym teacher in my blue one-piece racing suit. This gorgeous, golden surfer guy flirts with Mandy and invites us all to a party being held a few miles down the beach tonight. He says that with a driver's license, we can rent mopeds at the front desk.

After lolling in the warm water all day, lying on the hot sand, playing volleyball, and recounting stories about the Flight From Hell, we change for the party and rent mopeds. About forty people our age have gathered around a bonfire and it's like a scene out of a movie—people dancing, guys wrestling, and kayaks fitted with lanterns being paddled around the lagoon. There are big barrels of wine, a chest of cold beer, and a grill where you can buy hotdogs and hamburgers for a dollar.

A guy with wavy black hair; a wide expressive face; and dark, soulful almond-shaped eyes offers me a glass of wine and asks where I'm from. I tell him about the school project and the white-knuckle flight over the Pacific.

He's a native Hawaiian and explains how his people originally came from Tahiti, that his name, Ailani, means High Chief, and that he's part of a movement for Hawaii to secede from the United States.

"The decision to join the U.S. was not representative of the native people, but forced upon us by emissaries from Washington." Ailani says this with great seriousness, despite the merrymaking and making out going on all around us.

"I have a friend back home who would be very interested in your cause." Wait until I tell Olivia that I have a new subject for one of her editorials.

Ailani gets two more glasses of wine and begins teaching me Hawaiian. "*Mahalo* is 'thank you' and *Pehea 'oe* means 'how are you?'"

When I try to say these words, he laughs like crazy.

"If you ever find yourself short of consonants, maybe you can borrow some from Eastern Europe," I suggest.

But Ailani is not giving up easily and teaches me to say, "I'm fine," "no problem," and "where's the bathroom?"

We stroll down the beach and let the warm surf race across our feet. The moon appears from behind a bank of clouds.

"Come see where I live," says Ailani.

Strange land, strange man—not a good idea. On the other hand, I can no longer make myself worry about any of the things I used to worry about. Or else I've become a fatalist. If I survived that flight, then maybe it really isn't my time to go yet and I'm still supposed to do something on this Earth. But what?

Ailani steers my moped down a deserted stretch of road as I cling to his waist and my new philosophy of living in the moment. "So I guess you don't have any interstate highways here," I joke.

"Actually, we have three," he says. "Anything built as a result of the Federal Aid Highway Act of 1956 is called an Interstate even if it doesn't cross state lines."

Wow. He really knows his Hawaii.

What I imagined as Ailani's *Survivor*-style beach shack turns out to be a two-story almost all glass house, perched on a bluff overlooking the ocean. The front yard is covered with voluptuous tropical flowers so bright they shimmer in the gathering darkness. Once we're inside, Ailani pops open a bottle of champagne and mixes it with dark red fruit juice. The concoction tastes delicious, but I don't know how good an idea it is to mix the beer from this afternoon with the wine from this evening and now a bit of bubbly. He flicks a switch on the wall, and the room is suddenly filled with upbeat ukulele music.

"That's pretty," I say.

"Don Ho—our Elvis. I'm always amazed that Hawaiian music is so cheerful, when the native people have so much to be angry about. There were about three hundred thousand of us living here when Captain Cook brought his syphilis, flu, and concept of real-estate ownership. A few years later, two-thirds of the native population was dead."

"I'm sorry," I say on behalf of imperialists everywhere.

Ailani laughs. "I'm sorry—you've just arrived in Hawaii, and it's my job to show you the beauty of my native land, not bore you with history." He leads me to the balcony and we stare out over the Pacific, where long rolling waves wrinkle the dark surface. Birds and insects rustle in the trees, and the air is heavily perfumed with the scent of ungoverned nature. All my senses are elevated, and yet I still feel completely drained.

"You're not having a nice time," he says.

"I am," I say. "It's just that I feel like I've been through a war. My father died two years ago, and things were finally starting to look up, but there was a mistake at school so I couldn't graduate on time. Then right before leaving on this trip, my mother got remarried and my boyfriend broke up with me."

"Ah, you need herbal medicine." Ailani brings out a small wooden box and begins to roll what appears to be a joint.

"No thanks, I don't smoke," I say.

"It's not like that," explains Ailani. "This is the healing power of the Valley Island."

Without a doubt, an incredible citrus aroma emanates from Ailani's herbal remedy. When I try a small puff, there's a wonderfully smooth, fruity flavor like Strawberry Yoo-Hoo mixed with a pinch of lemon and mint. As the darkness unfolds, the soft glow of houses surrounding the beach resembles a pearl necklace. Waves continue to crash in the distance, even though we can no longer see them, and my worries begin to recede. I realize that all the problems in the world could be solved if we'd just love one another—not merely hugs and handshakes, but wild and unrestricted love, like the sea rushing toward the shore.

Chapter 26

The next morning I'm lying naked atop an enormous waterbed, and Ailani is standing over me with a glass of orange juice.

"Aloha," he says.

"Who? Where? What?" This has gone way beyond what my elementary school teachers would call a "teachable moment."

"Ailani, Hawaii, love." He smiles down from above.

Morning splashes over me like a bucket of cold saltwater. "Oh my God, what time is it?"

"Ten after nine," he says.

"The meeting is in twenty minutes!" I yank on my clothes while trying to run out the bedroom door and tumble forward.

"Hallie, I know this sounds crazy, but I want you to stay here," he says.

"Huh?" I'm sitting on the floor with my jeans now making a straitjacket around my sun-splotched legs.

"I think I'm in love with you," he declares.

Do I dare tell him I don't remember *one thing* that happened after we came inside last night?

"I like you too, Ailani, but I have to finish this project and get the last four credits I need to graduate."

"But the assignment just started, right? You can take sociology at the University here," he says.

Oh, my gosh—this guy is totally serious!

"I don't mean to brag, but my family has a citrus company, and we're very wealthy. Just stay here for a semester and let's try it out."

Someone pounds hard on the front door while shouting, "Hallie! Are you in there?" As addled as my brain might be at this moment, it's crystal clear that this summons is quite the opposite of Jesus calling for me softly and tenderly.

Zipping up my pants, I race to the front door.

Josh is practically hopping up and down. "One of the guys told me you left with Ailani. We've got exactly nine minutes to get to the breakfast hut or we both fail!"

Josh and I scramble down the steps, leap onto our mopeds, and go full speed down the road with the Doomsday Clock ticking loudly in our ears. "We smoked something and I'm not sure what happened after that," I shout over the wind. "All I remember is floating on a cloud of love and thinking I could single-handedly bring about world peace."

"Maui Waui!" Josh yells back.

"What?"

"It's high-octane pot—they grow it here."

"I don't remember anything that happened after that!"

"I think someone got *lei'd*," jokes Josh.

We pull up to the hotel in the nick of time and dash directly to where the others are gathered, studying some local maps.

Ms. Pritchett is back to being her insufferable self. She glances at her watch and acts as if they've been anxiously awaiting our arrival for hours.

"We're visiting the museum to study native culture for any history that might have ramifications with regard to the moral attitudes of the locals," she informs us latecomers.

I raise my hand and Ms. Pritchett calls on me. "Do you mean stuff like how when Captain Cook discovered the Islands, he brought diseases that killed two-thirds of the population, and that Native Hawaiians are trying to secede from the U.S.; so if they find a wallet, it might be returned if they think it belongs to a Hawaiian, but not to someone originally from the mainland or a tourist?"

Ms. Pritchett looks surprised and says, "Yes, that's exactly the sort of thing." Then she adds snidely, "Apparently you've already been *involved* in some research."

Banjo points toward a blue van pulling into the driveway and calls out, "Exit, stage left." He seems to have a partiality for Snagglepuss dialogue.

As we head off, all I can think is that now Josh will never ask me out. In the parking lot of the museum, I quietly explain to him that the Ailani thing was a mistake.

However, Josh stops me. "It's cool," he says. "We're like a rock band on tour. You know, what happens in sociology stays in sociology." (People seem to enjoy using this Vegas catchphrase on me. Now if only I looked like a showgirl.)

Still, Josh must think I'm such a slut. "Seeing as how Craig and I broke up right before the trip, I just…"

"You did?" asks Josh.

"Yeah…uh, I guess I didn't tell you then…huh?"

Josh smiles and suddenly appears very interested.

Chapter 27

*I*t isn't until we're rising through the clouds on the plane to Australia and I'm gazing down at a receding paradise that I actually consider Ailani's offer. What if I were to chuck everything and move to Hawaii? It might be just the thing for my Quarter-life Crisis. Let's just say it's not out of the question, and I know how to find that house on the beach if I decide to return when this project is finished.

Ms. Pritchett is not a relaxed air traveler, so even though we arrive early in the morning, she gives us the first day to recover from the long flight. Next to our hotel in Sydney is an Internet café, and most of us find our way there to catch up on e-mails and tell our parents that we're still alive...for the most part.

Olivia has sent me a weather report from back home. At first, I think that's very odd, since I won't be home for several months. However, the title of her e-mail is "Out of Ohio." A clue, perhaps? When Olivia tutored me in high school English, we read *Out of Africa* by the Danish writer Isak Dinesen, and Olivia showed me some letters the author had written home from her coffee farm in the Ngong Hills of Africa. One said that no matter where she was in the world, she would always wonder whether it was raining in Ngong. (And Bernard quipped that no matter where *he* was in the world, he was certain that Meryl Streep could successfully imitate the local accent.) Olivia closes with, *P.S.: Watch out for person-eating sharks.* The Unitarians prefer gender-neutral descriptions, thus their crusade to promote clothing manufactured from hemp rather than "person-made fibers."

I send Olivia a long message about Hawaii and how I almost stayed there, as much to share the experience with someone else as to try and sort it out for myself.

An e-mail from Bernard contains three attachments about skin cancer, with a paragraph in bold about how cloudy days are actually the worst because you get lulled into a false sense of security. Bernard also copies me on his daily journal about the girls' activities, which he refers to as his *Momoir.* Gigi scored very high on a private-school admissions test, and now the idea is that once she's a famous genius, he'll do the talk-show circuit. Bernard informs me that the *Momoir* will not only be a best-selling childrearing guide, but also contain a recipe section at the back for all those wondering how to properly nourish their gifted offspring.

This serves as one more example of why Olivia insists that Bernard suffers from "the spotlight effect," meaning that he thinks people are constantly thinking about him, when in reality, they're not thinking about him at all.

Mom and Pastor Costello went to see Louise's play in New York, which received a mixed review from a downtown newspaper, but contained a nice mention for "the stunning ingénue." Apparently, Louise removes her blouse in one scene. However, Mom assures me that it's in a *doctor's office,* as Louise plays a young woman diagnosed with *breast cancer,* and that she *keeps her bra on the entire time.* (Okay, Mom doesn't *italicize* in print, but I can still *hear* it.) And based on what Louise recently told me about her fast and fabulous new life in New York City, Mom didn't go out with her after the show. Nevertheless, I'm relieved. When Lady Louise told me how much she'd spent on an apartment share and clothes she just *had to have,* I was afraid Mom would find her on a street corner in the theater district wearing a WILL WORK FOR SHOES sandwich board.

There's a short note from Auggie, who was my boyfriend for about five minutes in the crazy months after my father died. I think of him sometimes when I'm lonely, and also whenever I see a Jacuzzi. That night we spent together was so nice. He attaches a story he wrote that recently won a prize. It's called "Lucky 7, Hard 8," and it's about a girl gambler. It's true that I find a substantial number of similarities between me and the main character, who is named Holly, but for the most part his words are very flattering.

I congratulate Auggie on his success and explain how Craig gave me an ultimatum and I skedaddled out of town like the big chicken that I am. If Auggie is writing a story about that relationship, then at least now he has the ending—lucky at cards, unlucky in love.

Cappy is under the impression I've already graduated from college and offers up a few lines of congratulations in his own inimitable style. *Good race. Well done. Enjoy yourself—it's later than you think. Nature always bats last. Yours in Chris (Chris McCarron—youngest jockey ever to achieve both $50 million in career earnings and three thousand wins). Cappy.*

In the afternoon, Mandy, Josh, Banjo, and I climb to the top of Sydney Harbor Bridge, which is called "the coat hanger." We're actually given breathalyzer tests before being allowed to start our ascent. Banjo says it's as spectacular as the Golden Gate Bridge in San Francisco, but never having seen that one, I wouldn't know.

From the top, we have an incredible view of the harbor and can peer down at the equally famous Sydney Opera House, which looks like a ship at full sail. After climbing down, we stroll along the waterfront, basically a gift shop ghetto where thousands of tourists wearing shirts from the Jimmy Buffet collection and fanny packs take photos and stockpile souvenirs.

Even though it's late in the day, the sun is still hot, so we duck into a bar where they serve kangaroo and emu as snacks. I definitely won't be telling Olivia the Animal Rights Activist about this. A funny Aussie song called "Pub with No Beer" is playing on the jukebox, and it's easy to spot the locals because they sport deep tans and look as if they rock-climb to work every day.

Upon hearing our American accents, one exceptionally weather-beaten patron with a body like Popeye hoists his bottle of beer and announces, "I'm glad they sent the convicts to Australia and the Puritans to America." I'm pretty sure this is a slight, but he laughs uproariously, as does the bartender and a few others who look as if they operate carnival games for a living, so we smile and toast to our being insulted. Why not? Based on the man's apparent lack of access to modern dentistry and weakness for serpent tattoos, it would appear that he's referring to his own ancestors.

Dropping the wallets in Sydney takes much longer than it did in Toronto or Maui because the city is spread out, and I have to use ferries and then buses to get from one place to the other. The beaches all seem to be covered in hard-bodied men with surfboards in tow and alluring bikini-clad women with hard-bodied men in tow.

After dinner, it's necessary to study because Ms. Pritchett is giving the first of three tests tomorrow morning. Her last lecture was on how different religious beliefs can influence the honesty of a culture or particular ethnic group. So in three hours, I need to memorize the basic tenets of thirty different religions, when I can't even remember all the rules and regulations for being a good Christian after five years of Sunday School.

About three-quarters of the wallets end up being returned here, which is a lot better than in Maui, where we only got back five out of forty-eight. And that was after writing the phone and address cards in both English and Hawaiian.

Meantime, Toronto still holds the record for the most turned-in wallets. An e-mail arrived yesterday reporting one more was found, so now we're only missing two. My guess is that those were picked up by Canadian raccoons and they'll figure out a way to get them back to us as soon as the weather turns warm.

Chapter 28

As wonderful as it would be to spend my last morning in the Antipodes learning how to surf in those gorgeous sapphire blue, shark-infested waters, or at the very least walking around the Royal Botanic Gardens and visiting Sydney's world famous aquarium, Ms. Pritchett's agenda prevails.

The test begins promptly at 9:00 AM, and the way she marches around the conference room with a number-two pencil tucked behind her ear, gives me flashbacks to taking the SAT in the high school gymnasium. Only this is much harder, because it's all short-answer questions with no multiple-choice or true/false. What makes it even worse is that I didn't get past page fifty of the handout, which is SO incredibly BORING. A trickle of sweat drips down my forehead as I watch Mandy and Josh turn to the second page (of ten!) while I'm still stuck on question number three. However, when Proctor Pritchett announces that our time is up, everyone looks as if they could have used an extra hour. Our pinch-lipped leader rather downplayed the academic rigor of this little project in her initial sales pitch, if you ask me.

After the test is done, there's only time for a quick lunch before heading to the airport. By this point we're all saying "g'day mate" to everyone we meet, as if this makes us sound like something other than buffoonish Americans who've been watching too much

Crocodile Dundee. And I'm getting used to uttering the words: "Nothing to declare."

Our next stop is the Malaysian capital of Kuala Lumpur, which Banjo informs us was founded by tin miners in 1857. The guy is a walking guidebook of bizarre information, and yet the only things I ever see him reading are comic books. Before setting us loose, Ms. Pritchett orders that Amanda and I do not wear shorts, because it will offend the Muslims, and warns us all that homosexuality is punishable by imprisonment or caning. Josh vigorously denies being gay, even though Ms. Pritchett didn't ask about anyone's sexual orientation. I guess if you're a soft-spoken guy with a mop of sandy brown curls and an earring, who also happens to express an interest in the arts, people can get that impression.

"I wasn't implying anything," says Ms. Pritchett. "In some parts of Latin America gays are celebrated as a third gender, and it's considered good fortune to have a homosexual son in the family. Likewise, in Native American cultures, transgendered people were respected and often considered healers."

While we're riding the elevator up to our rooms, Josh asks, "Do you want to go out and explore the city?"

"You mean instead of trying to hook up with our homosexual lovers?"

"They're not mutually exclusive." Josh uses Ms. Pritchett's favorite terminology for making it sound as if we're wrong every time we attempt to answer one of her questions.

I'm reminded that I love Josh's impish, but intellectual, sense of humor. Plus, he now has an amazing tan that makes him ruggedly handsome, like those movie stars who play rogue CIA agents that turn out to be the good guys in the end. So I agree to go sightseeing, but can't help wonder if once again Josh has invited the entire group.

When I arrive in the lobby, he's waiting there by himself, studying a map, and the two of us head out into the sticky, tropical heat.

The streets of Kuala Lumpur are an odd mix of gleaming,

futuristic skyscrapers with austere windows that rise above colonial-era buildings, slender businessmen scurrying about, and locals in tattered clothes operating pushcarts. Factory pollution and car exhaust mix with the steam and sizzle of fried noodles sold by street vendors out of grimy-looking pots. People drive by on mopeds with not only their entire family hanging off, but dead goats and pigs strapped to the back, lending a whole new definition to the words "takeout food."

We come to a crowded marketplace that's an assault on the senses—a fusion of colors, smells, dialects, and drum music. More important, it feels as if Josh and I are on a date, and I can't help but wonder if something might finally happen between the two of us. Fortunately, he doesn't seem to be holding the Ailani dalliance against me.

"Are you hungry?" asks Josh.

"Sure." However, I can only imagine what the doctor who gave me my vaccinations would say about eating in a place like this.

We cut through a narrow back lane of plank-and-stucco houses with laundry hanging overhead and approach one of the hole-in-the-wall restaurants.

"Do you think it's safe?" I ask. "Banjo said they eat dogs here."

"It's fine so long as we don't drink the water," says Josh. "And we'll only eat dog if they have golden retriever on the menu!"

However, it's impossible to tell if dog is on the menu or not since we can't read it and the waiter doesn't speak any English. A Norwegian tourist at the next table suggests that we try the stinky-but-delicious durian fruit and laksa, a spicy coconut noodle soup.

We agree, and the Norwegian guy, whose name turns out to be Gunnar, gives the waiter our order. After a brief exchange in a foreign language, the tourist asks if we want "air kelapa," which is coconut water, or else "tuak," the name for Borneo rice wine.

"Definitely wine," says Josh, and winks at me.

Gunnar explains that he's an agriculture student from Oslo backpacking through Southeast Asia during his vacation. "You should stop at Taman Negara National Park and go on the canopy walk," he says in perfect Minnesota English, "and also go snorkeling off the Perhentian Islands. Crystal-clear water—unbelievable!"

"We're here doing a school project, so we don't have that much time for sightseeing," I explain.

"Whoops!" he says and laughs. "I thought you were on your honeymoon."

Josh and I both laugh at this. And yet at the same time, I can't help but hope it means he thinks we're a good couple.

Gunnar pays his bill and gets up to leave. "At least find time to visit a tea plantation. It's one of Malaysia's most important crops."

The waiter arrives with our food, and everything is delicious. I try to figure out what spices are in the coconut noodle soup so I can tell Bernard about it. Josh and I discuss the radical change in Mandy's appearance and speculate as to whether it's temporary or permanent. Certainly the blue sparkly nail polish that she'd picked up in Sydney would come off easily enough.

"I invited her to come with us, but she was off to get hennaed," says Josh.

"She just added purple streaks!" I say.

"I'm pretty sure that she meant her *body*." Josh bursts out laughing.

"So, what are you majoring in these days?" I ask. "Sorry, but I lost track."

"I know," says Josh. "I've switched a few times. But it's definitely modern, urban architecture now. That's one of the reasons I came on the trip—to see buildings like the Petronas Towers." He points in the general direction of the tapering, twin polygonal office towers connected by a sky bridge that we'd spent a long time looking at from different angles.

I nod my head as if I believe him. But the truth is, Josh has changed his major more like a dozen times. Presumably, Clown College is just around the corner. Suddenly, my eyelids feel very heavy—I don't know if it's the wine or the long flight—but I yawn.

"I'm kind of tired too," says Josh. "Want to go back and take a nap?"

A nap? Does he mean together? And does he mean a nap or a *nap*?

"Sure," I say.

As we enter the lobby, Josh asks, "Want to come back to my room? Banjo won't be there."

"Okay," I say.

Only Banjo is there. And he's freaking out—ripping up the beds and throwing the drawers on the floor. Clothes are strewn everywhere. "I've been robbed!" he shouts. "Three thousand dollars in cash!"

"Did you check all of your pockets?" I ask.

"I hid the money in my backpack and then put it under the bed while I went out!"

Josh and I help him search through the rubble.

"What are you doing with so much money?" asks Josh.

"Ms. Pritchett gave it to me for safekeeping, while she went off to meet some village dukan."

"Dukan?" I ask.

"A witch doctor," says Banjo.

"*A witch doctor?*" Now it's Josh's turn.

"Alice did her master's thesis on tribal healing remedies, and an academic press has suggested that she turn it into a book," Banjo begins to explain, but he's distracted by the missing money and kneels down to check underneath the bed for the fifth time since we've been there.

Josh and I look at each other but don't say it: *Alice?* Ms. Pritchett had made it clear that she'd be known as Ms. Pritchett throughout all of our lifetimes, and I can only assume on St. Peter's roster, as well, when she *tries* to get into heaven.

We call the manager, and he insists that the hotel staff is completely honest and *perhaps* the money was misplaced. Though

I can tell from the look on the man's face that he doesn't believe a bunch of scruffy backpackers in their twenties had that much money to begin with, and we're just trying to run some sort of scam. To completely relieve himself of any liability, he points to the sign on the door that instructs travelers to place all of their valuables in the hotel safe.

Banjo puts his head in his hands. "That was the expense money for the rest of the trip!"

"We'll explain to Ms. Pritchett what happened," says Josh. "It wasn't your fault."

"But it *is*," says the distraught Banjo. "I told her I was staying in the room to add the results from Hawaii and Sydney to the database. And then I left—the guy at the desk told me there was a really good casino not too far from here."

"You didn't use the money to gamble, did you?" I know it's disloyal, but after being around gamblers, you quickly learn that nothing stands between them and a bet. Also, the fact that his ragged beard has been shaped into a satanic goatee doesn't exactly help matters.

"No, I swear!" says Banjo. "But she'll never believe me because, well, last year I had sort of a problem with Internet gambling, and Ms. Pritchett helped me out with a loan...so I'm lending a hand with her dissertation and the book to pay it back." Banjo looks down at his worn Merrell clogs. "I know she comes across as being firm, but Alice is really a very sweet woman. It's just that there's a lot of pressure in academics."

Okay, there's a small chance I believe him about the money, but no dice when it comes to Ms. Pritchett being a very sweet woman.

We search the room from top to bottom and the money definitely isn't anywhere to be found. No one mentions the irony of being robbed while we're here to test the honesty of the local citizenry.

"So how was the casino?" I finally ask. "Did you win?"

Banjo shakes his head, indicating that indeed he did not.

"Hallie can play poker," says Josh. "She's really good."

I'm pleased not so much by the compliment but that Josh recalls the time we played strip poker together. Though in many ways, I try not to remember because it was the night that Dad died.

"I'm better at blackjack," I say.

The guys both look at me with increased interest, and I can tell we're all thinking the same thing.

"That's where you get the best odds in a casino," I add.

They continue to stare and I feel compelled to keep talking. "Blackjack is uniquely beatable because the stream of cards coming out of a dealer's shoe makes the future predictable."

"I have a hundred dollars left," volunteers Banjo. "But to be totally honest, I don't think I could ever consider gambling again— it's brought me nothing but bad karma."

Cappy once told me that 99 percent of the time the words, "to be totally honest," are directly followed by a lie of outrageous proportion.

"I have about eighty bucks," I offer.

"Three hundred," says Josh. "Let's go see if Mandy's back."

This trip is quickly turning into one of those Brady Bunch episodes where they go on vacation and have all manner of cartoonishly crazy adventures. Only *our* Alice isn't nearly as lovable.

Chapter 29

We find Mandy back in the room, looking every bit the Pirate Queen, her arms and hands covered with reddish brown designs that would make excellent camouflage if she were hiding in a mulch pile. Banjo sums up the current situation, carefully leaving out the distinct possibility that he may have gambled away the supposedly missing funds.

I explain that if we all help, I can turn the odds in my favor at the blackjack table. I'm not sure what the Mennonite view on gambling is, but the distinct lack of appliquéd cats on their clothing makes me think that slot machines and the like are probably not high on the list. However, upon hearing the words, "nearby casino," Mandy's eyes light up and she grabs for her purse. "I've never been to a casino!"

Mandy donates $220 to the gambling fund, and I can see she still has a few hundred dollars left, possibly earmarked for her various beauty treatments. I'm rather surprised, because for some reason I didn't imagine a Mennonite girl would have such a large bank roll, and I guess it shows.

"My heifer won first prize at the county fair," Mandy proudly informs us. "It sold for almost two thousand dollars."

I guess I won't be complaining about the high cost of steak from now on.

We hurry to the lobby and catch a taxi. It's almost 8:00 PM.

"I left a note saying that I put the money in the hotel safe and went to Kampung Kuatan to see the fireflies and won't be back until early in the morning," says Banjo. "So we have all night to win back the money."

"Counting cards isn't like using an ATM machine," I try to explain on the way over. "Plus, to make it work, you should really have a much larger stake."

"You can do it, Hallie!" Josh positively beams at me.

Suddenly I know how my brother, Eric, must have felt out on the football field with everybody depending on him to win the game, including his girlfriend, who believes him to be the most amazing and talented guy in the world.

"And the staff is trained to look for card-counters and throw them out," I continue my warnings. "Or worse! They have cameras in the ceiling to watch how everyone gambles. It's not hard to spot a card-counter because they substantially raise their bets when the deck is full of aces and picture cards."

No one is listening to me. They're excited about this new project and I can tell by their smiles that they have full confidence in my abilities to turn $500 into $3,000 like some sort of magician.

The cab driver drops us in front of a building that resembles a Buddhist temple, except with modern curves, reflective glass, and an enormous waterfall out front. On both sides of the flashing pink neon KANDAR PALACE sign are granite Goddesses with four sets of arms and hands apiece, all steepled together as if in prayer. I guess that makes sense, since the old codgers hanging around Cappy's office liked to say that the only difference between people praying in church and praying at the track is that the ones praying at the track really mean it.

A thick layer of cigarette smoke clouds the air, and I search for the blackjack tables. The roulette wheels are in front, and their electronic screens flash enormous sums that can be won simply by playing the correct number. Banjo's eyes are practically reflecting dollar signs, the way cartoon characters do when they imagine coming into a sizable amount of cash.

"Why don't we try here?" he points at the nearest roulette game.

Whether Banjo gambled with the trip money is still unclear, but it's now become obvious why he left the casino empty-handed.

"Because the Law of Independent Trials says that if red comes up thirteen times in a row on the roulette wheel, there is no greater or lesser chance of it coming up in the next spin," I explain the math to him. "So a player has no edge. But in blackjack, the past affects the future. For instance if a ten is dealt—"

Banjo stares at me as if I'm speaking in a foreign language, reminding me of the sign above Cappy's desk: *There are three kinds of people in this world—those who are good at math and those who aren't.* I attempt to come up with a simpler way of making the case against this particular game. "Albert Einstein said the only way to profit at roulette is to steal money from the table when the dealer isn't looking."

Gathering our group together, I nod toward the small black domes spaced out every few feet on the ceiling. "Those are cameras called 'the eye in the sky.' They follow every move we make."

"You mean they watch us pee?" asks Mandy. She automatically smoothes down her short black skirt in case someone is looking up it right this very minute.

"They're not supposed to," I say. "But cheats know that, so the restroom is where they're most likely to wire themselves with electronic gizmos or hand cash off to a partner they don't want the casino to know they're in cahoots with."

Instead of listening to me, Josh and Banjo are transfixed by the hubbub of sexy cocktail waitresses in tight tops, explosive clanging and ringing of slot machines, and the daggers of bright light from a half-dozen disco balls slicing through the smoky haze. Shouts of joy and dismay come from a roped-off area where high rollers play baccarat.

"Who knows how to play blackjack?" I call out over the din.

Banjo is the only one to respond in the affirmative.

"Okay, you and I will pretend to be a couple and sit together at a table. Josh and Mandy will keep a look out for any security guards headed in our direction. If you see one, raise your hand and run it through your hair until we acknowledge the signal and then we all head for the exits. Got it?"

"But I thought you said this 'card-counting' wasn't illegal?" Josh is watching two burly security guards forcibly moving a man through the crowd and toward a door in the far wall marked "Private."

"It's not illegal—I'm keeping track of the cards in my head. When more high cards are left in the deck, the player has an advantage over the house. It's a simple math problem, whereas cheating is deliberately breaking the rules and manipulating the game to your advantage dishonestly, such as by using an electronic device," I say. "But the bottom line is the bottom line, and casinos like losers a lot more than winners."

"I feel like I'm in a James Bond movie," says Josh.

Josh and Mandy head for their lookout station while Banjo and I search for two seats among dozens of crowded blackjack tables. "We'll make chitchat about school as if we're students on vacation," I tell him.

"Can you count cards and talk at the same time?" he asks. "There must be six or eight decks in those shoes."

"I don't actually keep track of every single card," I explain. "I try and match the high cards against the low ones. And if there are a lot of big ones left in the deck, then you bet BIG, whereas if there are a lot of little ones left, you bet LITTLE. So follow my lead on betting, and remember to always split aces and eights."

Finally, we find two seats next to each other and I cash our seven hundred dollars in for chips. The dealer doesn't care that I'm telling Banjo when to stay or take another card, since a lot of players give advice, even to people they don't know. By winning more rounds than we lose, at fifty bucks a pop, we eventually work our way up to being a thousand dollars in the black, and Banjo is becoming increasingly excited that his problem might soon be solved.

Despite our having fairly good hands, the dealer suddenly gets three blackjacks in a row and this wipes out almost everyone at the table. We're forced to start over with only sixty dollars, so I insist on reducing our bets to ten dollars apiece. Three hours later, we're still grinding away and can never seem to get past the thousand-dollar mark. At one point, the count in the deck becomes very favorable for the players, and I have two aces, which I split. Theoretically, this should amount to at least one blackjack. But the first hand busts, and the other only makes nineteen, while the dealer squeaks out a twenty, and the guy to Banjo's left and the woman to my right both get blackjack. This just goes to prove that there must indeed be such a thing as luck—how else do you explain it when the *other* players win?

We're both frustrated, and Banjo announces that I'm not betting enough.

"We don't have enough money to bet more," I explain. "You should never put more than five percent of your total nut at risk unless it's a double down or…" I don't want to say "the count is in your favor," because that will tip off anyone who is listening.

However, Banjo remains firm that we start betting a hundred dollars per hand, despite my warnings. Our stake quickly grows to almost $1,900, but then we start losing when the dealer keeps drawing low cards and not busting. My intestines are tying themselves into square knots and suddenly it's easy to remember why I stopped doing this.

We're down to our last hundred dollars and the count shows a lot of high cards are still in the deck. I tell Banjo to stick on his thirteen because the dealer is showing a five.

"I feel really good about this one." Banjo thumps his index finger on the felt to signal the dealer that he wants another card. It's a queen and with a quick sweep of the dealer's hand, the last hundred-dollar chip disappears into the casino's pocket.

"Bad luck!" says Banjo.

Yes, Lady Luck is always to blame, or in this case, a distinct lack thereof. Tin-foiled again, as Bernard likes to say. "That's that." I pick up our remaining five-dollar chip off the table and hand it to Banjo. "Oh well, they say that it's only when a gambler loses everything that he can be reborn."

"C'mon." He pulls me toward a slot machine advertising that a win earns the player ten thousand dollars. "Maybe we can hit the jackpot."

"A drunken monkey could play the slot machines," I say. "Do you have any idea how bad the odds are? One-armed bandits are how casinos make almost all of their money, hence the word *bandit*."

Josh and Mandy appear from behind a row of slot machines. They could tell by watching our stack of chips at the table that we lost.

"Don't feel bad." Josh puts his arm around me and whispers, as if our current situation is entirely my fault.

As they say in pulp fiction, I felt as if I'd fallen into the gutter and then bounced lower.

Banjo has exchanged the chip for tokens. He asks Mandy to blow on them for good luck and begins plunging them into a machine with a *Desperate Housewives* theme. The first three tries don't pay off, but the last token causes the machine to ring and sputter until ten more tokens come out. "You see!" Banjo shouts dementedly and performs a rockabilly dance. He is truly what I'd call an "odd number."

Banjo, unencumbered by self-doubt, quickly plays the winnings. One token after another disappears down Wisteria Lane. "Cold machine!" He smacks the side of the slot machine in frustration when nothing happens. Nothing aside from the realization that we didn't save any money for a taxi back to the hotel.

Chapter 30

The four of us huddle together on the red carpet in front of the casino evaluating our options for traveling the six miles back to the hotel. There are plenty of shiny, black stretch limousines waiting, but not to carry away the losers.

"Hallie?"

I turn to see a very tan, well-built forty-something guy with graying hair and a neatly trimmed mustache, dressed in a tuxedo.

"Seymour?"

"Imagine meeting you outside the devil's workshop!" says the Aussie guy from Cappy's Texas Hold 'em games back home. "Actually, I can imagine it quite easily after the shellacking you and your pals gave me in poker."

Seymour looks terrific, like a man who has been dealt all the right cards. And who could easily be our source of cab fare. I introduce him to the others. "We're going around the world doing a project for school," I say, without incorporating enough details to make it clear exactly how this has landed us at the front door of a casino.

"Of all the casinos in all the towns in all the world, she walks into mine." Seymour pretends to be Humphrey Bogart in *Casablanca* and flares a lighter beneath his cigar.

"Do you own this place?" It wouldn't surprise me, because

Seymour is very rich. He travels around the world buying small companies to build up and then sell, or else list on a stock exchange.

"No no, I'm merely on the road for the bitch Goddess." He pats the healthy bulge in his jacket pocket to indicate that the deity in question is less formally known as *success*, or even better, just plain *money*. "But I might buy it after another run like the one I've had tonight."

Banjo's eyes light up like the neon casino sign. "You really cleaned up, huh?"

"Not quite another wool boom, but it will pay for a new fence," Seymour jokes in his thick Aussie accent.

"Our luck wasn't so good tonight," I say. Only it's two in the morning and tonight is now tomorrow.

"How about I stake you at some poker? The guys at my table are real stiffs—no sense of humor. You'll liven things up."

Mandy, Josh, and Banjo don't look as confident in my skills as they did before we started playing. If anything, they appear exhausted and ready to go back and face the music. Banjo is sticking to his story that he was robbed—how angry can Ms. Pritchett get?

"Let's talk," I suggest.

We head over to a restaurant across the highway, away from prying eyes.

Seymour even walks like a winner, with his football player's frame and gunslinger's gait.

A waiter brings us some tea and rice cakes.

"You know basic strategy for playing blackjack, right?" I ask Seymour.

"Sure, but it can take hours to win any serious money," he replies. "And it's boring. I like the action of poker."

"But there's a way to make it more interesting." I pull out a pen and begin writing on a napkin. "You're going to count aces while I keep track of the rest of the cards. There are twenty-four aces in a shoe of six decks. When there are twenty left, say something to me that includes the word 'score' in it, since that means twenty. For instance, 'I wonder what the score of the basketball game is.' When there are sixteen aces left, say something using the word 'sweet' for 'sweet sixteen.'" I write the key words next to their respective numbers.

Everyone except Seymour looks at me as if I'm completely nuts.

I continue on down the line. "When there are ten aces left in the shoe the key word will be Hamilton because he's on a sawbuck."

Seymour is now smiling and making suggestions of his own. "I'll use the word 'pool' for eight because that goes with eight ball, and I'll say 'beer' for six because that goes with six-pack."

"'French' will mean there are only four aces left since it's in that Christmas song—four French hens." I finish the list and hand it to him.

"I hate the French," says Seymour.

"You should thank them," I say. "The French designed our playing cards—the kings of spades, hearts, diamonds, and clubs are David, Alexander, Caesar, and Charlemagne, respectively."

Josh is now staring at me as if I've just announced that I was Marie Antoinette in a previous life.

Rising from the table I say, "I need a two-hundred-dollar advance and then for you to meet me at the bar next to the high rollers' blackjack table in thirty minutes."

Seymour peels two bills off his wad and hands them to me. He looks positively giddy to finally be having some fun. "I feel like a man in a trench coat has whispered 'the monkey hunts at midnight' into my ear before disappearing into the fog."

Hurrying over to the fancy hotel across from the casino, I go inside to the dress shop. Thank goodness it's open twenty-four hours, but then anyplace catering to a casino usually is. The cheapest evening gown, and also the ugliest in my opinion, is a floor-length Jolly Rancher red sequin number that's cut almost down to my navel. I pull my hair out of its ponytail holder and apricot waves fall almost to my waist. After adding a pair of spiky gold heels, I feel like I'm ten years old and playing dress-up. But I can't be betting thousands of dollars at the high rollers' table wearing jeans and a Donald Duck T-shirt, which I stuff into a plastic bag.

"You wook wovewy," says the eager saleswoman.

"I look like I robbed a showgirl's dressing room," I reply as I hand over the money.

Josh lets out a low whistle when he sees me walking toward them, trying not to get the heels of my shoes caught in the bottom of the dress. I take Seymour's arm and say, "Ready, darling?"

"Indeed!" He grins. "Though ready for what, I'm not sure."

"To be my spotter," I say.

"Yes, of course."

We move a few thousand dollars back and forth while nothing much happens with the cards. Amanda and Josh are in their previous positions, watching for security guards, and Banjo is holding the plastic bag with my clothes. I lose a round that we really should have won, according to the probability of drawing a high card. The problem with blackjack is that it's only in the long run that the law of averages kicks in—thus the need for a bankroll.

Seymour asks to cash in another five hundred dollars for chips. The dealer calls for a pit boss to okay it. A burly Asian man dressed all in black, with a gold pinky ring the size of Pluto, looks us over and nods. The steely-eyed South African guy to my right loses three thousand dollars on a single hand without flinching. He must have ice in his veins.

The table is suddenly very hot. With one deck left before the shuffle card, the shoe is bursting with color in the form of kings, queens, and jacks. Meantime, Seymour has just told me that he'd love to "see our old friend *Hamilton* again," signaling there are still ten aces to come. I can feel the pulse in my neck thumping, which would be bad in a poker game because people could see my heart racing and deduce that I was probably bluffing. But in blackjack, it doesn't matter; the dealer has to take a card based on the total of his cards, and not what the other players have or what he *feels* like doing. Seymour places his hand on my thigh. I'm not sure if it's intended to calm me down or heat me up. But I hope it's supposed to be part of our act.

Before the next round is dealt, we bet two thousand dollars apiece, up from our normal hundred dollars per hand. To any good pit boss watching over his flock of sheep supposed to be getting fleeced, this is the tip-off that we're counting, a sudden and sizable increase in our bet. Seymour stays with a queen and a ten, while I double down and take a hit on two fives. An ace appears. Blackjack! The dealer busts when a queen is added to his fourteen. Suddenly I see a couple of lumpy guys in suits heading toward our table, and my central nervous system begins to spin on its axis.

"Grab the money and let's go!" I whisper to Seymour, while quickly scooping up thousands of dollars in chips.

"C'mon, let's keep playing," he argues. "We're on fire."

"Exactly." I grab his arm and drag him away from the table to the front door. "The brighter you burn, the hotter it gets."

"But we aren't doing anything illegal," protests Seymour.

We head back to the restaurant, our designated meeting place if anything goes wrong. I pour all the chips into Mandy's purse and tell her to go and cash them.

"Why me?" she asks.

"Because they'll think you're really nice," I say. What I don't tell her is that prostitutes working casinos often receive chips as payment for services rendered, so the cashier will think nothing of her having several thousand dollars' worth in her handbag.

Mandy smiles broadly, thrilled to be part of the action, and heads off on her mission.

Seymour-the-businessman is still arguing that we should go back. "In fact," he says excitedly, "we could do this at casinos all over the world. Why don't you become my partner?"

Josh and Banjo stare at the two of us with awe, as if we're masters of the dark arts.

"Because people protecting their money don't necessarily stick to laws like in the U.S.," I inform everyone. "They don't just threaten and strong-arm card counters in back rooms, but they actually *kill* them." I'd heard stories from Cappy about teams of card counters from M.I.T. getting into so much trouble overseas that they had to quit if they wanted to keep breathing with any sort of regularity.

"We could form a team!" Banjo eagerly chimes in. "Only we wouldn't get caught!"

"Shhh!" I put my finger to my mouth. "If we're not careful getting this money out of here, it's going to be daylight in our livers," I tell them. "In a foreign casino, death by lead poisoning doesn't mean swallowing a pencil."

Mandy returns with the bundles of cash just as the sun is peeking above the mountains, and we count up twelve-and-a-half thousand dollars. Seymour hands me half—my cut, based on our agreement. A monastery bell tolls from a nearby hill.

Sunlight creeps across the floor and Josh says, "Oh no! We have to be at the breakfast meeting in fifteen minutes!"

After saying a quick goodbye to Seymour, we scramble into a taxi. I shove the wad of bills toward Banjo. The cab driver's eyes widen and I realize maybe it wasn't such a good idea to pull the money out right now. But we don't have the fare if it doesn't come from our winnings.

"Wow!" says Banjo. "If I were you, I'd definitely quit school and play blackjack full time."

His enthusiasm reminds me of the first big hit I made at the racetrack, when I was only fourteen—suddenly I was freed from one sort of life, but at the same moment imprisoned in another. So I don't hesitate with my response, since I've spent a lot of time considering this option over the years. "Aside from the risk of having my face rearranged with a tire iron, you don't exactly create anything of lasting value by playing cards for ten hours every day."

"Money has lasting value," says Banjo as he caresses all those hundred-dollar bills. "At least it will last until you die, and after that who cares?"

I don't bother to ask if Banjo has ever sat at a table concentrating hard for so long that his limbs go numb, his brain feels like it's underwater, and his neck has turned into a rod of steel. Or that, based on my experience at Cappy's betting parlor and the racetrack, full-time gamblers care more about playing than anything else in life, sometimes including life. They exist as candle flames—flickering, flaring, falling, fading.

Instead, I yank off the high heels and throw them onto the floor. Honestly, I don't know how anyone can walk in these torture devices.

Banjo lovingly removes three thousand dollars from the stack of bills to replace the trip money, hands everyone back their initial stake, and then passes the balance to me. I briefly consider donating the remainder to charity. Only we did win it fair and square, and having a little spare cash might make the rest of the trip a lot more fun. I give Josh, Mandy, and Banjo five hundred dollars apiece, keep five hundred for myself, and say that we'll give a thousand to the beggars on the streets for good karma, or else leave it at a temple.

When the taxi pulls up in front of the hotel, we all leap out. There's only five minutes until meeting time. I hand the driver a hundred dollars to (*a*) start our good karma program immediately and (*b*) make sure he doesn't take out a gun and help himself to the rest. The way I figure it, a person who is Buddhist and believes in endless reincarnation may not be all that worried about what happens to him in *this* life.

Josh tosses me the plastic bag with my clothes in it. "We'll find Ms. Pritchett and tell her you ate something that made you sick, but you're on the way."

As we barrel through the lobby door, there she is, staring at me as if I'm now working nights as a streetwalker. I speed off in the opposite direction, toward the room. When I show up at breakfast ten minutes later, the others are already gone. Ms. Pritchett places my twelve wallets on top of the map showing where they're to be dropped. Then she hands me my test with a bright red D at the top. Karmic retribution.

"You're on serious probation." Ms. Pritchett stares at me as if I'm the finger in her chili. "One more mishap, Ms. Palmer, and you'll fail this class and go home. And they're not mutually exclusive."

I sigh. You win some; you lose some.

Chapter 31

The first thing Ms. Pritchett does when we reach New Delhi is take Mandy and me aside to inform us that India has one of the highest rates of Chlamydia in the world, and so we probably shouldn't get too friendly with any of the residents. Gosh, she really thinks I'm out hooking during the off hours or that we're both so darn hot, it will be hard to resist so many advances.

"What's Chlamydia?" Mandy asks as soon as she leaves.

"Obviously, you've never been to the school health clinic," I reply. It's a little hard to miss those forty-by-sixty-inch posters with the handsome guy holding hands with the stunning young woman, and then underneath them in big, violent orange letters: You Could Be Looking at Somebody with Chlamydia.

The Taj Mahal is only 125 miles from our base of operations in New Delhi, and Ms. Pritchett says there won't be any seminars while in India so we can "achieve maximize cultural absorption." Once we've finished dropping the wallets, we're free. I think this is really nice of her until Banjo informs us that she's already made plans to fly off to a town called Pune and study communal living. (And it suddenly becomes clear how the STD rate might have skyrocketed.)

"It was started by some dodgy guru who ended up owning

around a hundred Rolls Royces," explains Banjo. He seems rather angry about the situation.

"Did you want to go with her?" I ask. *Who knows, maybe there's a floating crap game in that area.*

Banjo shakes his head as if he's damned if he does and damned if he doesn't. "That woman can be very difficult to please," he answers without really answering. "But now it's time to exit, stage right!"

Ms. Pritchett has organized us into teams, not because New Delhi is dangerous, so much as because Westerners are just constantly hassled for money. Josh is with Mandy-the-Former-Mennonite, and I've been assigned to Banjo-the-Human-Guidebook. Working in pairs gives us twice as many wallets to drop, and with the confusing maze of streets and crowded buses, it takes a full day to get them all in place. Furthermore, I don't expect to see a single one of them ever again. If I were as poor as so many of these people, there's no way I'd return twenty dollars, when it could feed my family for a year.

"Some parents actually maim perfectly healthy children so that they'll earn more money begging," Banjo informs me.

"And how is it that you know so much about everyplace we go?" I finally ask him.

"We lived all over the world when I was growing up," replies Banjo. "My father is a diplomat and my mom is a science teacher, originally from Lebanon."

"Cool," I say.

Banjo sighs as if there's some terrible sadness bottled up inside him. "They're divorced now. My dad lives in Brussels with a vacation house in the south of France, where he'll probably retire, and my mom moved back to be with her family in Beirut. But with all the problems in the Middle East, a lot of *them* have scattered around the world. Sometimes I think it'd be nice to be like Mandy and have all your relatives within a few square miles and a place to call home."

"I'm not sure that Mandy likes it so much," I say. "She's really letting her hair down on this trip. I don't think her family back home would even recognize her right now."

"But she knows it's there and that they're there," says Banjo. "I bet her ancestors are in a little cemetery down the road, and the family pets have all been buried under an oak tree in the backyard. I was never even allowed to have a fish."

As the city deepens into dusk, the hubbub of daily life increases; and the women's brilliant red, orange, and emerald green saris look like giant birds flashing by. One has a neckline and shoulder sash trimmed with strands of gold, and I can't help but imagine Bernard starting to sing, "The Sari with the Fringe on Top."

Everything I'd ever heard or seen in movies about India is true, from cows in the streets and rickshaws, to snake charmers crouched over baskets and computer geeks carrying laptops. The legal limit to the number of people allowed in the numerous overcrowded taxis is apparently "one more."

When we eventually meet up with Josh and Mandy, I'm surprised to find that Josh is the one who is now hard to recognize. He's gone native, dressed in rainbow-colored pajamas with a long top, and pointy-toed shoes in navy silk embroidered with bright, copper thread—the kind the Oompah-Loompas wore in *Charlie and the Chocolate Factory*.

"Are you in charge of the taffy-pulling room?" I joke.

"Why?" he shoots back. "Is your name Violet?"

"Who wants to see the Taj Mahal tomorrow?" asks Banjo.

Of course, we all want to go. Though not at four in the morning, when Banjo books us the taxi—but he explains that we have to view it at dawn and then leave before it gets hot and crowded.

The sun is just peeking over the horizon when we arrive. It makes the white marble dome shimmer and appear to glow with white light.

"Wow!" I whisper to no one in particular.

We all stand there, mouths agape, staring in amazement. A guide informs us that the forty-two-acre complex includes mosques, minarets, and acres of gardens on the banks of the Yamuna River.

Not to be outdone by a lowly tour guide, Banjo chimes in, "The Shah Jahan's wife died giving birth to their fourteenth child, and her heartbroken husband spent the next twenty-two years building her this monumental tomb, before eventually joining her there."

There's a lot to see, but by eleven the site is indeed sun-scorched and crawling with tourists. The hawkers keep trying to sell me postcards and souvenir books, while hundreds of children chase after us asking for money.

"How about a boat ride on the Ganges River?" suggests Banjo. "It's the sacred spring of India."

"Sounds cool to me," says Mandy, who has her long purple and black hair tied up in a knot under a big straw hat.

Josh yawns and wipes sweat off his brow. "Let's do it."

Banjo instructs the taxi driver where to take us, and for a mere two hundred rupees apiece (about four dollars), we get seats on a houseboat and cold glasses of *lassi*, a sweet yogurt drink that's like swallowing pure pleasure. I'm amazed at the wildlife that manages to thrive along the banks of the river despite the pollution. We see hundreds of different-colored birds, a crocodile, two turtles, and even an antelope. Oversized billboards urge villagers to protect the environment by not using soap or detergent when washing themselves and their belongings in the river. Indeed, I do see a number of people bathing, but unfortunately, by the looks of things, I'm guessing they're not trying to be eco-friendly so much as they don't *have* any soap to use.

Suddenly a group of tourists on the opposite side of the boat go berserk and start pointing. After my experience in Hawaii, I wonder if the yogurt pick-me-up was actually Indian joy juice, laced with amphetamines.

We make our way across to where the excited throng is leaning over the rail and see a big fish slip underneath the boat. "It's a river dolphin," a woman with binoculars explains in a clipped British accent.

The boat operator cuts the engines so that everyone can watch and take photos.

Staring at the spot where the creature disappeared, sure enough, a few seconds later, the silver-gray dolphin gracefully leaps alongside the stern.

"River dolphins are blind," explains birdwatcher-woman, "because in the silt-filled waters of the Ganges, their underwater vision is useless. So they navigate and hunt for fish with a highly developed echolocation system."

The dolphin puts on a show for about ten more minutes before disappearing downstream. Some kids on the boat wave at the fishermen standing on the banks and they wave back and smile.

A breeze kicks up, the engine murmurs hypnotically, the boat slowly makes a U-turn, heads back toward the dock, and we all doze a bit.

Josh announces that he has to return to the hotel to meet a family friend who is working in India as a cartographer. It won't surprise me if by dinner he's decided to become a mapmaker. Meantime, the rest of us wholeheartedly agree that it's time for a rest. And definitely some studying…in my case.

We pile into a taxi and head back to the hotel. The city center is reaching its late-afternoon frenzy, and horns are applied liberally. Banjo points to a cow clogging an intersection and announces, "There are fourteen million people in New Delhi and forty thousand cows."

In the meantime, motorists cut each other off, mopeds hop up on the sidewalk when traffic is stalled, and pedestrians dart out with no regard whatsoever for traffic signals. Driving is like playing the final board of a video game, only one that involves avoiding bovines instead of dragons.

Chapter 32

When I awake from my nap, Josh is sitting next to my bed dressed in his Indian party pajamas and reading the Hermann Hesse book that Olivia gave me.

"Why didn't you wake me up?" I ask sleepily. "This handout is like general anesthesia. Doctors could save a fortune having people read it before surgery and during childbirth."

"Listen to this." Josh turns back a few pages in *Journey to the East.* "He who travels far will often see things far removed from what he believed was truth."

"Deep," I say. "Just like my sleep."

"You want to go out?" asks Josh. "I heard about this great carnival that's like the Coney Island of New Delhi."

"I've never been to Coney Island," I say.

"Even better," says Josh.

"Where are Mandy and Banjo?" I glance around the room as if they might jump out of the closet.

"On their pilgrimages," he replies mysteriously.

"Huh?"

"Banjo *said* he was going to some temple or other, but when I was looking around I noticed a big casino only a couple of blocks from here. As for Mandy, who knows—she's probably having rings drilled through her nose."

It was true that when we left Kuala Lumpur, Mandy had two holes in each ear that I swear weren't there when we were in Sydney.

"I pinky-promised my friend Bernard—you remember, the muffin man—that I'd visit the Mughal Gardens and give a full report."

"Pinky-promised?" asks Josh.

"You know: where you extend pinkies and briefly intertwine them," I explain. "According to Bernard, it's stronger than a regular promise, but not as serious as swearing on your mother's life."

Josh nods as if it's the most normal thing in the world to be doing pinky-promises with the man who was sobbing, waving a hanky with the British Union Jack on it, and shouting, *"Au revoir, les enfants!"* as we climbed onto the bus.

The shade is open a few inches and darkness is falling fast. "But I guess that's something for tomorrow."

"Perfect," says Josh. "Let's go. I'm starving."

"You're always starving," I say. "Yesterday, Banjo informed me that cows have four stomachs. Are you a cow?"

"You'll have to ask Mandy," jokes Josh. "She's apparently the cowherd around here. Almost two thousand bucks for a single heifer! Did you hear that? She makes money while she sleeps."

These days Josh often talks about Mandy as if they might be more than friends, which depresses me. "My father grew up on a farm and couldn't get a civil service job fast enough."

Josh doesn't appear convinced. "Maybe I should transfer and change my major to agriculture…"

I groan and head out the door.

"Kidding!" he calls after me.

We catch a rickshaw over to the carnival where the air is filled with the smell of curry and the sound of psychotropic wailing to a dizzying dance beat. At the front of the park are row upon row of food stalls. Josh buys donuts covered with chili that make our eyes water, spicy hot tandoori chicken, and several curried items served on sticks. A vendor pours us paper cups full of fermented palm sap, which turns out to be surprisingly sweet and smooth. We forget to use bug spray and clouds of mosquitoes feast on our uncovered arms while we eat. Visions of Dr. Doom warning me about malaria flash in my mind's eye.

There are a number of rides, but they are truly man-powered, with guys spinning the wheels or running back and forth across teeter-totters. We climb into a cart pulled by two ponies, while just a few feet away men jog in a circle waving rings of fire and blowing sparks out of their mouths. I'd think it was some sort of a trick if I didn't see them taking the hot coals directly from the fire with my very own eyes. Aggressive young boys thread their way through the crowds selling electric yo-yos and skinny mongrel dogs roam everywhere, but neither appear to be dangerous.

Josh places his hand on top of mine. Then he leans over and whispers in my ear, "I'm glad you came on the trip."

"Me too," I say. "Though I'd better pass the next test or else I'm not going to get credit for it. Ms. Pritchett *hates* me! Not to mention she thinks I'm picking up extra cash as a hooker."

"It's safe to say the two of you won't be making out anytime soon," agrees Josh. "But don't worry. Ms. Pritchett is just one of those teachers who likes to make everyone work harder by giving them bad grades at the beginning."

"I'm on probation, whatever that means."

"Technically, it means that if you're late for another session, then she sends you home and you flunk."

"Great," I say.

Josh plays a game where he tosses a hula-hoop over a square and wins a small, stuffed tiger. When he turns to hand the prize to me, a little girl with wide eyes the color of black onyx and outstretched hands magically appears between us, a Bollywood star in the making. We both laugh at her amazing timing and agility, and Josh hands the toy to the child instead. It'd be nice to think that she'll be able to enjoy it, but most likely someone is waiting for her and the stuffed animal will be sold, possibly even back to the vendor.

Josh apparently reads my mind. He nods toward the man running the game and says, "She's probably the guy's daughter."

Suddenly my stomach is leaping around and I wonder if drinking the fermented palm sap as a chaser for the curry was such a good idea.

"I don't feel so good," I say. Uh-oh. I want to look for a trash bin, but before I can even turn, I've vomited all over the front of Josh's beautiful party pajamas.

After wiping his new shirt with his hands, and then rubbing them clean on his new pants, Josh says, "I think we'd better get you back to the room."

Josh leads me out of the park and to a taxi. Back at the hotel, he takes me up to my room, where I proceed to be very sick in the bathroom. The minute I come out and flop down on the bed, Josh goes in and throws up. Though whether it's from eating the same food or else having me puke all over him, I can't be sure. I'm hot and sweaty and feel another wave of nausea heading in my direction.

I vaguely remember Mandy coming in with some local man who checks my pulse, feels my forehead, and pronounces the words "Delhi Belly" in a knowing but singsong voice. The next twenty-four hours are a nightmare of crawling from the bed to the bathroom. Mandy and Banjo take turns watching us, and she must eventually go and sleep in Banjo's or Ms. Pritchett's room, as mine has become the infirmary.

At one point, I truly just want to die. I'm lying on the bathroom floor, my entire body burning up while my hair is wringing wet with sweat and hopelessly tangled. There aren't any of the good things about being sick—dry toast, ginger ale, and Bernard's Sister Wendy DVD collection. Why did I ever come on this stupid trip in the first place? It's ended up costing me the best thing in my life. The more I try to forget Craig, the more I remember him and how good we were together. Suddenly I burst into tears.

Josh enters the room, apparently recovered, and puts his hand on my shaking shoulders. "You'll be okay," he says.

I'm a little embarrassed to be sobbing over the toilet bowl, especially in front of the guy I thought was serious new-boyfriend potential before I got sick all over him, and so I say, "It's just my hair—it's disgusting. It looks like something you buy during intermission at a circus! I want to cut it all off."

"But you have such pretty hair." Josh places his hand on top of my head, a strategic move since the gnarly parts are more toward the bottom.

"I hate it!" And it's true. I'm tired of sweltering in the heat, and then when it's cold, needing an hour to dry my hair before putting it in a ponytail if I don't want mold to start growing on my scalp. And with the humidity in this part of the world, I could probably pass for a Goldendoodle.

"I can cut it for you, if you really want," offers Josh. "My grandfather was a barber."

I nod in agreement. Josh goes off presumably to find scissors. When he returns, I sit atop the toilet and close my eyes while the blades go snip-snip around my ears, and thick clumps of strawberry-blond hair cascade to the floor. Hugely relieved to be rid of the mess, I climb back into bed and fall into a deep slumber. The dizzying sound of an unidentifiable stringed instrument drifts up from the street. Or else I'm in heaven and the angels are playing on broken harp strings.

Chapter 33

It's the middle of winter and outside my window is the pin-drop hush of a snowy morning. Mom's reassuring voice echoes in the stairwell, "Go back to sleep everyone—it's a snow day!" Miracle of miracles—a snow day! My eyelids flip open. However, Ms. Pritchett is sitting on a chair at the end of my bed.

"Hello, Hallie," she says. "How are you feeling today?"

This is it. I'm fired. "Mostly better, thanks. A little tired."

"That's good!" says Ms. Pritchett. "I applaud your diving in and sampling the local cuisine."

I take it to mean she's referring to the curry of mass destruction.

"I'm just sorry that it made you ill." Gone is her usual haughty disdain.

Wow. This is the first nice thing the woman has said to me the entire trip. But I don't entirely trust Pleasance Pritchett. The woman is a totem pole of disguises, carefully selecting the mask that will achieve her goal; one minute, charming desk clerks for upgrades, and the next, berating bellboys for not delivering her luggage first.

These waters need further testing. "We saw a blind river dolphin and the Taj Mahal," I remark. "Not many people back in my hometown can say that."

"How *interesting*," declares Ms. Pritchett. "Now then, I've changed our schedule to give you an extra night to recover. Do you think you'll feel well enough to go to Egypt tomorrow morning? Otherwise, we'll get too far off the schedule, in which case you should just probably stay here until you're well, and then fly directly home."

What? She's going to abandon me among the snake charmers, fire breathers, and stilt walkers of darkest New Delhi! I promptly sit up in bed. "I'm fine, all ready to go!" Only it's at this moment I realize I'm not fine, but legally bald. For some reason, I thought that Josh chopping off all my hair was only a dream.

Ms. Pritchett notices my alarm. "I see that you've had a haircut. My, doesn't that style look so much easier to care for?"

This coming from a woman with a Jiffy Pop perm! She's definitely reverted back to her *supercilious* self. Olivia taught me that word when we were reading Henry James, and I wasn't sure I'd ever see the definition come to life so perfectly.

"Why don't you rest up, and we'll meet you in the lobby at 6:00 AM sharp to catch the shuttle bus to the airport." Ms. Pritchett rises from the chair.

"Sure," I say. The minute she leaves, I race into the bathroom and examine my cranium. Scalped! What was almost waist-length hair is now three inches at the *longest* point, and barely an inch around the top. With this apricot fringe surrounding my washed-out complexion, the mirror holds the reflection of a drug addict. Or else an exploded possum. I check the garbage cans, thinking that if my mane is still in there I might be able to somehow glue it back on. Only it's gone. I flop back down onto the bed and cry.

Mandy arrives and tries to comfort me. But seeing her sheet of long black and purple hair only makes me more tearful. "No guy is ever going to look at me again! What was I thinking?"

"Nonsense! It may be short, but it's a nice cut," insists Mandy, becoming a Women's Travel Olympics semifinalist in the cutthroat category of cockeyed optimism. She hauls out an enormous bag of cosmetics. A wrist full of copper bracelets with dozens of tiny bells dangling from them jingle jangle with every move. "You just need a little makeup is all."

Mandy applies a raccoon's share of mascara, bronzy-colored blush, and mocha lipstick. Then she roots around in her suitcase and takes out a pair of dangly earrings with copper-colored stones dripping from gold-link waterfalls. They resemble something that June Hennipen at Bernard's shop would wear—the same June whom Bernard likes to say never really made it back from Lilith Fair.

However, when Mandy holds up the mirror, I have to agree that I look less heroin-chic and more pottery-class-for-beginners. It's definitely different, but a lot better than the drowned rodent I felt like fifteen minutes ago.

I dry my tears and flush the tissue wad in my hands down the toilet, which immediately starts to back up. Oh gosh, where is Pastor Costello when you need him? The lavs at church were constantly overflowing and he was always running to the rescue while cheerfully calling out, "You get the animals, while I get the ark!" I'd often heard people say that he was a man with Christ in his heart and a plunger in his hand. Whenever it was suggested that someone else should take care of that sort of work, Pastor Costello insisted that it was all part of God's plan for him.

Mandy grabs the towels from the bathtub and tosses them onto the floor, but as the toilet water reaches the top of the bowl, the moon must change phases because the tide begins to recede. Meantime, if God has a plan for *me*, aside from not eating any more coconut fish curry at carnivals, it would really help to know about it as soon as possible.

By the time we board the plane for Cairo, I'm feeling better, but also bound and determined to find the only foreign restaurant I'm interesting in eating at, which would be a Scottish joint called McDonald's. People around us begin to pray when the plane takes off and the flight attendant says *"en shallah"* as an all-purpose disclaimer after almost every sentence, which Banjo informs us means, "God willing." Since Pastor Costello does the same thing back home, I guess Ms. Pritchett would consider this as an example of a "cross-cultural behavior pattern."

"Have you ever been in rehab?" Mandy inquires as the beverage cart arrives.

"No!" I realize that I've been doing a bit more drinking than usual on this trip, but honestly.

However, Mandy sighs like a furnace and only looks disappointed. Nothing about my personal life ever seems to please her.

"Why, have *you?*" Though I don't know what it would be for. Is there a rehab center for using too much robin's egg blue eyeliner?

"Hardly," says Mandy, as if this is something to be ashamed of. "I just think it'd be so cool to start sentences with, 'When I was in rehab…'"

In the hotel lobby, Ms. Pritchett gathers us together for one of her pre-activity briefings. "Once again, you girls can't wear shorts, culottes, or even capri pants. Furthermore, Cairo is known as the City of a Thousand Minarets. Be sure to take off your shoes before entering any mosques."

Ms. Pritchett informs us that in place of our usual lecture, a van will be taking us to see the pyramids the day after tomorrow. It doesn't sound optional, but then who wouldn't want to see the pyramids?

To distribute my wallets, I traverse smog-blanketed streets filled with donkey carts, beat-up taxis, way too many honking horns, stalls selling tacky King Tut souvenirs, and finally, become lost in a spice market that seems to specialize in fertility treatments and aphrodisiacs rather than salt and pepper. Around the corner from the Museum of Islamic Art, a goose vendor peddles poultry— dead or alive. Olivia definitely wouldn't like that. In more than one neighborhood it's impossible to tell whether the apartment blocks are in the process of being constructed or demolished.

Street vendors smile brightly and say, "*Salaam alaikum.*" I thought they were hawking salami until Banjo explained it's the traditional greeting which means "peace be upon you," and told me how to respond. Only, I won't be trying that again after the first guy I said it to pointed me in the direction of a shoe repair shop.

Finally, I stumble into a workshop that creates wedding tents and has an Internet café upstairs. Several women who don't appear older than fifteen are examining fabrics with great seriousness. Clearly, I won't require the services of that business anytime soon, if ever. In the front section of the café, men play dominos and backgammon while they smoke water pipes, sip tea, and argue. Behind a beaded curtain, I find men looking mostly at pornography on computer screens. I'm the only woman in the place, but no one says that I shouldn't be there or even looks at me funny.

There are lots of e-mails from friends and my siblings, and even Mom and Pastor Costello send a newsy note about what's going on back home. It mostly contains activity lists for all the kids and a description of how a heavy snow caved in part of the church roof, but nonetheless it gives me pangs of homesickness. Bernard writes that he's been throwing a sheet over his head and running around the gardens late at night in an attempt to scare the bevy of noisy young neighbors into moving. He stole the idea from an old movie called *The Ghost and Mrs. Muir*. Olivia, the family firebrand, is in Washington D.C. protesting to protect her right to protest— apparently the government has been cordoning off agitators in pens rather than allowing them to freely assemble. Bernard says that on the bright side, Olivia doesn't have to worry about anyone stealing her car down at the local train station because of all the outrageous lefty bumper stickers that are attached with gorilla glue.

Bernard wants to know if I've seen any musicals in the West End of London and proceeds to explain that when Noel Coward's play *Blithe Spirit* ran during World War II, audiences were told that in the event of an air raid the show would go on. Before signing off he warns me, "Don't eat asparagus after Ascot." I have to keep reminding him that England isn't on the itinerary.

Auggie writes that he's moving to San Francisco next month. He's getting an apartment with some friends and asks if I want to join them. Everyone knows that Silicon Valley is a terrific place for an aspiring graphic designer. Wouldn't that be something, to leave flat old Ohio for the glorious hills, salt air, and clanging trolley cars of San Francisco? Auggie's friends are probably artists and writers, and I'll bet they're renting a loft near a cool coffee shop, and it'll be like one of those TV shows where a bunch of hip, young people hang out together sporting great clothes and hairstyles, even though you never see them actually earn any money.

Olivia has forwarded me a couple of petitions to sign and pass on, as usual. She closes with a quote by some guy named Martin Buber: "All journeys have secret destinations of which the traveler is unaware." Only she doesn't say who exactly this Buber is and so I assume he's the guy from her church who goes hiking, excuse me, *trekking* in Bhutan every summer.

Finally, my brother Teddy writes that he's attempting to sneak into the year-end photo of every club at school, though he isn't a member of even one. This exercise is intended as part of developing a theory he has on the philosophy of belonging. Sure, whatever.

Nothing from Craig. I decide to send him an e-mail—just a chatty, "Hey, how ya doin'?" After all, he'd only said that he wanted to see other people, not that he never wanted to talk to me again. It takes me almost an hour and a hundred drafts before I have a five-line note. Finally, I force myself to hit the SEND button before I can change it again. The signing off part had been the hardest. "Love, Hallie" doesn't work anymore. "From" just makes it obvious that I didn't write "love." Eventually I gave up on a closing. Based on the address, he'll know that it's from me.

At five o'clock the next morning, we all pile into a hired van operated by a shifty-looking driver with a random collection of teeth all racing toward the exits, and a long uneven scar traversing the left side of his face from brow to jaw. I don't know what it is about seeing archeological wonders at the butt crack of dawn, but it does appear to be the custom in the East. It's like farmers back home milking their cows early in the morning. I mean, what do the cows care if it's before breakfast or after dinner? For me to be a successful farmer the hours would definitely have to be changed.

167

Although Mandy is wearing slacks and not shorts, the tight midi top barely covers her underwire. Ms. Pritchett's dark eyes remain in dead-shark mode, but I can tell the words "white slavery" are flashing across the overhead projector of her mind. Even I have to admit that Mandy is now merely one navel gemstone away from joining a harem, voluntarily or otherwise.

Josh and I appear to have fallen into a state of permanent friendship. I guess our first real date having ended with me yakking curry all over him was the opposite of romantic. We're sitting next to each other on the way to the pyramids when Josh leans over and whispers, "Pay attention—it's all going to be on the test."

On the bright side, Ms. Pritchett has organized a terrific tour. "No one has solved the mystery of how the pyramids were built." Our driver and guide, Ephraim, says this is not entirely true and we all love hearing Ms. Pritchett being corrected. Ephraim explains what archeologists have recently determined about the building of the pyramids and, despite his bar brawl looks, he's quite knowledgeable on the subject. "A French architect believes they used an internal ramp and counterweight system. Not a single stone was wasted!"

Josh is so entranced by the information on early excavation methods that I'm pretty sure he's on the brink of changing his major again, for real.

There's hardly any traffic outside the city at this hour, but Ephraim takes corners like a homicidal maniac on roads that are unpaved, washboarded, and full of potholes. We're lucky if two wheels are on the ground at any given time. He said he's been a guide for eight years, and if you ask me, it's a miracle he's still alive, especially after the Hail Mary pass along the edge of a cliff with no guardrail. I guess that explains all the religious symbols painted on the outside of his van. Ottavio, on the other hand, would love driving in Egypt. All speeding, all the time.

You'd think Ms. Pritchett would say something to Ephraim before we're all lying in the Cairo morgue waiting for our dental records to arrive from the States. But no, she fancies herself one of those naturalists, tramping around Africa watching lions kill cute little baby giraffes, academically bound not to interfere with the natural order of things. According to Ms. Pritchett, we're here to "study the native ways and not impose our manners, customs, and attitudes"—the whole *only take pictures, only leave footprints* deal. So what if we become part of her statistics? Heck, maybe it will mean a bigger book deal for her thesis if a couple of us become road kill along the way.

In the parking lot a vendor sells fresh strawberry juice that's cheap and delicious. Meantime, Ephraim spreads out a chart of all the ruling dynasties against the back of the van and explains who is entombed where, along with all the different burial rites, funeral masks, mummification techniques, and what have you. Ms. Pritchett, Josh, and Banjo stand glued to the visual aids while Mandy and I guess at how you say "too much information" in Arabic. Ephraim has turned out to be incredibly friendly, and he's also cloud-shaped, huge, and looming; so by staying slightly off to his left, we're able to carve out a nice wedge of shade in which to stand. I'm tempted to ask if anything is going on with her and Josh, but I'm not sure we've reached that level of girlfriendhood. And what if Mandy asks why I want to know?

Next, we stop at what is supposedly the oldest monastery in the world and Ephraim says that if we hike to the top we can see a hermit living in a cave. I'll probably be a hermit by default within another year, so really, what's the point? The boys and Ms. Pritchett eagerly trek up the dusty red hill while Ephraim perches at the bottom smoking and, every few minutes, calling out directions and pointing.

Mandy and I sit on a heap of rocks, whereupon she undoes her bag, removes some tobacco and Egyptian rolling papers that say CK DRAGONIS on them, and proceeds to turn out a perfect cigarette practically one-handed, like a cowboy. Holy smokes, I'm impressed! If I had to say which student on this academic endeavor is "learning" the most, it would definitely be Mandy.

She offers me a cigarette, but I decline. Pink skin and apricot hair with yellow teeth isn't a good combo, even under the best of circumstances.

We end up talking about gardening, of all things—particularly in the middle of the desert. Her parents have a huge vegetable garden back home, and the only way they'll let her plant flowers is if she sells them at the farmer's market, which she does every summer.

"Our garden is mostly flowers," I say. "Though we have some herbs and occasionally grow tomatoes for the deer to graze on. Bernard suggested that as a substitute for my going on this trip, we could just plant exotic flowers like proteas and pink ginger, and... what was the other one...he had a whole list of stuff that began with the letter P."

"This Bernard guy sounds like quite a character." Mandy says this wistfully, as if she wishes her family members might bust a move once in a while.

"Somehow, he manages to make each day feel like a festival. And Bernard has a story to go with everything. While pitching the exotic garden scheme to try and make me stay home, he told me how a great banker named Lionel de Rothschild once said that the real art of gardening is to make a plant that has come from a distant land not only look at home but feel at home." My voice rises with enthusiasm and I realize how good it feels to think about home, at least parts of it. "I'm not saying that Bernard just makes things up out of thin air, but I'm pretty sure he edits so the anecdotes always support his point of view."

It's peculiar how the sun-baked horizon, if you stare at it long enough, appears to turn inward upon itself. Talk of my old life brings thoughts of Craig to mind. Nothing special, just the mundane moments that become links in the chain that make up a life—*this desert wouldn't be a good place for a pond-building business...those long winter nights we spent playing "Clue" and drinking hot chocolate in the Stocktons' living room, until the house was quiet except for the chiming of clocks and sputter of a fading fire...his passionate embrace...*

"Hallie—are you okay?"

Mandy's voice sounds far away. The sun is too bright to look at anymore.

"Yeah, I was just wondering..."

"I thought you were seeing one of those mirages people are always talking about. You know, an oasis in the desert."

"It's really hard to find a guy our age who likes board games," I tell her.

Mandy gives me a peculiar look. "If you say so."

The others arrive back and Ephraim zooms us over to the massive Bent Pyramid of Sneferu at Dahshur as if there's a solid gold cup waiting, or else he has to pee real bad. I don't know what the rush was for, since we end up having it all to ourselves.

"The pyramids at Giza claim all the attention, but Egypt boasts dozens of pyramids," he explains.

Ms. Pritchett has been taking furious notes throughout and, on the drive back, I'm suddenly worried that everything we heard really is going to be on the next test, which is tomorrow morning. When we arrive back at the hotel, Ms. Pritchett and Banjo head off together to see, I assume, if any of the wallets have been turned in. Mandy, Josh, and I take off across the street to Burger King. It's not that the falafel stands don't look and smell appealing, but I'm not quite ready for another stab at local cuisine, despite Ms. Pritchett's honorable mention for being culturally adventurous.

Once we've finished eating, the others tell me to go back to the room and get some rest. I suppose they're right. I do feel tired. And it wouldn't hurt to study. Josh says that he and Mandy won't be long, they're just going to explore the Citadel, which essentially serves as a museum of Islamic architecture. Only, from the way Mandy giggles, I get the feeling that's not all they're going to explore. Note to self: Try not to barf on the next guy you'd like to be your new boyfriend.

Chapter 34

*E*arly the next morning there's no sign of Mandy and her bed hasn't been slept in. However, she shows up in the breakfast area just as Ms. Pritchett is passing out the test papers and gives me a big smile. "All cured?"

"Yes, thanks," I say. Though I might have slept better had I not been waiting half the night for her to come back and kicking myself for not going with them.

A big part of the test is to list reasons why we've received about half the wallets back in Cairo, while only two out of eighty were returned in New Delhi. Obviously poverty is one reason, but there's a lot of that here in Egypt as well—beggars on the streets, and women with babies lying next to them selling fruit and trinkets by the side of the road.

As we head to the airport, I ask Banjo the reason for our increased success, and he tells me the Arabs believe that money found in such a manner will bring them bad luck. "Didn't you hear the guide talking about it?"

We travel to Istanbul for five days, and then it's off to Romania. Ms. Pritchett and Banjo seem to be having some sort of procedural tiff, so for whatever reason, Banjo has taken it upon himself to teach me the names of stars and constellations. Mandy and Josh are exhausted by his endless displays of knowledge, therefore as the traveler most likely to die alone, this is apparently my Northern Cross (also known as Cygnus) to bear. The way I figure it, if I don't get credit for the trip, I'll be able to pass an astronomy class.

Mandy switches places with Banjo so she can sit next to Josh on the plane, and I'm in a bad mood by the time we reach the capital city of Bucharest. Apparently, so is the guy driving us from the airport to the hotel. He experiences road rage and curses up a storm while trying to overtake a horse-drawn cart on a winding, mountain switchback. Josh is goofing around pretending to be Dracula since Transylvania is in Romania, and threatening to bite Mandy's neck.

"I vant to suck your blood!" He lunges at her throat from behind.

"Don't!" She giggles in that girlish way that so clearly means, "Please do!"

No sooner have we checked in than Mandy and Josh are off to some medieval town with a castle. At least they invite me to go with them this time. However, I say no, that I need to send some e-mails. The truth is that I've been thinking more and more about Auggie's proposal to move to San Francisco and want to research the job market out there.

"Think before you ink!" I call after Mandy. Surely she's planning to hit a tattoo parlor and come back with a tramp stamp on her butt. I mean, what's left, short of plastic surgery?

On the way to an Internet café, I pass a little shop that specializes in telling fortunes. I'm sure it's just a tourist trap. A woman sitting in a cane chair out front asks in fairly good English, "It's worth five dollars to find your future?"

I still have most of my share of the casino money left. And the skinny kids playing in the yard certainly look like they could use a good meal. I agree, and she leads me inside while yelling something to an unknown entity. It's a shabby little room with a cast iron stove at one end and a dilapidated mattress on the floor at the other. An old lady wearing a bright, flowered babushka peers out from behind a curtain and then shuffles over in black velvet slippers with the toes cut out. She's the first woman I've ever seen with sideburns.

We sit down at a rickety table covered with a worn, plastic tablecloth, the red and white checkered kind you see in Italian restaurants. There's no crystal ball, tarot cards, zodiac charts, or anything else. She just lights a few candle stubs and runs her gnarled fingers over the ridges of my palm. The old lady doesn't speak English like the younger woman, who I assume is her daughter, and makes a few grunting noises to get the party started. In the dusky light it's possible to make out a stuffed Garfield with suction cup feet stuck to the tiny window in the corner. The old lady begins to mutter, but I can't understand any of it. She turns my hand over, studies the top for a moment, and then scrutinizes the other one, front and back.

When the old woman rises from the table, I haven't deciphered one thing that's been said. However, she shouts for the younger woman, who it turns out is not only the sales and marketing agent, but also the translator and fee collector. The daughter informs me: "You use brain and hands in the work, you will fight a great battle—maybe sickness or child having, there's a special man you keep sending away, and you will make four children." She smiles as if four children is the biggest blessing in the world, takes my money, and then hurries off to hustle up the next customer.

Only this brings up more questions than it answers. I follow her out the door asking, "Do you mean that I currently work with my brains and my hands or that I *should* work with them? And most important, *what man?*"

The woman shrugs and turns her attention to a guy in a suit carrying a weather-beaten attaché case.

I continue pondering what she's told me. The man they're referring to must be Craig. Or maybe Auggie? What about Josh? Though I didn't really push him away—he more or less ran on his own accord. Understandably so.

The man disappears inside, and I ask the woman, "Is the guy I sent away the one I'm supposedly having the four children with?"

"Five more dollars," she says.

It's at this moment I realize that I've turned nuttier than a Tim Hortons maple log, pleading with the daughter of a fortune-teller on the streets of Bucharest for the answers to all of my problems.

Chapter 35

The heading on Bernard's e-mail reads DEATH BY ART in bold letters.

The text is in telegram style. REMINDER. STOP. DO NOT DRIVE IN FRANCE! STOP. RENOWNED ART DEALER AMBROISE VOLLARD WAS KILLED IN A CAR CRASH WHEN STRUCK IN HEAD BY SMALL BRONZE SCULPTURE BY MAILLOL HE KEPT IN CAR. STOP.

Okay, he needs serious medication, or else he's bored out of his mind without me there to torture. Certainly, no one else in the family will stand around and listen to him recount the history of Beef Stroganoff or Chicken Marengo or whatever other dish he happens to be preparing that day. I've now told Bernard a dozen times that we're *NOT* going to France. He's getting to be like Charles Ryder's father in *Brideshead Revisited*, who keeps insisting that their dinner guest is from America when it's perfectly clear that he's not, and the old man is merely amusing himself at everyone else's expense.

The Internet quickly leads me to believe that there's a brilliant future out in the San Francisco Bay area for a self-starting young person with a degree in graphic design and gumption to spare (and willing to work cheap). Some of the companies don't even occupy ugly office buildings, but these way-cool "campuses" that have air hockey and even daycare for pets!

It feels like only an hour has passed when the friendly proprietor taps me on the shoulder to indicate that he's closing up shop. The wall clock says that midnight is fast approaching and since "assembly time" is 7:30 AM, I make a beeline back to the hotel. However, that night when I drift off to sleep, instead of thinking about how stupid I was not to stay home and take that job in Cincinnati, the words GO WEST, YOUNG WOMAN flash across my mind like a billboard in Times Square.

Just one wallet is returned in Romania while we're there, only we never actually get it back, because the guy who brought it to the hotel demanded a hundred-dollar reward and the original twenty was already gone. Sociologically speaking, Bucharest appears to be a finders-keepers culture.

Warsaw is our next stop, and after two days of tramping around in a horrendous snowstorm, we're more than ready to move on. If any of the wallets are returned, I imagine it will be after the spring thaw, which from the looks of things, arrives in late July.

That Ms. Pritchett has multiple personalities now goes without saying. She'll give us all Ds on a test and then offer to take us to see the opera *Turandot* at the famous Mariinsky Theater in St. Petersburg. At this point, it's just a question of how many people are in there and how nasty is the one grading us on this project going to be. Meantime, Ms. Pritchett hasn't said a word about me being off probation, even though I haven't been late for any more wallet drops or morning powwows.

Russia is cold, but the sun shines brightly from a storybook blue sky, casting a perfect silhouette for architecture that surprises at every turn, with extravagant glories tucked in among the drab legacies of the Soviet era. Incredible pastel palaces stand alongside ugly, gray cinderblock buildings. Turn a corner, and you see a candy-striped cathedral, gilded domes shining in the winter light, and a bridge across a canal lined with apartment houses the color of Easter eggs. Walk in another direction, and there's a tumbling-down, concrete slab warehouse. Some of the subway stops are so beautiful they could pass for museums. Banjo the Human

177

Guidebook informs us that Winston Churchill described this country as a "riddle wrapped in a mystery inside an enigma." I'm now convinced that Banjo came out of the womb with his hand raised. He knows everything except how to gamble properly. Why is it we always seem to be drawn to that one thing that *doesn't* come easily? Or that one person?

Maybe it's staring at a statue of the great poet, Alexander Pushkin, that's causing my heightened state of brooding about the past and what could have been. Or perhaps it's what Auggie once said after living in Russia for a year, that something about the country makes a person want to search his soul, whereas the go-go forward-looking out-with-the-old-in-with-the-new U.S. of A. doesn't encourage such introspection. Tomorrow is always supposed to be a better day. Well, what if it's not?

On the way to the theater we stroll past the magnificent green and white Baroque-style Winter Palace that now serves as the Hermitage Museum. This is on Bernard's short list of galleries for me to visit, because there isn't an overload of abstract art, which he likes to call "the sanctuary of the talent-challenged." Bernard is typically against any canvas or sculpture where the tour guide begins, "It's supposed to be..." Leaning down to whisper in my ear, Bernard unfailingly asks, "Then why isn't it?" No, Bernard much prefers Renoir, who believed that art was for pleasure, and therefore rarely painted anything disagreeable.

Meantime, I can't wait to tell Auggie that I saw so many of the places he's talked about. Banjo informs us that Peter the Great built the Winter Palace for his daughter, the Empress Elizabeth, but she died before it was finished.

Wandering around the globe the past two months has certainly made one thing clear, it's highly doubtful that anyone is ever going to build a monument for me—certainly not a three-story palace, and most likely not even a ranch house with a two-car garage.

Chapter 36

The narrow streets of Amsterdam are crowded with backpackers, strollers, bicyclists, and people hawking everything from canal rides to adult entertainment. After an hour of wandering around, it's easy to see how a tourist could spend a grand or so window-shopping, what with the red-light district being perfectly legal and directly adjacent to licensed cafes selling 101 types of cannabis. It seems that here you can get anything you might want for a few hundred dollars. Or at least, anything you *think* you might want.

The city center is definitely the world's largest outdoor museum. And not just because of all the tourists, slackers, sex workers, skateboarders, street musicians, potheads, headbangers, dreadlock dudes, and hippies past their sell-by date, but as a result of government regulations that ensure businesses and homeowners preserve the architecture the way it was hundreds of years ago. There are lots of tall, narrow houses in pretty colors and, if you want to move in your piano or waterbed, it has to be hauled up the front of the building on the outside. Being a mover in this city must require an engineering degree or at the very least a firm knowledge of applied physics.

I don't know what chance we have of getting the wallets back here. Despite the Netherlands having a general reputation for honesty and square dealings, when I go to rent a bike, the woman hands me not one, but two locks, and warns me to be very careful that it doesn't get stolen. She claims that a million bikes go missing every year in the city of Amsterdam, and yet there are only 500,000 to start with, so that means every bike is stolen twice.

The locals all speak English, along with Dutch, and at least three other languages, which is a good thing, because the Dutch language was created by dumping a box of Scrabble letters onto a table and then putting a blindfold on and combining them into words. The airline we flew here on is called KLM, simple enough, but no, it stands for Koninklijke Luchtvaart Maatschappij, which translates as Royal Dutch Airlines. Still, the fact that the locals speak English doesn't help much, since they appear to have a penchant for messing with dumb tourists. For instance, I ask this normal-looking guy (aside from the man-purse, but they're rather common here) dressed in a charcoal-colored, pinstripe suit how to find a street called Jacob Catskade, and he says, "Go to the end of the canal." As it happens, the canals are all connected—all 170 of them!

Surprisingly, only two wallets aren't returned. The hotel manager tells us that theft is regarded as undignified, and the people who steal bikes are mostly organized rings of thieves.

Banjo the Human Guidebook adds, "The Dutch are reputed to be the tallest people in the world; there are more canals in Amsterdam than in Venice; and Dutch ovens were actually invented in Pennsylvania." Okay, now he's just showing off.

The hotel provides e-mail inside the rooms. Auggie has sent me the lyrics to that old song "San Francisco" which begins, *If you're going to San Francisco, Be sure to wear some flowers in your hair.* He goes on to say that I inspire him to write, and the idea of being someone's muse is not only flattering but downright romantic. I write back that Number 1, I have no more hair, and Number 2, I'm still exploring the job market out there, because I don't feel comfortable just showing up without so much as an interview. I finish off with, "Amsterdam = bikes, dikes, clogs, tulips, windmills, Heineken, and now it's time to Van Gogh."

By the time we depart for Ireland, everyone is looking a bit thin-lipped and weary. Josh and Banjo have five o'clock shadows that you could shine the floor with. Mandy hasn't added a piercing, body stenciling, or even a new hairstyle since the body perm in Cairo. Whether it was the Amsterdam nightlife that wiped everyone out, or just plain *road rash* after twelve weeks of hotels and about 30,000 air miles, is hard to tell. Late last night, we could be found in the hotel bar downing Heinekens mixed with Dutch gin, a local favorite known as *kopstoot*, which we were told translates to "a knock on the head." Ten hours ago, the name was a mystery, but now it's crystal head-banging clear.

Because we're going to Donegal, which is on the border of Northern Ireland, a finger-jabbing Ms. Pritchett warns us that we have to exercise caution with regard to the touchy political situation. "If anyone asks whether you're Protestant or Catholic, just tell them you're *American*." That's funny, because our guide in Egypt said that if we were wandering around the city and anyone asked if we were American, to say that we were *Canadian*.

As the plane descends over a field of deep green, the pilot announces, "Welcome to Donegal in the northwest of Ireland. Please take a moment to set your watches back to 1928."

Though we land smoothly, everyone claps when the plane touches down, which is fine, I think, so long as they're prepared to boo and hiss if we crash. Banjo leans over and informs me that the Irish are very superstitious. He taps the top of my apricot head and says, "Fisherman think redheads are bad luck and won't allow them near their boats."

"Cut it out," I push his hand away.

"It's true!" says Banjo.

Knowing him, it probably is. "Well, I wasn't planning on going fishing," I inform Banjo. At least not *that* kind of fishing. To be honest, I wouldn't mind meeting a nice guy. Amsterdam makes a person think a lot about sex. And Heineken mixed with gin provides a certain clarity that you just don't get from chocolate Yoo-Hoo. Perhaps it's time for me to be proactive in creating a new and improved life for myself. I mean, I don't have anything against patience, because that's something you need to be a good gambler, or good at almost anything worth doing. Then there's Pastor Costello, who is always going on about how patience reveals our faith in God's timing, especially when our twenty-year-old toaster is going into extra innings. But what exactly am I waiting for? And what if it's for something that's not ever going to come?

Chapter 37

*D*ropping the wallets in Donegal is easy, because it's not a big city and the street signs are in English, or else both English and Gaelic. Ms. Pritchett's study also compares the level of honesty between those who reside in towns versus cities. The people in Donegal are friendly and eager to help. Only, while the Canadians accompany you to where you're going, when you ask the Irish for directions, they just keep standing there and talking, explaining who lives in every house along the way.

After releasing my third wallet into the wild, I suddenly realize that I'm in the wrong place. There's a triangular market square called the Diamond, which leads to Main Street, only I need *Upper* Main Street. Ms. Pritchett is very particular about her locations, so after consulting the map, I retrieve the dropped wallet and toss it back into the bag.

A police officer with a large wooden stick attached to his belt asks, "Can I help you, Miss?"

"I'm looking for Upper Main Street," I say. "There's supposed to be a hospital."

"May I see what's in the bag, Miss?" he asks in a thick Irish brogue.

I open the shopping bag and explain about the experiment. But after poking around at the different styles of wallets, he apparently thinks the project involves working as an international pickpocket. No amount of telling him to look at the return address inside the wallets or the fact that they all contain twenty-euro notes will halt our march to the local police station.

Eventually, Ms. Pritchett arrives and acts as if this is all *my* fault. "Didn't you show him your school I.D.?" she keeps asking with that steel-trap mouth while glaring at me with those bird-of-prey eyes.

"Once the policeman saw all those wallets, he wasn't interested in the story about the project or anything else," I insist. Apparently, the Irish have a reputation for being good storytellers—perhaps the man has already heard it all.

Anyway, the cops don't want to deal with Ms. Pritchett either. They quickly release me into her custody, and she loudly instructs me to go finish distributing the wallets. The police can be quite certain they'd better not make any more attempts at impeding her academic dreams.

Once we're outside the station, she casually remarks, "Josh tripped and had to go to the hospital."

"Is he okay?"

"It's just a sprained ankle, but Banjo will have to finish dropping his wallets." Ms. Pritchett sounds far more concerned about the effects on her project than she does about Josh's health and well-being. I really am getting tired of this woman.

"I've hired a local guide to take you around this afternoon," Ms. Pritchett informs me as she takes off up the hill with her purposeful stride. "We've had enough trouble for one day."

But apparently, we haven't. When I arrive back at the hotel, Banjo is frantically searching for his passport. Here in Donegal, Mandy and I are sharing a suite with the boys—two bedrooms are connected by an open archway, with a tiny kitchen and lounge area in between.

"Just check to see if it's in any of your bags," he pleads with Mandy and me.

"It has to be here somewhere," says Josh, who is hopping around on crutches. "You must have had it yesterday, because you went through immigration."

The phone rings, and the desk clerk tells me that our guide is here. "You'd better send her up, because we might not be able to go," I inform him.

"Are you *sure* that you didn't drop your passport as one of the wallets?" asks Mandy.

Banjo suddenly looks horrified.

A stunning young woman with bright blue eyes and long flowing deep red hair that seems to be half-liquid, half-solid appears in the doorway. There's no doubt in my mind that all the animals of the forest gather around to help her dress when she wakes up every morning.

As she waves at us and says, "Hello, I'm Brigid," I think that Mandy might suddenly keel over from plain astonishment.

"Hey," says Josh. "We're not having a very good day—Hallie was almost arrested, I tripped and sprained my ankle, and now Banjo can't find his passport."

Brigid smiles knowingly. "Sounds as if the fairies are bringing you some bad luck," she says worriedly, but nonetheless with a delightful lilt to her voice. "When they're bored or angry, they like to play with the lives of humans."

We all laugh at her little joke. Only, Brigid is completely serious. And she's so wide-eyed and Disneylike that we immediately stop chuckling.

"Yes, I suppose that's one possibility," Josh agrees diplomatically.

With charm and authority, Brigid takes over the proceedings. "What you must do is turn your clothes inside out."

I look at Josh and he looks at Banjo. It's been a long day for everyone, and I don't know that turning our clothes inside-out is really what any of us have in mind at this juncture.

However, Mandy is enthusiastic about the idea and has already pulled off her shoes. "Underwear too?" she asks.

"Just the outside clothes should do it," replies Brigid.

Mandy and I go into the next room and dutifully begin removing our clothes, while the boys do the same in their bedroom. As I'm yanking off my jeans, I hear Banjo shout from the bedroom. "Found it!"

We stumble through the archway to where Brigid is waiting in the tiny sitting area. Banjo stands there in his boxer shorts, looking not unlike a pipe-cleaner sculpture, holding up his cargo pants in one hand and passport in the other. "I've been looking through all my bags, when it was in the side pocket of my pants the entire time!"

Brigid simply nods as if the fairies have been outfoxed once again. "Well, who wants to do a little sightseeing before it gets dark, then?"

We all agree. Hopefully our little streak of bad luck has ended.

"I'm sure you've all heard of the singer Enya," says Brigid. "Well, she's from Donegal, and one of her cousins lives right next door to me!"

I'm not entirely convinced about the existence of fairies, but there's certainly something to be said for cruel fate. And oh, how it mocks me!

Chapter 38

The town of Donegal is a jumble of medieval and modern buildings, which pleases Josh to no end, as he's now fervently interested in architectural conservation. Brigid shows off a fifteenth-century castle, and then leads us down a path to an old abbey sitting in a peaceful spot where the River Eske meets Donegal Bay.

Pointing to where some seals are frolicking, Brigid informs us, "selkies are seal fairies. The females can shed their seal skin and become beautiful women."

"Oh, how wonderful!" says Mandy, who has been hanging on Brigid's every word.

"Yes, but she'll break a man's heart if he falls in love with her and hides her skin to prevent her from going back to the sea."

While meandering back to town, Mandy and Brigid discuss the particulars of selkies and how exactly they cause men to pine and die for them. Finally, we stop to take some pictures in front of a pub called the Blarney Stone.

"What's blarney?" asks Josh.

"Crap," says Brigid. "It's our most successful export, after the pub. For some reason, Irish cookbooks don't sell all that well." Brigid laughs. "Some people say the cuisine was created on a dare."

"The Irish drink more tea per capita than any other nation," announces Banjo.

"More Guinness, too," Brigid adds cheerily. We venture inside the pub, where the walls are plastered with rugby posters, some possibly from before I was born, and she orders us all shandys, which are made with Guinness stout and red lemonade. They taste refreshingly cool and totally delicious.

Two men are playing music in the far corner. One is a wizened old character with a fiddle on his shoulder, while the other is young and able-bodied, pounding on a strange-looking drum. The notes are rapid and lively, much the same way as people here talk.

Mandy has downed her third shandy when she leans over and whispers, "Hallie, will you do me a big favor?"

"Sure," I say. "I mean, as long as you don't want me to pierce your eyebrows or something like that."

"My family is unbelievably strict—honestly, it's a miracle I've been able to attend college," explains Mandy. "And the real reason I came on this trip was to see what it's like to be with a woman." A quick pink sweeps over her face as she takes a deep breath and looks up at me.

Huh? I tell myself that maybe it's the Guinness talking and try to be cool. "I'm really flattered and everything, but—"

"Not you!" exclaims Mandy, as if I must be totally insane.

"Oh," I say. Though I don't know whether to feel relieved, angry, or extremely self-conscious. Just, generally speaking here, what's so bad about *me*?

"Brigid!" whispers Mandy. "I think Brigid is gay and that maybe she likes me. Can you find out for sure?"

Oh, my gosh! And I thought fairies and selkies were a lot to digest in one day. "How exactly am I supposed to do that?"

"Have you ever been to a gay bar?" asks Mandy.

"Not exactly," I say. "But I sort of live in one back home."

Mandy looks momentarily perplexed before continuing, "Ask Brigid if she can take us to one."

"I don't know that rural, northwest Ireland has a real happening gay and lesbian nightlife. Couldn't you have thought of this when we were in Toronto or Sydney?"

"I chickened out," says Mandy.

"And what about *Amsterdam?*" I add to the list. "All those naked women in windows…"

"I'm not going to pay for sex. That's gross!" says Mandy. "It's just that I thought this trip would be the perfect way to hook up without anyone finding out. But now it's almost over and on Friday we go to Morocco…"

"Where I believe the king chops people's heads off for that kind of thing," I finish the thought for her.

Mandy looks horrified. Only now, I've just given her all the more reason for going ahead with this little personal sociology project right this very minute.

"Wait a second—what about that night in Cairo when you and Josh took off and never returned? I assumed that you guys hooked up and…"

"I wanted to smoke kif, so I made him take me to a place in the old quarter," says Mandy. "We got really stoned—that's all."

"So you're not into guys?" Just to be clear here.

"I don't know."

Where's Bernard with his gaydar when I need him? Obviously, mine is nonexistent—having thought Pastor Costello was gay before he married my mother.

Mandy looks down and fiddles with her empty glass. "Have you ever…"

"No!" I say.

"Aren't you curious?" asks Mandy.

My mind flashes back to the time when Joanne at the garden center asked me out, and even though I said "no," I did think about it for a minute. "Not particularly."

"Will you please just ask Brigid if there's someplace to go?" pleads Mandy.

Is there a sign on my back that says DOPE FOR HIRE? I walk to the other end of the bar where both Banjo and Josh are flirting so hard with Brigid that they may soon need oxygen. Taking her aside for a moment, I frame Mandy's request for an alternative lifestyle venue, without going into her particular infatuation with our guide.

Then I report back to Mandy. "Brigid knows a place that's not a gay bar per se, but all the artsy people hang out there, and it's friendly to tourists."

"Fabulous!" says Mandy. "What time are we going?"

"We?"

Brigid comes over and flips her gorgeous coppery red mane to one side. She pulls out her cell phone and says in that seductive lilt, "I'll ring up some friends and we'll meet there tonight. On Fridays, they have really fine music."

"Sounds perfect!" Mandy smiles shyly.

Banjo and Josh hurry over in case Brigid needs assistance closing her cell phone.

"Ready to hit the next pub, babes?" asks Banjo. "I hear that the Tul-Na-Ri has disco on Friday nights!"

Josh lifts himself on his crutches, performs a spin, sort of, and almost topples over, but Brigid catches him.

"Looks like you lads are on your own—we're going to have a lasses' night out," says Brigid.

The guys appear crestfallen for about two seconds, until Banjo spots a dartboard across the room. "Darts! C'mon—I'll bet you a dollar a game."

Josh hobbles after him. "They use euros here."

We gather up our things and follow Brigid to the exit.

"Leave the door unlocked," Josh calls after us. "Our key is in the room."

Chapter 39

*W*andering up Castle Street, we come to a building with rickety wooden steps that leads to a place called the Dew Drop Inn on the second floor. The walls and ceiling are supported by exposed wooden posts and beams like the interior of a colonial farmhouse. There's nothing to identify the place as a gathering spot for the alternative lifestyle crowd, but the people are generally younger than those in the Blarney Stone, and more creatively dressed. Also, a female disc jockey, dressed as a train conductor, is spinning a recording of Rod Stewart's *Hot Legs*.

Leaning in close to Mandy I say, "Tell me again what I'm doing here."

"Moral support," she shouts over the music.

"Not quite the words I would have chosen…"

But Mandy is entranced by the action on the dance floor and no longer paying attention to me.

The décor consists of about a thousand 45-RPM records tacked to the walls and some beat-up posters of bands such as the Undertones, Hothouse Flowers, Stiff Little Fingers, Pop-Tarts, and B Jesus. Oh, Pastor Costello would like that last one. I'll have to see if I can get a CD for him. Behind the bar is a signed photo of the Irish band Clannad. For some reason, it catches my eye and I move in closer. Sure enough, there's Enya! She's following me! The woman behind the bar catches me staring and smiles. "Occasionally her cousin comes in here on Friday nights," she says. "I'll be sure to introduce you if I see her."

"Thanks," I say and quickly move away.

There are some long couches in the back and a girl waves in our direction through a haze of swirling smoke. Almost everyone holds a large glass of dark beer in one hand and a cigarette in the other.

"Do you know her?" Mandy asks Brigid.

"It's Donegal," says Brigid, "I know everyone."

Mandy is wearing a formfitting gold Lycra mini-dress that turns more than a few heads. I'd say that it's so tight you can see her underwear, but I'm pretty sure it's so tight you can tell she's not wearing any. I hate to take my mother's side when it comes to clothes, but when Louise tried to escape in a similar outfit, I had to give Mom points for barring the doorway and saying, "Just because it comes in your size, doesn't mean that you should wear it!"

We order drinks and take them to the back, where it's mostly women and a few guys who are either gay or else trying out for a Madonna tour. They've gone to a lot of trouble to construct some wild outfits. Though I should talk—with my super-short haircut and chandelier earrings, I fit right into the scene.

A young woman with a curtain of dark hair and vivid green eyes asks if we're here tracing our ancestry. "That's usually the only reason that Americans come to Donegal."

Mandy and I explain the sociology experiment, and they mostly look at us as if we're crazy—flying to different countries to throw money away.

"You'll get all your purses back in Donegal," says the young woman. "But only because the folk who find 'em will be afraid of bad luck! They'd keep 'em if they thought they could and not be harmed."

"They've already had an encounter with a fairy," announces Brigid, and nobody laughs or even looks remotely amused.

"A solitary fairy?" asks the young woman.

"Aye," says Brigid. "But after turning the clothes inside-out they immediately found the lost passport." Brigid nods toward the young woman. "The fairies are always giving Colleen a hard time and making her forget things. Isn't that right, girl?"

Colleen wags her head as if this is indeed the case. "You're lucky. That fairy must have been in a hurry."

"But I always thought fairies were good," I say.

"Like the tooth fairy," offers Mandy.

The girls laugh like crazy and then take big sips from their drinks. Brigid must eventually feel sorry for us, because we appear so dumbfounded. "We only say 'good fairy' in case they're around and listening," she explains in a voice you'd use for talking to a stupid child.

"Right." I nod my head as if this information is solid gold, right up there with the Periodic Table.

A woman with a short dark pixie cut, jewel-like blue eyes, and milky white skin leans across the back of the couch and introduces herself as something that sounds like "Chevron."

"Your name is Chevron?" I have to shout because Janis Joplin is wailing, *Freedom's just another word for nothing left to lose*, from a speaker directly above our heads.

She laughs heartily, an inviting laugh, like the distant measures of dance music heard through opening and closing doors, but otherwise, there's an air of inscrutability about her. Is she or isn't she? And do the black rubber pants with all the zippers translate into bondage or just less time in the restroom?

"S-i-o-b-h-a-n," she spells it out for me. "*Chevonne*—it's the Irish version of Joan."

I nod. "You're not Enya's cousin by any chance?"

She shakes her head. "Disappointed?"

"More like relieved," I say. "You have such unusual coloring."

"Dark Irish." She rearranges her willowy frame so that we're sitting next to each other.

"Dark?" Siobhan is the whitest person I've ever seen!

"Some say it's from when the Spanish Armada failed to conquer England in the late 1500s, and the shipwrecked sailors were washed ashore on the west coast of Ireland," explains Siobhan. "Others believe we're descended from the selkies."

"Those are the seal fairies, right?" I hope Ms. Pritchett has lots of fairy questions on the final exam, because I'm becoming a real expert.

Siobhan smiles, and I'm not sure if the twinkle in her eye means that she actually prefers this theory or she's pulling my leg so hard that I'm going to slide off the couch in another second.

The floor begins to sway when the first lines of Pink's "Missundaztood" begins playing, and practically everyone jumps up and begins to dance. While Mandy appears to be having a wonderful time talking with Brigid, Siobhan leads me out to the middle of the floor. It's hardly a couples dance, more like we're all out there hopping around together, as if it's an exercise class. At least that's what I tell myself. Great dance tunes play one after another, and there are several more trips to the bar. Before I know it, the lights are dimmed, and the DJ is announcing the last song of the night.

Barry Manilow's "Mandy" begins playing and I swear *our* Mandy looks at me as if this is a Sign From God. I sit on the couch taking the final few sips of my drink and thinking about the times Bernard and I would go to the Garden of Eatin' when one of us was depressed and order a mound of blueberry blintzes with sour cream and play "Mandy" on the wall-mounted jukebox.

Suddenly I don't know whether it's the half-a-case of Irish Red Ale making my stomach feel queasy or a full case of good old-fashioned homesickness.

Chapter 40

After the bar closes, the four of us dash through a light rain and pile into Brigid's tiny Renault like we're clowns in a circus act. Mini cars are very popular here and remind me of something from the Lego village in our basement. To carry my family around, we'd need at least four of them.

Mandy has invited Brigid and Siobhan back to the room, and a six-pack of beer is miraculously produced from the trunk of Brigid's car, which they refer to as "the boot." I'd be just as happy if I never saw another beer in my life. In fact, I think I might be going through chocolate Yoo-Hoo withdrawal. The company should sell patches to confirmed addicts who will be out of the country for an extended period of time.

Inside the apartment, Mandy cranks up the radio, and then she and Brigid promptly disappear into the bedroom we're supposed to be sharing. My legs feel like weights are attached to them and my thoughts are becoming increasingly vague. I look at Siobhan and she looks at me. Through the blurriness inside my head, I realize that I've just been going with the flow tonight, having decided that to announce, "by the way, I'm not gay" would sound like an insult to everyone there. The beers came one after another and I never worried about it again.

Siobhan sits down next to me on the couch and then leans over and kisses me on the lips. *Oh my God, I'm kissing a girl.* Right *now* would be the moment to stop. On the other hand, I'm thousands of miles from home with a woman I'll never see again. The whole trip is an experiment, after all.

Suddenly the door opens and the laboratory lights go on. Josh tumbles in on his crutches with Banjo right behind, looking like he's been through a carwash without the car. It's definitely a sitcom moment.

"Check it out, Josh," Banjo drunkenly slurs, "a little girl-on-girl action."

"Now there's a bet I would have lost," says Josh.

"Please don't stop because of us!" exclaims Banjo and flops down on a chair but misses and winds up on the floor.

"It sure explains a lot," says Josh. "I thought it was *me.*"

"What do you mean?" I have a sudden moment of clarity.

"Is that your boyfriend?" asks a confused sounding Siobhan.

There's luck, and then you have its weak-tea sister, chance. Which is why when it comes right down to it, every good gambler knows that life is not only short, but also rather absurd.

As the guys stumble in the direction of their room and Siobhan moves toward the door, all I can think about is sleep. Whispers and giggles can be heard coming from my room, and so I curl up on the couch.

I dream about snow. Eric and Louise and I are little and playing catch in the backyard. Eric, already a Little League star by the age of eight, is pounding Louise and me with direct hits and we shield our faces with our hands. The softballs are suddenly scones, and I'm not in the backyard but on a couch in Ireland.

"Wake up, sleepyhead," calls out a male voice that is definitely not Mom's. "It's almost noon, and lesbians all over the world are rolling off camp cots to search for their Harley boots while the radio plays k.d. lang songs."

I throw a scone back at Josh, and even though he's on crutches and can't easily duck, I miss by a mile. Glancing at my watch, I find that it really is noon. We were supposed to be down at breakfast by ten o'clock this morning! I leap up to search for my clothes but discover they're still on my body, mostly right where I left them. That has to be a good sign. At least when compared to Hawaii.

A shirtless Banjo appears in the archway between the boys' room and the common area. "There was a bombing outside of Marrakech. Morocco is cancelled. We're going straight to Peru."

"It's probably just as well," says Josh and nods at my fair skin. "You lying on a Moroccan beach would be like putting a spoon in the microwave."

Mandy appears from our bedroom wearing fresh clothes and a towel wrapped around her head. There's no sign of Brigid. "Has anyone noticed that the towels here are about as thick as the toilet paper back home?"

"We're really not going to Morocco?" I ask.

"Ms. Pritchett is off changing the tickets right now," replies Banjo.

"Darn," I say. "I wanted to see a garden designed by the painter Louis Majorelle and restored by Yves St. Laurent. My friend Bernard is forever talking about his use of cobalt blue. Did you know that the Arabs believe heaven is an actual garden, so the ones they create are meant to represent paradise on earth?" Uh-oh, the longer I'm away from Olivia, the more I'm beginning to sound like her.

"Why do you care so much about gardens?" asks Mandy. "I hate our garden. It smells like cow manure and all I do during the summer is weed."

"It'd be cool to see tropical flowers instead of the dahlias and hydrangea that I'm used to back home; just like it's fun to look at pictures of formal English gardens next to the less-structured designs that came into vogue after the Arts and Crafts Movement."

They all stare at me as if I've just announced my candidacy for President, and Josh asks, "And you know so much about this because..."

"Osmosis, I guess."

Never to be outdone when it comes to the laying on of factoids, Banjo dives into the conversation. "When we lived in Sacramento for a year, this dude down the street had the most amazing garden—only it turned out he'd been murdering hitchhikers and burying them there."

"Really!" Mandy's hennaed hands fly up to her heavily glossed lips.

Our phone rings and Banjo answers. "Exit downstage in fifteen minutes," Snagglepuss purrs into the receiver while shooting me a look that says, *You'd better hurry!*

There's no time to worry about the chainsaw that's playing "Da Doo Ron Ron" in my head. Fortunately, everyone is suffering after the late-night pub crawl and there's an open box of Alka-Seltzer on the table. As I stumble toward it, Josh raises his crutch in the air. "To the few, the proud, the hungover!"

When we arrive in the lobby, Ms. Pritchett stares as if she's the General of some ragtag army that's fast disintegrated in her short absence. "All the wallets were returned," she states matter-of-factly. "Though six were left with local barkeeps, and I had to go around and pick them up."

First, there's the short hop to Dublin. Then we catch a plane to Barajas airport in Madrid, where we'll change for a flight to Lima, Peru.

As usual, Mandy and I have seats next to each other. She puts her pillow against the window and prepares to doze off.

"Hey, not so fast," I whisper. "What were the results of your experiment?"

"Oh gosh, I was so drunk I can hardly remember it. That Irish Ale we were drinking is *not* normal beer!" exclaims Mandy. "So, do you want to find a gay bar in Peru?"

"No," I say. "What I want is for you to tell Josh that I'm not gay!"

"He and Banjo said they broke in on you and Siobhan going at it." Mandy covers her mouth so she doesn't laugh out loud.

"We kissed, that's all," I say. "I was thinking about what you said—it was my big chance to kiss a girl, you know, just for the hell of it—the plane was leaving in five hours. But it's very important that you tell Josh I'm not a lesbian...NOW."

"OH—I get it!" says Mandy. "You want to hook up with Josh."

"It's crossed my mind," I say. "One night about three years ago we were getting all touchy-feely at this party, and then I suddenly had to go and—"

"Why'd you leave if things were getting good?" asks Mandy.

"Well, actually, my Dad was in the hospital...he died that night."

"I'm so sorry!"

"Thanks," I say. "Anyway, everything was crazy after that. I took a year off from school, and when I finally went back I was seeing this guy from home—my old high school boyfriend. But right before the trip, we broke up."

"How come?" asks Mandy.

"I've thought and thought about it, and at the end of the day, I'm not sure exactly," I say. "I guess people just change over the years and sometimes they forget to tell each other."

"So, you've had this crush on Josh for a long time but couldn't act on it." Mandy narrows her eyes thoughtfully and seems to be enjoying this latest bit of intrigue.

"Josh hasn't made a move, and then suddenly last night he acts as if he's been sending me signals the entire time." I cover my face with my hands as if the story can't possibly get worse. But it does. "And now he thinks I'm gay!"

"I read in *Cosmo* that guys find the lesbian thing totally hot," says Mandy. "So you should have a much better chance after last night."

"You really think?" Where is Bernard when I need him? Or maybe this is one for Olivia. Guys are so confusing.

"Josh definitely likes you," Mandy assures me. "He talked about you for half the night when we went out in Cairo—how you're really determined and know exactly what you're doing with your life. He's aware that people laugh at him because he changes his major, like, every week."

Undoubtedly, Mandy is trying to make me feel better, but at this point, I don't care. It's impossible to tell whether it's the hangover, homesickness, or a broken heart, but I'm becoming increasingly bewildered and upset. Tears form in the corners of my eyes. "I'm such a loser!" I blurt out. "My boyfriend breaks up with me, in almost four months I haven't managed to get anything going with Josh, and then to become a lesbian you opt for a perfect stranger instead of me." If I were four years old it's the moment my mother would say, "I think that *someone* is overtired."

Mandy puts her arm on mine. "Hallie, what if we hooked up, and then you were in love with me, and I found out that I *wasn't* gay?"

There's something actually sensible in all of that, but right now I can't for the life of me figure out what it is. However, just trying to decipher it brings me back from the brink of tears.

"Josh definitely likes you," insists Mandy. "I can totally see you guys getting together in Peru."

"But *how?*" I practically whine. Olivia always used to say that trying to make someone love you, or make yourself love someone else, for that matter, is like trying to plant cut flowers. If my life had a soundtrack, now would be the moment for a wailing sax solo.

Mandy pats her latest ten-pound stack of women's magazines as if they hold all the answers to the mystery that is love. "We'll make it happen, I promise. You helped me in Donegal and I'll help you. That's what girlfriends are for!"

I take Mandy's arm and close my eyes. It's official; I've become one of those needy people I always used to despise. All that's left is to pray for identity theft.

Chapter 41

I barely remember changing planes in Madrid, just hours of glorious sleep while gliding through dreamy blue skies. When we arrive in Lima, the blood red sun is sinking behind brooding Andean peaks. It's a short drive from the airport to our hotel, and we all meet for a late dinner in the dining room before heading off to bed. Ms. Pritchett locates us and offers to have a guide take us to see some nearby ruins tomorrow after we finish dropping all the wallets. Josh and Banjo are enthusiastic and so Mandy and I pretend that we are too.

The public transportation system isn't very efficient and taxis are cheap, so I treat myself by handing my map over to the driver and ride around like visiting royalty behind a Plexiglas partition. He thinks I'm insane to be leaving these wallets and keeps shaking his head and mumbling "Loco," and I can tell that he really wants to pick them up himself.

It's impossible not to be disturbed by the extreme contrast between the staggering affluence and heartbreaking poverty on the streets of Lima. In a wealthy section of the city, mansions sit on the lawns like gigantic wedding cakes, while in the poorer neighborhoods entire families can be found begging on the side of the road.

At two o'clock in the afternoon we all gather for some casual sightseeing. Mandy is the last to arrive, and at first, I don't recognize my roommate of thirteen weeks. Her hair is back to being pale blond, hands are free of geometric patterns, fishing-lure earrings are gone, and her nails are stripped of polish and fake tips. So much for her starring role in *Mennonite Girls Gone Wild*. We really must be going home tomorrow night!

The four of us wander around the Main Square buying a few postcards and looking at beautiful, hand-knit baby blankets, while a group of Native American men wearing colorful clothes play a Beatles medley on panpipes. Beside them, petite women in bright taffeta dresses with multiple petticoats underneath sell handicrafts and also rides on a llama decorated like a Dr. Seuss character. On top of the women's heads are quirky, black stovepipe hats, a bit like the kind you sometimes see in photos of Abraham Lincoln, and they give us big grins even though we browse without buying. The late afternoon air slowly fills with the weight of humidity and the spicy thick scent of tobacco.

"Look at that sixteenth-century Spanish architecture!" exclaims Josh. "I really think I'm going to switch to cultural anthropology when we get back and, you know, do that whole gun, germs, and steel thing..."

"Haven't you already changed your major enough times?" I ask. "How will you ever get enough credits to graduate and actually start working?"

Mandy elbows me in the ribcage. I suddenly remember how Craig and I broke up the time I nagged him about school and his career. "I mean, I can certainly see how that would be very interesting."

He smiles at me. I smile back.

We pass a woman hawking vegetables from a tiny stall decorated with strings of dried peppers. "Peru introduced the world to tomatoes, peppers, and potatoes," Banjo informs us. If he ever decides to give up gambling, writing vacation guides really wouldn't be out of the question.

When we arrive back at the hotel, Mandy suggests having a

party to celebrate our last night of traveling together. The only problem is that the final exam is in the morning, and Ms. Pritchett has made it clear that Mandy and Josh and I are in danger of not being given a pass. It's hard to tell if Ms. Pritchett is just bluffing, but we don't dare skip studying.

"We can't *not* go out—we may never see each other again!" declares Mandy. "I know, we'll go back to our rooms and study until ten, and then meet in the lobby."

Banjo needs some time to update his records on whatever wallets have already been turned in, and so everyone agrees on this strategy.

Mandy and I bring a couple of tall bottles of Inka Kola back to the room. It tastes like bubblegum flavored fizz. Apparently, they've never heard of chocolate Yoo-Hoo down here either. I should really apply for a job with that company and take charge of global distribution.

"Our room is so perfect!" declares Mandy. There's a separate living room area with a couch; so her idea is that after some club hopping, Josh and I will have the bedroom to ourselves, and then she can sneak in later and crash on the couch.

I'm not at all convinced her plan is going to work, but I'm certainly willing to try it. Like Mandy said, we may never see each other again, so there doesn't seem to be anything to lose. In the meantime, we lie sprawled across our beds, digesting the results of some fifty-page study that Ms. Pritchett threw at us this morning. It's about whether the characteristic of altruism comes from socialization or genetics. A professor at Kansas State claims that people are predisposed to being cooperative and helpful even if they aren't aware of it, so long as they're in an environment where others act in similar ways.

I decide that I hate sociology. If you work at it long enough, I'm pretty sure you can make a case for or against just about any theory imaginable and find results to back it up. I begin to nod off.

"*La noches es larga,*" says Mandy.

My Spanish isn't very good but I take that to mean "the night is long."

The bed begins vibrating, and I assume Mandy pushed a button on the wall to jolt me awake. I haven't seen a vibrating bed since staying in some cheap motor lodge when I was a little kid and we visited my grandparents.

The phone rings and, although Mandy picks up the receiver and puts it to her ear, I can clearly hear Ms. Pritchett shouting, "There's an earthquake! Stand in a doorway!" The line goes dead. Panic rises in my throat like some of that bad seafood Bernard warned me about.

By now, the entire room is shaking and the overhead lamp comes loose from the plaster ceiling, while books and pens slide to the floor. We fling open the hall door and stand underneath it. A room service cart goes flying past. Families run screaming down the hall toward the stairway. Time slows down, and every heaving second seems like an hour.

"Oh, my God!" says Mandy while crouching down and placing her hands over her head. But the walls don't crack and tumble down on top of us.

The trembling finally stops. I don't know if it's over or just taking a breather. Say what you want about the bad winters in Ohio, we don't have earthquakes, tsunamis, or volcanoes. The worst warning you're ever going to hear there is *Stop, drop, and roll!* Speaking of which, the fire alarm begins ringing and the hallway sprinklers start squirting us. We rush toward the stairs. Roaming around out front searching for us are Banjo and Josh, still on crutches, and Ms. Pritchett, who is wearing that god-awful velveteen cranberry blazer over her nightgown.

"Are you girls all right?" asks Ms. Pritchett, her eyes wild with distress.

"Yes, fine," we answer in unison.

"Are you sure?" She looks us up and down as if someone might be trying to conceal a rotator-cuff injury.

We wait outside for two hours, everyone exchanging stories,

talking to other tourists—a sudden extended family created by an emergency. I tell them how whenever anything bad occurred back home, my Uncle Lenny always liked to say, "Worse things happen at sea."

The hotel manager eventually comes over and explains that the earthquake triggered the fire alarms and sprinklers, and that we can go back inside as soon as they're turned off. He says there isn't any structural damage to the building, just a lot of broken dishes, lamps, and that sort of thing. Only the rest of the city hasn't been as fortunate. We can hear ambulances and fire engines racing up and down the side streets.

Does Ms. Pritchett cancel the test in the morning? Hell no. She tells us to be downstairs at eight on the dot with pencils sharpened.

Chapter 42

So much for Mandy's and my big plans for our final night in Peru. We end up back in our beds studying for the test, and the next thing we know, Josh is banging his crutch against the door saying that it's morning and time to go downstairs. The earthquake knocked out the phones, so there was no wake-up call.

Sitting down to the three-hour exam, I have this fantasy that after we've done all this work, Ms. Pritchett wouldn't dare fail us. On the other hand, I've seen enough of Ms. Pritchett in action to know this might be an entirely false supposition, or what Bernard likes to call "a Fig Newton of my imagination."

The test is bloody hard. (We all say "bloody" regularly, ever since that night in Ireland when it was uttered in every sentence of every story told.) One of the questions is on experimentation procedure, which was explained in a photocopied book chapter our fearsome leader had presented to us the first day, and I assumed was just background material, not something to memorize! She also wants us to explain how the earthquake affects our results in Peru, and if they should still be included. I have no bloody idea.

After collecting our papers, Ms. Pritchett announces that the airport is undergoing some post-quake repairs and our 6:00 PM flight this evening can't leave until the same time tomorrow. The cable TV is down, and there's no Internet service, so we have to kill a day hanging out.

This is what I'd call your classic "good news/bad news" situation. We're all anxious to get home, yet it's another chance to celebrate our last night together. And this time, without a test hanging over our heads.

Mandy leans over and whispers, "Disaster brings people together." She follows this with a wink and a nod toward Josh.

We escape Ms. Pritchett to go and see how a city looks after an earthquake. This morning's newspaper reported that it was a 7.9 on the Richter scale, the third worst since they started keeping records a hundred years ago. However, the epicenter was up north, and so the capital city sustained minimal damage in comparison to outlying towns and villages. The driver of an old black Dodge with a Virgin Mary painted on the side and an army of plastic saints marching across the dashboard offers to take us around for a reasonable fee. It would appear the only buildings that caved in or sustained severe damage were in pretty bad shape to begin with. As usual, it's the poor who suffer the most.

Upon seeing a little schoolhouse that has a partially collapsed wall and the kids gathered out front, we decide to stop and see what we can do to help. Josh and Banjo assist the men in clearing debris and attaching a tarp to the roof, while Mandy and I hail a street vendor with a cart and buy them all some lunch. It only costs the equivalent of forty U.S. dollars to feed thirty people, and so we go find a store where we can also get them some paper, pencils, crayons, and workbooks.

It feels good to be able to help, even if it's just a little bit. I consider joining the Peace Corps and coming back here to build irrigation systems, set up clinics, and teach English. Although it would probably help to know Spanish.

By the time we arrive back at the hotel it's dinnertime, and after showering we go to a steakhouse where a group of guitar players walks from table to table serenading customers. Next, we head to a nightclub that's more punk than Latin, with a live band covering songs by The Ramones, The Clash, The Cure, and a few other bands starting with "the." My sister Louise would be in heaven.

"I'm going to pop across the street for a little while," says Banjo. He points in the direction of a strip of casinos ablaze in neon that we passed on the way into the city from the airport. "It's a lucky country—a place where former shoeshine boys become president."

"And where casinos apparently have backup generators," I add.

Banjo exits, stage left.

Mandy leaps up. "I'll go too."

She practically winks at me, and I wonder if Josh can tell that this is a setup. He orders two more pisco sours, a strange but delicious drink made with grape brandy.

"Methinks our friend Banjo has a major problem." Josh shakes his head.

"So do I," I tell Josh. "I'm worried that I flunked the test."

"Don't," he says.

"Even with all the work we've done, I honestly believe Ms. Pritchett would be heartless enough to not give me credit."

"You did flunk the test," says Josh. "You, me, and Mandy—we all did. None of us were expecting that question on procedure."

"So she's going to fail all three of us?" I ask.

Josh smiles. "Not exactly."

"C'mon, you know something." I give Josh a friendly push, forgetting that he can't put weight on the one ankle yet, and he practically falls off his bar stool.

"You know how we helped Banjo out of that mess in Malaysia—especially you?"

I nod my head.

"Well, Banjo felt that he owed us a favor," explains Josh. "At the beginning of the trip, he and Ms. Pritchett were an item—he never returned to my room at night. I think they broke up somewhere between Sydney and New Delhi. Anyway, it's unethical to have a fling with a grad student. At least at our college it is."

My eyes widen and I suddenly remember how Banjo would slip up and call her Alice. "Banjo threatened to turn Ms. Pritchett in if she flunked us?"

Josh smiles. "Maybe not in so many words, but it's safe to say that we're all going to pass."

I'm relieved and actually begin to laugh as I imagine Bernard describing the situation as Banjo and Ms. Pritchett having become "overly-familiar." This was one of his favorite expressions, right up there with "home-knitted" for those customers he deemed mentally unbalanced.

"Banjo and Alice!" My eyes widen—you may as well just return me to the Mother Ship.

"Probably best not to create a mental picture," adds Josh.

"You know, I'm not a lesbian," I suddenly blurt out.

Now it's Josh's turn to laugh. "Well, it turns out that I *am* a lesbian, and I think I'm attracted to you. Is that weird or what?"

We talk for a while, and then without discussing where we're going next, Josh and I wander out into the night, where stars quilted onto a black-velvet southern-hemisphere sky make the constellations appear upside-down to our eyes, with Orion the great hunter standing on his head.

Chapter 43

*B*ack in the hotel room Josh tries to find some music on the radio but only gets static. Outside we can hear the chink chink of metal hitting brick and the hiss of buzz saws as the power company works through the night. It's been four years since I first developed a crush on Josh my freshman year of college, and now we're finally getting together. Excitement rises in me like a tide.

Josh balances his elbows on his crutches and kisses me on the lips. As we continue kissing, his crutches fall over, he hops on one leg toward the bed, and I follow him. We tug at each other's clothes occasionally, but mostly take off our own. Josh removes some condoms from his jacket pocket and tosses them onto the dresser. *Does he carry those around all the time,* I can't help but wonder? Did he think we might hook up tonight? Or is he just always ready for action?

After we're naked, Josh moves slowly, in fact so slowly that my mind starts to wander. I'd been so desperate for something new to read that I'd borrowed a copy of *The Little Prince* from the traveler's library in the lobby this morning. The bizarre illustrations of snakes and rosebushes and faraway planets have been sloshing around in my head all day. I now know what it feels like to hurtle through space and time, not sure that you'll ever make it home again.

"I've been studying the Kama Sutra," Josh informs me.

I heard of that somewhere, possibly biology. I can't believe that Josh has chosen this moment to tell me he's decided to change his major again!

"Particularly tantric sex," he adds.

"What?" I finally ask.

"It means that I can make love to you for hours," he says.

As he drowns me with another soggy kiss, I silently question whether he may be in possession of an overactive saliva gland that's gone undetected until now. Otherwise, this entire experience is so odd—I'm trying to feel something, but I'm not. A change, like a shift in the wind, comes over me. The landscape of my own heart is at this moment foreign terrain, playing tricks on my mind and body that I don't understand. And now he's telling me that this might go on for a very long time!

For years I'd been lusting after Josh, and now it turns out we have no chemistry together whatsoever. Why couldn't I have found this out four months ago? There should be a test you can take as soon as you meet another person, perhaps by touching your index fingers—if they both turn red you're on. Meantime, if they turn black, it's a dead loss. I could invent sex mood rings and become a millionaire.

Josh continues making love to me. Is it possible to feel lonely when you're physically with somebody? And for the mind to be flashing these mundane images, such as whether I should have ordered the seafood paella tonight? Mandy's dinner looked so good. It seems as if it would be really rude to stop Josh and say, "I left a jacket in the closet that I don't want to forget to pack." Then it hits me—I've heard about women faking it. I just never thought that I'd be one of them. But if I don't do something soon, I'm going to be the one on crutches for the trip home.

"Oh Josh," I say. "I don't think I can last much longer."

"Try to hang on," he instructs. "Think about something else for a moment."

Unfortunately, all I've been doing is thinking about other things. "No really, this is it."

I huff and I puff and I fake an orgasm. It feels pretty contrived to me, but he seems to accept it as fact and doesn't ask for proof. We curl up together in the bed, but suddenly I feel as if I'm going to burst into tears. And not ones of joy and satisfaction. I nudge Josh awake. "I guess you'd better go back to your room since Mandy will be coming in soon."

"She won't care," he replies sleepily.

I'm now pushing him out of the bed. "We have to get up early." I go and fetch his crutches. Josh finally dresses and leaves, but not before supplying me with a hug that's more like a first down.

I lie wide awake on the lumpy mattress where I'd just faked my first orgasm. It was as if an unseen hand had given a final shake to the kaleidoscope and a new pattern emerged where all the questions of the last fifteen weeks had settled down into one perfect and stunning frame.

Craig. I wanted to marry Craig. The splendor of being in his arms transcended life and even fate. When we were together, the world's sharp edges were smoothed, and I felt well-defended against the dark. It's not imagining my life *with* him so much as that a life *without* him suddenly seemed impossible!

I just want my world back to the way it was before this trip. What are the odds of breaking even?

Chapter 44

By the time we're gathered in the lobby with our bags, Mandy has completed her transformation back to the Mennonite girl I first met at the start of the trip, at least on the outside. The Broadway-strength makeup is gone and the leftover permanent has been blown straight with a hair dryer. The gray muslin dress has been unfurled, ironed, and donned.

After we finish checking out I place *The Little Prince* back in the traveler's library—along with the dozen John Grisham books and one copy of *The Da Vinci Code* in German—so he can share his simple wisdom with the next pilgrim. The little prince's powerful secret, according to author Antoine de Saint Exupery, goes as follows: *It is only with the heart that one can see rightly; what is essential is invisible to the eye.* And now I too am ready to return to my planet.

As the minibus driver perilously darts through mobs of pedestrians and around rubble, Ms. Pritchett hands back our final test papers. Mandy, Josh, and I have Cs at the top. "I was hoping that you all would have done better," she informs us.

We nod as if we're also very disappointed in ourselves, but what's really going through my mind is, "I hope that I never ever have to see you again." Oh, I'd learned plenty, all right. It's just that none of it was on any of Ms. Pritchett's tests.

As for the experiment itself—how many wallets were returned overall and where—Ms. Pritchett presents us with some preliminary conclusions in the form of a long boring essay, complete with a graph that tracks social mores in the context of an economic matrix. Basically, people living in small towns turned in the wallets more often than those in large cities, same with places where employment was high, versus low. However, religion or superstition occasionally altered that pattern, which appears to be what our mad sociologist was after.

My own take on things is that aside from clothes, creeds, and tolerance for curry dishes, citizens of the big blue marble aren't all that different. The places we visited were similar to those back home in that most people try to be honest, but a few don't always succeed. Then again, if everyone in the world had a decent, stable income, I'm convinced that a lot more folks would be able to afford honesty. Because if my family was starving and I found some money lying in the street, I'd probably sleep just fine knowing that I'd put food on the table. In fact, most people, if suddenly upgraded to middle-class life, would most likely give away a little more than they should, remembering how rotten it was to be poor.

Finally, there's me—lying to myself and others in order to make my actions sound less selfish. The truth of the matter is that I yearned to go on this trip due to some vague lack of fulfillment at a moment when my entire life wavered on the edge, and I'd had a crush on Josh for years. I did exactly what I wanted to do—running away from something...or to something, I don't know. But I expected Craig to wait for me while I was out searching for a more exciting boyfriend and a more thrilling existence, which in hindsight seems pretty unfair. I should've just told him the truth, that I was no longer sure about our plans and needed some time to think and explore.

Maybe I'd imagined a grander life for myself. And it was a matter of discovering all the people I wasn't meant to be, the things I wasn't meant to do, and the places I wasn't meant to live. Through the slow (and often painful) process of elimination, all that's left is the not so grand, but genuine, boring old me. An imaginary trumpet blares, and Gil is smiling over my shoulder, a guardian angel dressed as William Shakespeare in doublet and tights saying, *"To thine own self be true."*

There's a long wait at the Lima airport as work crews continue to deal with the aftermath of the earthquake. Then we have a four-hour layover in Houston. I'm tempted to call Craig from the airport and tell him that I've changed my mind, but decide it will be more exciting to wait until I see him in person. The last leg of our journey is only three hours; we should be home by suppertime. I phone Bernard from Houston to ask if he can pick me up at the airport in Cleveland.

"It's so good to hear your voice!" Bernard shouts as if I'm calling from Antarctica. "We watched the earthquake on television and I was certain that you were buried alive!"

It feels wonderful to finally chirp, "See ya later, decorator," into the receiver and know that I'll be face to face with him again in just a few short hours!

Weariness magically disappears as everyone becomes excited about arriving home. Even Mandy, as she leaves her trashy novels and women's magazines on a chair in the Houston airport for the next traveler, appears happy at the prospect of returning.

It's impossible to sleep on the final leg of our journey. We've been on dozens of flights and they were all basically the same, but this being the one home somehow changes everything. Josh wanders up the aisle and hands me an envelope.

"What's this?" I ask him.

"Open it," he says.

Inside is a long lock of strawberry blond hair that looks as if it's been taken from the tail of the clown horse in a rodeo. "My hair!"

"A memento," he says.

And from the way he says it, I can tell he doesn't have any plans for us to see each other again. I guess Josh didn't feel that much for me either. What's the opposite of mutual attraction?

"So did you decide to change your major to archeology or cultural anthropology?" I ask. "Or conservation or cartography?"

"Naw." He shakes his head. "I've got to finish up school and start my career. The trip was really great from that point of view—there's so much in the world to be interested in, but I don't necessarily have to major in all of it. It's just as easy to read a few books or go on a vacation to discover something new."

Mandy/Amanda has been frantically scribbling some sort of a list as we fly from Texas to Ohio. I don't know if it's because all her magazines are gone or she's planning to launch an invasion on Monday. "Do you ever wish you were someone else?" she asks me.

"Of course!" I say. "I wish I were beautiful like my sister, Louise, and brilliant like this guy Brandt I went to high school with, and rich like, well…a rich person." Then I laugh.

"What's so funny about being smart, rich, and gorgeous?"

"It's my stepfather—he's always saying that you *have* to be yourself, because everyone else is taken."

"Theoretically speaking, I suppose that's true," replies Mandy. "But it doesn't mean people can't try to change, if not themselves then at least their lives."

"So, what's on your agenda for when we get back?"

Mandy flips to the first page of her notes and puts her finger on the top line. "The first thing I'm going to do is break off my engagement!"

"You're *engaged?*"

"Didn't you see that guy with them when we left?" asks Mandy.

"I thought he was your brother."

Mandy moves her finger down the list. "I'm never going to make it as a real painter, but I still love art. Seeing Rembrandt's "Nightwatch" in the Rijksmuseum was just so amazing that I started to cry right there. I went straight to an Internet café and submitted my application to the University of Maryland for a graduate degree in art history or criticism. Eventually, I'd like to get a job at a museum or maybe even open a gallery someday."

"Cool," I say. I don't ask Mandy what she decided about men versus women. One journey can answer only so many questions. Meantime, it also has to create some new ones.

"What about you?" asks Mandy.

"Look for a job," I say.

"Be glad you don't have anyone trying to ruin, I mean, *run* your life." She smiles at her intentional slip.

"Yeah, that's a relief. Only I don't have anyone to blame when things get screwed up."

Mandy laughs crazily as if there's no way a person could mess up her own life.

The pilot announces that we're getting ready to land and it's almost sixty degrees outside. Winter somehow disappeared, replaced by a pale spring brightness.

I remove the black silk rope containing the crystals from around my neck and hand them to Mandy.

"Will this help me find true love?" she asks eagerly.

"It worked for me."

And Mandy can see that there's no reason not to accept the gift, as the look on my face declares that I've indeed found love.

I dash through the doors and Bernard is standing there waiting for me, as steadfast as the earth's orbit around the sun, with an enormous smile on his face, and carrying a large first-aid kit in his right hand. Please tell me that's a joke. Or it's filled with muffins. Either way, I feel like planting a flag in the soil.

Chapter 45

" Your Botticelli hair is gone!" he shouts before we've even had a chance to hug each other.

Parents and friends are waiting for us in the luggage area, making for fast and jumbled goodbyes. We've all written down e-mail addresses and promised to stay in touch.

I'm proud of Ms. Pritchett. She manages to remain in character right until the bitter end, waving goodbye to all of us, looking every bit the frown in a pantsuit.

As Bernard and I walk to the car I'm worried that he's going to know I've changed my mind about Craig's proposal and squeeze it out of me, when I want my fiancé to be the first to know. However, it turns out there's so much to tell each other that the subject of Craig doesn't even come up. I'm talking stream-of-craziness about the trip—Pyramids, Taj Mahal, earthquake. And Bernard is thrilled to report that he finally had the neighbors evicted.

As we drive past the hospital and into town it feels so good to be home! The month of May is exactly the same old boring wonderful way that I remember it. The air exudes the scent of those familiar spring showers that thaw the winter earth. Fresh grass cuttings splotch driveways scattered with bicycles. The flaking bark of the sycamore trees make a mosaic of silvery gray and shiny white as slanted rays of sunlight play on the interlacing boughs. Sheets flap on clotheslines. Everyone around here has a dryer, but no fabric softener can give you the same soft touch and heavenly perfume as spring carried by a breeze. The sign out in front of the high school says CONGRATULATIONS GRADUATS. That's encouraging. Not.

For a while there, I was no longer sure of who I was. But as we drive through town, I suddenly remember. And all is finally right in my world. I can just feel that things are going to work out!

"Rose looks adorable in her Little League costume," says Bernard.

"Uniform," I correct him.

His hand flies up to his mouth. "She keeps yelling at me for referring to the watchamacallits as 'rehearsals.'"

"Practices."

"Yes, of course," says Barnard. "It's a whole new lingo of batters and bases, and not the kind I'm used to!"

Bernard pulls the car into the driveway very slowly, and it bounces up and down as the tires plunge into a half-dozen enormous potholes. "Have you hit upon hard times while I was away?"

"I dug them myself," Bernard announces proudly as he switches off the engine. "Some people drive too fast where children are playing."

It's clear that "some people" is Ottavio, who uses the driveway more as a runway for taking off and landing, gunning the car from zero to seventy within a matter of seconds, and slamming on the brakes with equal swiftness.

On the back of Olivia's cherry red Buick I spot a new bumper sticker that says: THE FIRST BOAT PEOPLE WERE WHITE. "I see that Olivia's been busy, as usual."

Bernard shakes his head. "Her latest cause is the census being overly focused on racial and ethnic identity, or something like that. Have you noticed that Mother's causes never have colored ribbons that you can pin onto your lapel?"

"Oh, my gosh!" The house next door has a pile of rubble for a garage, there are giant scorch marks across the once-pristine white front, and part of the roof is collapsed. "What happened?"

"To make a long story short, the Schultzes sold me the house at a very fair price, since they were losing their lederhosen as absentee landlords," explains Bernard. "And then I finally managed to evict the students. The ringleader was charging kids a few bucks to attend parties, and so Al and Officer Rich helped me get them out on a zoning violation. However, they had one final blowout bash— what Pastor Costello would most certainly call 'a real humdinger,' complete with fireworks being launched from the roof. The only thing missing was a concert by The Who. The police *and* the fire department had to come. Oh my *garage*, you should have seen it!"

Bernard regularly substitutes "garage" for "God" since the disaster area attached to the house is bursting with broken antiques, stage props, and junk, it's basically ten times more chaotic and dangerous than any conceivable Apocalypse scenario.

"Wow!" I say. "That must have been some party."

"When a rocket hit the power lines there was an actual fireball! Fortunately, the insurance was comprehensive and up-to-date," replies Bernard. "Now, I've made a special dinner in honor of your travels—chicken fricassee with wild mushrooms and Bleu de Bresse baked potatoes. I went back and forth all week—fricassee or fricandeau, fricassee or fricandeau? Then I whipped up some spaghetti and wheatballs for mother, which, in case you're not in the mood for poultry, has a gustatory appeal all of its own, especially since I was able to obtain some fresh basil for the artisanal marinara sauce. On weekends, they've started a farmer's market in the town square! And for dessert, we're having a Mexican floating island with kahlua custard sauce and sesame pumpkin seed brittle. It's what Katharine Hepburn and Spencer Tracy ate in the movie *The Desk Set*, only theirs was made with raspberry coulis, of course."

If God is in the details, then Bernard is a deeply religious man. I decide not to remind him that we didn't travel to France, Italy, Mexico, or Hollywood.

"I was hoping to take a quick shower, and then go and see Craig." I bite my lip knowing how hard Bernard must have worked on dinner.

"Of course!" he says as if he momentarily forgot what it's like to be young. "I'll make up a plate and leave it in the fridge."

Dropping my things in the summerhouse, I quickly shower and head over to Craig's. I'd been rehearsing my speech on the plane the entire way home, and even imagined his response. After a few soft practice knocks, I bang on the door of hope.

Only when Craig appears, the entire speech flies out of my head. It isn't so much my nerves as the expression on his face. He doesn't exactly look happy to see me.

"Hi," I say.

"Hi." He stands in the doorway without coming out or asking me inside.

"I'm back." Suddenly I'm trembling with nerves, afraid to breathe or not breathe.

"I can see that." Craig's once inviting tone of voice is now cold as a moonbeam on a frozen lake.

"We had an earthquake in Peru—the bed was vibrating and everything!" What a *stupid* thing to say!

"Glad you're okay," he says.

"Can we talk?" I ask.

"I'm sort of busy right now." Craig keeps his hand on the door. He's still not stepped out or invited me inside. I may as well be collecting for UNICEF.

"Oh," I say. It certainly doesn't seem to be the right moment to announce my momentous decision.

"Maybe tomorrow," I say.

"I have to get up early and drive to Doylestown." His features remain as hard and cold as those stamped on a coin. "I just landed a really big job there—a pond with two waterfalls and a fountain."

"Oh, congratulations then," I say.

"Thanks." He closes the door in my face.

With a sinking heart, I turn around and walk back down the driveway. My wondrous discovery of true love—that it's not a red red rose or never having to say you're sorry, but a great passion where there exists something to fill the mind, the heart, and the senses—will forever remain nothing but an undelivered letter. For whatever reason, I'd assumed Craig's offer was open-ended. Does he have another girlfriend? Or worse, does he hate me? He didn't even mention my haircut. How did I get everything so wrong? Two days ago the answer seemed obvious—when you're no longer sure of who you are, go back to where you were when you knew.

It's at moments like this I could really use a message from the Emergency Broadcast System telling me where to go and what to do.

Chapter 46

I realize that I should stop and see my family but I'm just too heartbroken. Mom doesn't know that we cancelled Morocco and isn't expecting me until Saturday and so I decide to let it slide until I've pulled myself together. Because my mother takes unsmiling children personally, unless of course she told you not to do whatever it was in the first place, which I suppose in this case she sort of did.

On the long tearful ride back to the Stocktons' I remember something that Robert Louis Stevenson wrote in his essay "El Dorado": *To travel hopefully is a better thing than to arrive.* Just four hours ago I was on top of the world. Now it's as if I've fallen off the edge of one of those old Byzantine maps, into the uncharted area inhabited by dragons and sea monsters.

Sitting in the driveway, the evening slowly withdraws. I watch the sky turn from blue to pink to violet while a perfectly round moon outlines the rooftop like a stage set. The front porch is where Craig and I had our first kiss. Around back, in the summerhouse is where we first made love. The miraculous discovery of intimacy and sharing the most delicate yearnings of my soul with another person had been the most profound experience of my life so far.

When I used to live at the Stocktons', tomorrow seemed all

possibility. Now my dreams of the future are tempered with regret, and every day will be a day's remove from what was supposed to be.

I'm inclined to bypass the dinner table altogether and head directly to bed, but that will draw even more attention to my wretched situation.

"That was fast," Bernard calls to me from the dining room. "Come sit down. We've only just started."

"Craig wasn't home," I lie. But the life has gone out of my voice and I can't hide my distress so easily.

Bernard gives Olivia a look that says he feels a Billie Holiday song may be in order.

I slump into an empty chair.

Gil politely says to Bernard, "Pass the potatoes, please."

Ottavio dashes into the kitchen and quickly returns with another place setting.

"Tho' much is taken, much abides," says Olivia, who has a quotable quote for every occasion.

"Betty Friedan?" Bernard guesses the founder of the women's movement just to aggravate her.

"It's what Alfred Lord Tennyson said about Odysseus' journey in his great poem *Ulysses*," Olivia informs us. "Although Robert Graves later wrote a book questioning whether Homer's original *Odyssey* may have actually been scribed by a woman."

"Who better than a woman to know a coup d'etat from crudités?" retorts Bernard.

Olivia proceeds to ask me lots of questions about my trip, especially Egypt and the pyramids. She loves the story about the blind dolphins in the Ganges River. "Mandy said they'd bring us good luck. She's Mennonite and her family has a big hex sign painted onto the side of their barn to keep away witches."

"The dolphin was a symbol of ambiguity in William Butler Yeats's poem *Byzantium*," says Olivia.

"I'm sure he's probably right," I say, tempted to add, "based on my life since the day of the boat ride."

Ottavio seems very confused by the fact that we didn't visit Italy.

For some reason, talking about the trip is starting to depress me. I would have enjoyed it more if I'd known how terrible life was going to be when I returned.

Bernard senses that I'm flagging. "Can you believe that none of my poor culturally-deprived girl scouts knows who Dorothy Draper was?"

"Who was Dorothy Draper?" I fall for the distraction, as usual.

Bernard looks as if he might faint into the wheatballs.

"The Martha Stewart of her day," Gil enlightens me. "If I recall correctly, she was very much against beige."

"She only made interior design a profession!" proclaims Bernard.

This conversational gem dies a natural death, as no one else seems to have a Dorothy Draper story to tell.

"I'm thinking of moving to San Francisco," I announce. Saying it somehow makes it seem more real.

Bernard coughs and reaches for his water glass.

"It's a good place for graphic designers, you know—Silicon Valley and all that," I add.

"A wonderfully progressive city," says Olivia. "They're experimenting with some innovative legislation for helping the homeless."

Bernard rolls his eyes as if I'm talking about moving to Neptune and Olivia should have been committed years ago. "You could work in the garden until you find something suitable around here. The town is growing like it's going out of style. Why, there are a million different things you can do right here in Cosgrove County!"

Yes, I suppose that's the essence of probability—everything is possible and yet only one thing happens. "Thanks for the offer, but let me see what happens with the résumés I send out tomorrow. Honestly, I'm starting to wonder how much control we actually have over our lives. I mean, are we just pawns of a higher power, or can we really determine our own destinies?"

"We can control how we behave and certainly our appearance," argues Bernard. "As Olympia Dukakis said in the movie *Steel Magnolias*, the only thing that separates us from the animals is our ability to accessorize."

"No matter what you say, I'm never going to wear scarves and brooches," I tell Bernard.

"Fine, but a nice gold bangle bracelet once in awhile can't hurt," he counters. "At least for interviews!"

"There was an Army recruiter on campus in December," I say. "They have jobs for graphic designers in public relations. Or with my computer skills, I could even apply for the engineering corps."

Bernard suddenly looks like he's been shot.

"I don't know that I'd join an army that gives you a medal for killing men and a discharge for loving them," declares Olivia. "Love is illegal, but not hate—no, that's encouraged."

"I have a play opening this Friday." Gil tactfully introduces a new subject. "We're finally doing *Mrs. Warren's Profession* by George Bernard Shaw."

"I can't wait." Olivia claps her hands. "All my friends from church are coming."

"After much lobbying by Livvy," adds Gil.

"Will the Department of Homeland Security allow some eighty-*odd* Unitarians to congregate in a public place without a permit?" asks Bernard.

Olivia ignores him. "Shakespeare is fine, but he didn't write many good parts for women the way that Shaw and Ibsen did."

As soon as Bernard and I are alone in the kitchen he declares, "It would appear that we need a master plan to get Craig back."

"I don't think so," I say. "I had this crazy idea about marrying for love."

"Of course," says Bernard. "And you will. But everything requires a little help once in a while, even love. That's what seasonings are for!" He points to the enormous spice rack and then places his hand over his heart as if mourning the passing of a great leader. "The famous food writer and foremost authority on American cuisine, James Beard, once said, 'I believe that if ever I had to practice cannibalism, I might manage if there were enough tarragon around.'"

Bernard pauses and maintains his pose, as if waiting for my applause. Instead I blink back a tear. "He doesn't love me anymore."

"I'll tell him you've been blinded by pesticide, or the victim of a car accident like Audrey Hepburn in the movie *Wait Until Dark*," suggests Bernard. "I'll say that you were careless because you were so carried away thinking about him while driving, and then he'll insist on marrying you."

"I'd have to pretend to be blind for the rest of my life!"

"Audrey was only pretending in the movie," says Bernard. "And she looked absolutely gorgeous. I did stop to wonder how a blind woman was able to apply her makeup so perfectly. You could be the best looking blind woman in town!"

Olivia enters the kitchen with the leftover wheatballs, and being that she was the only one who ate them, there are a lot. Apparently, Olivia heard at least the last line of Bernard's most recent Lucy and Ethel plot. "Bernard has the right to remain silent, but unfortunately not the ability." She turns directly to her son and says, "Stop meddling—if it's meant to be then it's meant to be." Her voice is quiet but sharp

Bernard places his hands on his hips and shoots back in his best I-Told-You-So voice, "I warned you from the beginning that this trip was a terrible idea! Even your mystical muse Ranier Maria Rilke knew that humans were put on earth to experience the beauty of *ordinary* things, not go dashing about the globe in search of I don't know what!"

"Indubitably," replies Olivia. "But how do you know what's ordinary until you've seen the extraordinary? And the excruciating?"

"I don't know why you bothered to have me if you were just

going to argue with me the entire time." Bernard appears to be addressing his query to the heavens above.

"Because I had no way of knowing it was going to be *you!*"

As Olivia turns to leave, Rocky the chimpanzee sashays into the kitchen. He opens the fridge door, stares into it for a while, and then closes the door without removing his usual bowl of fruit salad. Bernard offers him wheatballs, but he only sniffs at them and shakes his head. He lumbers back through to the den where he always watches *Animal Planet* after the girls have gone to bed.

"What's wrong with him?" I ask. "I barely got a 'hello' when I arrived back."

"They won't let him be a room mother at Gigi's school anymore," says Bernard. "The principal found out about it and said, 'What if he bites one of the children?'" Bernard snorts. "Ridiculous! Based on what I've seen, I think we should be more worried about one of the little monsters biting *him*. I wanted to inform those petty humanoid bureaucrats that even back in his drinking days, Rocky never bit anybody, but all they would've needed to hear is that he's a reformed alcoholic. He'd probably be banned from walking Gigi home from preschool in the afternoons."

"It's a clear case of discrimination," I say, sounding not unlike Olivia catching the first whiff of a new cause.

"The larger problem is that Gigi has made a lot of new friends at school, and then she has dance classes and gymnastics on weekends," says Bernard. "Don't get me wrong, Gigi still adores Rocky, but she no longer wants to spend every waking moment with him. It's hard for him to understand and..."

"And..."

"I'm worried that he's going to start drinking again. Yesterday, he made Ottavio and Mother planter's punches and poured a whopper for himself—a cocktail the size and strength of which I'm quite certain doesn't fall under the guidelines of the *moderation* program."

"Didn't the woman who started that program end up in prison for killing someone while driving drunk?"

"Two people," Bernard corrects me. "I've never been convinced about the plan myself."

"It sounds a lot like telling yourself to love someone in moderation," I say. Only, this comes out sounding maudlin and not like the joke I'd intended.

"Or eat muffins in moderation," says Bernard.

Suddenly I'm awfully tired. "I think I'm going to say goodnight."

"Of course," says Bernard. "Sleep with the pillows at the opposite end of the bed so you don't wake up looking at the Shultze's old house. I have a crew covering the roof so we don't get any water damage."

"What are you going to do with another house?" I ask. Whereas most sons would probably want to move their mothers next door, I happen to know that Bernard loves having Olivia under the same roof, even if they do bicker most of the time.

"Oh, nothing." Bernard turns away from me and begins re-drying the dishes that I've just dried.

"Well you must have bought it for a reason," I say.

Bernard faces me, presses the dishtowel to his brow as if he's received a crushing blow to the head, and manages to look completely devastated. "I was thinking that maybe you and Craig might rent it for awhile; and then if you decided to stay in the area, I could take back a mortgage—you know, your payments would go toward buying it."

Once again, Bernard has somehow managed to become the embattled heroine of *my* story.

"That's very sweet of you." I give Bernard a hug. "But I think you'd better just sell it."

"Not a chance. And risk people with macramé planters and pole lamps moving next door?" exclaims Bernard. "Until Rose and Gigi are old enough to live there with their husbands, I'll rent it out to some nice professional lesbians or a sweet old man with a cat that he believes is the reincarnation of his dead wife."

"Are you kidding me? First off, Rose and Gigi are only five and three." Then I realize that Bernard is kidding, and I'm the one losing my sense of humor. Or if he isn't, then he's well aware that it's extremely wishful thinking.

Heading to the summerhouse, I think how nice it will be to crash in my own bed. Only it's a fitful night's sleep, filled with dreams about all the things that time has taken away. Finishing college was supposed to give me this great life filled with opportunity. So when does that start?

Chapter 47

When I wake up, it's with an emotional hangover. Oh, for the good old days of reckless promiscuity, binge drinking, and vomiting the night away in New Delhi. Plus, *what* was I thinking giving away my crystals? I suppose it would be incredibly rude to ask Mandy for them back. Perhaps she'd consider loaning them to me for a few weeks.

Maybe this is how Dorothy felt upon finding herself back in Kansas after all those adventures in Oz. The thought makes me wish that my trip had been nothing more than a dream, with my old life right here where I left it. But there aren't any farmhands surrounding the bed and Toto doesn't leap into my lap. From outside comes the lazy beat of raindrops along with the familiar smell of 100 percent bona fide Cosgrove County mud, the glue that binds winter to summer.

After gathering up the trinkets I bought for the paste-eaters, I fix my hair to look as unsquirrel-like as possible and head over to my mom's house. Bernard insists the new style makes me appear very "gamine," like Audrey Hepburn in *The Nun's Story*, but I looked gamine up in the dictionary and it clearly stated: "street urchin or homeless person."

Driving down my old street the first thing I notice is the FOR SALE sign on Mrs. Muldoon's lawn. When I walk in through the garage door, Pastor Costello gives me a warm ministerial-sized hug. "We weren't expecting you until Saturday! I can't wait to hear about your adventures." Then he announces he's late for a deacons' meeting and hurries out the door.

"Welcome home, Hallie!" Mom gives me a kiss and quickly looks me up and down to check for broken bones. "Your hair is gone!"

"I thought it would look more professional for starting work."

"Do you have a job?"

"Not yet, but I'm sending out a lot of résumés over the next few days. I'll land something soon." I'd read on a website that a person must exude confidence when hunting for a job—for instance, don't say "if," but "when."

Mom appears to be in a rush. She grabs hold of Roddy and starts putting on his sneakers. "I'm taking the twins to the pediatrician. I think there might be something wrong with Reggie's hearing. Or maybe it's just another ear infection."

Mom used to think there was something wrong with *my* hearing, but it turned out I just wasn't listening. "Do you want me to stay here with Roddy?" I offer.

"Thanks, that's sweet of you," says Mom. "But the doctor likes to see them both, because the healthy one can act as a baseline or control factor or something...as if they're an experiment."

I put on their little spring jackets while Mom works on Reggie's sneakers. "I see that Mrs. Muldoon's house is for sale."

"It's a travesty that she has to move," says Mom. "When her arthritis is bad she can't turn the taps, open the refrigerator, or even a doorknob, and it's too expensive to have a person over there full time."

"That's so sad," I say. Everyone knows how much Mrs. Muldoon loves this town.

"Sometimes, I'm afraid she's just going to lay down her burden and pick up her gospel armor."

Mom had acquired this expression from Pastor Costello, who uses it in reference to older women at church who had worked hard all their lives, mostly for the benefit of others. For some odd reason you never heard him say it about a man.

"Mrs. Muldoon isn't an alcoholic, right?" I ask.

"Hallie!" exclaims my mother. "In the twenty-four years we've been neighbors, I've only once seen her have a glass of sherry, and that was at their fortieth wedding anniversary party. Why would you even *say* such a thing?"

"Because if she likes chimps I think that Rocky might be looking for a new gig," I say. "He's sort of at loose ends now that Gigi is busy with school and dance classes."

"Oh, really?" Mom grabs her car keys off the counter. "The house hasn't sold yet, why don't you go over and talk to her?"

We walk out the door together. "Good luck at the doctor," I say.

"I'll have a welcome-home dinner for you tomorrow night," offers Mom.

"Just promise not to serve Indian food."

Mom looks briefly puzzled. I suppose it's because she's never once made Indian food.

"I was going to have meatloaf," she says slowly, as if perhaps my jetlag hasn't worn off.

"Sounds perfect." I wander across the lawn to Mrs. Muldoon's house. If her problem really is mostly about opening things, well, I remember that one bender Rocky had where he must have uncapped twenty bottles of liquor. Plus, he regularly cranks open cans of peaches using a can opener and pops the tops on applesauce jars for the kids. In fact, Rocky is so strong that we always hand him the pickles when we can't get the lid off. My nerd friend Brandt says that an adult male chimpanzee has five times the strength of a human.

Mrs. Muldoon is so excited about the prospect of a simian assistant, especially one who works for fruit salad, that I'm forced to call Bernard and ask him about it right away.

"It's full time?" he asks. The man who didn't want Rocky to

begin with is now incredibly anxious about losing him. "The girls do love having Rocky tuck them in at night."

Mrs. Muldoon is sitting right there, eagerly staring at me. "Well, she's not an invalid—the arthritis in her hands just prevents her from opening things, turning handles, and doing a lot of household stuff. She gets around fine. I mean, he wouldn't necessarily have to live here."

Bernard asks me to wait while he consults with Olivia. Eventually Bernard comes back on the line and says, "It's hard to ask Rocky a question like this, so Mother says she'll drive him over and show him the situation."

"Olivia thinks it's a good idea?" I ask.

"It would appear so—she's quoting Maya Angelou, something about making a living isn't the same as making a life," replies Bernard. "And I suppose it's no problem for one of us to pick him up and drop him off. I'm practically a taxi driver anyway these days, what with all of the girls' activities."

Mrs. Muldoon is so convinced that this is going to work she has me yank out the FOR SALE sign on the way to my car. Now, if I can only do as well finding *myself* a job. Maybe I should open an employment office for primates.

The car radio announces that it's ten o'clock in the morning. Only ten o'clock? Wow. No tests, no jobs, no kids to look after. Free at last. It's a glorious feeling.

No boyfriend, no money, no prospects. Having lots of time to think maybe isn't such a great thing after all. In fact, it's possible to see how a person with a certain number of hours to spare could easily start developing conspiracy theories and writing manifestos condemning industrialized society. Or else study to become a mime.

I decide to go and check out what's happening at the garden center. With all the new houses going up in the area they'd expanded and doubled the inventory. On the downside, everything gets picked over twice as fast.

Chapter 48

"Hi, Hallie," Joanne, the manager, calls out from behind some baby dogwood trees. "Where's Bernard?"

"Just me today," I say. "Scoping things out."

Joanne emerges from behind the potted trees. She has a strong build and medium-length dark blond hair that is sort of like a bird's nest—filled with moss, twigs, seeds, and usually a pencil or two. "Wise move. People are placing phone orders without even coming to look at the stuff first."

"Okay then, I'll just wander around for a bit."

"Be sure to check out the canary ivy," says Joanne. "A lot of people are using it instead of English."

"Will do."

"Hey, I love your haircut!" Joanne calls out after me.

"Thanks," I say. "It was time for a change."

Passing the bird feeders, garden gnomes, and tomato cages, I head out to where the seedlings and flowers are on display. Looking between the racks, I'm almost positive that I spot the trademark boating cap of my bookie friend Cappy in the last aisle. Only what's he doing at a nursery—buying a wreath for the winner's circle at the racetrack?

I lean across some flats of ivy. "Cappy?"

"If it isn't the calculator kid." He gives me the once-over. "Or rather the calculator lady, though it doesn't have the same ring to it."

My hands automatically reach for the sides of my head. "It's just a haircut."

"You can say that twice and still repeat it," says Cappy. "Makes you look all grown up."

"What are *you* doing here?" I say.

"I want to surprise Sharon with some bluebonnets," says Cappy.

"For real?"

"As real as a royal flush," replies Cappy. "They're the state flower of Texas, sort of what the shamrock is to Ireland."

"That's so romantic," I say.

Cappy waves me off with his right hand. "It's just so she doesn't get homesick. We're not zoned for cattle and I wouldn't know what to feed an armadillo."

"Of course," I say. As a person who's oftentimes on the receiving end of gambling debts, Cappy doesn't like to be seen doing anything too touchy-feely in public.

"I talked to my grandson, Auggie, in San Fran yesterday—he got a contract for his book. One of his professors liked a story he wrote so much that she sent it to her own publisher." Cappy still appears rather stunned by the idea. "Just goes to show you that life is a game of chance and not necessarily one of skill. Apparently this editor wasn't even taking any new writers."

"I'm thinking of going out there if I can line up some interviews," I say.

Cappy doesn't ask my reasons for such a move. He's a big fan of *never complain, never explain.*

"You wouldn't by any chance have some work for me in the meantime?" Cappy has been asking me to join his bookmaking business as far back as I can remember. "I could use a little cash just to get organized."

"I don't hire college graduates. You didn't spend all that time and money to become a bookie. Keep trying. Something will turn up. Good times are good for the shoe salesman and bad times are good for the shoe repairman."

I'm both hurt and surprised. "But you've always offered me a job."

"Your dad wouldn't like it."

"That never stopped you before."

"It's different now that he's dead."

I don't understand. In fact, I'd think it would be the opposite and that Cappy wouldn't have to worry about what my father might think now that he's gone.

Cappy can see the look of confusion on my face. He's by nature a superb reader of not only cards but people. "Besides, the business is changing—no lettuce in it anymore unless you want to become a software engineer and offer Internet gambling. I'm afraid the local bookie is going the way of the dodo bird." He pauses while rubbing his chin. "There's no future in the past."

This last line is the one Cappy employs to console his losing customers, usually while encouraging them to bet double on the next race.

I tell Cappy about meeting Banjo and how he admitted to having had an Internet gambling problem.

"Playing on some computer isn't nearly as much fun as a regular game, in my opinion, but it's convenient and offers more privacy," says Cappy. "However, it's only a *problem* if you're losing."

Joanne comes over with two trays of bluebonnets. "This is all we have right now, but I'll be getting more in next week."

"That should be enough to establish a beachhead," says Cappy. "Bulls, bears, and pigs, right?"

This loosely translates to people who make intelligent decisions with their money tend to make reasonable profits over the long haul, while those who become greedy get slaughtered, like livestock. It'd taken me almost a decade to be able to understand Cappy, and it's a shame I can't find a way to make use of this rare skill, such as in a United Nations for bookies, where they might need a translator.

Cappy and Joanne walk to the checkout counter while I go

and look at the climbing plants. The fence around the pool at the Stocktons' had to be a particular grade of metal for safety reasons, and Bernard wants to see if we can do a better job of camouflaging it.

As I'm leaving, Joanne catches me in the parking lot. "Hey, Hallie, I overheard you talking about a job. We need some seasonal help here, you know, May through September."

"Oh, really?" I ask.

"Ten dollars an hour," says Joanne. "I know it's not a lot, but… we have fun. Plus, you've been coming here so long that you know the inventory and can explain how to care for everything."

I suppose she's right. It turns out I'm the accidental gardener.

"I might be taking a job in San Francisco," I tell her. "Is it okay if I let you know in a week or so?"

Joanne hesitates. "Okay. But definitely by next week. Nature doesn't wait!"

Chapter 49

When I arrive back at the house, Bernard is yanking the convection oven cord out of the wall and hauling the appliance off the counter. "I'm breaking up with the convection oven."

"I didn't know the two of you were in a relationship," I say.

"Not anymore!" replies Bernard. "It's tried to kill us with salmonella for the last time by not thoroughly cooking the Almond-Crusted Catalan Chicken."

He heads toward the garage with the unfaithful oven, though I don't know how he's going to find room in that junk repository.

"Why don't you just put it out at the curb?" I suggest. "Tomorrow is garbage day."

Bernard's voice can be heard echoing in the back hall. "We may get back together if I have to whip up some of my Three-Berry Yorkshire Pudding."

The rest of the day and most of the next is spent whipping up cover letters and launching them into cyberspace along with my résumé. Based on some of the seniors in my class who had all these amazing internships and summer jobs, I can't imagine I'm all that desirable to a marketing, advertising, or software company. On a whim, I consider applying to cut topiary at Disney World, but they want to know how many years of horticulture school I've had.

239

At five o'clock I close up shop and hurry off to dinner at Mom's. The kids have made a WELCOME HOME sign and taped it above the grace plaque where Mom normally hangs the "Happy Birthday" banner. Apparently in all those boxes of decorations we don't have a pre-printed "Welcome Home" sign. I suppose that's because nobody in the family has gone anywhere until now.

I hand out the presents, mostly toys that I bought in the Far East, a handcrafted game of Mancala, and a doll wearing wooden shoes from Amsterdam for Lillian, who is amassing quite the collection.

"Rocky is such a blessing," says Mom. "Mrs. Muldoon is able to watch the twins again, which makes her so happy."

"Wait until Sunday, when they can go to church together," I say. "Rocky hasn't been to Mass in awhile. People probably thought that all this talk about promoting intelligent design over evolution scared him off."

"He's just wonderful with the boys," enthuses Pastor Costello. "They've met their match when it comes to energy."

"Where's Davy?" I ask the general population.

"Up in his room after using bad language," Pastor Costello informs me. "And I don't mean split infinitives."

It's all I can do to keep myself from saying that I'd like to add L-O-V-E to his list of four-letter words.

I go upstairs to bring Davy a desert treasure map that I picked up in Cairo. At the end of the hallway is a brand new highboy filled with a half-dozen trophies. *Are they Dad's old sports trophies?* I wonder. Getting up close, I can see that they're for karate, mostly first and second place, and all engraved with my little sister Francie's name.

Francie comes exploding out of her room in a white pajama-style suit belted at the waist. "I'm already a yellow belt," she announces and strikes a pose suggesting that I'm about to be chopped in two.

"Congratulations!" I say. "I guess no one in this family has to worry about being bullied from now on."

"There's a big tournament in Tampa the day after school is over." Francie slashes her hand sideways while kicking the air with her leg.

"Florida?" I ask.

"The coach is taking us to Busch Gardens afterward, whether we win or lose!"

The downstairs door opens and I hear lots of excited shouts. "Eric!" yells one of the little kids, who are really not so little anymore.

Sure enough, Eric and his girlfriend Elizabeth are standing in the living room hugging everyone.

Mom looks thrilled. "Surprise!" she says to me. Then she turns to Eric. "I was afraid that you were going to miss dinner."

"We got caught in traffic between here and Cleveland," says Eric. "Since when does this town have a rush hour?"

"I was hoping that Louise would make it too, but she had to be in Chicago for an audition," explains Mom. "Then it's off to summer stock in New Hampshire. But she's coming home to visit for two weeks starting on Thursday."

"How long are you guys staying?" I ask Eric and Elizabeth.

Eric shoots me a look, but it's too late. Mom is staring anxiously at her eldest child and his longtime girlfriend. Not having been around the past few months, I suddenly realize that I might be a little behind on everyone's plans.

"Don't you have a week before going back to Nashville?" asks Mom.

"Actually, we're moving to Los Angeles." Eric is now grinning from ear to ear. "I've got a job as an accountant for a record company!"

"Wow!" I'm thrilled for him. He's always loved music but never pursued it in high school because he was so busy with sports.

"Los Angeles!" Mom's hands fly up to her face as if Eric just said he's moving to hell. "What about Elizabeth?" It's no secret that Mom has been waiting for an "announcement," though certainly not the kind that involves her becoming a grandmother.

"We're moving out there together," says Eric. "A sports clinic has already made her an offer." Elizabeth has a degree in physical therapy, her specialty being sports injuries, which is how she met Eric. His knees are often sore and his left shoulder pops in and out.

Mom is *not* happy. "Los Angeles?" she repeats, though she may as well be saying "Californication." My mother, like many people, enjoys the notion that corruption and vice are the sort of things that could never happen in a small town, though Cappy and Officer Rich would be happy to tell her otherwise. In fact, Officer Rich says that boredom in small towns gives them a larger proportion of methadone addicts than you find in big cities.

"It's a good job," Eric assures her. "Lots of room for advancement."

Pastor Costello calls everyone into the kitchen for dinner. Davy insists on sitting next to Eric, his hero.

After we say grace and the meatloaf is passed around, Mom appears to recover from the shock of Eric's announcement, but I can see that she's hoping there might be some follow-up about "setting a date." At least when they were in graduate housing together she could pretend that they weren't so much living together as dealing with a campus real-estate crisis.

"We want to hear all about your trip, Hallie," says Pastor Costello. "But I think Teddy wants to share some news first."

Sure enough, Teddy looks as if he's about to burst. "I've been accepted at the University of Munich," he says. "To study philosophy."

I turn toward Mom, and she looks none too happy about this plan either, but apparently she's had several days to absorb the information.

"That's great, Teddy!" says Eric. "Congratulations."

Teddy puffs up his modestly built chest. Getting Eric's blessing is like having Dad put his stamp of approval on the mission.

"Munich, Germany?" I ask, like an idiot.

"I know," says Teddy. "I took Spanish in high school. But I've been studying German using a computer program, and then I'll take a six-week intensive before school starts in August."

"Teddy has to leave the week after graduation," says Mom. She's trying to sound cheerful but there's concern in her voice.

"Good for you!" But suddenly I'm feeling rather forlorn. Eric has his dream job in Los Angeles, Louise is doing theater in New Hampshire, Teddy will attend school in Germany, and even little Francie is off to Orlando to become a karate champ. Beyond the family, my friend Gwen is doing a fashion internship in Milan, Italy, and Jane is practicing with the Olympic soccer team down in Texas.

For some reason I always assumed that I'd be the one off doing exciting things. But all I have right now is an offer to be a clerk at the local garden center or else continue as a yard person. And even those jobs are only good until the fall. It's the first time in the book of my life that I'm almost afraid to find out what's on the next page.

Chapter 50

The following day is spent feverishly e-mailing more résumés and searching for job postings, not just in San Francisco, but everywhere! Yes, even Hawaii. So far, most of my queries, if they get any response at all, result in form letters stating that they appreciate my interest in their company and will be in touch if anything arises that fits my "particular skill set."

The problem is obviously experience. Or rather that I don't have any. It would appear that work is a lot like love in that way—experience comes just after you need it.

Meanwhile, Auggie loves living with a couple of video game designers in an amazing loft near Chinatown, which is part of an upcoming neighborhood that even has its own cool acronym, SoMa, which stands for South of Market. He says to just move out there and his friends will help me, worst case being that I take an entry-level job somewhere and quickly move up. It's worth considering. I've certainly read enough stories about people starting as secretaries in high-tech companies and ending up with millions of dollars in stock options.

Soon I find myself reading Craig's old e-mails, the ones from last fall, when I was finishing school and he was starting his business, and we couldn't wait to see each other every weekend. Without planning to do so, I start writing him—a long e-mail saying how it was just too much for me to consider getting married before the trip, but that while traveling I realized how totally right it was. To describe the moment I quote Hermann Hesse in *Journey to the East*—"When something precious and irretrievable is lost, we have the feeling of having awakened from a dream." I don't mention that I experienced this epiphany while in bed with Josh, but honestly, I would if I thought it'd help any.

At first I have no intention of sending this garbled stream of thoughts, which is only slightly more intelligible than the copy of William Faulkner's *As I Lay Dying* that Olivia made me read a few years ago. But somehow my finger hits the "send" button and I close my eyes as if making a wish.

Between scouring job banks, which all serve to confirm that I should have studied engineering, or better yet, nursing, I keep looking for a reply from Craig. Nothing. The want ads in the *Cleveland Plain Dealer* reveal a need for science teachers, telemarketers, and part-time data inputters; and there's a certain air of desperation surrounding children's birthday parties. If my search goes on for much longer, taking up balloon art is not out of the question.

Checking the status of sent e-mail reveals that Craig has received my missive. I can't stand it anymore and call him on my cell phone.

"It's me," I say. "Did you read my letter?"

"Yes."

"And?"

"Nothing has changed, Hallie." His tone is flat.

"Exactly," I say. "I went away and came back. We're both exactly the same."

"I mean that nothing has changed since before you went away and you didn't want to marry me."

"But *everything* has changed," I say and my voice begins to tremble.

"I don't see it," he says.

I hang up before starting to blub into the receiver. He doesn't *see it.* Just how exactly do you *see* love, anyway? Am I supposed to hire a plane to do some skywriting?

Tossing my laptop onto the bed, I go inside for a chocolate Yoo-Hoo. That always calms my nerves and helps me to think clearly.

The kitchen counters are covered in planters, baskets, moss, fruit, cut flowers, pale green Styrofoam holders that Bernard calls "frogs," colored ribbons, and a bag of bark. In the midst of all this, Bernard's racing from the kitchen to the dining room with an enormous bunch of baby's breath in one hand and a vase in the other. Meantime, Gil digs through the mess trying to find his keys.

Bernard hurries back to the kitchen, glances at me, and says, "You look like Maria Callas following the ill-fated Japan tour, after her voice was ruined."

"Thanks a lot," I reply.

"As they say in Madrid, '*al mal tiempo, buena cara*'—the worse things get, the better you should look."

"I'll work on it." At the moment, I'm not in the mood for any of Bernard's quips and celebrity stories designed to cheer me up. I don't think they even make a Hallmark card for the mess I've created.

"How's the job search going?" asks Gil.

"About as good as the one for your keys," I reply. "Joanne at the garden center offered me a job through September. It'd just be something to tide me over while I keep looking."

"Wonderful!" exclaims Bernard. He magically pulls Gil's key ring out from under some pinecones.

"What's so wonderful about it?" I ask. "I just spent a hundred thousand dollars going to school to become a graphic designer."

"But Hallie, you're a daughter of the soil," insists Bernard. "You know everything about *jardinage*. Like Emperor Augustus said, he found Rome brick and left it marble. You did the same thing for our yard!"

"It'd just be temporary," says Gil. "And you *are* very good with plants. If you've got the grits, you may as well serve them."

Bernard clutches the countertop as if he might lose consciousness. "Did I ever mention that Gil was kept prisoner on a horse farm in Kentucky until he turned eighteen years of age and realized that he was free to go?"

Bernard loves playing Duke of Normandy to Gil's Duke of Hazzard, especially whenever Gil tosses off one of his "down-home sayings," as Bernard calls them.

Gil jingles his keys and heads for the door.

"Aren't you going to have some blackberry pie?" Bernard calls after him. "It's just out of the oven. Or if you have a moment, I can whip up some cornpone instead."

Gil tips an imaginary cap at Bernard. "Mighty grateful, but I gots to slop the hogs, dig the well, and plow the back forty, all before supper."

Chapter 51

" Would you mind helping me bring some of these planters and baskets into the dining room?" Bernard begins singing "There's Lots of Fish in the Sea" from *The Mikado* as we move everything out of the kitchen.

A moment later the doorbell rings and a gaggle of girls laughing and chatting enters the living room. They seem to be filled with all the delights of spring.

Only, the last thing I'm in the mood for right now is young people enjoying themselves. Maybe I'll go for a drive. I've never driven around aimlessly before by myself, but old people seem to swear by it. As I approach the front door, Bernard calls after me, "Hallie, can't you stay and help for a little while? I really need another set of hands familiar with the horticultural arts."

I try to come up with a quick excuse, but I don't have one—no studying to do, kids to care for, or job to go to. On the other hand, being with Bernard is really my only comfort these days. In a bathroom stall in Australia a previous occupant had scrawled: *A friend is someone who knows the song in your heart and can sing it back to you when you've forgotten the words.* Not only did Sydney rank well in the honesty Olympics, but I gave them high marks for graffiti, too.

Bernard has by now gathered his troop in the dining room to

begin a session on flower arranging. Andrew opens a brand new notebook with a sunflower on the front cover.

"Botanicals are part of our lives from cradle to grave, and they accompany us through all the special occasions in life," begins Bernard. "Births, christenings, bar mitzvahs, birthdays, weddings, anniversaries, and for those who have departed. There's no occasion that flowers aren't appropriate for—hostess gifts, hospital visits, to freshen up the office, the list goes on and on."

"My sister wore flowers in her hair to the prom," chimes in one girl.

"There you go! They have oh-so-many uses. However, there's a very fine line between *taste* and *travesty*." Bernard gives a cautionary wave of his right index finger. "And that's what we're going to learn about today."

It's hard to tell if wearing flowers in your hair falls under the category of taste or travesty, but Andrew diligently scribbles something in his notebook.

"Whatever your level of skill in floral arrangement, the most important rule is to select blooms and foliage you like, and then arrange them in a manner that emphasizes their natural grace. Over-arranging is the most common pitfall of the amateur and it makes the blooms appear stiff and static."

"What's your favorite flower?" one of the girls asks Bernard.

"Gold Medal or Pillsbury Softasilk," replies Bernard.

But Andrew and Bernard are the only ones who laugh at his little *flour* joke.

"I enjoy different flowers depending on the occasion and my mood," Bernard says more seriously. "The Japanese art of floral arrangement is called *ikebana*. It emphasizes balance, harmony, and form, which is perfect for weddings and dinner parties. Garlands are an ancient form of flower decoration dating from the fourteenth century BCE, when floral remnants were discovered in Tutankhamen's tomb. They're festive and always appropriate for a spring fling or the local harvest festival. Likewise, in the depths of winter, a display around candlesticks is lovely and cozy.

During the summertime, one can never go wrong with a 'garden in a basket'—fresh cut flowers trailing foliage and lacy ferns."

"Remember when we watched *The Prime of Miss Jean Brodie* and she called chrysanthemums 'serviceable flowers'?" asks Andrew.

"Miss Brodie was supposed to be a snob," explains Bernard. "Some people hold to the impression that flowers must be expensive in order to be appropriate. But even the simplest daisy can be the star of a stunning and well thought out display. A good host or hostess doesn't need to have the *best* of everything, so much as to make the *most* of everything. What do I always say?"

"Presentation is everything," calls out a girl in the back.

"That's correct," Bernard beams at her.

"My father always brings my mother a dozen red roses after he's made her mad," offers Amy.

"Yes, well, we're all thorns trying to be roses," says Bernard. "Now let's break into groups and work on our different occasions."

Bernard leaves the wedding team to labor in the dining room while he sends the Valentine's Day squad into the living room. "Hallie, would you help with autumn—that's what all the gourds are for."

Bernard instructs everyone, "Keep in mind at all times what you're trying to say, and let the arrangement speak for you. Flowers have a language all of their own."

Suddenly it hits me. "Sorry Bernard, but I have to go." I rush toward the front door, tripping over a huge basket of pink and white carnations that scatter everywhere. But I don't even stop to pick them up.

Chapter 52

*O*utside is a gray-washed world. The sky is low and soft with fog, the streets are slick with rain, and the sound of drops thrumming against the car roof, which would normally be soothing, only serves to agitate me even more. Passing the gas station and the Star-Mart, I hurry to the ATM and remove my life savings, which is all of $106. However, what I lack in cash, I make up for in conviction. Sure, fate plays a role in determining all of our lives, but who says you have to accept it. I'm going to master it!

As I storm the garden center, Joanne appears pleased and asks, "So you've decided to take the job?"

"I need all those marigolds you started in the greenhouse," I say.

"They won't bloom for another week," says Joanne. "It's so early in the season, you may as well just buy the seeds and grow them yourself."

By now I'm practically frantic. This is at least as crazy, if not more so, than Bernard's suggestion to try to make Craig think he was losing his mind, the way Ingrid Bergman's husband did to her in the movie *Gaslight*. Furthermore, the odds are a lot longer than I'd like them to be. But the older I get, the more I'm beginning to think that life really is a lot like poker, and sometimes it's a matter of playing a poor hand as best you can.

I take a hundred dollars in twenties and toss them down on the counter. "I'll pay full price. I just need them all now. It's a marigold emergency."

Joanne helps me load sixteen trays of marigolds into the trunk of the car and we set two on the backseat.

When I arrive back at the house, Olivia is writing a May Day editorial (she's one of few people who can work the rites practiced by Flora, the Roman Goddess of Spring, and the rights of janitors to a livable wage and healthcare benefits into a single coherent sentence) while Gil and Bernard are wrangling the girls toward bath time. Rose is bopping everyone with a big foam bat and shrieking, "You're out!" every time she lodges a direct hit, which is often.

"It's true what they say," jokes Gil. "You spend the first few years teaching them to walk and talk and the next twenty years telling them to sit down and be quiet."

"Ha! Come over to my house," I say. "The kids have stopped asking where they come from and refuse to tell anyone where they're going."

"Speaking of going," says Bernard, "we should leave in forty-five minutes so as not to be late for poker."

"I don't really feel like poker tonight."

Bernard clutches his chest as if he's having a heart attack. Then he places his hand on my forehead. "You don't feel like playing cards? I knew it! You caught some sort of plague on that trip."

"I'm fine, really," I say. Absolutely fine, except for a broken heart.

"Henry David Thoreau said 'there's no remedy for love but to love more,'" offers Olivia. "Though he was most likely a closeted homosexual sublimating his desires in a passion for nature."

Before a full interrogation can be launched or further supposition on how gay life was at Walden Pond, I grab an apple from the kitchen and beat it for the summerhouse. My heart is heavy with regret and yet simultaneously beating with hope.

Sometimes it feels as if it's just going to stop altogether or else explode.

I wait until almost midnight before pulling on a black sweatshirt and driving to the end of Craig's block. It's like the old days when Bernard and I used to "liberate" clippings. Only this time, I'm planting instead of confiscating.

The showers earlier in the day have left pools of water standing in the street and the soft earth sinks slightly under my footsteps, while the air hangs over my shoulders with the stillness of a heavy tapestry. Using a spade and a flashlight, it takes me almost two hours to put all 192 plants in the middle of the front yard. By the time I'm finished, the marigolds spell out MARRY ME and are about the same height as the grass. In a few days, depending on the weather, they should bloom. Then he'll be able to "see it." And so will everyone else.

Chapter 53

*A*fter three days of sunshine, I'm certain that the flowers must have bloomed, and yet there's no word from Craig. And I'd know if he'd called since this cell phone has not been out of my hand for one second in the past seventy-two hours. Is it possible someone mowed the grass before he saw them? A small part of me hopes so, or else I'm going to be the laughingstock of the entire town. Because it's true what they say about small Midwestern communities—if you don't want anyone to know about it, then don't do it.

Finally, I can't stand it anymore and drive past his house, slowing just enough to see that the lawn has been cut *around* the marigolds. A row of birds perched on the power line appear to be looking down at them. *Why can't I be like a bird?* Despite storms and sudden changes in the direction of the wind, they never seem to lose their balance.

I go back to the Stocktons' and check my e-mail, again. Surprise—a company in San Francisco is actually requesting an interview. It's just for an entry-level position working on the bridal registry website for a fancy department store, but at least it would be actual on-the-job experience. And from there, who knows, one day I could end up in charge of gift wrap!

It's hard not to call Craig's cell phone. Maybe he's out of town working on one of his ponds and hasn't seen the front yard yet. But then who mowed around the flowers? Craig always cuts the grass because his Dad has allergies.

Sleep is only a rumor from my bed of thorns. The hours between midnight and sunrise are filled with bad reruns and night-sweat dread. The following morning, I go back and look again. The marigolds are still there, some of the petals falling to the ground like teardrops, but not a word from Craig.

On the fifth night I can't stand it anymore. It's impossible to fall asleep, and I think I'm actually one step from the booby hatch. First thing in the morning I'm going to phone Craig, and if he still says no, then that's it. San Francisco or bust! If I don't get the bridal registry job, I'll just do what Auggie said and wait tables until something comes up. Worst-case scenario, I end up a derelict in Las Vegas, wandering around casinos finishing people's drinks and cigarettes.

With a firm plan in place, I finally begin to calm down. What's the big deal, anyway? Craig is just a guy. And like Olivia told me during the Ray fiasco(a.k.a. dating the son of a big mafioso), never chase after men or buses, because another one will be along in a minute.

Then it hits me. Maybe Craig *has* given me his answer. After all, he was the one complaining that he couldn't "see it." I grab a flashlight from the night table drawer and hurry outside. The air is cool and moist and the night hangs like cobwebs around my shoulders. I carefully begin combing every inch of the lawn for some sort of reply. When I shine my light into the bushes, they rustle and a loud shriek pierces the night. I'd successfully located one of the peacocks.

A moment later, a light goes on inside the house and Bernard appears on the front porch wearing a robe and slippers. I suppose I could hide behind the bushes, but then he might think a prowler is casing the place. Yet, if I tell him the truth—that I'm looking for a sign from Craig—he's going to think I'm rolling dice without the dots.

I shine the light onto my face so Bernard can see it's just me. "I thought I dropped some money," I explain. That's a dumb thing to say, since I won't have any money until I do some yard work for Bernard or take that job at the garden center.

Bernard looks puzzled. "Won't it be much easier to find it in the morning, when it's light out?"

"I suppose so," I say. "Goodnight then." I head around the side of the house and keep waving the flashlight across the lawn to search for some sort of response from Craig. So far there's nothing but a bunch of dandelions that don't spell out anything except that we need to buy weed killer.

The house next door is all boarded up. Bernard is having a contractor come by next week to give him an estimate on repairs. Before the fire, it was a charming old two-story home with a stone foundation, high ceilings, wonderful dormer windows, and carved wooden sunbursts above the fireplace.

Suddenly I'm overcome by a wave of black despair. If misery loves company, then why am I so alone? And that's the moment I realize I have to leave here as soon as possible. In *The Journey to the East*, Hermann Hesse wrote, *Next to the hunger to experience a thing, men have perhaps no stronger hunger than to forget.* I never thought I'd want to forget Craig and all the good times we had together, but right now, it hurts too much to remember. Everything here reminds me of Craig. And as Cappy is fond of saying, life is too short if you're happy and too long if you're miserable. Spending the remainder of my days around this place will make for a very long stretch of time indeed. Basically a life sentence. It's time to follow that horizon, go around the big bend in the river, and be carried on the wind. Where is The Rapture when you need it?

Passing the pond on the way back to the summerhouse, I shine my light in to take one last look at the fish that Craig and I put in there together. Something glints back at me, as if there's a broken mirror at the bottom. Sure enough, lying on the black gravel are about fifty shiny silver dollars spelling out the word Y-E-S. I have to stare long and hard to make sure it's not a trick of the moonlight, or else that I'm imagining things—that my eyes, or even the fish, aren't playing a terrible joke on me. But there it is, for anyone to see! And even though the night is dark, it's like breathing in the sun.

Chapter 54

The minute the clock hits 7:00 AM the next morning I phone Craig.

"It took you long enough," he says.

"I'm slowing down in my old age."

"Are you sure?" he asks. "Really really sure?"

"I've never been more sure of anything in my life!" I guess every marriage is a long shot. But this is one time I don't mind trusting the feeling in my gut that it's right, as opposed to being guided by any statistics or probabilities. "And you?"

"Anything else would be second best!" he says.

"Bernard wants us to take the house next door," I blurt out. "You'd have tons of room for your pond stuff."

"Hang on a minute," says Craig. "I thought we were planning to move. Are you just going to throw away four years of college and be a yard person for the rest of your life?"

"I'll look for something in Cleveland and commute. Until then, I can work here and at the garden center." I say this with enthusiasm. I'm just so thrilled we're really getting back together that everything else seems secondary. In the past few days I've made a big realization: that I'm not striving for the exotic so much as the ordinary—to live simply with the person I love. I don't know, is it possible to have a growth spurt at the age of twenty-one?

"I have a better idea," says Craig. "Can you be ready in half an hour?"

"I'm ready now!"

"Okay, I'll come by in ten minutes."

The urge to run inside the house and tell everyone is strong, but I need to make sure that I'm not delusional. Dressing carefully in my best faded jeans and favorite T-shirt (the light blue one with Mr. Bubble on the front), I yank on my good white high-top sneakers and then hurry out to the driveway.

Craig picks me up in the blue Chevy truck he traded for his Audi so as to haul around his pond building materials. We drive an hour southwest to Doylestown and Craig pulls up in front of a falling down mansion that doesn't look all that different from the house in East Hampton where Big Edie and Little Edie lived in *Grey Gardens*.

"It's going to be torn down next week and completely rebuilt. They want hedges, gardens, pathways—the works!" announces Craig. "It's a good budget, and they need someone for the landscaping. Are you interested?"

"You mean in designing the garden?" I ask.

"Everything outside—where the trees will go, a patio, hedges, and shrubbery for around the pool house and tennis court!"

My mind immediately turns to the space station I created on the computer for a final project last fall. Using the same software I could easily map out some proposals. "Yes, definitely!"

"When it's finished we can feature the results on the website, along with the Stocktons' yard—and who knows, maybe have a business together!"

"And run it from the new house," I say. It's too good to be true! Especially when it hits me that I'd be able to wear my jeans all the time.

Craig bends down so that one knee is resting on the damp earth. "Hallie, will you marry me?" He produces a ring from out of his pocket—a square yellow diamond in a platinum setting with tiny diamonds around the band. "It was my grandmother's," explains Craig. "But if you don't like it, we can have it reset."

"No, it's beautiful," I say. "It's old-fashioned, like those antique rings I've seen at Bernard's estate sales."

We hug each other and I cling to him as if he might suddenly vanish. When Craig puts his mouth to mine I taste the sun on his lips and feel his kiss down to the depths of my soul.

"How about next summer?" I say. "I just know that Bernard will want to have the wedding in the backyard."

"I was thinking more like this fall," says Craig. "In the spring my mom and dad are leaving on a world cruise for their twenty-fifth wedding anniversary."

"Oh," I say. "Well, Eric is moving out to the West Coast next week to start a new job, Louise goes directly from summer stock in New Hampshire to a play in Chicago, and Teddy leaves for Munich right after graduation. Maybe everyone can come home for Thanksgiving?"

"I don't think the Germans celebrate Thanksgiving," says Craig.

"Christmas?" I say uncertainly. It feels as if the excitement is draining out of our big moment.

Apparently, Craig feels it too. "How about *now?*"

"Now?" I say. "Don't we need a license? And don't you want our families—"

"I mean *now* in a week or two," says Craig. "After all, your stepfather is a minister, right?"

Love roars down like gale-force wind. And I immediately know that marrying as soon as possible is right, for so many reasons.

Craig looks at me with anticipation.

"Gosh, my mother would love it if we didn't *live in sin.*" I add the italics so that it carries the same level of disapproval she always lends the phrase.

"Will she think you're too young?" asks Craig.

"I doubt it. I'm going to be twenty-two. Mom was married and expecting a baby at seventeen!"

Craig takes my hand carefully, as if there's a chaperone nearby, and leads me toward the pool house. "We've been using this as the onsite office." He opens the door to a small but many-windowed room that contains a faded tan couch, Ping-Pong table, and some poolside furniture—four blue molded plastic chairs set up around a rusty, glass-topped metal table. Gauze curtains blow in and out of open windows. Yet the spicy thick scent of pipe or cigar smoke still hangs in the air.

"What do you think?" he asks.

"You've started smoking."

"That's the contractor," says Craig.

This time, when his lips meet mine, our passion flows like a river, one that had divided into separate channels and is now merging together again with great force. Everything buried inside me is suddenly reaching outward. It's all so clear now that what I ache for in body and soul can't be found by boarding a plane to the other side of the world. True love is right here in this small shabby room on the outskirts of Nowheresville, USA. Through the windows untended roses bloom wild among dark cascades of leaves and for the first time spring isn't just something happening around me, but deep within in my soul, as well.

The maps of our bodies are so deeply rooted in each other's consciousness that we know instinctively the ways in which to give each other pleasure, yet making love is still the greatest of all refreshments; bringing joy, release, and even moments of laughter and sheer playfulness.

When we've finished, Craig whispers into my ear, "Want a cigar?"

Lying on the old, faded couch, the two of us savor the sweetness of our reunion and set about the task of mending the torn fabric of our relationship. Maybe it won't be exactly the same, but hopefully, it will be different in a good way. The main thing is that now when we talk about the future, we mean our future together.

Chapter 55

Craig drops me off out front because he wants to go home and check his parents' calendar for a week from Saturday. They have a busy social life and often attend charity events in Cleveland and, lately, weddings for the children of his father's law partners.

Craig is going to call me if he can clear the date; I'll check with Pastor Costello; and then we'll just have to send out e-mail invitations. Bernard will have a fit about that!

However, back at the Stocktons', Bernard is nowhere to be found. And yet for some reason, he simply has to be the first person that I tell.

Instead, I come across Olivia sitting at her desk in the den. "Hello Hallie, how's the search for gainful employment going? Because I was talking to a friend at church who's working to free imprisoned journalists in Latin America and he needs someone to help create flyers. Though I don't know if he can pay all that much."

"Actually, I'm pretty sure that I found something," I reply. "Um, have you seen Bernard?"

"He's on a field trip with the Girl Scouts," she says.

"A field trip?" This is certainly a surprise. "*Outdoors?*"

"Good gracious, no! Pottery Barn," says Olivia. "Troop Bernard is doing a session on decorative pillows, if I recall correctly. At least his *cri de coeur* on the way out the door was, 'Less isn't more anymore!'"

"Oh." I try not to appear too excited, but Olivia can tell that something is up. Unlike Bernard, however, she operates on a need-to-know basis.

"Is there anything that I can assist you with, Dear?" asks Olivia. "You're all right?"

I shove the hand with the ring into my jeans pocket. "It's nothing, thanks." As Bernard is fond of saying, it's not a lie so much as saving a secret for later. "Are you writing an editorial?"

"My obituary," Olivia replies lightheartedly and hands me a sheet of paper.

"Are you dying?" I ask with alarm.

"Heavens no. I mean, not that I know of. But of course, we're all dying, aren't we?"

"Then why…"

"I don't want anyone censoring my life," says Olivia. "Furthermore, my legacy should be a call to action—a butterfly beats its wings, a domino falls, suddenly it's winter…"

At that moment, the door bursts open and Bernard's entire troop pours in carrying Pottery Barn bags. Ever the self-promoter when at the mall, he's wearing his Google Me T-shirt. Bernard is absorbed in giving a speech on how it's important to use the same good manners whether talking to a duke or a doorman. Uh-oh, one of the girls must have slipped when dealing with a salesperson. Just saying "please" and "thank you" isn't nearly enough for Bernard. If you don't ask about business or at least comment on the weather during a transaction, he considers it downright rude. And heaven protect the customer chatting on a cell phone while making a purchase!

"The British philosopher Thomas Paine said that 'manners are the highest achievement of a civic culture,'" concludes our resident anglophile.

Olivia whispers to me, "I'd classify Tom Paine more as an

American revolutionary." Then she calls out to her son, "Welcome home from the pillow wars!"

"Isn't this a great country!" proclaims Bernard. "You can buy anything you want and put it wherever you like!"

"Unfortunately, we do the same thing in other countries too." Olivia can't resist injecting some good old-fashioned American hegemony into the exchange.

"Mother, you're a terror!" pronounces Bernard.

"One man's terrorist is another man's freedom fighter." She picks up the small Iraqi flag on her desk and waves it at him.

Bernard rolls his eyes toward the ceiling, drops his packages, and pretends to be deflated. Yet we all know it's hardly possible that anything could ever dull his galloping enthusiasm after a successful shopping trip. In a stage whisper he announces to the girls, "Once again, Mother is exercising her right to be wrong."

From the back corner of the room I give Bernard a little wave.

He takes one look at me and gasps, "You're pregnant!"

"No!" I practically shout.

The girls all giggle.

"Then you've reconciled with Craig!" He throws his arms up in the air the way referees do to announce a touchdown. "Like Judy Garland and Mickey Rooney in *Girl Crazy*."

I open my mouth to tell him the news, but Bernard beats me to it.

"You're getting married!"

I close my mouth as Bernard is now so far ahead of me.

"We'll have the wedding here! Is there a date?"

"It looks like a week from Saturday," I say.

Bernard simultaneously reaches for the couch and one of the girls. Theatrically speaking, the performance is just shy of a swoon. Having such a large audience only encourages his natural thespian tendencies. "A week from Saturday! Has your Roquefort slipped off its puff?"

"It's my family—they're taking off in every direction, and I don't know when we'll all be together again. Besides, it's better this way." I hesitate to say this next part in front of an entire Girl Scout troop, but all eyes are on me and what the heck, they may as well learn from my mistakes. "I almost ruined the best thing that ever happened to me, and I'd rather not leave enough time to screw it up again."

Bernard flutters his hands in the air. "Girls! Girls! Andrew! New badge—wedding planning! I know that today was supposed to be our last meeting before summer break, but anyone who wants to learn how to create a truly tasteful wedding is welcome to continue through to the big day." He pushes the shopping bags to the side and assembles himself on the couch. "Notebooks out! Ruth Ann and Sarah—there are two pitchers of mint lemonade in the fridge. Serve over ice, garnish with orange slices, and be sure to add sprigs of mint. Andrew, run into the den and make your troop leader a very tall, cool martini."

Olivia chimes in from the back, "Bertie, why don't you just use a catheter so you never have to leave a room again and miss what anyone is saying."

"Because if it's about me I know that it's all going to be good!" he quips back.

One of Bernard's more diligent students points to her watch. "But you taught us that 5:00 PM is cocktail time, and it's only half-past three!"

"Yes, Julie, but there's a little corollary to that." Bernard offers the audience a broad smile, which anticipates his applause line. "It's always five o'clock somewhere."

Chapter 56

*T*he minute dinner is finished I head over to tell Mom the big news and ask Pastor Costello if he'll marry us. The dusky evening light lingers as if it might never end. Summer is just around the corner. And there's no place in the world I'd rather be right now than here. Once in awhile you have to leave everything that's good in order to find out just how good it really is, and that all a person desires isn't necessarily somewhere else. The nameless thing inside of me that's been floating loose for so long has finally found its home.

My brothers and sisters are in various stages of doing homework, getting ready for bed, and playing video games. Pastor Costello is helping Darlene with her speech-therapy assignment, and she's very frustrated, practically in tears. He patiently waits for her to try again. "You can do it," Pastor Costello encourages Darlene. "The only difference between try and triumph is the '*umph*!'"

"I saw a saw that could outsaw any other saw I ever saw!" The words flutter from Darlene's lips as unexpectedly as butterflies or bats.

"There you go!" Pastor Costello beams at Darlene and everyone else as if we've just witnessed a miracle of biblical proportions.

"I have something to tell you guys," I say.

Mom freezes in her tracks and suddenly looks horrified. "You're pregnant!"

"No," I say. "That would be impossible."

They appear relieved. Though I think they may have taken "impossible" to mean that I'm a virgin. Suddenly Mom and Pastor Costello are all smiles.

"Then what's wrong?" Mom asks with great concern in her voice.

It's at this moment I have to ask myself why people always think something is *wrong* whenever I have something important to say, whereas my brother Eric's announcements (about awards, scholarships, and job offers) are always greeted with anticipation. Oh well. "I'm getting married!"

Mom looks surprised. "To whom?"

"Craig, of course!" I realize that I probably should have brought him with me, but he had to submit the design for some ponds at a retirement community.

Mom and Pastor Costello give me big hugs and we sit down together in the living room. Knowing the crazy schedules of all the kids, they understand why we're having the wedding so soon.

"Christmas wouldn't have worked because Eric and Elizabeth are going to her family reunion in Texas," says Mom. "It's the first time one of you kids won't be home for Christmas!" Mom looks as if she's about to cry at the very thought of it, and Pastor Costello puts his arm around her.

"Maybe we'll go out and visit them for a few days in California," Pastor Costello reassures her.

I slap my hands on my knees as if to signal that the negotiations can now begin.

"So," I say to Pastor Costello. "Will you marry us?"

"In the church?" he asks.

"Uh...no," I say. "The wedding is going to be in the Stocktons' backyard."

Mom turns and looks at Pastor Costello. He frowns, and it's obvious he's thinking that somebody needs a faith lift.

"It's where Craig and I fell in love." This isn't exactly true, it was on the front porch, but close enough, and we don't want a church wedding.

"Will you start coming to church again?" asks Pastor Costello.

This is a good sign—we're entering phase two.

"Not necessarily," I say. "Craig's family is Lutheran, and we aren't exactly churchgoers at the moment."

"I didn't think so." Pastor Costello looks down at the carpeting with the Oreo minis scattered about like shrapnel.

"Is that a deal breaker?" I ask. At dinner Olivia had informed me that the Unitarians will marry or bury anyone for two hundred dollars. They even do pet funerals.

Pastor Costello glances at Mom and then turns back to me. "Not necessarily."

"I was hoping it wouldn't be," I say.

"Will you reconsider when you have a family?" asks Pastor Costello.

"Amen to that," I say.

We all smile. But my eyes land on the old family photo perched atop the end table. I can't say that I was one of those girls who fantasized about getting married, but I guess I always assumed that Dad would be there to give me away if I did.

Mom takes both my hands in hers. "Your father would be delighted that you're marrying Craig."

I nod in agreement. Dad liked Craig a lot. And I know he was hoping that all his daughters would get married. Dad was really into that whole family thing.

Chapter 57

I'm still trying to yank on this enormous heap of a wedding gown when Bernard sticks his head over the top of the changing room asking, "Are you decent?"

"Isn't it a bit early to discuss morals?" I ask him. The truth is that Bernard doesn't care if I'm dressed or not. Due to the fact that women parading around in their underwear don't excite him, he assumes that likewise, his presence doesn't bother them.

"If you need to come out you can throw a fur coat over your slip the way Tallulah Bankhead used to do," advises Bernard.

"I'm not wearing a slip. And this embroidered foliage is ridiculous!" I finally come tripping out of the dressing room looking not unlike an ecru version of the man-eating plant in the *Little Shop of Horrors*.

Bernard gazes at the monstrosity with glassy-eyed admiration and adjusts the satin belt. "But you *love* flowers and leaves."

"Growing out of the ground," I correct him. "Not draped across my butt and slithering under my armpits!"

"It's like the fairy queen Tatiana in *A Midsummer Night's Dream*, dancing and playing with her sprites!" announces a satisfied Bernard.

"It's like a TOTAL NIGHTMARE and not going to happen

as long as there is breath in my body!" I begin tugging at the zipper.

"Well, you can't wear jeans, an Atlas Tires T-shirt, and those storm trooper boots on your wedding day!"

"Well, I can't wear any of *these* either!" I gesture toward a rack of tulle, lace, and pouf that could only have its origins in the principle that the bride is a bouquet. "We've tried on over a dozen dresses so far and they're only getting worse!"

Bernard ignores my pleas and hands me another cotton ball on a hanger. This one isn't as froufrou, but the neckline plunges practically to the waist.

"You've got to be kidding!" I tell him.

Bernard attempts to keep the mood light as he senses that I'm fast descending into serial killer bride mode. "You know what they say, nothing risqué, nothing gained."

"It's going to take more than a pair of socks and a box of tissues to make that one a possibility." I shove the dress back at him.

Bernard yanks a white silk sheath dress off the rack that isn't covered in frippery and flounces or the bouncy white netting you use to scrub pots. It doesn't have one of those God-awful trains, hang all the way to floor, or look like there's a matching rhinestone tiara and armpit-length white gloves to go with it. He pushes me into the changing room and hurls the dress in after me. "I was afraid it would come to this!"

A few minutes later, I emerge smiling. "It's not at all terrible, for a *dress*."

"I suppose we could ask them to make it in denim." Only Bernard's quip doesn't sound very quippy. I look over and he has a tear running down his cheek.

"Why so glum, sugar plum?" I parrot Bernard's favorite expression for when the girls become upset.

Bernard quickly wipes at his face with one of the tissues from the wads we'd been using to pad the dresses that are too big in the bust (most of them). "Nothing."

His nothing is always *something*. It's more like *nothing* plus five minutes. I sit down next to him on the bench.

"It's just that when Gil moved back in, right before we adopted the girls, he thought that we should get married." Bernard removes another tissue from the nearby heap.

Okay, whereas the general assumption here would be that Bernard is tearful at seeing how grownup I look as a bride, in actuality, he's wondering if he's ruined his own chance of ever being a bride.

"So why on earth didn't you say yes?" I ask.

"It seemed so silly at the time," says Bernard. "I mean, we couldn't really get *married.*"

"But you can have a ceremony!" I say. "And then go out of state or to Canada and apply for a real marriage license."

Bernard perks up a bit. "I've read about so many couples who are doing it these days."

"It's settled then," I say. "Tell him 'yes' and we'll have a double wedding! How can Gil possibly object when *Much Ado about Nothing* and *Twelfth Night* both end in double weddings?"

At the words "double wedding" Bernard's entire face lights up. "In the musical *Calamity Jane* starring Doris Day there's a double wedding at the end with Katie marrying the lieutenant and Bill marrying Calamity Jane!"

"Does this mean I get to wear my jeans and boots?"

"Good gracious homes and gardens, no! The whole point of the movie is that Calamity Jane becomes *more* feminine after falling in love."

Bernard is suddenly back to his old party-planning self. Heading out of the dressing room, he calls over his shoulder, "Have the woman fit you for this dress! We'll need the tuxes cleaned and more food and flowers and how will we ever find an open-minded minister on such short notice…?"

Chapter 58

*T*hree days before the weddings Craig comes by with some old high school friends who now run a construction company to see what sort of work needs to be done on the house next door. I've begged him to please try and restore it to the original plans as much as possible, which Bernard has helped me piece together using his books on architecture. According to these, it's an antebellum house in the Federal Style, built before the Civil War. I'm supposed to know this because of the front and rear center entrances, evenly spaced windows, gable roof, and end chimneys.

At the same time, Bernard is going gangbusters in the backyard—shouting orders at delivery people, flower vendors, and a phalanx of carpenters. His invitations—featuring the British spelling of "honour," much to the protestations of spell-check and also Gil—have gone out by overnight mail. Being that Gil's family is from Kentucky, Bernard had asked whether he should include "no firearms please" at the bottom.

The area between the pond and the summerhouse has sprouted an altar (which Bernard refers to as "the stage") with an arched trellis covered in blue and white roses. In front of that will go the chairs, and off to the side, a real wooden dance floor surrounded by two dozen tables. Following the ceremonies, the makeshift altar will become the bandstand. Covering all of this is a billowy white tent large enough to hold a trapeze act.

One potential caterer has set up a table filled with samples of food, a local baker is standing over several trays of cakes and cookies, and a florist is putting the finishing touches on some possible altar arrangements. They all want Bernard's business because he has the ear of just about every well-to-do woman in town.

Meantime, a cadre of Girl Scouts is working on candle centerpieces and seating charts with Bernard helicoptering above them. "The table decorations should never be so high as to obstruct the guests' vision and thereby impede conversation." He holds up a notepad containing the guest list. "A green check mark means over-imbiber and a red check mark connotes those who are one egg-white short of a soufflé. With regard to the seating chart, we want to *group* the alcoholics, whereas we *intersperse* the crazies."

Gil is on the sidelines with Rose and Gigi, basically trying to stay out of the way, yet still be on hand to rubber stamp Bernard's choices, which can best be described as *always say "yes" to excess.*

"The good news is that Saturday is supposed to be gorgeous," Gil says to me.

"Then why the tent?" I ask. "Are we having a circus?"

Gil shakes his head in disbelief. "It's definitely turning into a Cirque du Soleil production."

"Bring on the acrobats," I say.

A guy standing on a platform next to the arched trellis holds up some plastic vines and shouts, "Where do ya want these?"

"Center stage!" responds Bernard.

"Where's that?" asks the man.

Bernard leaps up onto the platform. "Center stage is wherever I am, if I might quote the great American dancer and choreographer Martha Graham."

Yes, indeed. Bernard is in rare form. At breakfast he'd berated Olivia for spending time trying to organize a poets' union and not fulfilling her duties as "Mother of the bride." *And these duties would be what, exactly?* I want to ask, because Bernard hasn't allowed the rest of us to make even the tiniest decision so far!

"Aren't you supposed to be sampling wedding cakes?" Gil asks me.

"I'll puke if I take one more bite of hazelnut frosting," I say. "Besides, I caught a glimpse of Andrew's notebook and under the dessert section there's already a photo of the six-tier cake that Princess Grace of Monaco had at her royal wedding."

Ottavio comes around the corner of the house, looks at all the preparations, and more or less bursts into tears before going inside.

"I think Ottavio rather wishes that he and Olivia were getting married," says Gil.

But Gil doesn't really need to say anything, since Ottavio has never made a secret of his desire to tie the knot.

"Olivia told me that she doesn't trust contrived rituals," I explain.

Craig walks over with a hammer in his hand. "Why is the side of the house being covered with a white tarp when it doesn't matter if the garage gets wet and the entire roof is going to be replaced?"

"Be serious," I reply. "An eleven-year-old Girl Scout named Andrew knows more about what's going on here than I do."

My fiancé looks puzzled.

"Hey Andrew," I call out.

The neatly dressed boy with a fountain pen tucked behind his ear scurries across the yard, careful to step over the power lines that have been laid for the floodlights. "Is there a problem with the boutonnière?" Andrew consults his notes. "Bernard and I ordered one blue rose with white baby's breath for B and G-1."

"B and G-1?" I ask.

"Bride and Groom One," says Andrew. "Which reminds me—how should your stepfather's place card read—his full name or Reverend Costello, since he's performing your ceremony?"

"Anything is fine," I say.

Andrew jots down a note and ticks another item off his list.

"Uh, G-1 has a question—why is the house next door being covered with white tarpaulins?"

"It's just until after the wedding day—for aesthetics," explains Andrew. "Bernard doesn't want people looking over their shoulders and seeing all that ugliness."

I glance at Craig as if to say, "Well, there's your answer."

A confused-looking worker is about to set a pillar down near the table where the wedding cake samples are spread out. Andrew dashes over to the man. "Over there!" he points to the front of the tent.

Bernard strides across the lawn and hands me a song sheet with one hand while wiping fake sweat off his brow with the other. He's in full "I before U" mode, not unlike an aristocrat who's just suffered the indignity of a minor car wreck that wasn't his fault. "These klutzes are worse than the workmen in *A Midsummer Night's Dream!*"

"It will all come together," I assure him.

"I'm glad that I caught you two lovebirds because there needs to be a list of songs the band and disc jockey will play at the reception. I was thinking that to kick off the dancing we'll start with 'Marrying for Love' from *Call Me Madam*. Ethel Merman sang it in both the stage and movie versions."

"Don't forget to make sure they have Credence Clearwater Revival's version of 'Ooby Dooby,'" says Gil. "And not the Roy Orbison one."

"I've instructed the DJ to play that last, when we want to clear everyone out," replies Bernard. "Right after 'My Old Kentucky Home.'"

Craig looks at me to see if I'm hiding a song list up my sleeve, but I just shrug, since it's the first I've heard of it.

Without so much as glancing up, Bernard continues with manic merriment, "We also want 'What I Did for Love' from *A Chorus Line*. And of course 'Can't Help Lovin' Dat Man' from *Show Boat*." Bernard takes the list back from me and starts going down it with his finger. "Definitely 'Come Rain or Come Shine.' That was one of Judy's best." He begins walking away while making notes. "*I'd* better take care of this."

"Fine with me," I call after him. Not that it matters. "So long as there isn't any Enya."

Olivia strolls over carrying some freshly cut daisies. "The gardens look lovely for this early in the season."

"Thanks, I cheated by putting in some potted flowers. Joanne offered me a good deal to clean out her leftover spring stock," I reply. "The real miracle is that Bernard is letting me do the gardens however I want."

"Of course, you're a professional now," says Olivia. "And what a noble profession indeed. When it came to preserving our souls through building strong communities, Ghandi said that 'to forget how to dig the earth and tend the soil is to forget ourselves.'"

"I guess." I mean, as gallant as that may sound, I hadn't actually *chosen* this life so much as it seemed to up and choose me. "Last night I was thinking how if I'd never seen your sign for a yard person down at the Star-Mart five and a half years ago, none of this would have happened."

Bernard comes racing over carrying a silver ladle in one hand and an ice bucket in the other. "My Alaskan king crab recipe for a pair of tongs!"

"In the dining room with the chafing dishes," I tell him. "Do you want some help?"

"You kids just worry about writing your vows," says Bernard.

This had been Craig's great idea—that we write our own wedding vows. And I agree, the traditional ones about honoring and obeying are outdated, but I didn't realize that I was agreeing to an English project. Craig's vows are apparently all finished, whereas I haven't gotten past, "I, Bride One, take you, Groom One, to be my..."

Olivia is, of course, thrilled by this decision, believing that the customary vows call for the woman not to tie the knot so much as sacrifice at the altar.

Chapter 59

The night before the big day I lie awake for what seems like hours, my train of thought taking the scenic route, running a hundred different versions of the movie of my life: What if I'd stayed in high school? What if I'd gone to Las Vegas instead of college? What if Dad hadn't died? What if there was no chocolate Yoo-Hoo and only strawberry? A hoot owl cries from somewhere nearby and gives me the jimjams.

At two o'clock in the morning I'm still staring at the ceiling. Off in the distance a train whistles. It's probably only going to Cleveland, but from there I could catch a bus or a plane. If I'm so excited about getting married, why am I suddenly thinking of ways to flee?

From the window I see a light go on in the kitchen. Please tell me that Bernard hasn't decided to make the food himself. Last time he tested the stuffed mushrooms and wontons he told me that our caterer put the "sewer" in connoisseur. The truth is that Bernard won't admit to liking *anyone* else's food.

Gil is sitting at the kitchen table drinking a can of root beer.

I take the chair across from him and pick up the deck of cards lying next to the napkins. When I'm nervous it helps to shuffle and practice one-handed cuts.

"Nervous?" asks Gil.

"Nope," I lie and riffle the cards together. "You?"

"Reflective," says Gil. "A few years ago I made this offhand remark about getting a domestic partnership certificate, and now suddenly we're getting married. It was just to ensure that if anything happened to either of us, the other would have full responsibility for the children."

Oh, wow. Here I pictured Gil proposing to Bernard by placing a ring on top of a marshmallow sundae or something romantic like that. "And now you'd rather not do it?"

"I just don't see how it will change anything," says Gil.

"Sometimes I wonder…" This definitely requires a chocolate Yoo-Hoo, and so I go to the fridge. "I think that perhaps…I just wanted to marry Craig because it suddenly looked as if I'd lost him for good…and maybe it was like losing a game. You know, because I like to win games."

Gil opens his eyes wide and leans back from the table as if indeed that's a good one.

"I have an idea," I say from inside my bridal black hole. "We'll each cut the deck once, and if the total of the two cards is greater than twelve, then we both go through with it, and if it's eleven or less, then we both bail."

Gil looks as if this is the most insane but also the most brilliant idea he's ever heard. "Great! Let's do it."

I shuffle the cards and place the deck squarely in front of him. Gil neatly cuts the deck and turns up a six of hearts.

We both stare at it for a long moment, calculating that another six or higher is needed for the nuptials to proceed. This time Gil shuffles the deck and places it in front of me.

I hear delicate footsteps on the stairs that surely belong to Olivia. We both panic. In my attempt to hide the cards I accidentally fling them onto the floor, and Gil knocks over his can of root beer.

"Is everybody awake with *excitement?*" Olivia's voice rises and falls in a sweet singsong.

Gil dives in first. "We were just…"

"Trying to decide on a poem to read," I chime in. "As part of my vows."

"What a lovely idea," says Olivia. "Although the older I get, the more I think the best way to popularize poetry is to ban it—make the possession of verse a felony punishable by a fine and community service. Dealers get a life sentence. So now, what poems are under consideration?"

Alarmed, I quickly look to Gil, who is wiping up the spilled root beer.

"Uh, yes, we thought perhaps maybe something from the Bard."

"At my wedding we read from the work of Anna, the Comtesse of Noailles." She begins to recite: *I will leave of myself in the fold of the hills the warmth of my eyes which have seen them in blossom, and the cicada perched on the branches of the thornbush will be resonant with the piercing cry of my longing.*

When Olivia finishes I don't know what to say other than, "Wow!"

"But in French, of course," adds Olivia.

"Of course," says Gil.

"Did you know that *coeur*, which is French for heart, and *courage* are both from same Latin root word?" asks Olivia.

Aha! She does know that the two of us are down here with our feet soaking in buckets of ice.

"Marriage is a rather large step," Gil finally admits.

"Love makes the world bigger and smaller all at once," says Olivia.

"So Livvy, why don't *you* get married?" asks Gil.

"Yes," I say. "What about you and Ottavio?"

"We could have a group wedding!" offers Gil.

Olivia places her hand on her heart and her eyes widen. "When I hear the word *group* for some reason it brings to mind a lynching mob. Besides, I've already been married. And my child has grown up."

We all look doubtful about that last statement.

"Well…he's of legal age," she amends.

Bernard floats around the corner in three-quarter time, as if a waltz is playing in his head, and cheerily announces, "I just tell people that Mother can't remarry because she's still in mourning."

I wonder how long Bernard has been listening in. "No offense," I say, "but the Judge has been dead for almost five years."

"Queen Victoria mourned the death of Prince Albert for over two decades." Bernard states this proudly, as if Vicky were a close relative. Then he points up at the clock. "I know I told everyone to be ready early, but not at half-past three!"

"We were just helping Hallie decide on a poem for tomorrow," says Olivia.

Gil and I exchange glances, relieved to be off the hook. Bernard would have a fit if for one second he thought that all of his planning was about to go to waste because of a couple of runaway brides.

"Ah yes," trills Bernard, "finding the perfect words for going from *me* to *we*." He clasps his hands together and smiles lovingly at Gil, as if tomorrow can't come soon enough.

"How about something by the American poet Laura Riding?" Olivia can propose female candidates for just about anything. "The already-married writer Robert Graves was so in love with her that when she tried to commit suicide by jumping from the window of an apartment building, he jumped out after her. They both survived, but his marriage ended."

"I think Hallie is looking more for a straightforward *I Love You*, rather than *I Love You to Death*," offers Gil.

"T.S. Eliot said that 'genuine poetry can communicate before it's understood,'" adds Olivia.

"T.S. Eliot also said that 'humankind cannot bear very much reality,'" adds Bernard. "This was the man who hid from his wife until she had to be institutionalized, and then following her death, which was most probably a suicide, he married a secretary thirty-eight years his junior."

"I never should have taught you poetry," says Olivia.

"It can and will be used against you. Free verse in particular." Bernard claps his hands as if organizing a kindergarten class. "Everyone back to bed this instant. The helium man will be here at 7:00 AM sharp."

Gil and I glance at each other. *The helium man?*

"Over two hundred balloons need to be inflated and strung along the aisles," Bernard informs the less informed.

"None of them had better take flight!" warns Olivia. "Balloons kill birds."

Bernard looks as if he'd also like to have someone killed. Someone standing right here in this room.

"Everything is happening so fast," I say.

"Wait until you get older," says Olivia. "It happens even faster."

"Angels on your pillow!" Bernard calls after me. It's been his favorite line since reading that torch singer Peggy Lee used to say it to her children every night at bedtime.

281

Chapter 60

S oon there's a chink of light in the East and the lawn turns from silver and gray to green as the morning dawns gloriously sunny. It's a perfect end-of-spring day and I'm no longer a flight risk. The uncertainty of the night before has vanished along with the morning dew, and I've never been so sure about anything in my life. There are no guarantees when it comes to relationships, but much like in gambling, some forms of uncertainty are better than others. Craig is fantastic, and I'd be crazy to spend the rest of my days waiting for someone better to come along. First off, no one would. But let's just imagine that despite those one-in-a-million odds he did. What are the chances of said someone being willing to put up with me?

In honor of the wedding, Olivia has added a new bumper sticker to her cherry red Buick: ARMS ARE FOR LOVING. She's also banned throwing rice, saying it causes the birds' stomachs to explode, and put out containers of birdseed to toss instead.

Heaven forbid I try to put on my dress and fix my hair behind a locked door. From all the way downstairs, Bernard's satellite-dish ears locate the sound of the garment bag being unzipped. "I'll be right up!" echoes in the stairwell.

After quickly pulling the dress over my head, I squeeze into the horribly uncomfortable high-heeled sandals.

"All ready." I smile and hold out my arms so he can admire the dress.

"Very funny!" says Bernard. "Come into Mother's room where the light is better and we can do your makeup."

"I already put on some mascara and lip gloss so that in the photos I don't look like an Alpaca guinea pig with red eyes and exploding hair."

"Granted, you're young and we don't need full *maquillage*," says Bernard. "But we're never too beautiful for shadow, shading, and contour!"

Why is he suddenly saying WE? I dutifully follow Bernard to Olivia's vanity table, with its array of cosmetics and moisturizers that weren't tested on animals, produced at the expense of a rainforest, or packaged by Third World children who should have been in school. The truth is that Bernard does the makeup for all of Gil's shows and is quite skilled at it. When he's not engrossed in a Biedermeier furniture book, Bernard can often be found studying *Making Faces* by Kevyn Aucoin or scanning *Cosmo* and *Glamour* magazines at the grocery store.

"Now, have you decided how to wear your hair?" he asks.

"What do you mean?" I ask. "Like *this*." The regrettably short hairstyle I arrived home with has now grown out a bit and, with my natural wave, doesn't look bad at all. At least that's what I'd thought.

Bernard laughs as if this is the best joke of the day. "Not exactly enough here for a French twist, or a chignon, so we'll keep it down but use a little mousse and some lacquer..." (Don't ask me why Bernard insists on using this 1950s term for hairspray). "Modern, but still princessy—bouncy, yet swept back on the sides..."

There's the dreaded *we* again. *Why don't we just move into a nursing home together?*

Out comes the hairdryer. He mutters something about Sandy Duncan in *Peter Pan* while grabbing a circle brush, and then attacks my head as if he's whipping up a batch of meringue.

"Ta-da!" Finished with me, Bernard lifts his arms like a

gymnast sticking a fabulous landing, and then dashes off to survey the setup in the yard one last time before changing into his own bridal ensemble.

Alone at last. Only, it's as if I've entered a funhouse. Staring back from the large oval mirror is a woman I've never seen before. She's dressed in a simple and unadorned, yet stunning, white Shantung silk dress (instead of muddy garden clothes), with a powdered and perfumed presence so delicate, it's a happening. Where is the Hallie Palmer who normally puts the casual into "casualty"?

This private reverie is broken by Bernard operatically shouting, "My kingdom for two 1953 Queen Betty shilling-coin cameo cufflinks!"

You'd think the Brits were losing the empire all over again. I mean, he has hundreds of cufflinks. And at least a dozen royal family-themed ones.

"Betty, Betty!" calls out Bernard, as if Queen Elizabeth II is going to suddenly answer back, "Bertie, Bertie—in here!"

He races into the room and quickly scans the top of Olivia's vanity table. Not only has Bernard stitched his Girl Scout Do-Dad patch onto the tuxedo lapel but, in the past twenty minutes, either his tux has turned several shades lighter or his skin has gone several shades darker. It's as if an eclipse has occurred across his face.

"Are you wearing man-tan again?" I ask.

"Of course not." Bernard pats at his cheeks. "It's just a healthy summer glow."

"Well summer hasn't started yet, and there's a great big fault line on the right side between your healthy face and your pale neck."

Bernard races off in the direction of the hall bathroom, I assume to smooth out the mancake that he denies ever using, but which nonetheless leaves orange rings on the inside of his shirt collars.

Olivia comes down the stairs looking radiant in a lilac-colored silk dress with a pleated skirt and a cream and purple scarf tied around her neck. On the left side she has a pretty amethyst starburst brooch, and on the right is a big plastic button that says, "SUPPOSE THEY GAVE A WAR AND NOBODY CAME?"

"Oh, Hallie!" Olivia's hands fly up to her cheeks. "That dress is lovely! It's absolutely perfect for you."

"Thanks. I wish I could say the same for the shoes. They pinch absolutely everywhere, and I'm kicking them off the minute the ceremony is over!"

"It's easy to see why men abandoned wearing high heels in the late 1800s," says Olivia. "Now if only the Madison Avenue-Hollywood-Milan shoe conspiracy would allow us girls to do the same."

Bernard reappears from the downstairs bathroom with his tan sufficiently evened out. "Oh, but Mother, I adore you in heels. It means that I can hear you coming." He turns to me and adds, "Mother has no natural predators, much like the marsupial and the manatee, and therefore she's able to roam freely."

Olivia adjusts her scarf and attempts to sweep past her son, but Bernard throws himself into her path. "Now Mother, I know you despise holidays and special occasions, but I've organized a family photo prior to the nuptials, out in the Chinese tea garden."

"Actually, I enjoy weddings," says Olivia. "Everyone is so optimistic—the woman thinking that she's going to change the man, even though she won't, and the man convinced that the woman won't change, even though she will."

Bernard takes Olivia by the shoulders and steers her toward the door.

Troop Bernard arrives early to set out the place cards, string balloons along the aisle, and make sure the centerpieces are watered and spritzed. Andrew wears a dove gray sport jacket and black slacks with a mint green shirt and dark green tie instead of the traditional Girl Scout pantsuit and sash.

At ten o'clock the wedding party begins to arrive. Just like the kids in our family have never had to organize a play date, there's no need to search outside the family for a wedding party. Aside from my friends Gwen and Jane, who are bridesmaids, the Palmers take care of the rest—Eric is best man for Craig, Louise is my maid of honor, Francie and Darlene are flower girls, Roddy and Reggie are ring boys, and Davy and Teddy, along with Rocky, are ushers. Gil found the ushers some tuxedos and top hats in the costume closet, so they look like they're right out of the Ascot opening-day scene in *My Fair Lady*. Everyone wants their picture taken with Rocky, and Teddy is practicing his German by greeting guests with *"Willkommen"* and *"Guten Morgen."*

My mother gushes about how beautiful I look, which is nice, but everyone knows that you can't trust your own mother as a barometer of public taste. Out of her bag she starts pulling items like a magician. "Take my lace handkerchief—that counts as something *borrowed*. This sapphire ring is adjustable, and it's *blue*." She slips it on the third finger of my right hand. "Your dress is, of course, *new*." A small black velvet satchel appears next. "These were your grandmother's pearls. They're very *old*, but I had them restrung. These will be yours now, since you're my oldest daughter. And then, when your daughter gets married, you'll pass them on to her."

I almost say, *"My* daughter?" But it doesn't sound quite as fanatical or farfetched as when she'd previously mentioned my "one day having a family." Instead, I hold the delicate single strand of ivory-colored pearls around my neck and Mom clasps them together in the back with an audible sigh. She's very big on tradition. Roddy and Reggie, the twin ring boys, come galloping over with their hair mussed and miniature matching suits slightly askew. Mom automatically goes to work sorting them out.

Mrs. Muldoon came early with my family and every ten minutes Rocky goes to check on her. They've ended up getting on very well indeed, and between the meals sent over by my mother and Bernard, have managed to prevent Mrs. Muldoon's daughter from forcing her to move out West.

Gil's father arrives, who looks like an older version of Gil: tall, lean, and long-jawed, though more dour than sunny, and Bernard whispers to me that Gilbert Senior would be perfect playing the part of a bony-fingered Lutheran minister in an Ingmar Bergman film. Gil's sister Kathleen has come with their father, along with her longtime boyfriend Sam, and we've been warned not to ask if they're getting married, because it's apparently a touchy subject. Bernard has invited his Uncle Alvin, who is busy recording all the food that's being served in a small spiral notebook. He strolls over and politely asks me how to spell *broccolini*. Since this hybrid vegetable is a cross between broccoli and Chinese kale, Bernard felt that it counted toward including the girls' Asian culture in the proceedings. This was actually a great relief, because for a while there, Bernard considered hiring a band that played zither, dulcimer, oboe, and a gong, until he said WWJOD—What Would Jackie O. Do?—and quickly returned to his senses. It didn't hurt that Gil discovered the demo tape.

When I finish assisting Uncle Alvin with his food list, Gil leans over and whispers, "He has all of his teeth but none of his marbles." However, Gil isn't exactly exaggerating in this particular instance. Uncle Alvin has a list of everything he's eaten dating back to 1971.

My old high school classmate and Louise's ex-boyfriend Brandt flies in from Massachusetts for the occasion. Though no longer a couple, they've remained friends.

If anyone is going to get married next in this family my guess would've been Eric, especially since Elizabeth told me ahead of time *exactly* where she'll be standing when I toss the bouquet. However, yesterday Eric confided in me that after finally landing his dream job in Los Angeles, the last thing he wants to do is "snap on the ol' ball and chain." I said, "Thanks for sharing your optimism right before the most important moment of my life." Brothers!

Rose and Gigi are adorable in pink taffeta dresses with little white silk flowers embroidered on the skirts. Though I don't know how long Rose's outfit will last, the way she's tugging at it. Gil is following them around saying, "No more somersaults! I mean it this time!"

The garage is locked securely, so that no small children can wander in never to be seen or heard from again. Gil had wanted the (*"Oh, my garage!"*) door cordoned off with police tape, but Bernard wouldn't hear of it, since yellow and black would clash with his silver and Prussian blue color scheme. (After heliotrope and mauve met with a resounding *no*.)

It's time to start, and the violinist hasn't arrived yet; so Bernard is of course freaking out, warning the waiters to slow down so we don't have an "hors d'oeuvres gap," and asking the DJ if he can spin a disc of the "Wedding March" if it comes to that.

"I requested 'Forever in Blue Jeans' to be played at the reception, but we can just as easily walk down the aisle to it." A little joke to relieve the tension.

Bernard stares daggers at me and states, "We'll play 'Siegfried's Funeral March' from *Götterdämmerung* by Richard Wagner before a single note of the Neil Diamond oeuvre." Though whether it's going to be for Bernard's funeral or my own he doesn't make clear.

"Fine, so we'll wait," I say to Bernard. "What's the big deal? It's not as if the backyard is reserved again at five o'clock. Besides, it's a gorgeous day and everyone is having a marvelous time."

And it's the truth. We look around and people are admiring the Chinese tea garden, pointing at all the different birdfeeders, and wandering around the gazebo trying to catch glimpses of the peacocks. The hum of dragonflies is in the air and the fountain at the center of the pond trickles a merry tune. Many of the flowers aren't in bloom yet, but the roses look gorgeous, the daffodils are blowing their trumpets, and I put some hyacinth and anemones purchased from the nursery into beds where I'll plant other things in a week or two.

Guests who aren't strolling around happily snack on appetizers and sip drinks. A waiter threads his way through the crowd with a tray of champagne, mimosas, and plain orange juice.

One of the servers approaches us and asks, "Are you Bernard?"

"What's left of him," replies Bernard, anxiously glancing toward the street for any sign of the delinquent violinist.

The waiter holds out his tray. "The chef wants me to make sure that you try these."

Bernard bites into a miniature piece of toast with some sort of red and green spread, and his facial muscles begin to spasm. "Is a classic Tuscan crostini too much to ask for?" he sniffs as if his Cordon Bleu instincts are reeling.

The waiter flees in the direction of the kitchen. Another server appears with a silver tray, and this time, Bernard seems pleased by what he tastes.

Suddenly I hear the unmistakable notes of a familiar tune. "What is *that?*" I ask Bernard.

"Artichoke fritters," he says with the air of a satisfied gourmand. "Aren't they delicious? I gave that imbecilic chef my own recipe."

"That *song!* It's Enya, from the *Shepherd Moons* album!" One of the peacocks lets out a bloodcurdling shriek, and I wholeheartedly concur. Turning to rush the DJ's table, Andrew intercepts me. "I called the violinist and she's five minutes away. Her car wouldn't start."

Bernard appears greatly relieved. He nods his head toward the lawn party. "Check out table five with the beehive hairdo and, I dare say, matching orange rayon pantsuit."

I look over and see Mrs. Gilchrest, the organist from Pastor Costello's church, who firmly believes: The higher the hair, the closer to God.

"It's so out that it's practically in," remarks Bernard.

"So wrong that it's right," says Andrew.

They both giggle and Bernard continues, "Did you see that shiny black Mercedes SUV that George Rittenhouse rode up in? I don't think his mother has been in the ground more than two weeks and they're spending like it's going out of style. Not four months ago Brenda was begging me to come to another one of her Tupperware parties."

I consider mentioning that not four years ago Bernard loved

flashing his silver Alfa Romeo all over town, until the girls arrived and he traded it in for a Volvo.

But Andrew turns out to be the one with the comment ready. "That money is so new the green is practically coming off on their hands!"

A woman carrying a loaded violin case races toward the tent and so I go to rescue Craig, who has been sequestered inside the house, since Bernard is another stickler when it comes to wedding traditions, at least the ones he approves of. Although he had to settle for locking up Craig instead of me, since there's no way I was going to be stuck in the house with Bernard hovering over the caterer in a mode that had quickly crossed from helpful to harmful, and by breakfast time was one pear phyllo star away from a restraining order.

Upon seeing my dress for the first time, he gives me two thumbs up, which is Craig's highest rating for anything.

"Are we ready?" he asks.

"So ready that we're bordering on a hostage situation." I grab his hand, we head for the back door, and a wild excitement flares up inside of me.

It's been decided that Craig and I will go first. This way, anyone not prepared for the shock of two men having a commitment ceremony can make an early escape, even though it means missing out on the commemorative sterling silver candy dishes Bernard had made especially for the guests to take home, with our names and the date beautifully engraved on the front. (And the name, address, and website for his antiques shop on the bottom.)

Chapter 61

$\mathcal{B}$ernard's Girl Scouts are in full-dress greens, lined up like an honor guard as we walk down the aisle. Our church is the garden, with the white, blossoming apple orchard as its dome.

By the time we reach the altar, where Pastor Costello presides with his Bible in one hand and wire-rimmed half-glasses in the other, I'm such a nervous wreck that the folded piece of paper containing my vows is disintegrating in a pool of hand sweat.

Pastor Costello warms up the crowd by reminding them why we're all gathered here and tells everyone how long he's known us. Then he launches into the actual ceremony with the usual stuff about how love is patient and kind and endures all things.

Bernard hired a guy to make a video, and having him leaning over my left shoulder only increases my anxiety. I can feel the rivulets of perspiration gathering underneath my bangs, preparing to create a waterfall.

Finally, Craig reads from his carefully typed index card with pure contentment in his voice:

I, Craig Larkin, take you, Hallie Palmer, to be my wife, my constant friend, my faithful partner, and my love from this day forward. In the presence of our family and friends, I offer you my solemn vow to be your faithful partner in sickness and in health, in good times and in bad, and in joy as well as in sorrow. I promise to love you unconditionally, to support you in your goals, to honor and respect you, to laugh with you and cry with you, and to cherish you for as long as we both shall live.

There's a rush of feeling from my stomach to my throat, as if I'm going to burst like a ripe seedpod.

Craig smiles at me. Women in the audience sigh. Pastor Costello nods and says, "Hallie..."

My vows are terrible next to *those*. They compare marriage to a plant that grows best with lots of care and attention. I've obviously spent way too much time under the dangerous and harmful rays of Gro-Lights. I grab the index card from Craig's hand and switch the names around. After all, isn't that the whole point of getting married—to share everything?

When it comes to the part about promising to be his "faithful partner," I stumble and accidentally say "fitful partner." Everyone in the audience laughs, though it's hard to tell whether it's because of the mistake or because they know it's probably true.

Before long I hear the words, "I now pronounce you husband and wife!"

My hands begin to tremble in the magic and wonder of the moment. I look down at the front row and Mom is dabbing her eyes with a tissue. As soon as she glances away for a second, I quickly wipe my forehead with the palm of my hand.

After kissing me, Craig takes my hand, and we walk past our guests, who are flanked by several hundred silver and (Prussian) blue balloons, to Bach's "Air on the G String" (yes, Troop Bernard had some fun with the name of *that* tune). After making our grand exit, we double back and take our places behind Mom and Pastor Costello for the next event.

The minister from Olivia's Unitarian church walks onto the stage. He's a tall man who looks more like the drummer in an aging rock band than a minister, with thinning, silver hair that hangs down almost to his shoulders and a turquoise bolo tie. His robe is a vibrant green with what appear to be waves etched along the sides and back, and underneath it, he wears brown Crocs dotted with sunflower Jibbitz.

The minister introduces himself like a waiter at a fancy restaurant, "Hello, my name is Forest, and I'll be performing your ceremony today." During the rehearsal Bernard had said we're just lucky he isn't named Moon Glow or Tree Stump.

Surprisingly, no one gets up to leave. I guess they don't want to miss this show. Or, at the very least, they want to be able to tell their friends, "You'll never believe what I saw this past Saturday right here in Cosgrove County!"

Bernard and Gil take their places at the altar, and the minister talks so much about the earth, sky, and air that it'd be easy to think you'd dropped in on a conference to stop global warming and save the rainforest. Ottavio has tears streaming down his face to the point where a bystander might think he's absolutely desperate about the ozone layer and greenhouse gases.

Finally, the minister gets around to asking if anyone objects to the union, which I decide is a pretty big gamble with this crowd, especially the ones from *my* church.

Olivia raises her hand.

"*Mother?*" Bernard's eyebrows go up drawbridge-style, so that they're almost vertical.

Chapter 62

*O*livia stands up. "I don't object, I was just wondering if there's room up there for one more couple?"

Bernard stares at her with his jaw hanging down, the same way he looked when he spotted a chunk of bruised pineapple in the fruit salad earlier on.

"Why, I do believe this is the longest Bernard has ever had his mouth open without anything coming out of it," Olivia states to the, by now, mesmerized guests, who won't be able to get on their cell phones fast enough after this spectacle.

However, the minister doesn't appear at all surprised. Based on the number of times Olivia told me that she and Forest have been arrested over the years, and even bombed with tear gas back in the late 1970s, it apparently takes much more than a last-minute wedding to surprise *him*. Forest peers over his half-glasses and says, "As the great composer Arthur Rubenstein once remarked, 'life is the game that must be played.'"

I take it that's Unitarian for "yes" since Olivia clasps Ottavio's hand, they bound up to the stage and stand on the other side of Forest, opposite Bernard and Gil.

Bernard finally sends his chin back up to rejoin the rest of his face, and from my second-row seat, I can hear him say, "But you don't have a license."

"Neither do you," she whispers back.

Pastor Costello hurries forward to lend Ottavio his ring. The UU minister talks some more about walking lightly on the planet and then reads poetry by William Blake, who is apparently a patron saint of the Unitarians, at least if you judge by the way Olivia is always going on about him.

He who binds to himself a joy
Doth the winged life destroy;
But he who kisses the joy as it flies
Lives in Eternity's sunrise

As soon as the ceremony is over, Ottavio, Olivia, Bernard, Gil, and the minister perform a group hug, while everyone claps, and Gigi and Rose dance down the aisle tossing white rose petals from baskets decorated with silver and (Prussian) blue ribbons. Mom leans over and kisses me while Pastor Costello shakes Craig's hand, and it crosses my mind that the only one missing is Dad.

Suddenly there's a huge gasp among the guests, and the ghost of Dad comes stomping across the yard directly toward us, as if aged by a computer, with a mane of wild white hair and a walrus mustache added for shock value.

"Uncle Lenny!" shouts Lillian, who doesn't remember Dad, but will never forget her great Uncle Lenny and his infamous bedtime stories—fractured fairytales which rarely failed to include the phrase, "I was tits up in a ditch when suddenly, out of nowhere...."

Roddy and Reggie simultaneously shout, "Santa Claus!"

Mom, who was hospitalized throughout the entire Uncle Lenny episode, practically collapses into Pastor Costello's arms.

Uncle Lenny, sporting navy slacks and a white captain's jacket, complete with gold trim, epaulets, and a stiff white cap with a shiny black brim, scoops Lillian into his arms like she's an oversized mackerel and shouts "Ahoy, Maties!" in his booming bass voice. As Bernard likes to say, he's right out of central casting.

"Are you really dead?" asks Lillian.

Uncle Lenny laughs uproariously and the rest of the kids hurry to his side.

He bends down and begins telling them, "We were taking a yacht to the owner of a rubber plantation in the West Indies when a mighty storm rode up…and before you know it, I've slipped cable and am bobbing along with only the boom mast to keep me afloat, and not so much as a skillygallee. That's when, out of a dark black cloud, sailed the pirate ship…"

I look at the assorted guests, who have now spread the word that this is the Palmers' (thought to be deceased) salty sailor uncle. The only person who does not appear at all surprised by this surprise appearance is Bernard. And then I recall the one place with no name card at my parents' table.

"Why do I get the feeling that you knew about this?"

"He contacted me first because he was afraid your family would think they'd have to give the money back if he wasn't dead. But your Uncle Lenny is fine with his Coast Guard pension, which has been reinstated now that he's officially alive again."

"And…" I say.

"He wondered how you would all feel about him coming to live here now that he's retired. I believe his exact phraseology was to 'become a landlubber.'"

"Uncle Lenny wants to move *here?*" I ask. "Gosh, Cosgrove County is so boring compared to what he's used to."

"Sometimes it just takes one other person to create excitement," Bernard says mysteriously.

Sure enough, I look over and Uncle Lenny has extricated himself from the children to give Mrs. Muldoon a deep-sea-sized hug. I can't believe it—the two of them! And right under my nose.

Uncle Lenny holds up a glass of champagne and bellows that he'd like to toast the bride and groom. Mrs. Muldoon leans in close and apparently corrects him by saying that there are now three brides and grooms, or rather two brides and four grooms, or something like that. The orchestra stops playing and Uncle Lenny raises a flute of champagne. *The wind that blows, the ship that goes, and the lass that loves a sailor.* Then he clinks glasses with Mrs. Muldoon and she *giggles!*

Louise turns to me and says, "Oh, my God! Do they have a *thing* going on?"

"Stranger couples have happened." I nod toward Brandt, who (at one time in the not too distant past) Louise claimed as her "soul mate." However, I know what she's really thinking. "Uncle Lenny and Mrs. Muldoon are only in their sixties," I assure her.

Louise scrunches up her face as if 60 is the new 600.

Marching over to Bernard, Uncle Lenny shakes his hand and then hoists his glass once again. "Here's to a triple wedding—just like in *H.M.S. Pinafore!*"

Bernard and Uncle Lenny immediately burst into song:

Oh joy, oh rapture unforeseen,
The clouded sky is now serene,
The god of day—the orb of love,
Has hung his ensign high above,
The sky is all ablaze.

If you ask me, it's not so much the traditions as the surprises that make a wedding memorable.

Cappy strides over wearing his best boating cap along with a double-breasted, wide-lapelled white suit that, although it might clearly say "wedding" to him, undoubtedly suggests a career in extortion to everyone else. A haze of cigar smoke engulfs his head in a vaporous cloud and leaves a white ribbon trailing in his wake. I'd seen Cappy and his wife, Sharon, slip into the back row right before the ceremony began. Though with the amount of yield-sign yellow sequins rounded up for Sharon's gown, you don't really "slip into" anywhere without causing a certain amount of retina damage.

"Here's looking up your address." Cappy hands me an envelope.

"As they say in racing, breed the best with the best and hope for the best. Craig Larkin is one lucky fellow."

"I thought you didn't believe in luck." Finally, after all these years, I've caught Cappy out!

Cappy nods over to where Craig is smiling and shaking someone's hand, his entire body exuding self-assurance and contentment. "I'll let you in on my biggest secret—confidence gives the illusion of luck, and most of the time that's all you need. Bet on yourself, kid. Always bet on yourself." To make sure things don't turn serious, he quickly adds, "So long as you don't take any wooden nickels."

I shake the envelope Cappy just gave me as if to check for any such counterfeit currency. However, in reciting his "final secret," Cappy has reminded me of what I'd wanted to ask him in the first place. "What's this Al tells me about you being down at the courthouse almost every day? Is the mayor trying to put you out of business?"

"Online gambling has already done that," replies Cappy. "The town is growing and needs more fundraisers, but golf tournaments don't raise enough lettuce anymore. So we're organizing charity poker games—black tie, open bar, everything on the up and up."

"You're kidding?" I say. "You've gone legit!"

Cappy nods as if this may be so and may not be so. "Only bad thing is that there's no smoking. And of course this way the wives know where we are." He gives me a wink. "But they play poker too, and absolutely love it. All this time, I assumed that agreeing to marry a man was enough of a gamble for any sensible woman."

As if on cue, Cappy's wife calls him over to talk with Officer Rich about something. He grins and says, "Must obey the War Department."

I hear strains of Neil Diamond's song *Be* from the *Jonathan Livingston Seagull* soundtrack wafting out over the lawn and watch Bernard make a beeline for the disc jockey as if he's planning a flying tackle. When Olivia had slipped the man a twenty-dollar bill earlier on, I thought she was just giving him some change or perhaps a tip. Bribery is more like it.

Suddenly I'm alone at the edge of the gardens. The voices around me melt into a loud happy hum and, for a moment, I stand listening to leaves shuffle in the spidery thatch of towering trees above. It's no longer the end of one season but the beginning of another. Great bursts of bright green grass surround the flowerbeds. Birds warble and crickets chirrup in the speckled half-light. On one side of me, guests are talking and laughing, while on the other the gardens flash and shimmer. To the left is the summerhouse, where so many things have happened, and off to the right, my new home. It has been a long journey, though only a hundred yards in actual distance.

Mom calls from somewhere underneath the tent. "Hallie, where are you? Eric and Elizabeth have to leave, or they'll miss their plane to California!"

"Coming!" I take one more look around, attempting to capture the fading past while contemplating the as-yet-unwritten future. My eyes brim with tears as I bid farewell to those days, and still I feel no regret. Life is indeed a crooked road, but fortunately time spreads it out so things don't all happen to a person at once. The good comes right along with the bad, winter into spring, summer into fall, and there's no big finish at the end. Every day is a bounty and your best bet is to make it count, just like the flowers come up after the darkness and the rain, not in spite of it, but because of it.

The End

A Reader's Guide

A Conversation with Laura Pedersen

and

Questions and Topics for Discussion

A Conversation with
Laura Pedersen

Julie Sciandra, longtime friend of the author and bowling alley heiress, talks to Laura about her new novel.

JS: Does the school that Hallie attends really exist?

LP: No. With peripheral elements like that, my objective is simply not to distract the reader from the characters and story. Also, I wrote for the *New York Times* for ten years and burned out on research. As a reporter and columnist, you spend hours fact-checking.

JS: Am I having flashbacks to my ninth grade English class, or are there similarities to *The Odyssey* in *Best Bet?*

LP: There's no fooling you private school students when it comes to the classics. But I can't say it's supposed to be a great metaphor for anything, aside from the fact that Hallie is on the adventure of her life. Otherwise, I just drew a few parallels for fun, such as the storm on the way to Hawaii, a.k.a. the Land of the Lotus Eaters. It probably would've been going too far if Rocky were the only one to recognize Hallie when she returned home, like Odysseus's dog.

JS: But in your books, it's almost always the girls who get the exciting parts.

LP: So many stories are about men going off on secret missions

302

or to seek their fortune. I do enjoy having the gal light out for the Territories and making the guy wait for her. Or not.

JS: I loved the ending to *Last Call*. But it was sad. All the Hallie Palmer books end on a more upbeat note.

LP: The poet must die, so the rest of us can live! However, I'm a positive person and find there's enough bad news in the paper every day, so one sad ending is enough.

JS: But Rocky didn't get a particularly happy ending. He leaves the Stocktons'.

LP: Rocky is like Mary Poppins in that he goes where he's needed. If you want to get really deep, let's say he's representative of the answer to most spiritual quests, which, in my opinion, is to be of use.

JS: Although the Hallie Palmer books are usually shelved in general fiction, I've seen them in the Young Adult section. Did you have a particular audience in mind when you started them?

LP: There's definitely a crossover audience with teenagers, especially girls—*Beginner's Luck* is now on high school reading lists. I didn't have a particular audience in mind when I wrote them, but you'd probably need a high school education in English and history to appreciate all of the references. Fear not, there's absolutely no math or science necessary. At readings and signings, it's mostly adult women who show up, but I see a few men there too. We also have crossover with FOBs.

JS: FOBs?

LP: Friends of Bernard—alternative lifestyle.

JS: The gay guys get better parts than the lesbians.

LP: Maybe Joanne from the garden center will be given her own series—the way *Rhoda* was spun off from *The Mary Tyler Moore Show.*

JS: Where do you get ideas for the scenes in your books?

LP: Many of the incidents have happened in some form or another to me or people I know, including the passing acquaintance with an alcoholic chimpanzee. Actually, I consider most of the fictional events to be tame compared with my real life experiences, so it's always funny when a reviewer says something is farfetched or unrealistic. The craziest things are usually true. For instance, I had a college advisor who was a half bubble off-plumb and made the same horrible mistake with my transcript.

JS: I know that you usually have one main thought for every novel and then casually drop it somewhere in the story. Can you tell me what it was with *Best Bet*, or would that be breaking the secret code?

LP: Since it's the final installment, I suppose we can break the silence without having to enter you into the Federal Interviewer Protection Program. In chapter 44, Hallie sums up the findings of the "honesty experiment" and concludes that she lied to herself when justifying going on the trip in the first place. She wanted to go—maybe to get away for awhile, to try being with Josh, or for any number of reasons. Basically, she wanted Craig to wait for her while she looked to see if there might be something better over the rainbow, which is a little unfair in my book.

Questions and Topics for Discussion

1. At the beginning of the story, Hallie's mother remarries. Although Hallie likes Pastor Costello, do you think this is still difficult for her to accept? Could it factor into her decision to leave town rather than move in with her boyfriend?

2. With more young people going away to school and taking jobs far from home, they tend not to live close to their families and childhood friends. What are the positives and negatives of this? Would you like to go back and live in the place where you grew up? Or if you're young, would you like to live permanently where you are now?

3. Is it difficult to justify spending large amounts of money on higher education when you might not be able to find a good job in your field? Does college offer other valuable life experiences that make it worth the cost?

4. How do you decide whether to pursue a career that will be financially stable or one you're passionate about that probably won't pay as much?

5. Should everyone travel before settling down? Or live in another country for a period of time? How has travel changed your perspective so far? Where would you like to go next?

6. Does growing up in a large family make a child more or less independent?

7. When a person asks you to marry him or her, do you think if your gut response isn't an automatic overwhelming YES, that this means it's a bad idea?

8. Can living together help determine whether a marriage will work? What about breaking up for a period of time?

9. Could Hallie have handled Craig's proposal better, or did she get what she secretly desired—freedom?

10. Banjo's parents have lived all over the world, and he doesn't have a place to call home. How important is it to be connected to a place and the people in that place, if at all?

11. If you spend your childhood on the move, what skills might you learn that will serve you well in adulthood? What might you miss out on?

12. When deciding whether or not to have children—and how many— does whether you grew up in a large or small family make a difference?

13. Is it wise to wait until a certain age to marry in case you both change a lot? What is a good minimum age to make such an important decision?

14. Is it necessary to take big risks in life to reap big rewards?

Made in the USA
Lexington, KY
02 January 2010